THE BIRD IN THE CHIMNEY

Fanny was an orphan who had been brought up at Darkwater, her Uncle and Aunt's sinister old house on the moors. She in turn was now looking after two young relatives, orphans from China who were also kindly being taken into the household by her Uncle. She had previously dreamed of going to work abroad in the Crimea but now she became increasingly dedicated to giving Olivia and Marcus her full devotion.

Fanny and her cousin Amelia compete for attention and hope for their romantic longings to be fulfilled...

The ghost in the chimney was a white bird which had died at the same time as a previous mistress of Darkwater, and now it was a portent of disaster.

THE BIRD IN THE CHIMNEY

Dorothy Eden

MAO ES

First published 1963
by
Hodder & Stoughton Ltd.

This edition 2001 by Chivers Press
published by arrangement with
the author's estate

ISBN 0 7540 8586 4

Copyright © 1963 by John Burrows

British Library Cataloguing in Publication Data available

Printed and bound in Great Britain by
Redwood Books, Trowbridge, Wiltshire

1

As the swirling smoke of the engine cleared, the little group was etched forever in Fanny's brain—the outlandish figure of the Chinese woman in her black trousers and high-collared smock, and the two children in their quaintly old-fashioned clothes, the girl with black hair, stick legs emerging from her pantaloons, and tense eyes staring unwinkingly, the boy smaller, unexpectedly fair, his eyes dreamy and lost.

And the smoke clouding over, then clearing again to show the tall dark figure of the man.

She had known at once that the man belonged, although he stood a little distance away. He was watching her too hard, seeing the effect that the sad wrinkled alien face of the amah and the two waif-like children had on a young lady of obvious wealth and fashion.

In her mind, for a moment, like a view enclosed inside a bubble, bright and impermanent, was a picture of Darkwater, the faded rose many-chimneyed house, the lawns, the trees heavy with summer, the strutting peacocks, the distant flicker of the lake. Nowhere into the picture came this little trio. Instinctively she knew that they would be forever strange and unwelcome.

Yet her immediate impulse was to sweep the children into her arms and say, 'Don't be afraid. You're safe with me.'

Safe... It was true that the chilly grey summer day, the hissing of steam, the shouting and bustle of a busy London railway terminal, and the constantly belching smoke, did constitute a menacing atmosphere to such new arrivals from another world.

She couldn't be sure whether the watching man was part of the menace.

She only knew, with frustrated anger and bitter grievance, that from this moment her life had to be changed, that it must follow a very different course than the one she had planned so hopefully when she had packed her bag at Darkwater.

2

At the bottom of her bag Fanny laid her modest pieces of jewellery, the silver locket which sprang open to hold a miniature or a lock of cherished hair—it was empty, and Fanny scarcely knew why she kept it since it was unlikely ever to contain anything—the seed pearl necklace, the ring set with garnets and seed pearls, the gold brooch that had been her mother's. She had never known what had happened to the rest of her mother's jewellery, unless, more than likely, she had been too poor to have any.

She had come from Ireland, and the Irish were not renowned for their wealth. She had been beautiful, they said, but it had been a foolish marriage for Papa to make. He should have married an heiress. Not only had she been poor, but also too delicate to survive childbirth. Her name had been Francesco. That had been given to Fanny—that and her deep blue eyes and black hair. And her life. So great a gift as the last was the main reason for Fanny's secret plans at this moment. She must make the most of something so dearly given.

Over the shabby morocco jewel box in her travelling bag she laid her underclothing, two sets of everything.

Dora would have done her packing for her. Fanny was not encouraged to give the servants orders. This was a tacit understanding between Aunt Louisa and herself. But Dora, recently promoted to the upstairs, adored Miss Fanny and would even have risked Hannah's disapproval to do her behests.

As it happened, Fanny preferred to do this task alone. She couldn't let even loyal Dora see that for one night in London she was taking two of everything, and her summer as well as her winter gowns.

She was on fire with excitement. Ever since her cousin George had come home wounded from the Crimea she had been waiting for this opportunity. She had made and rejected a dozen plans, but this chance had been handed to her out of the blue. It was meant to be taken.

The only way she could explain her suppressed excitement,

at breakfast that morning when she could eat nothing, and it was left for the rest of the family to eat heartily from the array of dishes on the sideboard, was to say that the train journey and the visit to London were such an adventure. Not to mention meeting the new cousins, poor babies, who had travelled so far.

Uncle Edgar had smiled indulgently, but Aunt Louisa had compressed her lips, not with scorn for Fanny's naïve excitement, but with the thought of the new arrivals. Aunt Louisa had never cared for children who were not her own. At the tender and vulnerable age of three Fanny herself had made that discovery.

It was left for George to say to the table at large, 'Fanny looks deuced pretty when she's excited. Doesn't she? Deuced pretty.'

His eyes, ever so slightly vacant, rested for an embarrassingly long time on her face.

Aunt Louisa said sharply, 'Don't forget the time, George. Mr Maggs comes to give you your treatment at nine.'

'Yes, Mamma,' said George mildly. He still stared at Fanny. The doctors said he would eventually recover from the head wound he had received at Balaclava—perhaps they didn't care to tell his parents otherwise. All Fanny knew was that the lofty scorn and small sadistic cruelties with which her cousin George had been accustomed to treat her had been metamorphosed into this distressing and embarrassing affection. Where once she had defied him, she was now ever so slightly frightened of him.

It was one more reason for her desire to escape. Long ago she had begged Uncle Edgar to let her take some employment, she was young and active, she hadn't Amelia's chances of making a good marriage, if indeed she made any at all, and above all, she was bored. She refused to be content with a life full of trivialities and invented occupations.

Uncle Edgar was shocked and adamant. A Davenport to go into service! Besides, above all, she was his ward, a sacred trust to him from his poor cousin Edward. He would carry out that trust to his dying day.

'There are plenty of ways of occupying yourself in this house,' he had said repressively.

Fanny knew all about that. Running errands for Aunt Louisa and Amelia, stitching at the household linen with Hannah, because she sewed so neatly, reading to old Lady Arabella, feeding the screeching peacocks, playing and singing to Uncle Edgar in the evening when he was in the mood for a little music. She was a puppet pulled this way and that. A puppet everlastingly dependent, everlastingly grateful...

Gratitude could turn sour, Fanny thought, as she folded her last garment. Indeed, she was unnatural enough to feel none at all. It hadn't been her fault that her mother had died at her birth nor that her father had contracted a consumption that carried him off before she was three. And Uncle Edgar and Aunt Louisa had so much. This enormous house, the gardens, the lake and the parkland, the little village where the villagers doffed their caps deferentially, the church and even the parson.

One small bewildered child, arriving from the hot sun of the Italian Riviera where her father had gone to die, should not have had to feel gratitude.

Perhaps it was her look of defiant independence that most antagonised Aunt Louisa. Fanny looked at herself in the tilted mirror on her dressing table. At this moment excitement had heightened her colour and her dark blue eyes were brilliant. In spite of the drabness of her grey poplin gown she looked very pretty. She had a long slender neck and a waist that Amelia bitterly envied. Her blue-black hair, smooth and luxuriant, made her look foreign, Amelia said. English men like fair-haired women. And Aunt Louisa considered that Fanny had too bold and direct a way of looking at them. Amelia knew how to lay her thick fair lashes prettily on her cheeks. Not that Fanny hadn't long lashes, too. She must remember to use them modestly. She must remember her position...

While she stayed at Darkwater, she could never forget her position. But she would go on looking directly at people, too. It had never amused her to flirt. She ran rings round giggling Amelia when it pleased her to do so, but in the end the young men discovered that it was Amelia who was the heiress, and the slow significant coolness came into their manner.

Fanny despised all of them. Some day she would meet a man to whom money was of minor importance. But not, intuition told her, while she stayed at Darkwater...

There was a knock at her door, and before she could speak Amelia came bursting in.

'I say, Fanny, have you packed? Papa wants to see you in the library when you're ready. I really do think he could have let me come with you.'

'Perhaps you'd like to go instead of me?' Fanny said coolly.

Amelia flung herself into a chair, pouting.

'What, and be a nursemaid to two children!'

'That's what I'm to be.'

Amelia's round pink and white face, too plump and already uncannily like her Father's, remained unconcerned. She never saw any point of view but her own.

'Oh well, that's different, isn't it? But we could have gone shopping. Will you bring me some French ribbon, anyway. To match my pink bonnet?'

'If I have time, and you give me the money.'

'Oh dear! I've overspent my allowance. I shall have to ask Papa.'

'He won't refuse you.'

'Well, after all, he is my Papa,' Amelia pointed out. 'If yours had remained alive, I expect he'd have been glad to buy French ribbons for you, and seen that you had a respectable dowry. Fanny, who do you think will marry you?'

The question stung.

'Someone who loves me,' Fanny replied calmly.

'But who will that be? I mean, without a dowry——'

'I don't intend to sell myself.'

Amelia sprang up, her cheeks pink.

'What a revolting thing to say. You mean that men prefer me to you just because I'm rich. In other words, that I'm selling myself.'

Fanny gave her direct gaze, without speaking. Amelia's eyes glinted with anger and hurt pride.

'Very well, you have an eighteen inch waist, but Mamma says men prefer women not to be too thin.' Her eyes went to the lovely curve of Fanny's bosom, and fell. She stamped her foot childishly.

'Fanny, you are exasperating. All right, I'm sorry I asked who would marry you. It must be a question that hurts. You can't change customs, and it is important to have a dowry, whatever you say. But I'm sure you'll find someone suitable. Only there isn't that much time, is there?'

Amelia was referring to the fact that Fanny was in her twenty-first year. Fanny chose to misunderstand her.

'No, there isn't, and if I'm to see Uncle Edgar in the library before I leave——'

'I didn't mean that sort of time, but never mind.' Amelia had recovered her good nature. 'Do you think having these children in the house is going to make much difference? Mamma says it will, but Papa says if they're kept out of sight we'll hardly know they're there. And anyway how could he refuse to have his own brother's children. It's awfully lucky Papa's so generous, isn't it? First having you as a ward, and now these two. And coming all the way from China. Mamma's afraid——'

'Afraid of what?' Fanny asked, as Amelia hesitated.

'We just don't know who Uncle Oliver married in Shanghai. Wouldn't it be terrible——'

'If the children were Chinese?'

Amelia's eyes were round and shocked.

'They couldn't be completely because Uncle Oliver wasn't. But they could be—sort of half—and even if they are Mamma says Papa will insist on their coming to church with us on Sundays. Imagine us with ivory-coloured cousins!'

Amelia began to giggle, but she was still anxious. It was easy enough to read her thoughts. She was wondering if even a substantial dowry would tide her over that sort of scandal.

'Mamma thinks it was awfully inconvenient of both Uncle Oliver and his wife to die in that typhus epidemic,' Amelia went on. 'But Uncle Oliver always was in trouble, and I suppose this was his climax, so to speak.'

'Your father must have been glad when he decided to go out to the East twenty years ago, and didn't come back.'

'He must have,' Amelia said in a heartfelt voice. 'Dear Papa, who's so respectable. I believe it wasn't only money with Uncle Oliver, but'—she lowered her voice—'women! That's why Mamma says these children could be anybody.'

Fanny tried to remember the distant day when she, a mere baby, had made the long terrifying journey to Darkwater. She remembered the dark muffling folds of a blanket, and much later the strange strident noise which sent her into floods of tears, but which proved to be only the elegant and haughty peacocks on the lawn. She could have been anybody, too.

'They're your own flesh and blood, Amelia,' she said reprovingly. 'Your father sees that. He's the only one, it seems to me, who does see it.'

Amelia flounced across the room. She had still to learn to move gracefully.

'Oh, Fanny, Don't be so righteous. I know what one's duty is, as well as Papa, and as well as you. But it's an awful bore having to explain about infant cousins all the way from China. And if they should have slant eyes—well, I don't care, I'm not going to let them interfere with my life.'

Poor babies, Fanny was thinking. No one wanted them. Not even Uncle Edgar, really. And she was callously planning to run away, and let Hannah, who would accompany her to London, bring them home.

But she had to seize this opportunity! If she didn't do it now, the war in the Crimea would be over, Miss Nightingale wouldn't require any more volunteers, she would have no alternative but to apply for a position as a governess or a companion, both impossible without references, and both nauseating to think about. At least, in the Crimea, one would be doing a worthwhile task, and probably meeting at last a man to whom integrity, a warm heart, and a little beauty, too, meant more than landed property or stocks and shares.

The children were travelling with their Chinese amah who would remain with them. They would be adequately cared for.

'Fanny, you're not even listening to me!' Amelia said peevishly.

'Yes, I was. I was thinking how we all try to protect our own lives.'

Amelia's pale blue eyes, a little prominent, like her father's, widened.

'But what have *you* to protect?'

'My heart beats, the same as yours,' Fanny said dryly. Then, because she was fond enough of Amelia, who was selfish and undiscerning and remarkably empty-headed, but who did not, at least, have her brother's sadistic qualities, she said reassuringly, 'I'm sure you're worrying unnecessarily. The children will stay upstairs in the nursery and the schoolroom, and you'll hardly see them.'

Amelia shrugged. 'Yes, I expect so. After all, what are servants for? But don't stay in London a minute longer than you need to. I shall have to read to Grandmamma while you're away. You know I can't endure that.'

Both Aunt Louisa and Uncle Edgar were in the library. Aunt Louisa was walking up and down as if this were the end of an argument, and one which, as usual, she had lost, for her lips were compressed, and the tip of her large nose flushed. Uncle Edgar was watching her with benevolence. Arguments seemed to amuse rather than anger him. He rarely lost his temper, a fact which drove his wife to fury. She could have coped with a hot temper, she couldn't cope with the unbendable unbreakable iron beneath her husband's soft, plump, pleasant, facetious, and good-natured exterior.

When Fanny came in they both turned.

Uncle Edgar said at once, in surprise, 'My dear child, why are you looking so shabby? You're not proposing to travel in those clothes?'

Fanny had meant to scrupulously leave behind her fur-trimmed coat, her striped silk gown, and her dark blue bonnet with the velvet ribbons. They were her best clothes and as good as anything that Amelia or Aunt Louisa wore. She considered that they still belonged to Uncle Edgar, and anyway, in her new circumstances, she would have no use for them.

'I thought, for a train journey, with the dust and smuts——'

'Which is very sensible and prudent,' said Aunt Louisa.

Uncle Edgar shook his head.

'On the contrary, Louisa my dear, that's quite wrong. Fanny is representing me. She must look her best, in any case, we always like her to look her best.'

When he noticed her, Fanny thought privately. For he had a curious trick of seeing her, and probably his own family, too, only through the eyes of outsiders. She could wear a faded and shabby house gown the entire week, without comment, but as soon as visitors were expected, or, more particularly, when she followed the family procession into church on Sunday mornings, she had to be expensively and fashionably dressed so as to do him credit. So that people could say that Edgar Davenport was remarkably generous to his penniless niece?

It was only in her darker moments that Fanny believed that last assumption. Uncle Edgar was a fair and kindly man. He was absent-minded at home. He truly didn't notice what his family was doing or wearing unless they drew attention to themselves. He spent a great part of the day in the library with his stamp collection, his erudite books, his correspondence on charitable affairs which he meticulously looked after himself, and his committees. He looked just a little eccentric, with his high domed balding head with its ruff of hair that would one day be saintly shining silver, his prominent mild blue eyes, his full-lipped mouth. In the house he liked to wear a shabby wine-coloured velvet smoking jacket, and was given to extravagantly-coloured waistcoats. A heavy gold watch chain lay across his chest. The watch concealed in his pocket was a chiming one. He had used to make it chime for the children when he was in a jovial mood. It had often stopped tears and tantrums. Fanny wondered if its magic would be called upon for the new children. She hoped it would, for if Uncle Edgar were not kind to them, who would be?

'You will go upstairs and change,' Uncle Edgar was saying. 'You have plenty of time. The carriage has been ordered for half past eleven. The train leaves at twelve. Now repeat to me again exactly what you have to do.'

'Yes, Uncle Edgar, I'm to take a cab from the station to the shipping office to make enquiries as to whether the *China Star* has arrived, as expected, and which train the children will be on. I'm also to ask if an official has been sent to meet them and escort them to London, and later to suitably reimburse him.'

'What is suitably?'

'A guinea as you suggested, Uncle Edgar.'

'Correct, my dear. What next?'

'After we've been to the shipping office and ascertained our time-tables Hannah and I are to go to our hotel and wait.'

'Correct again. You see, Louisa, Fanny is quite capable of taking charge of this business. It saves you a journey which I'm sure you don't want, and it's quite impossible for me to get away. I'm far too busy. I'm a man of many affairs.'

'Too many,' said Aunt Louisa tartly. 'If you'd taken a little more interest in your brother when you were both young, we might never have been in this contretemps.'

'I don't think my influence would have stopped Oliver going to the bad,' Uncle Edgar said seriously. 'He was always uncontrollable, even as a small boy. Anyway, I wouldn't refer to this matter as a contretemps. It merely means our family is a little larger. What of that? There are enough empty rooms in this house. It will keep the servants up to the mark.'

'The children will have to be taught.'

'Ah, yes. You mean the problem of a governess.' Uncle Edgar's eyes flicked to Fanny and away so quickly that she couldn't be sure he had looked at her. 'Well, we don't need to take all our fences at once. And anyway, my dear, we've been over this matter often enough. Oliver has made the children my wards. I have no alternative, have I, even had I wanted one. Which naturally I don't. I shall enjoy the little beggars.'

He gave his wide beaming smile. And Fanny knew that he didn't want these strange children any more than, seventeen years ago, he had wanted her. But he was a man of principle and it worried him that he should have uncharitable thoughts. He was busily convincing himself and his wife that he hadn't.

Aunt Louisa got up, in her fussy bossing manner.

'I won't have Amelia's chances ruined.'

'My dear, whatever do you mean?'

'You've promised her a dowry of ten thousand.'

'Did I suggest reducing it?'

'No, but you frequently talk as if money is short, and now there will be extra expense. You can't deny that. And the other thing is,'—Aunt Louisa hesitated, biting her lip—'must we let it be known the children are coming until we see what they look like, I mean, supposing——'

Uncle Edgar threw back his head, guffawing heartily.

'You mean, supposing the little beggars are yellow? There's not a chance. Oliver was a fool, but not that much of a fool.'

'How do you know?' Aunt Louisa said tightly.

'Why, the devil take it, because he was a Davenport.'

Uncle Edgar was feeling in his breast pocket. His expression had changed. His brother Oliver's undisciplined life and inconvenient demise had been put out of his mind, and he was smiling with anticipatory pleasure.

'Come here, Fanny. Your aunt and I thought we would like to make you a small gift. You've been with us a long time now and you've given us a great deal of help, not to say pleasure.'

Fanny looked swiftly from one to the other. Aunt Louisa's expression had not changed. She was still thinking petulantly of the awkwardness and inconvenience of having to give a home to the strange children arriving from Shanghai—or was she thinking of the unsuitability of giving Fanny a gift?

But Uncle Edgar was smiling and waiting for Fanny's response.

She bit her lips. Whatever the gift was, she wasn't sure she could accept it gracefully.

'Look,' said Uncle Edgar, opening a small red morocco box.

The jewel gleamed on the red velvet. Fanny's self-possession left her and she gasped.

'But Uncle Edgar! Aunt Louisa! It's too valuable!'

Uncle Edgar picked up the pendant and swung it from his plump forefinger. It was a dark blue sapphire set in diamonds and gold filigree.

'It belonged to an aunt of mine,' said Uncle Edgar. 'A great-aunt of yours. So you're entitled to it just as much as Amelia would be. That's what you're thinking, isn't it?'

Fanny looked again mutely at Aunt Louisa. Aunt Louisa said in her tart voice, 'Don't thank me. I personally think your uncle is spoiling you. Just because you're going on a short journey which is no doubt a great excitement and pleasure to you.'

So she was expected to take charge of the children when they had settled down at Darkwater. Aunt Louisa could not have told her more plainly. She was full of indignation and confusion, for she didn't mean to come back, anyway. So how could she accept so valuable a present?

Fanny had inherited from her Irish mother not only her luxuriant dark hair, but a mobile mouth whose lower lip protruded when she was hurt or angry. It was something she couldn't control.

'Why are you giving it to me, Uncle Edgar?' she asked

aggressively.

Uncle Edgar's expression remained amused, benevolent, just a little unreadable.

'Because it pleases me to. It's as simple as that. Your aunt thought we should have waited until your twenty-first birthday. She didn't agree that this was the right occasion on which to make you a gift of this kind. Why not, I said? Fanny's like a daughter to us. We must do all we can for her. After all, she has only her looks to get her a husband. I've no doubt they're more than sufficient, but a bauble or two may help. Come here, my dear. Let me put it on you.'

Some people, Fanny thought, were born to be givers and some takers. Neither appreciated the other. She must accept this gift gracefully, although it couldn't have been made at a worse time. This was not the moment to begin feeling grateful, otherwise her strength of purpose would weaken. After all, she could leave the jewel behind. Amelia would eventually pounce on it greedily and claim it as her own.

Uncle Edgar's plump hands, remarkably soft, on the back of her neck made her flesh prickle. Once before she had felt them there. It was a long time ago. She was dripping wet from her fall into the lake, and he was caressing her beneath her soaking hair, reassuring her. She remembered that she had been still trembling with fear and shock.

The sapphire lay like the touch of a cool finger-tip against her throat.

Aunt Louisa had thawed sufficiently to give a frosty smile and said, 'It's very becoming, Fanny. You must wear it at Amelia's coming-out ball.'

'Yes, Aunt Louisa. Thank you very much. Thank you, Uncle Edgar.'

(And people would say, Where did you get that magnificent pendant? Your uncle? Isn't he the most generous person in the world! . . .) But she wouldn't be there. She would be far far away in the Crimea, in a useful world she had found for herself. Fanny's lashes fluttered, and Uncle Edgar cried joyously, 'There! She's looking delighted. Aren't you, my love?'

He gave his throaty chuckle and patted his wife's cheek.

'I hope you will look as delighted the next time I give you a piece of jewellery. Eh, my dearest?' He was using his playful tone, which meant he was in a high good humour. 'But of course you will. You always do. That's one of the most charmingly predictable characteristics of the fair sex. Now, Fanny,' his voice changed to his brisk business-like one. 'You have only fifteen minutes in which to change before Trumble will be waiting. So run along, and see that Hannah is ready, too.'

3

DARKWATER... The name had come from the peculiarly dark colour of the water in the moat that had surrounded the house until the last century. The brown soil and the frequently lowering grey sky had made the water look black. Now the moat had been drained and the sloping lawn was green and innocent, but the lake glittering beyond the yews and the chestnuts had the same tendency to turn into black marble on a dark day.

The drawbridge had gone, the Elizabethan façade of time-mellowed brick, diamond-paned windows, and rows of tortuously shaped chimneys, remained. Extensive restoration work had been done at the beginning of the century, but there were still the cavèrnous fireplaces, the winding stairways, the elaborately carved oak ceilings, darkened with time, and the tiny minstrels' gallery hanging over the long dining room.

There were twenty bedrooms, as well as those of the servants in the attics. The house and parkland lay in a gentle fold of the hills. Only from the upstairs windows were the moors visible. The wind blew across them and into the house which was always full of draughts and ancient creaking noises.

It was only in the summer that the place was innocent. Then the tattered and writhing shapes of the oaks were concealed beneath green leaves, the yellow flag irises swayed on the edge of the lake, and the water reflected the passing clouds. Sun shone through the diamond-paned windows of the house, and the whining edge had gone out of the wind. In the downstairs rooms there was an old, old smell, impregnated in the walls, of pot pourri, beeswax, woodsmoke, and roses. The warmth of the sun brought it out.

In the summer Darkwater was beautiful. It was as if its happier ghosts—perhaps there were summertime ghosts—lived then.

But in winter the picture was entirely different. The gardens and parkland were desolate, leafless, and stricken. Clouds and mist hung close to the ground. The Chinese pavilion by the lake, built by the same Davenport who had restored the house, its red and gold paint flaked and faded with the years, looked barbaric and completely alien. The wind battered on the windows and the heavy draperies made slow deliberate movements. Logs smouldered in the great fireplace in the hall day and night and fires had to be maintained in the living rooms and bedrooms. With the curtains drawn and the lamps lit the rooms took on a cosiness that deceived all but the most sensitive. These might be nervous maids who spilt hot water or a scuttle of coals in the passage because a curtain billowed out, or a voice cried. Or it was more likely to be the children who didn't care for the long passages at dusk and screamed if a draught blew out the candle. Amelia used to cling to Fanny's skirts. Fanny remembered once taking a wrong turning and instead of opening her bedroom door finding herself in a completely strange room, with a fourposter, and the dark shape of a form in the bed.

She had been sobbing with fright when the maid found her.

'It's your own fault, Miss Fanny! Running ahead like that, thinking to be so clever.'

'There's s-someone in the bed!' Fanny stuttered.

The maid held the candle high. Its flickering light fell on the plump coverlet and the long shape of the bolster. The bed was empty.

'You see! There's no one there. This room hasn't been used for ages. Not since my time here, anyway. You're a silly girl to be frightened.'

But the little maid, not much taller than Fanny, was frightened, too. Fanny knew that by the way the candlestick shook in her hand. They had scurried back down the passage, round the right turning, and safely to Fanny's room, the little narrow one next to Amelia's and the nursery.

That was when Fanny first began to hear sounds in the wind, voices, laughter, and sometimes footsteps.

But that was partly Lady Arabella's fault for the unsuitable stories she had used to tell the children before their bedtime. She would begin an innocent fairy tale, and then, when the three children's attention was completely engaged, the tale would become subtly and indescribably sinister, this somehow made worse by Lady Arabella's own plump kindly and cosy appearance. Only her eyes showed a curious glee. They were the wolf's eyes looking out of the amiable sheep's head.

Amelia used to burst into sobs and have to be comforted with sugar plums. Fanny had never cried. Once she had put her fingers in her ears, and Lady Arabella had chuckled with what seemed to be gentle satisfaction. But mostly she had been driven to listening with a terrible fascination. She was not always able to eat her sugar plum afterwards, but put it in the pocket of her apron to be enjoyed in a calmer moment. George, of course the eldest and a boy, never showed any nervousness or fear, but it was significant that now, in his delicate state of health as a result of his war wound, he frequently had nightmares and cried out, not about the charging Cossacks, but about the human head beneath the innocent piecrust, or the clothes in the wardrobe that came out and walked about in the dusk.

George was too old now to be conforted with sugar plums. He kept a bottle of brandy beside his bed instead. It was on the doctor's recommendation.

When Edgar Davenport had bought Darkwater some three years after his marriage, Lady Arabella had come to make her home there. She hadn't been interested in sharing the young couple's quite modest manor house in Dorset, she had bitterly opposed her daughter's marriage to a young man whom she had considered a nobody. She was the daughter of an earl herself, and had thought that Louisa could have done a great deal better for herself. But Louisa hadn't any great beauty and since Lady Arabella's husband had squandered her own fortune, and then drunk himself to death, Louisa's chances were considerably marred. At the age of twenty-three, she had been very glad to take Edgar, as perhaps her only chance. And anyway, if he was a quietish sort with no dashing looks, he was still a pleasant and amusing young man, with none of his young brother's tendencies towards wildness. As it turned out, he was a very good catch, for when the ancient great uncle in Devon died, and Darkwater came on the market, it appeared that Edgar had more resources than he had divulged.

Darkwater, he said, must not be allowed to go out of the family. He would buy it himself, even if it meant economising for years to come. His wife demurred, it was late autumn when she saw Darkwater for the first time and it depressed and vaguely frightened her. The leaves were falling and the clouds hanging low. The house indoors had the shabbiness to be expected after the eighty year occupation of a bookish and solitary bachelor. It made Louisa shiver. Or perhaps this was only because she was at that time expecting Amelia, and pregnancies didn't agree with her.

But Edgar had no intention of asking his wife's opinion. He was the master and the decision was his. He had made up his mind the moment he had heard of his great uncle's death.

So, just before Amelia's birth, the family moved to Devon, and Lady Arabella accompanied them. It was necessary for a mother to be near her daughter at such a time, she said. Her innocent myopic eyes told nothing, but it was clear enough from the start that she considered Darkwater a fitting residence for herself, the descendant of a noble family. She meant to spend the rest of her life there.

She had no patience with Louisa's fancies about the place. Anyway, Louisa's blood had been considerably watered down by the unfortunate father she had had, and one wouldn't expect her to fit so easily into this environment.

Edgar took immediately to the life of lord of the manor, with his stable well-stocked with good hunters and his house with servants, his tenants eagerly welcoming a landlord who was interested in their welfare, the village church no less, for it needed restoration and a vicar less old and doddering, and the sparse social life of the moors desperately wanted an infusion of new blood. Lady Arabella also took to the mingled charm and desolation of Darkwater. She found that it suited her temperament. The closing down of the mist filled her with excitement, she adored the wind-petrified shapes of the leafless trees, she simply put on another shawl if the draughts were too bad.

She selected two large rooms on the first floor and made them uniquely hers. As the years went by the rooms shrank, for they were so cluttered with her possessions. These included a life-size marble statue of her mother, the Countess of Dalston in Grecian robes which stood imposingly in a corner. At dusk, before the maids had brought in the lamps, it looked terrifyingly like another person in the room. Even more so when Lady Arabella had negligently tossed one of her shawls, or perhaps her garden hat, on to it. But this was strictly her privilege. No servant or child was allowed to take such liberties.

For the rest, there were innumerable small tables, knick-knacks, paintings, low chairs with uncomfortably sloping backs, an astonishing edifice of seashells and fishes beneath a glass dome, an enormous globe on which she was wont to make the children trace all the countries of the British Empire, a birdcage empty and a little morbid since her parrot had died, heavy plush curtains heavily ornamented with bobbles, gilt-framed mirrors, cupboards filled to overflowing with a hotch-potch of stuff, and in the centre of the room the chaise-longue on which Lady Arabella spent a great deal of her time, doing her needlwork or pursuing what she called her historical readings. She was deeply interested in history and folklore, particularly regarding the part of the country in which she lived.

Or she might simply sit idle with her cat Ludwig in her lap.

'Do you know why he is called Ludwig?' she used to ask the unwillingly enthralled children. 'Because once I was in love with someone called Ludwig. Oh, yes, stare if you like, but it's true. He was a German prince. He had moustaches, so!' Lady Arabella puffed her cheeks and caressed imaginary moustaches. She was a born story-teller. 'But he wasn't permitted by his parents, or protocol, call it what you will, to return your Grandmamma's love. And anyway I was only sixteen, which was much too young even in those days, when we were all wearing muslin dresses that looked like nightgowns and pretending to be afraid of Napoleon Buonaparte. So now I have only a cat to love me. Unless by some chance any of you children do.'

She stared at them so hard with her round short-sighted eyes that they murmured affirmatives, Amelia going so far as to cry, 'I do, Grandmamma. I do.'

It was always George, her favourite, to whom Lady Arabella looked for a display of affection.

But it was only Ludwig, the big dark tabby with the flat supercilious face who sat on her lap and rubbed his head insinuatingly against her. Fanny was sure he was the German prince reincarnated.

Those two rooms were a small world within a world. As a child Fanny had felt as if she had been on a nerve-wracking journey when she had had to visit Lady Arabella. It was only when she was grown-up and read to Lady Arabella daily that she lost her fear of the old lady. Or thought she did.

Louisa had grumbled continuously after the move to Darkwater. Finally her husband, in spite of his constant talk of economy, found enough money to buy her an elegant sable cape and muff. So Louisa made the discovery that an expensive gift could do a great deal towards mending hurt feelings. She never let her husband forget that again.

When Fanny, the difficult precocious three year old, who already showed that she was going to have more looks than Amelia, arrived, Louisa found that a diamond brooch made her more tolerant towards the child. During the years, various crises were suitably marked by trinkets, a new bonnet, silk for a gown. Edgar Davenport was an indulgent husband. Or perhaps he just liked peace.

Needless to say, Louisa was already debating the price of the orphans from Shanghai. This could be a high one, because the situation was getting ridiculous. Edgar's relatives seemed to have a habit of dying like flies and leaving their offspring in his devoted care. To have three penniless children foisted on one was not amusing during the course of one's marriage. Not to say that Fanny wasn't quite useful now, so long as she kept her place. But with the worry of George's health and the launching of Amelia into society, there was just no time or place in Louisa Davenport's life for small foreign children.

George was waiting at the turn of the stairs when Fanny, dressed now in her best, came down. He sprang out at her and seized her hand. She started violently. She hadn't seen him there in the shadows. He was always doing this sort of thing now, lying in wait for her, and then laughing immoderately, especially if she screamed.

He wasn't laughing today. Instead he put her hand to his lips, pressing a passionate kiss on it.

Fanny tried to snatch it away. She couldn't until he chose to let it go. He had a frighteningly strong grasp.

'I wish you wouldn't do that, George. It's absurd, and I don't like it.'

'Absurd?' The word faltered. He was hurt, his confidence ebbing. He was such a good-looking young man, tall, broad-shouldered, a high glow in his cheeks. When he had joined the 27th Lancers he had looked so proud and arrogant in his uniform. But now, although he had suffered no physical disfigurement, his long body had that vaguely shambling look, his eyes changed too quickly from uncertainty and hurt to intense excitement. His actions, too, were unpredictable. He would want the groom to saddle his horse at midnight so that he could ride over the moors, or he would walk about the house calling out softly to see who was awake and would talk to him.

All the doctors said that a long period of rest and quiet was essential. After that he should be able to lead a normal life, not too strenuous, perhaps. His army career was certainly over. But there seemed no reason why he shouldn't eventually marry.

'George!' That was his mother's voice from the foot of the stairs. It was sharp. Although it was addressed to George, the sharpness was for Fanny. She was annoyed by this attachment her son had formed for Fanny, and blamed Fanny for it. It was easy enough to cool a young man's ardour if one wanted to. Fanny obviously didn't want to. After all, George was quite a catch.

'George, Tomkins had been walking up and down with your horse for half an hour. He said you wanted it by eleven. Don't keep the poor beast waiting any longer.'

'Oh, lord, I forgot.' George was an abashed schoolboy, the passionate lover gone. 'Well, good-bye, Fanny. Have a good time. Don't stay away long. We'll miss you.'

Why, this might be the last time she ever saw him! The knowledge swept over Fanny, making her forget George's recently developed disturbing habits, and remembering only that he had always seemed to be her brother.

'Good-bye, George,' she called fondly. 'Take care of yourself.'

George turned to give a gratified wave. His mother said tartly, 'Since you'll be gone no more than two nights, Fanny, nothing much can happen to George or any of us in that time.'

'Things can happen to people all the time,' Lady Arabella was shuffling down the passage from her room. 'I fancy I heard the bird last night.'

Once, only once, long ago, when she had been less than ten years old, Fanny, too, had heard the bird. She had lain petrified for hours after the scuffling noise had stopped. The legendary bird was reputed to be imprisoned in one of the many chimneys, though in which one no one was ever quite sure. It had been a white bird, the legend said, though when finally it fell lifeless into the hearth it was pitifully soot-streaked. It could have been a white barn owl, people said, or a dove. Or there was the fantastic story that it had been a white heron, its long legs hopelessly entangled in the narrow space. That had been why the fluttering and screeching had been so loud. Its imprisonment had coincided with the death of the young mistress of Darkwater at that time. When the dishevelled creature had fallen into the hearth, her young face had lain like snow on her pillow.

As the years and then the centuries passed, the struggling bird was heard again and again. It always portended disaster.

'Mamma, there was a gale blowing last night,' Aunt Louisa said. 'That's all you heard.'

'That's what you'd like to think,' said the old lady portentously. 'But remember the last time I heard it. We had news about George soon after.'

Aunt Louisa clucked impatiently.

'Goodness me, it's a good thing we haven't all got your imagination. If I'd listened to all your omens I'd have been frightened out of my life years ago. Now watch your step. Where are you going?'

The old lady lifted her voluminous skirts an inch or two and peered short-sightedly at the stairs.

'To say good-bye to Fanny, of course. Should I be left out of the farewells?'

'First George, and now you. Anyone would think Fanny was going on a long journey and not coming back.'

Lady Arabella had reached Fanny's side. She was out of breath and wheezing a little. She tucked a crumpled package into Fanny's hand.

'Sugar plums, my dear. Eat them on the journey. Keep one or two for the children. They will find them comforting. You always did, do you remember?'

'Yes, Great-aunt Arabella. Thank you very much.'

Fanny's eyes pricked with tears. It was a good thing the old lady was too short-sighted to see them. Anyway, she had turned to remount the stairs. She had two woolly shawls around her shoulders. Her head, with its slightly awry lace cap, sank among them cosily. With her short broad stature and her skirts tending towards the crinoline, it was virtually impossible to pass her on the stairs. She was more comical than sinister. Surely she wasn't really sinister, at all. That had been only childish imagination in a dusk-filled room.

Now she had been kind, and Fanny wished passionately that she hadn't been. First it had been Amelia with her request for French ribbons, then George urging her to hurry back, and now Lady Arabella giving her comfits for her journey.

But she mustn't let these things shake her resolution. She wouldn't be back at Darkwater. Never again . . .

Hannah had appeared with the baggage, and Uncle Edgar came in briskly to say that the carriage was at the door.

'That's better,' he said, looking at Fanny's smart appearance. Her fur-trimmed cloak, the smart shiny boots peeping beneath her silk skirts, her bonnet tied with velvet ribbon, all marked her as a young lady of taste and fashion. 'You must look your best, my dear, otherwise you may find people trying to take advantage of you. Hannah!'

The elderly servant in her modest dark attire came forward.

'Yes, sir?'

'I expect you to take good care of Miss Fanny. Don't let her do anything foolish.'

Hannah's lips went together. It wasn't for her to say that the master must know Miss Fanny could be unpredictable at times. Didn't he remember the storms and tantrums at intervals in the past? But one had to admit she looked a well-bred well-behaved young lady at this minute, so perhaps all would be well. Personally she couldn't wait until the nerve-wracking journey in one of those fast smoky trains was over, the perils of London safely avoided, and all of them home again in the peace and quiet of Darkwater.

'Fanny! Fanny!' Amelia was flying down the stairs, her skirts billowing. 'Here's the money for the ribbon. Papa gave it to me. Don't forget, it's to be striped. And if you can't get the exact shade, get the nearest you can.' Amelia's cheeks were as pink as the ribbon she hoped Fanny would bring back from London. She was a silly little affectionate thing, and one didn't want to disappoint her . . . Reluctantly Fanny put out her hand for the money. Hannah could bring back the ribbon. Uncle Edgar was smiling indulgently. Aunt Louisa said, 'Really, Amelia! You and your fal-lals. I hope you're not neglecting the serious reading Miss Ferguson recommended every day. Then come, Fanny. Trumble can't wait forever.'

Darkwater . . . All the way down the curving drive, Fanny's head was thrust out of the carriage to look back. The sun was out from behind the clouds, and the house looked the way she loved it most, warmly red, the windows shining, smoke curling from the twisted chimneys. It was like a jewel lying against its backdrop of gentle green hillside. The flaring red of the rhododendrons marked the path to the lake. The lawns were velvet. The peacock and the peahen strutted near the rose garden. Rooks cawed in the swaying elms.

'Put your head in, Miss Fanny, do.'

Fanny fumbled for her handkerchief. She couldn't let Hannah see the tears on her cheeks. It was Hannah, long ago, who had told the children, and the avidly interested Lady Arabella the legend of the bird in the chimney. She had heard it from the previous housekeeper who had been in employment at Darkwater for forty years. And before that it had come from another superstitious and nervous servant.

It was only a legend. No one really believed it, not even Lady Arabella, although it pleased her to make startling announcements.

Indeed, there must often have been a bird caught in one of those many chimneys, a swift, perhaps, or a starling. But not that white forlorn sinister one that was a portent.

Yet Fanny had sometimes likened herself to the unfortunate creature. She too, had been caught in her poverty, in her orphanhood, in her inability to live a free untrammelled life because an unprotected young woman had little place in the world.

That was why she had determined to escape before she, like the bird, suffocated in the claustrophobic atmosphere.

But today she loved Darkwater. If only the morning had been dark and gloomy, the clouds pressing down, the wind whining. But the sun shone and she had a sense of identification with the great faded rose-red house lying against the hill-side. It was as if she had known it, not only for the seventeen years of her residence there, but for centuries. She was going to long for it bitterly, as if she had left part of her heart behind.

A branch whipped her face. She drew back, a reason now for her tears.

'There, I told you,' said Hannah. 'Hanging out there like a great overgrown child. You're a fine one to be bringing little children safe home.'

Fanny dabbed at her reddened cheek.

'I'm sorry, Hannah. I do foolish things.'

'You don't need to tell me that, Miss Fanny.' Hannah had been at Darkwater for fifty years. She came from the village where she, and her seven brothers and sisters had slept like peas in a pod in the bedroom of the two-roomed cottage. Her father had been a labourer on the estate and her mother, in between being brought to bed with a new baby, had helped in the kitchen of the great house. Later, there had only been two brothers and a sister left. The rest, one by one, had withered away with a fever. Only four in the big bed had seemed lonely. Hannah had been glad at the age of twelve to begin work in the great house. Now she was sixty-two and had earned the privilege to speak her mind. 'I can see I'll have my hands full with the three of you.'

'No, you won't, Hannah. I'm going to be perfectly sensible.'

Hannah reached out a neatly gloved hand to pat Fanny's. Being the eldest of eight children had given her a maternal quality that she had never lost. Her face, apple-cheeked and prim, within the sedate circle of her bonnet was full of kindness.

'Of course you will, love. You can be when you wish. But don't look as if it's going to be such pain to you. Or is it that you're homesick already? Silly child. You're not leaving Darkwater forever.'

4

EVERYTHING had gone according to plan. Fanny and Hannah had arrived safely in London to find that the children were due from the ship docked at Tilbury by midday the next day. Fanny had contained her excitement about her own private plans sufficiently even to go shopping for Amelia's ribbon. She meant to go with Hannah to meet the children, take them by cab to Paddington and put them on the train for Devon, then take Hannah aside and say good-bye.

Hannah would be dreadfully upset, she might even be angry, but she was a servant and must do as she was ordered. She was quite capable of taking the children safely to Darkwater and breaking the news of Fanny's escape.

Escape? It was odd that that was the word that came to her.

Of course she didn't mean to tell Hannah where she was going. That could result in Uncle Edgar fuming and fussing to London to insist on her returning home. She would merely say she had a situation and was going to take it up that day.

It had all seemed so simple. The only thing she had overlooked was her emotional reaction to the new arrivals.

She hadn't thought they would look so small and desperately self-contained and lost. It hadn't occurred to her that she might see herself in them, herself as she had been seventeen years ago, just as frightened and lost, just as eager for a welcoming voice.

But there they were, the strange little trio, rooted to the ground with apprehension. Miss Nightingale and her nurses, the pride of doing a worthwhile task, the possibility of meeting some young man who would marry her for love, all swept out of Fanny's head. She was kneeling on the dusty sooty ground to gather the children into her arms.

The amah was bowing low. Behind her the strange man said, 'I take it you are Miss Davenport?'

Fanny straightened herself. The little girl whom she had embraced stood aloof, her black eyes still staring warily, but the boy's cold hand was curled within her own.

'I am. And you're the gentleman from the shipping company who so kindly met my little cousins.'

He bowed. 'My name is Adam Marsh.'

She hadn't needed to know his name. She wondered how she could best give him his guinea with dignity and bid him farewell. She thought he was behaving in a slightly too familiar way for a mere employee of a shipping company. He was really staring at her quite openly. His eyes were very dark brown, almost black.

'Thank you, Mr Marsh, for your help. My uncle will no doubt be writing to you. In the meantime, he instructed me to give you this.'

She held out the guinea in her gloved hand. She thought that for a moment Mr Marsh looked surprised, as perhaps was not to be wondered at. He would hardly expect to receive money from a young woman. But in a moment his fleeting expression of surprise had turned to what seemed to be amusement, and he took the coin with another bow. He was well-dressed, she noticed, his coat of excellent cut, his linen immaculate.

'My thanks to your uncle, Miss Davenport. But surely we're not parting immediately. I believe I was to see you safely on your train for Devon.'

'That's quite unnecessary. I have my maid waiting at the other side of the barrier. We have ordered a cab.' She looked up at the waiting young man. Something made her add, 'Though I would be grateful if you would see us to the cab and find a porter for the luggage . . .'

'The porter is waiting. And in the cab we'll perform introductions. I believe you don't yet know the children's names.'

He was very self-assured. It was scarcely his business, a stranger, to make her known to her own cousins.

But she couldn't help the relief of being capably looked after. The old Chinese woman looked so remote and unapproachable, and the children seemed likely to burst into tears at any moment. It was nice to see Adam Marsh swing the little boy into his arms, and tell the girl to take Miss Davenport's hand. It made them a little family, filing through the gates, the amah discreetly a few paces behind.

The cab was waiting. The luggage was hoisted on top, and the children, then Fanny, followed by the amah who was plainly terrified of this new method of transport, got inside. Hannah, who was relieved to have everyone safely arrived, climbed in next, and Mr Marsh told the driver to take them to Paddington station.

As Fanny was leaning out to repeat her thanks to him, he lifted a long leg on to the step.

'Is there room inside for me? I think so. Nolly and Marcus and Ching Mei take up the space of only one small person. Marcus can come on my lap.'

He settled down comfortably, his knees all but touching Fanny's.

'But, Mr Marsh——'

'Not a word, Miss Davenport, It's no trouble to me at all. Besides,' he patted his pocket, and surely the gravity of his face didn't conceal the irreverent amusement, 'I have been well paid. Now let me have the pleasure of presenting your cousins to you. This,' he took the little girl's hand, 'is Olivia, but I understand she has always been called Nolly. And this young fellow is Marcus. Shake hands with your cousin——' he hesitated questioningly.

'Fanny,' said Fanny reluctantly, and only for the benefit of the children. This stranger was taking too much on himself. Hannah was looking at him with disapproval. It was the way she should be looking at him, too. Yet she couldn't help liking the easy way he held the little boy in his lap. He surely couldn't be just a lowly shipping clerk. Perhaps he was the son of the owner, learning the business from the ground up, as some young men did.

'Your cousin Fanny,' he said, prompting the children, who reluctantly held out limp cold hands to be shaken.

The little girl spoke for the first time.

'Are we going to live with you?'

The unmistakably hostile and perfectly contained voice abruptly brought Fanny to a realisation of what she had let happen to herself. In a moment of emotion and pity and sympathy she had sacrificed her chances of happiness, happiness which for her lay only in living an independent and worthwhile life. She had gone down on her knees on a dusty smutty railway station and promised two strange children that they would be safe with her.

She never broke promises. She would particularly never break one made to a trusting child. But in the close confines of the cab the strange atmosphere of lostness and danger that had seemed to hang over the children had vanished, and they were just two children like any others, the girl with her cool hostile gaze, the boy not much more than a baby, his nose needing attention, his eyelids beginning to droop.

They would have been all right at Darkwater, with Hannah and Dora, and the little alien-faced amah who as yet had not said a word.

But now she had promised, and already they, or the girl at least, odd little precocious creature, was looking to her for reassurance. And anyway this interfering Adam Marsh obviously meant to stay until the moment the train left, with them all safely aboard. It wasn't any business of his. He was exceeding his duties. But one had to suppose he meant well.

Fanny's resentment against the children encompassed him, too. Did he think she looked the kind of person who would be content with living in the background all her life?

But how could he know she did that? She was the niece of a wealthy man. He probably saw her living a leisured and pampered life. Uncle Edgar had always meant outsiders to see just that.

Fanny impatiently loosened the fastenings of her fur-trimmed cape. It was hot in the cab. She could feel her cheeks flushed. And she was acutely aware that Adam Marsh was still subjecting her to his thoughtful scrutiny, as Nolly said again, patiently, 'Are we to live with you, Cousin Fanny?'

'With your uncle and aunt, and your cousins Amelia and George—yes, and me, too,' she answered meticulously.

'And her?' She pointed to Hannah.

'Yes, Hannah, and the other servants.'

'It sounds a great many people,' said Nolly, with her lack of expression. 'I don't think Marcus will care for that. He's shy.' And suddenly she flung round on the Chinese woman and began a flood of words in a strange language.

The woman replied sharply. The staccato exchange was over in a moment. Fanny noticed, with some bewilderment, that the amah's bright slit-eyes had gone over Nolly's head to Adam Marsh's almost as if in supplication. She murmured something more, and he nodded, as if he understood.

'What are you saying? What is everyone saying?'

Adam replied quietly, 'I think Nolly was begging to be taken back to Shanghai, and of course Ching Mei explained that was quite impossible.'

'Do you speak Chinese?'

'A little. I had a trip to the Far East when I was a boy.'

'Oh,' said Fanny, satisfied. 'So that's why you were chosen to meet the ship today. That was very sensible of the shipping company. It must have made everyone feel much more at home. It's very kind of you to take this personal interest, Mr Marsh.'

'I think I haven't mentioned Ching Mei to you, Miss Davenport. She has made a great sacrifice in leaving her country to bring the children safely here. It appears she promised their mother to do this. But you can understand it was a tremendous enterprise for someone who hasn't travelled before and who speaks little English.'

Fanny was too warm-hearted to let her own disappointments obsess her. She turned sympathetically to the amah in her high-necked black smock and impulsively touched one of the wrinkled yellow hands folded so quietly.

'You will be taken care of, too, Ching Mei. My uncle is very kindhearted and generous.'

The slit eyes in the little alien face stared back uncomprehendingly.

'She won't understand you,' said Adam Marsh. 'But may I say to you, Miss Davenport, that if your uncle could find the opportunity to send her home when the children are settled, it would be a great kindness.'

That was nothing to do with Adam Marsh, either. Uncle Edgar might decide that the cost of an old Chinese woman's return to her country was too high. But Fanny found herself nodding, and in her high unfamiliar voice, Ching Mei suddenly said, 'Velly kind.'

The cab was trundling through the dusty narrow streets that led to Paddington Railway station. In a few more minutes they would be there. If they could find an empty compartment the children could be bedded down on the seats and persuaded to sleep. Because she hadn't expected to make the long journey home, Fanny was now dreading it.

For no reason at all she was thinking of the sapphire pendant locked in her jewel box. She had purposely left it behind, disclaiming possession of it. Now she would have to wear it to Amelia's ball. It would mark her again as one of the family, and this seemed to her to be co-operating in a lie. She was no more one of the family than these children would ever be.

She realised she had never given a thought to the fact that their skin was as white as her own. She didn't think it would have worried her if it hadn't been, but at least Amelia would be profoundly relieved.

Mr Marsh had found them an empty compartment only one carriage from the dining car. He was efficient to the end. He helped them all aboard. Ching Mei, her bland wrinkled face showing no expression, though this must be one more tremendous ordeal for her, came last. Fanny helped Hannah settle the children then emerged into the corridor to see her lifting an intent face to Adam Marsh. He had just finished saying something to her. She gave the briefest nod, then with her neat silent movements, she left him, and he looked up to see Fanny.

'What were you saying to Ching Mei?'

He smiled very faintly.

'You're observant, Miss Davenport.'

'Perhaps. These people are in my charge now. Your duties are ended. There was no need for final instructions.'

He smiled more broadly.

'The final instructions you assume were merely reassurance. Don't you realise that poor little creature is scared out of her wits.'

'I don't see what is so terrifying about Hannah and me,' Fanny said coldly. 'Why wasn't she afraid of you, too? Was that because you spoke in her language?'

'She isn't afraid of you, Miss Davenport, but of this great monster.' He indicated the noisily steaming engine. 'Of the travelling, the strange language, the future.'

'You are very concerned about an old Chinese woman. Why not the children? Everything is strange to them, too.'

She felt his eyes dwelling with their serious intent regard on her face.

'The children will have a future. They will have you.'

'You have certainly summed up the situation in a very short time, Mr Marsh.'

He was too observant. He had caught the asperity, or perhaps the undercurrent of grievance in her voice.

'You speak as if the situation isn't entirely to your liking.'

Fanny lifted her chin. The momentary impulse to confide in him had been so strong and so surprising that she had to speak sharply.

'As far as it is in my power to make them so, the children will be happy. You have no need to feel so concerned for people who have crossed your path so briefly, and only as a matter of business.'

He completely ignored her rebuke. He said softly, 'I think you could make anyone happy, Miss Fanny.'

To her confusion the colour flew into Fanny's cheeks. She had been right in her first opinion. This young man exceeded his duties in the most extraordinary way. He assumed a too proprietory attitude towards a strange family and now calmly called her by her first name. This apart from the intimacy of his remark. And yet...

'I think the porter is about to blow his whistle, Mr Marsh. Isn't it time you stepped off the train?'

'In a moment. Perhaps we will meet again one day.'

'I should think it quite unlikely.'

'Our meeting today was unlikely. Who knows? I have a great liking for the Devonshire moors.'

With this remark he did step off the train. Fanny backed away to return to the compartment and the children, one of whom she could hear crying. But for a moment she was held, not quite understanding her upsurge of hope.

Perhaps there was to be something in her life, after all.

Because a shipping clerk, someone Aunt Louisa would call a mere nobody, had expressed a liking for the moors?

But then, if she were ever to marry, she couldn't expect a husband who was anything but a mere nobody. Unless, of course, he was someone swept off his feet by her beauty and tenderness, to the exclusion of all other considerations...

Mr Adam Marsh, standing on the railway platform looking up at her so intently, did give a vague impression that this might have happened to him.

Fanny's heart was beating uncontrollably faster. Then suddenly, folding the expensive material of her cloak around her, she realised that she looked what she was not, a rich young woman. Certainly rich by the shipping clerk's standards.

He was calling something to her.

'Remember——'

The steam was hissing noisily from the engine. She leaned forward.

'What did you say?'

'Remember me when we meet again.'

The words made their own beautiful shape in the confusion of sounds. Then a cloud of smoke enveloped the platform and when it cleared the whistle had sounded and the train was moving out. It was no longer possible to see the expression in Adam Marsh's face. He stood, a tall figure, raising his hand in farewell. He grew smaller and smaller as the distance lengthened, and Hannah was at Fanny's side saying crossly, 'Miss Fanny, come in, do. All that dirty smoke over your good clothes. And if you ask me, that young man had a great deal too much to say for someone in his position.'

This was all true. But for once Fanny was going to be illogical.

'Oh, I don't think so. He talked the greatest sense. Where would we have been without him?'

'Where we are now, of course,' Hannah retorted acidly. 'And with the boy crying his head off, and that Chinese sitting like a foreign image, I declare I don't know how this journey is to be got over.'

('I almost think, Hannah—I almost think I have fallen in love.') Fanny pressed her lips together, keeping back the impulsive confession. But she couldn't repress the flush in her cheeks, or her surge of gaiety. Now she was glad to be going back to Darkwater. Because if Adam Marsh liked moors he would make a point of spending time on them when he had the opportunity. He was certainly a young man who made his own opportunities. His company would have a ship sailing from Plymouth, perhaps, and he would break his journey down there to make a call at Darkwater to see how the passengers in whom he had taken such an interest were settling down.

Or he would invent some other reason. She had no doubt as to his versatility. And now his interest in the children and the Chinese amah no longer puzzled her. It had developed, of course, immediately after he had set eyes on her.

'Miss Fanny——'

'I'm coming, Hannah. Why are you worrying?' Fanny's voice was gay. 'We are going to have a completely pleasant journey.'

The children were sitting bolt upright. Nolly had refused to lie down, it seemed, so Marcus had done the same, a habit of imitation that Fanny suspected was frequent. There were tears still on his cheeks, and his large smoky blue eyes were woebegone.

Nolly, however, showed no distress. She sat primly, her feet in their shiny buttoned boots crossed, her hands clasped in her lap. She had something of the composure of the elderly amah, a discipline learned far too young, and hiding, Fanny guessed, a smouldering volcano. The black eyes stared with an unchildlike challenge. Small wonder that Marcus was dominated by a sister like this.

'They're not like children at all,' Hannah said in an undertone to Fanny.

'Oh, I think they are,' said Fanny. 'I expect they won't go to sleep because they're hungry. Unpack that hamper, Hannah, and let us have some lunch. Then everybody's temper will be better.'

This, however, was not a complete success. Marcus would have nothing more than a mug of milk, and his sister began a chicken sandwich which presently she laid down with the polite remark that she didn't care for the taste of it. Hannah's lips tightened, but Fanny merely said pleasantly, 'Then try one of these biscuits. I assure you they're very good.'

Nolly stared.

'Doesn't Marcus need to eat his sandwich either?'

'Train journeys,' said Fanny, 'are occasions when one isn't forced to eat anything one doesn't like. Naturally it is different at home. But we're not at home yet, are we.'

'Home?' echoed Marcus hopefully.

'Don't be silly,' said his sister. 'We're never going home again. You know that Mamma and Papa have gone to heaven and we have no home.'

'And that,' said Fanny, 'is something I never want to hear said again. Hannah and I have travelled hundreds of miles to get you and take you home. What a stupid little girl you are. Now will you please ask Ching Mei to have another sandwich.'

Nolly stared with her disconcerting unflickering gaze. She had a small slightly turned-up nose. Her mouth was soft and childlike. Dark ringlets hung beneath her bonnet. She was only a baby, one realised, if one could ignore her alarming composure.

'I don't think we care for you, Cousin Fanny.'

'I'm sorry about that.'

'Do you care for us?'

'Not immoderately at this moment.'

'Then we have no friends.'

'Don't be silly,' said Fanny exasperatedly. 'I'm your friend. So is Hannah. So is your Cousin Amelia and Aunt Louisa and Uncle Edgar.' She spoke firmly, making her words persuasive. But Nolly was staring at her, disbelieving. Perhaps afraid to believe.

'It's true,' said Fanny. 'And now will you please do as I ask. Pass Ching Mei a sandwich.'

The Chinese woman spoke suddenly in her high voice. Nolly pouted, then grudgingly did as Fanny had bidden her.

'There's going to be trouble with that one,' Hannah whispered to Fanny. 'You can't have her only taking orders from the Chinese woman.'

'From Ching Mei, Hannah. She has a name. And Nolly's accustomed to obeying her. She'll learn to obey us, too.'

'There'll be tantrums,' said Hannah darkly. 'Perhaps worse than yours used to be, Miss Fanny.'

'One only needs to have understanding,' Fanny said.

For she knew—Nolly was herself. Uprooted, unhappy, resentful, bewildered, impelled to fight dragons she couldn't see . . . The little girl pulled at her heart already.

Her own rebellion was dead. Or perhaps it was merely taking a different form. From now on she was to be the champion of these two orphans, and do her best to make them happy in an unwelcoming household. That was to be her purpose in life. That, and perhaps the visit of Adam Marsh to the moors . . .

'I don't know what's happened to you, Miss Fanny,' Hannah muttered. 'You're talking like an old woman. And you're flushed, as if you have a fever. Do you feel quite well?'

'I've never felt so well,' said Fanny, with truth.

5

LETTERS arrived for Edgar Davenport late that afternoon. One bore a foreign postmark, one came from London.

Edgar recognised the handwriting on each. He opened the one with the Chinese postmark first. He believed in facing bad news quickly.

It was, as he had suspected, from Hamish Barlow, the attorney who had first written to him about Oliver's death and the trust imposed in him regarding the two children. He fully expected it to contain a list of his brother's debts. This was not the case. Although the debts undoubtedly existed, Mr Hamish Barlow was, surprisingly enough, going to acquaint Edgar personally with them.

By the time you receive this letter I shall be on my way to England. I have a passage on the tea clipper, the Verity, *which, all being well, expects to make the journey in something like twelve weeks. So you may think of expecting me about the end of August or early in September. I have various business affairs to attend to, but I will not deceive you that the journey is being made chiefly in regard to settling your brother's estate. It has aspects which I would prefer to acquaint you with by word of mouth.*

Also, I made a promise to your brother and his charming wife, now so tragically gone from us, that I would satisfy myself as to the safe arrival of the children who should be with you on receipt of this.

I sincerely trust they completed their journey without mishap. The Chinese woman, Ching Mei, is of the highest integrity, and intelligence.

I am looking forward, my dear Mr Davenport, to making your acquaintance, and this I propose to do as speedily as possible after my arrival in London. I shall inform you when this event takes place.

'H'mm,' Edgar muttered, throwing the letter down.

He opened the other one. It was from his stockbroker. It informed him that much to the writer's regret it looked as if the Maxim Banking Company, an enterprise in which Edgar had invested a substantial sum of money, was, contrary to paying a dividend, likely to show a loss on the year's trading. The writer recommended salvaging as much money as possible at once, as he foresaw panic among the shareholders.

'I am sorry to say I predict your loss will be as much as seventy-five per cent, or even more,' the letter concluded.

Upstairs, Louisa Davenport was dressing for dinner. Since Hannah was not yet back from London, Dora, the new maid, was called in to help. She was slow and clumsy and terribly nervous. Louisa had little patience with inexperience. She increased the girl's confusion by ordering her to do too many things.

'Lay out my grey silk. No, not that. That's blue. Where are your eyes? The crinoline. Put it on the bed. Now come and lace me. How strong are you?'

Dora looked at her skinny arms. She was undergrown, plain, with crooked teeth, and only fourteen years old. She had just been promoted to the upstairs after two years of washing dishes and scurrying hither and thither for cook in the kitchen. The mistress had asked her if she were fond of children and she had said yes, because how could you say anything else? Anyway, it was true. There were ten brothers and sisters in the cottage on the moors and she found she had missed them painfully when she had come to the big house. She had been pleased and excited to be told that if she wished she could move upstairs and help to care for the new arrivals from far-off China.

But she hadn't known that would bring her to do anything so terrifying as lacing the mistress.

'I'm very wiry, ma'am,' she said nervously.

Louisa had found the new fashion of the crinoline much to her liking. The only drawback was that it necessitated a neat waist, and that she had not got.

'H'mm,' she said to Dora sceptically, 'We'll see. Take these two ends and pull. Oh, good gracious, girl, you haven't the strength of a fly. Amelia, is that you?' There had been a tap at the door. 'Come and help this incompetent creature.'

Amelia came bursting in, and promptly began to giggle.

'There's no need for impertinence, miss.'

'I'm sorry, Mamma, but you do look funny. Do you really want these awfully tight? You know it makes your face flush.'

'I shall have only six courses at dinner,' said her mother. 'Then I shall be perfectly comfortable. You know we have Sir Giles and Lady Mowatt coming.'

'They're so dreary,' Amelia complained. 'The governor of a prison. Uh!'

'Sir Giles is a man of importance. Your father likes him.'

'Papa! But when is there going to be someone for *me* to like? Someone young. Doesn't Papa realise I'm grown-up.'

'Of course he realises it. Don't be so stupid.'

'He never seemed to notice Fanny was. He never did anything about her. And now she's getting old.'

'Dora,' said Louisa, 'give me the hairbrush. I shall do my own hair. Miss Amelia will help me. You may go.'

Dora bobbed thankfully and withdrew. Louisa turned crossly to her daughter.

'Haven't I told you before not to discuss family affairs in front of the servants?'

'Oh, Dora,' said Amelia. 'She won't gossip because no one listens to her. And Mamma, it's true what I said. Fanny has hardly ever met a young man, and now I'm seventeen I don't intend that to happen to me.'

Louisa surveyed her daughter with mingled indulgence and criticism. It was a pity she wasn't ravishingly pretty. But her skin was good and she had animation. She would never be left sitting silent in a corner. Her fair hair tied in ringlets on either side of her face was quite charming. Being a little over-plump suited her style. She was a presentable daughter. There was only one trouble and that was one her father refused to admit or understand. Her looks faded to insignificance beside Fanny's. Fanny, when her emotions were aroused, had a way of looking incandescent. She reduced Amelia's chatter and smiles and fluttering lashes to the gauche tricks of a schoolgirl.

It was all very well for Edgar, with his exaggerated sense of fairness and responsibility, to insist on the girls being treated like sisters. But Edgar was a man, and men were blind to the subtler points of feminine behaviour. He had to be made to realise that this was Amelia's year, and Fanny must be kept in the background.

For instance, that extravagant unnecessary gift to Fanny of the sapphire pendant had been an error of major importance. It would only serve to make the girl flaunt her looks even more. Edgar refused to see that. But then Edgar always had been stupid. Stupid, stupid, stupid, thought Louisa, the comb snapping in two in her clenched hands.

Amelia sprang towards her.

'Mamma, have you hurt yourself?'

'Of course I haven't.' Louisa laid down the broken comb calmly. 'I was only wondering why you compare yourself with Fanny. The circumstances are entirely different. Your father and I will certainly make it our business to see that you meet plenty of young men, if not here, then in London.'

'London, Mamma!'

'It occurred to me we might open our house there for your ball. But that will depend on your father.'

Amelia clapped her plump small very white hands. (Some day someone would say to her, 'You have very little hands like water lilies, see, just curving open.' And then he would bend his head and kiss her palm.)

'Papa will do anything for me!'

'Will he, indeed. You know I won't permit him to spoil you. And don't be too confident. We have so much worry with George now, and these wretched children arriving are another problem.'

'Fanny will look after them,' Amelia said blithely. 'George will help her. He'll love it. His adored Fanny!'

Louisa frowned. 'Don't speak like that. I won't have this stupid infatuation of George's encouraged. It's nothing but an aspect of his illness. I'd ask you to remember, Amelia, that you are not the only person in the world whose happiness has to be considered.'

'Oh, Mamma! It will take so little to make me happy. Just a ball in London, and a husband I truly love. And a little money, of course, and jewels, and—and——'

Amelia had her face pressed to the window. The moors, dark fold on fold, stretched away to the edge of the earth. The sky was colourless, like river water. There was the far-off cry of a bird. A heron from the lake, perhaps, or an owl. Or the trapped bird in the chimney that Grandmamma was always talking about.

Suddenly Amelia shivered. At dusk she hated the moors, she hated the thought of the grim grey prison ten miles away in its bleak setting. She hadn't minded so much when the prisoners had been French. That had seemed romantic. She had imagined them singing *La Marseillaise* and wanting to die for their country. But now the cold dank cells were occupied by the riff-raff from the streets of London and Liverpool, thieves, forgers, would-be murderers... Sometimes one escaped and the countryside was in terror, with the hounds baying in the mist— for an escaper always chose a time of thick mist when his capture would be doubly difficult. Amelia would imagine she saw the bearded desperate face at her window, and would be torn between terror and a terrible fascination. If it ever happened that a prisoner did appear at her window, would she scream, or hide him beneath her bed and temporarily have the violent creature at her mercy? She didn't know why such thoughts came into her head. She only knew that they made her long to get away from here. She would marry and have six children and live in London where one could go to the theatre or a dinner party every night. And there would always be lights, and no lonely night wind.

'Mamma!' she turned slowly, her voice intense, 'I would do anything to get those things.'

Her mother was clasping her topaz necklace—good enough for the governor of Dartmoor prison—round her plump neck.

'What woman wouldn't! It's always been her aim in life, a good husband and security.'

'You got them, Mamma. You must be very happy.'

Louisa's mouth went down at the corners. Happiness didn't consist of a house full of servants, a wardrobe overflowing with expensive clothes, a warm bed, and a husband beside her who sometimes, but not now so frequently, woke to fumble beneath her nightgown. No, that wasn't happiness, she realised. But just as her mother hadn't pointed out that fact to her, she had no intention of pointing it out to her daughter.

'Of course I'm happy. Don't look so worried, child. You'll acquire all these things. But the effort will be as much mine as yours. I still have connections, even though I've been buried in the moors for so long. I'll do what I can with your father. Now run along and see if Grandmamma is coming down to dinner. If she is, see that she's wearing her cashmere shawl, and that her hair is tidy. Sometimes I believe she deliberately makes herself look like a scarecrow.'

Amelia, her spirits recovered, giggled. 'She does. She's naughty. George is the only one who can make her do things.'

Louisa frowned again, remembering the many ways in which her mother spoiled her handsome grandson. But she merely said sharply, 'Amelia, don't gallop out of a room like that. Learn to glide along quietly and gracefully.'

Amelia paused. 'Like Fanny, Mamma?'

'Nothing of the kind! I have never advised you to model yourself on Fanny.'

'I never have,' said Amelia blithely. 'Anyway, Fanny can dash about when she's in a temper. You ought to see her then. Oh, Papa—I'm just going.'

Edgar came into the room, scarcely noticing Amelia's departure. He was deep in thought.

'My dear, you haven't begun to dress. You must hurry. You know what a stickler for punctuality Sir Giles is. I suppose it comes from running a prison——'

'Louisa, don't chatter! Can't I have a little peace.'

Louisa looked at him in surprise. He was normally a good-tempered and placid man.

'What's the matter? Has something happened?'

'Only a trivial but worrying thing. My brother's attorney from Shanghai is seeing fit to pay us a visit. I must say I regard that as a little nosey-parkering. Probably he imagines me as improvident as Oliver. But even if I were, there's nothing he can do about that. My brother's last instructions must be carried out.'

'How old is he?'

Edgar stared at his wife perplexedly. He had never been able to understand the way a woman's mind worked, and had come to dismiss the whole process as unworthy of serious attention.

'Whatever has his age got to do with it?'

'Is he married? Or perhaps unaccompanied by his wife?'

'What are you thinking of?'

'What you should be thinking of, my love. Had you forgotten Amelia comes out this year? We shall require every eligible man possible if we are to have successful parties. Don't men ever think of these things?'

'Don't women ever think of anything else!'

'Now, Edgar, please don't get irritable. Amelia is your daughter and you must do your best by her.'

'Confound it, I've promised her a very generous marriage settlement.'

'So you have, love.' Louisa gave his hand a perfunctory caress. 'But a marriage settlement is of little use without a husband. I really think we must open the London house——'

'No! That's out of the question.'

'But, Edgar——'

'Don't argue with me. I say it's out of the question.'

'Oh dear. Amelia will be so disappointed.'

'Have you been discussing it with Amelia? Without consulting me?'

His wife's full eyelids drooped slyly.

'I'm afraid we shall need to be persuaded that there are advantages in having a ball here.'

'The London house hasn't been lived in for years. You'd find that everything needed re-decorating and re-furnishing. As it is, Murchison lives there and keeps a couple of rooms available for me, and that's all that's necessary. Advantages! My dear Louisa, it would only be a matter of several thousand pounds more to have the ball in London.'

'Then,' said Louisa, smoothly, 'Amelia and I will expect a much more generous allowance for our wardrobe. Amelia needs several new gowns, and as for me——'

'Stop it,' said her husband harshly.

'Stop it! Please don't speak like that to me! I am merely asking for one small fur tippett.' Louisa's full mouth pouted, reproachfully. 'Only it must be of white ermine. Lady Mowatt has something similar, but of muskrat. Ermine is a much more rewarding fur. And really it is to be such a summer, with these strange children foisted on our household—why I meekly put up with them, I can't imagine—and then the utter fatigue of Amelia's coming-out. But it's the children who are worrying me so much. Your brother's after all, and it's scarcely my fault that he turned out to be such a waster. I don't see why I, or Amelia, poor child, or any of us should be so put about——'

Again Edgar held up his hand to interrupt. He recognised the familiar grievance in his wife's voice. He knew that the ermine tippet would naturally extend to being a cloak costing a great deal more than he cared to think about. He also knew that life wouldn't be worth living until the cloak hung in Louisa's well-filled wardrobe.

'My dear Louisa, will you listen to me a minute? When I said that it would be out of the question to re-furbish the London house, I meant it. Money's short at present. I've made one or two bad investments lately and it's left me short of cash.'

Louisa was alarmed.

'Edgar, it's nothing serious?'

He laughed easily. 'Good gracious, no. It will right itself in time. Something else will come up. But in the meantime I'd be glad if you'd exercise a little economy in the house.'

This was not amusing. Louisa pouted again.

'That won't be easy with two extra mouths to feed and extra servants. Though it would be the least Fanny could do to offer some help. I hope you will speak to her, Edgar. And this, I might say, was certainly not the time to give her an expensive present. Why, that sapphire would have kept the children for a year, or——'

'Bought your ermine tippett?' Edgar observed. 'This was exactly the time to give it to Fanny, if we expect her co-operation. Besides, the child deserved it. Remember, she didn't get a ball, as Amelia is going to.'

'She'll share Amelia's. She can't expect more than that.'

'A very different kettle of fish, my dear. As Fanny would be the first to realise. Well, I suppose I must dress.'

Nevertheless, he sat heavily on the edge of the bed, making no move to go to his dressing room. He was sunk in thought.

'Edgar, what is it about this man from China that upsets you?' asked his wife shrewdly.

'Eh? What are you getting at?'

'Something's worrying you, and I know all that talk about money is merely a disguise.'

'Oh, you do, do you?'

Edgar surveyed his wife. She was laced into her stays and hooked firmly into her crinoline. The neck of the bodice was low and displayed a too generous amount of white flesh. Her hair style, with its tight sausage curls liberally flecked with grey, was more fitting to Fanny or Amelia than to a middle-aged matron. Her cheeks were flushed, and the tip of her nose swollen and bulbous. She had already arranged her face into the animated expression that would last until her guests left. After that, the pouting lips and the look of grievance would return.

When he was in his early twenties, Edgar had fallen deeply in love with a delicate and nymph-like girl called Marianne. He had laid his heart at her feet and she had laughed at him. She had said in her clear laughing icy voice, 'But, Mr Davenport, you look so exactly like a frog!'

Seven years later he had met Louisa who had not laughed at him. She hadn't been pale and nymph-like, but she was the granddaughter of an earl. Edgar had decided that ambition was a much more satisfying object to seek than love. Although he was not beyond expecting that Louisa's ample flesh might be pleasant. And so it was, if grudgingly given. Also she ran his house well, and for all her propensity to be a rattle, was shrewd. She had earned her diamond ear-rings and perhaps her ermine tippett. It was not her fault if he always saw Marianne's pale shadow behind her, and heard that cruel laughter.

'If you must know,' he said, 'I expect Hamish Barlow to arrive with a list of my brother's debts. It must be something serious to bring him so far. In honour bound, I shall have to try to settle them.'

'How vexing!' Louisa cried. 'Couldn't your brother have made a little money. I understand business people in China have.'

'Not Oliver, you may be sure.'

'Well, don't worry about it now,' Louisa said briskly. 'It's late and we must go down. Why don't we have a little music tonight? That always cheers you up. Amelia will play the piano. And next month Amelia and I must have a few days in London shopping. I shall have to find some reliable woman to make her ball gown. She will need a great many things'—Louisa swept up to kiss the top of her husband's head—'and we may look at furs, too.'

'You haven't listened to a word I said.'

'Oh, indeed, to too many.'

Edgar made haste in dressing, hoping for ten minutes alone in the drawing room with a glass of sherry before his guests arrived.

In this, too, he was disappointed, for he found Lady Arabella esconsed in his favourite chair. Wrapped in her fleecy white shawl with her stiff black skirts spreading about her, she looked cosy and gentle and half asleep.

'Well, Edgar,' she said in her husky voice.

'Good evening, Mamma.' His voice was hearty, easy. He had quickly overcome the irritation of finding her in his chair, and the room not empty.

'It was so chilly, I had the fire lit. The summer's late as usual.'

'Good idea. Nice and cheery. Are you dining with us to-night?'

'I thought I would. I miss Fanny. She reads to me.'

'Doesn't Amelia?'

'Oh, Amelia. That harum scarum.' The old lady's voice was indulgent. 'I'm looking forward to the new children. They'll help me to pass the time. Fancy, Edgar! Such skeletons in your family.'

'Hardly skeletons, Mamma. My brother had a past, I admit. But that's no business of the children's. We won't have any of this sins of the father rubbish. I'm a broad-minded man.'

'*And* wise and tolerant,' Lady Arabella approved. 'You know, I once thought my daughter was making a mistake in marrying you. But you've astonished me.'

'Thank you, Mamma. I hope I have been a good husband.'

The old lady smiled gently. Her eyes stared myopically into the fire.

'Giving her this splendid home, too. Do you know, I've discovered a new pastime since the children have got too old for stories. I've been delving into the history of Darkwater. If I had been a man I should have been an historian. These old tales fascinate me. Darkwater has quite a history, you know.'

Edgar had lifted the sherry decanter. He put it down again, listening politely.

'All old houses have,' he said. 'I suppose you're referring to the legendary bird. The bringer of disaster, eh?'

'Not just disaster,' said Lady Arabella enjoyably. 'Death.'

'Come, Mamma! How you love gloom.'

'Ah, yes, gloom. And successions, too. Family trees. All those pictures of fruitful trees with babies in the branches. So pretty.'

Edgar smiled indulgently.

'Where do you find all this stuff?'

'Oh, it's all here in the house. Some of the Davenports were admirable recorders.'

Edgar's smile had faded.

'The library is my preserve. I really can't have you ferreting about in there, Mamma.'

'All those books and no one bothering to open them,' Lady Arabella said regretfully. 'George and Amelia haven't inherited my literary tastes, which is a pity. One's mind should be cultivated. You mustn't deny me my little hobby, Edgar. Besides. I hadn't realised the Davenports were such an interesting family. This house has seen some times.'

Edgar stared at her. Her face was bland, innocent, lost in thought. She might have been telling this story to anyone. It wasn't directed especially at him. Or was it?

No one had rung for lamps to be brought in and the room was full of twilight. Sunk into the wing chair, with the uneven wash of the firelight on her wide black skirts and white lace cap, Lady Arabella looked like a monstrous mole. That's what she was, busily tunnelling her way into old books and diaries, all the musty paraphernalia of a very old house, swallowing the secrets and then letting them ferment inside her. She had a dangerous habit of embroidering and exaggerating. Not that it mattered much what scandals emerged regarding dead and gone Davenports. All the same, he should long ago have examined those old books himself.

'All old houses have seen interesting times,' he said, then realised that he had made that platitudinous remark before, and added, 'It won't see any more while I live here.'

'But how can you be sure?' Lady Arabella said vigorously.

She was embarking on her favourite theme. 'Events are forced on us. These strange children arriving, for instance. They will change the atmosphere and a changed atmosphere provokes things. Then there is George's war injury. You can't deny that has made him almost a stranger. We have to learn to know him all over again. And had you forgotten that this is the year Amelia puts her hair up, and Fanny comes of age. These are the seeds of drama.'

Lady Arabella's voice had become deep and vibrant as it did when she got to the terrifying part of a fairy story, the moment when she was going to deliberately shock and startle her audience.

'You will see, Edgar,' she said portentously.

'Come, Mamma,' said Edgar playfully. 'You're just like a child waiting to stir muddy water to see what lies underneath.'

The old lady pounced.

'Why is the water muddy?'

Edgar put down his glass of sherry, then picked it up and took a large mouthful.

'I don't know what you're talking about. I hope you will keep off such a cryptic conversation at dinner.'

'And why should I? It might liven things up. People enjoy hearing scandal about others.'

'Scandal!' Edgar's eyebrows shot up in surprise. 'What exactly are you referring to?'

Lady Arabella closed her eyes dreamily.

'How I adore other people's letters. So revealing. Your great-uncle was a talented correspondent. I fear it's a dying art in this family. Can you imagine George or Amelia writing really artistic letters. Fanny may, of course. She may have inherited the Irish gift for poetry.'

'I still don't know what you're talking about,' Edgar said good-humouredly. 'My uncle's letters would be with the recipients, not here.'

'Exactly my point. The replies, you understand, are still in existence. I find I have a knack with hidden drawers in desks. I'd have made an accomplished burglar. Then perhaps,' the old lady chuckled, 'I wouldn't have been coming down to dinner when you entertained your friend, Sir Giles Mowatt.'

Edgar was bending over her.

'What did you find?'

'The next thing I shall investigate is secret panels. I can't think why I never thought of this fascinating pastime before.'

'What did you find?'

'Edgar, don't breathe on me like that. I've told you what I found. Merely family letters. No secret hoard of sovereigns, unfortunately.'

'Show them to me.'

'Yes, indeed I will when I find them.'

'You said you had found them.'

'And since then I've mislaid them. Isn't it aggravating—I've grown so forgetful. But they'll turn up, and then certainly you shall see them.'

'Who were they from? You remember that, at least?'

'Someone called Philip. A connection of your great-uncle's. You've never explained the ramifications of your family to me. But he seemed to be a person of distinct literary talent. It's really a pity your children haven't inherited it. Still they do other things. Amelia is clever with her needle, and in spite of his illness, George still rides superlatively. And by the way, Edgar, the boy badly wants a new hunter.'

Their eyes met, Edgar's still and watchful, Lady Arabella's milkily dim. At last Edgar said, 'George has a tongue in his head. If he wants something, he must ask for it himself.'

Lady Arabella shook her head slowly. Her frizzy grey hair ringed from her lace cap in a frosty halo. She looked vague and gentle and only half-concerned with the conversation.

'He won't, Edgar. Since his illness he almost seems a little afraid of you. Isn't that odd?' Lady Arabella picked up her stick and poked playfully at Edgar's gently rounded stomach. 'Such a fine figure of a man are you. I used to say to Louisa before she married you that you were an unprepossessing creature, but perhaps you would improve in middle age. And indeed you have, dear boy. That watch chain now. It must have cost a pretty penny.'

'Mamma, keep to the subject. You were saying that George needs a new horse, but that he hasn't the courage to ask me for it himself.'

'Poor boy. He used not to be like that. It's a great tragedy. We must make his life pleasant for him until he recovers his health.'

'That doesn't involve pampering him. Do you know what a well-bred hunter costs? At least a hundred guineas.' Edgar began to walk up and down, thoroughly put out. What was he, an inexhaustible purse into which all his family dipped? A pool to be fished? A muddy pool, Lady Arabella had insinuated. The devil take her. What was the devious old creature up to? He didn't underestimate his mother-in-law. But he had never remotely considered her a match for himself. The very idea was ridiculous.

All the same, it would be as well to get possession of those letters. If they existed... She was quite able to make the imaginary more dangerous than the reality. What did emerge from all this was that her great love for her grandson was going to ruin the boy.

Edgar's irritation burst out.

'Amelia requires ball dresses, my wife seems to think she will freeze to death without new furs, I have two penniless children arriving to be supported, children I neither begot nor approve of, and now you—you on behalf of my voiceless son, see fit to demand another horse which will probably break his neck! What am I, Mamma? Simply a bank account?'

'How comical!' Lady Arabella clapped her hands appreciatively. 'What an apt description. Only you would have thought of it, dear boy. But that's what a lot of people are, isn't it? Mostly men, of course, but sometimes women, if they have the cleverness to keep their husbands' hands off their money. Such predatory creatures, men. You must admit, Edgar, a new ball dress or a piece of jewellery is negligible compared with what a man will desire.'

'And what's that, Mamma?' came Louisa's voice from the door.

Lady Arabella blinked myopically at her daughter.

'Good gracious, Louisa, you look very grand. I must say Edgar dresses you grandly.'

'What do you mean, Mamma,' Louisa said irritably. 'I've worn this gown a dozen times. I've just been telling Edgar that Amelia and I have a great deal of shopping to do. But why are you sitting here in the dark?' Louisa tugged at the bell rope. 'Why is this house always so dark and cold? Even on a summer evening.'

Edgar recognised the familiar tactics. They would go on until the new furs were bought. His family were leeches, he thought, with cold clarity. Only Fanny demanded nothing. Sometimes he wished she would so that he could be angry with her, too.

'Shall we tell George about his new horse tonight?' said Lady Arabella dreamily. 'The dear boy. He deserves it. He nearly died for his country.'

6

TRUMBLE was waiting on the tiny station platform. Hannah carried Marcus who was asleep. Fanny had attempted to take Nolly's hand, but the child had firmly withdrawn it. She walked at Ching Mei's side, small and upright and independent. It was half past eight and she should have been dropping with weariness. Indeed, her face was colourless, but her eyes stared out as brilliantly as ever.

Fanny could see Trumble staring as they approached. Ching Mei's pigtail and her trousered legs obviously fascinated him. He had expected a Chinese woman, but dressed respectably in skirts and petticoats.

There was mist in the air. The wind was cool and fresh, like cold water. Fanny breathed deeply, smelling the familiar loved smell of damp earth and heather. Perhaps she would have withered away with longing for this and the moorland wind if she had gone abroad or stayed in London.

Trumble had doffed his cap and sprung forward to help with the baggage. As they were about to climb into the carriage Fanny's attention was taken by another small group who had left the train. She stared in pity and horror. There was a man, handcuffed, between two warders. He was on his way to the prison. Fanny caught only a glimpse of his thin bearded face beneath the flaring station lamps before he was hustled off.

She shivered. Imprisonment. It was terrible. There were so many forms of it. The prisoner's face had been expressionless, like Ching Mei's. Like her own must be, at times.

Fortunately no one else seemed to have noticed the episode. And in the carriage, when Marcus woke, and began to sob, Fanny suddenly remembered the sweetmeats Lady Arabella had given her. They had been left untouched in her reticule. She produced the small brown paper bag and distributed the sticky sweets.

'There,' she said. 'We'll be home in less than an hour.'

She thought again, involuntarily, of the prisoner when the

carriage had come to a standstill outside the front door, and Trumble was helping them all to alight.

For either by accident or deliberately, the curtains had not been drawn across the drawing room windows and in the glowing lamplight the scene within was visible in every detail.

Lady Arabella was dozing in the high winged chair by the fire. Opposite her on the sofa Aunt Louisa, her topaz necklace catching the light, was deep in animated conversation with Lady Mowatt. Uncle Edgar stood smoking a cigar and talking to Sir Giles. Uncle Edgar was wearing his most benevolent expression. He looked well-fed and content, a man without a care. Sir Giles must have just said something that pleased him for he made a deprecatory gesture with his cigar. Sir Giles, unlike the hapless creatures in his custody, had a ruddy jovial face as if he habitually dined well and had a cellar as well-stocked as Uncle Edgar's. His wife was a quiet creature, soberly dressed. Aunt Louisa, with her honey-coloured necklace and her massive crinoline looked almost flamboyant in contrast.

Beyond them Amelia and George were sitting at the card table engaged in a game of cards. George looked remarkably handsome. From this distance one couldn't see the lines of difficult concentration on his forehead or his intermittently blank gaze. Amelia wore her sprigged muslin with the blue velvet sash. She had her curls pinned high in an adult manner, and looked very grown-up and sure of herself, the cherished daughter of wealthy parents.

It was a pretty picture. It required no one else in it.

Again Fanny had the overwhelming sense of being excluded from any genuine place in the family. The wind blew in a sharp gust, making her shiver again. The horses moved restlessly on the cobblestones. Hannah was saying, 'You can walk now, a big boy like you,' and had set Marcus down. And suddenly Fanny knew that the strange children, Nolly and Marcus, were looking in at the warm room, too. She felt a small very cold hand slipped into hers. She looked down. It was Nolly at her side. The child hadn't looked up, hadn't made a sound. Her bonnet hid her face. Only her chilly fingers spoke. Fanny reached out her other hand for Marcus, and for a moment the three of them stood there, irrevocably bound.

There was no other way, she realised. She was now passionately identified with them. She was not sorry she had come back.

Then the heavy oak door swung open, the light streamed out on to the cobblestones, and Barker was there, urging them to come in out of the cold. The family in the drawing room had heard the commotion, and Uncle Edgar's deep genial voice was to be heard saying with what seemed like pleasant excitement, 'I believe the children have arrived. Do come and meet them. Lady Mowatt, would you be interested to see my poor brother's children? Louisa my love——'

It really seemed as if they were welcome.

They came inside. Hannah was discreetly whisking Ching Mei up the stairs. Fanny stood with the children still clinging to her.

'Well,' said Uncle Edgar, putting his finger under Nolly's chin and gently lifting it. 'This must be Olivia. I'm your uncle, child. I hope you'll grow fond of me. And this is the boy. Tch, tch, tears won't do. Now I have something that will interest you. Would you care to see my watch? I warrant your papa didn't have one like it. It plays a tune.'

'Edgar, not now. Tomorrow,' said Aunt Louisa.

'Mamma!' That was Amelia, her voice louder than she had intended from relief. 'They're quite white.'

'From exhaustion, I should think,' said Aunt Louisa, and only Fanny saw her angry glance at her indiscreet daughter. 'And a little grubby from the long train journey.'

'By jove,' said Sir Giles, putting down his glass of port. 'They're of a rather tender age, Davenport. I must say I admire your generosity.'

'On the contrary,' said Uncle Edgar, 'the pleasure will be all mine. After all, who knows how imminently I'm going to lose my own children. Amelia makes no secret of being on the look out for a husband——'

'Papa!' Amelia shrieked.

'And Fanny is pretty enough to join her at any moment. So there you are, I have two to take their place. Come, my poppet,' he chucked Nolly's chin again, 'aren't you going to speak to your uncle?'

'They're very tired, Uncle Edgar,' Fanny said.

'She's pretty,' said Uncle Edgar, with great pleasure. 'I believe she looks a little like her father. He had all the looks in our family.'

'And see where they led him,' came Lady Arabella's wheezing voice.

'To an early grave,' said Uncle Edgar sadly, with admirable presence of mind.

'Fanny,' Aunt Louisa spoke authoritatively. 'Take the children upstairs. They look quite worn-out. Now, Edgar, don't interfere. They can see your watch tomorrow. Poor little creatures. They don't know what anything is about at this moment.'

Fanny curtseyed to the company and led the children to the stairs. She had to pick up Marcus and carry him, he was stumbling so badly from fatigue. Nolly followed silently.

At the turn of the stairs she heard Sir Giles Mowatt saying again, 'By jove, Davenport, I admire you. You take a thing like this in your stride.'

'Well, they're not exactly here under duress, like your guests,' Uncle Edgar said, and there was a great roar of laughter.

'They're really quite sweet,' Amelia said in her high voice. 'They look so innocent.'

'Ah, yes. Innocence. A precious quality, one I don't see much of. We must be off, I'm afraid. I, too, was expecting an arrival on this evening's train.'

'Oh, poor man!' cried Amelia. 'What has he done?'

'I'm afraid he escaped from Wandsworth prison where he was doing a sentence for theft. They say he's a desperate fellow, but I warrant he won't escape from Dartmoor.'

Ching Mei was standing in the centre of the room in which the children were to sleep. It was probably the first English bedroom she had ever seen. Her bewilderment simply took the form of rendering her motionless, her hands clasped in front of her, her slitted eyes pulled.

Dora was at the door, goggling. Hannah came bustling out muttering, 'That heathen woman, what's to be done with her? She's useless. Not a bit of unpacking done, and as for getting the children to bed——'

Fanny pushed the children into the room. She said sharply. 'Dora, how would you like to be stared at like that? Go down to the kitchen at once and get Cook to make a bowl of bread and milk. Hannah, will you get the bed in the next room made up?'

Hannah looked at her in surprise. 'For you, Miss Fanny? But it isn't aired! The room hasn't been used since the house party last November. Everything will be damp.'

'Do as I ask you, Hannah. You can put a bed warmer in.'

Hannah nodded slowly. She lowered her voice.

'I understand, Miss Fanny. You don't trust the Chinese woman.' Hannah was refusing to call her by her outlandish name.

'Only to the point that she, too, may be nervous in such a strange house.'

'But we're all upstairs, Miss Fanny! Just overhead.'

'And which of you would wake if a child cried?' Fanny asked sceptically. 'Besides, you know that Dora jumps at her own shadow, and so does Lizzie, and cook would say it wasn't her place, and none of you would wait on a Chinese woman. Would you?'

'Miss Fanny, you do say some things.'

'Besides, I want to be near the children. Tomorrow, I shall have all my things moved up.'

'Permanently, Miss Fanny?'

'Permanently.'

Hannah, with her tired elderly eyes, stared at Fanny. Fanny said, 'I know what you're going to say, Hannah. Start a bad habit and you'll have it always.'

'No, I wasn't, Miss Fanny. I was going to say, bless your kind heart.'

In the other room the children were chattering busily, but the moment Fanny went in, like startled birds, they were silent. All the same, their faces and hands were washed, they were dressed in their nightgowns and ready for bed. Ching Mei, when no strange eyes were on her, obviously worked swiftly and efficiently. She had even opened one of the trunks to get out the children's night things. Now she stood again in her familiar deferential attitude, with clasped hands and downcast eyes.

'That's wonderful, Ching Mei,' said Fanny. 'You are very quick. Dora is bringing up some bread and milk. Try to persuade the children to have some.'

The Chinese bowed. Fanny said perplexedly, 'How much English do you understand? You must have spoken it in my cousin Oliver's home in Shanghai.'

Ching Mei stared.

'Didn't she?' Fanny appealed to Nolly.

'Not much,' Nolly answered. 'She was just beginning to learn when—when——' She pressed her lips together, to stop their trembling. 'When we came away,' she finished flatly. 'After that we just talked Chinese.'

'There'll be no more Chinese spoken,' Fanny said firmly. 'Do you all understand?'

Ching Mei bowed again. 'Tly velly much, missee.'

Fanny felt a lump in her throat. If one wanted a lesson in self sacrifice and loyalty it was all there in this alien woman, with her sad wrinkled face, her expressionless eyes. Tomorrow she must tell Uncle Edgar what Adam Marsh had said. When the children were settled some way must be found to send Ching Mei back to her own country. She must not be allowed to die from homesickness.

The thought of Adam Marsh brought back a surge of warmth into Fanny's heart. Suddenly she wanted to be alone to think and dream. She kissed the children quickly, 'This is your bed, Ching Mei,' she said, indicating the narrow one placed at the foot of the children's, and was rewarded by Ching Mei's sudden giggle which meant understanding. But Ching Mei pointed to the floor, indicating she would prefer to sleep there.

Fanny nodded. 'Do as you like. I'll be next door if you want me in the night.'

'We're not babies to want people in the night,' Nolly said.

Fanny faced her reproving gaze.

'I wasn't suggesting you were. Such a travelled young lady as you couldn't have remained a baby. Indeed, I'm surprised you haven't already found a husband.'

Nolly pressed her lips together again, this time to prevent a surprisingly human giggle. Her hair stuck out in pigtails. She had, Fanny noticed, been hiding a doll under the blankets, for now its highly-coloured Chinese face and flat black hair emerged. She was only a baby, after all. Thank goodness, for her precocity had been a little alarming.

Only a baby... For in the night cold fingers touched Fanny's face.

'Cousin Fanny! Cousin Fanny! Marcus is afraid.'

Fanny sat up, fumbling for the candle at her bedside. She struck a match quickly, and the frail light showed her Nolly's nightgowned figure. She was clutching the Chinese doll in its gaudy red kimono. Her eyes were dilated.

'What is it, Nolly? Why are you afraid?'

'Marcus is afraid,' Nolly whispered. 'He thinks he heard something.'

Fanny wondered if George had been walking about, as he sometimes did long after midnight. The house, as she listened, was as still as it ever could be. She was so used to the infinitesimal creakings and rustlings that she scarcely heard them.

'Then come and let us see Marcus,' she said, picking up the candle and taking Nolly's hand.

If Marcus were frightened he was being remarkably silent about it. It required only one look to see that the little boy was fast asleep. Ching Mei, in her lowly position, wrapped in a blanket, didn't appear to have stirred.

Fanny was beginning to realise Nolly's tactics. Marcus was at once her scapegoat and her possession.

'Come on, Nolly, what was it you heard?'

The child looked round fearfully. The wavering candlelight cast moving shadows over the high ceiling and the panelled walls. In the long mirror of the wardrobe they were caught, two nightgowned figures, Fanny with her dark hair on her shoulders, Nolly with her pigtails and her intensely disciplined face looking medieval, the forlorn child in an old story. The breathing of the sleepers made a faint whisper. There was still no other sound.

'Something in the chimney,' Nolly whispered. She pointed to the dark mouth of the fireplace. 'Up there.'

A cool prickle ran down Fanny's spine.

'What sort of noise?'

'A sort of fluttering, and something falling down.' Her

fingers tightened on Fanny's. 'Has something fallen down?'

Fanny resolutely shone the candlelight on the hearth, and into the cavernous chimney. There was a smattering of soot on the tiles, nothing more.

'Look, that's all it is,' she said. 'Soot from old fires. It gets loose and suddenly falls. That's what you heard.'

Nolly stared. At last she said, 'It's dirty.'

'Yes. Dora will tidy it in the morning. Now get back into bed.'

Nolly went quite willingly back to her bed.

'It's a good thing Marcus didn't hear that,' she said. 'He'd have been frightened.' And the amah sat up abruptly, mumbling in Chinese. She blinked. The candlelight seemed to dazzle her.

'Trouble, Miss Fanny?' for the first time she used Fanny's name with a pretty deliberation.

'Nothing, Ching Mei. Go back to sleep, both of you.'

In the morning, which was grey and chilly, with a rising wind and the high tors black against the sky, Dora couldn't get the fire to burn. The sticks must be damp, she said, and a lot of soot seemed to have fallen down. Perhaps the chimney needed cleaning. With the fascinated children watching, she stuck the long poker up the chimney, and something fell to the hearth with a rush.

Nolly screamed. Fanny hurried to see the small light-as-paper skeleton of the bird, wings still outspread in its vain attempt for freedom.

'It's a starling,' she said matter-of-factly. 'Poor thing, it must have been caught there last summer and no one heard it.'

'I did,' said Nolly. 'I heard it in the night. You didn't, Marcus.'

'I did,' said Marcus. 'I did so.'

'Neither of you did,' Fanny said. 'That bird's been dead for a long time, poor thing. Take it away, Dora. And later today in the garden I'll show you some live starlings. They're coal black, but the sun shines like diamonds on their feathers. Dora, what are you waiting for?'

'I'd better not let Lady Arabella see, Miss Fanny. She'll

declare it was white, and that would mean——'

'Dora!'

'Yes, Miss Fanny,' Dora mumbled, balancing the light draggled burden on a shovel and hurrying away.

Omens, thought Fanny impatiently. They didn't exist. Intuition did, and perhaps a certain presentiment. But not omens. They were for the ignorant and the foolishly superstitious.

'Cousin Fanny, why was the bird in the chimney?' Nolly's clear precise voice demanded an answer.

'Perhaps it was building a nest. Perhaps it just fell down.'

'Why didn't it fly out again?'

'I suppose it couldn't. The chimney's dark and narrow, like a tunnel. It wouldn't be able to spread its wings.'

That was it exactly. Not being able to spread its wings... She had always thought so, from the moment she had identified herself with Lady Arabella's fanciful white bird.

'Then it should have flapped and screamed until someone came and rescued it,' Nolly said with nervous distaste.

'Yes, darling.'

'But suppose nobody rescued it?'

'That's enough about the poor bird. See, the fire's burning beautifully now.'

She stooped to hold out her hands to the blaze. It was absurdly chilly for mid-May. She felt very cold.

She had to go down to her own room to put away her finery from yesterday and get out the poplin day dress, faded from many washings. Amelia heard her and came bursting in in her usual unceremonious way.

'Fanny, what do you think? Papa is buying George a new horse!'

'Is he?'

'You don't sound at all surprised or indignant.'

'Why should I be?'

'Because George already has a perfectly good horse, and he knows he is free to ride any other of Papa's horses. Even my Jinny, if he pleases. But now he is to get a pedigreed hunter, and all I get is money for a paltry bit of French ribbon. You didn't forget to buy my ribbon, did you?'

'No, I didn't forget. I'll unpack it presently.'

Amelia subsided on to a chair, her skirts flouncing out. She was still pouting and looking like a schoolgirl.

'Mamma says Papa is talking economy all the time, and yet when George asks for something—or when Grandmamma asks for him, as Mamma says she did, not a no can be said. Fanny, do you think Papa is afraid to say no to Grandmamma?'

Fanny laughed. 'Don't be silly, Amelia. Your father isn't afraid of anybody!'

'No, I didn't think he was. But it's awfully unfair. This is supposed to be my year.'

'I expect you will get what you want eventually,' said Fanny, twisting her glossy hair into place. 'And after all, George——'

'Don't you say it, too! I know he nearly died for his country. But that was just the fortunes of war. After all, he had lots of splendid times with his regiment before that, and he wanted to go into the army. Oh, I suppose I'm mean and selfish to talk like this. Am I, Fanny?'

'And vain,' said Fanny.

'Oh, I declare! Fanny, you're the most unsympathetic person I ever met. And why did you sleep upstairs last night?'

'It's where I intend to sleep from now on,' Fanny said calmly. 'Dora is moving my things today.'

Amelia's indignation grew again.

'But what if I want you?'

'One flight of stairs doesn't mean I am living on the moon.'

Amelia giggled reluctantly.

'Fanny, you're in a mood this morning. I know Mamma thinks it will be nice if you take an interest in the children, but that isn't to mean you won't have time to do things for me. I must admit the children did look rather sweet last night. Papa was quite taken with the girl. And at least—wasn't it terrible the way I blurted it out—they're the right colour, so that worry is over. I may come up and see them in the nursery today.'

'May you, indeed? Your own cousins, and it may please you to have the whim to visit them.'

'Oh, I didn't mean it like that. Fanny, you are aggravating.

You've changed somehow since you've had this journey to London. Turn round and look at me.'

Fanny finished pinning up her hair. She turned with deliberation.

'Well, there you are. What do you see? The great metropolis written in my face?'

'No-o. But your eyes are so bright. If it wasn't impossible, I'd believe you'd fallen in love.'

'Impossible?' Fanny queried coolly.

'Well, how could you, with Hannah at your shoulder, and then the wretched orphans. And besides who would you meet on a train?' Amelia suddenly jumped up. Her voice dropped to a whisper. 'Fanny, you didn't see *him*!'

Fanny couldn't help her colour rising. How could Amelia know? Was her secret written so plainly on her face?

'If you mean the clerk from the shipping company——'

'Oh no, not him, I meant the new prisoner. The one Sir Giles said was arriving. Fanny, did you really see him?'

Fanny's voice was casual with relief. Amelia could be a destructive person with secrets, whispering them, distorting them . . .

'Just for a moment, yes.'

Amelia wrung her hands together.

'Did he look awfully starved and desperate?'

'I don't think so. Really, Amelia, I believe you think Dartmoor prison is full of caged tigers or panthers, with claws and blazing eyes.'

Amelia had gone to look out of the window. She was a little round figure with a cosy domestic look. A man would put his arm round that softly fleshed waist and think of warmed hearths and well-laden tables and filled cradles. He wouldn't think there was anything further to know about a young woman like that.

'I don't know why I have this longing to see one of them,' she whispered. 'I should be terrified, and yet——They are just human beings, aren't they, with a mother who once loved them. I suppose they have long forgotten about love . . .'

Fanny contrived to keep her colour when Uncle Edgar asked

her, at breakfast, about the young man from the shipping company.

'We didn't have the opportunity to talk last night. But I take it all the arrangements went well. The company sent a reliable sort of fellow?'

'Very reliable, Uncle Edgar.'

'Splendid. I shall drop them a line of thanks. I take it——'

'I gave him the guinea, Uncle Edgar.' Fanny lowered her head for this time she could feel the warm colour in her cheeks. She was more and more sure that the guinea had been pocketed by Adam Marsh simply to save her embarrassment, that he was quite unaccustomed to taking money from a lady. She was almost certain that they would laugh about it in the future.

'Fanny looks well, doesn't she, Louisa?' Uncle Edgar boomed. 'The little change has done her good.'

'I said she had fallen in love,' Amelia said boldly, then fell into her irrepressible giggle.

'Who with? Who, damn him!'

'George!'

His mother spoke so sharply that George fell back into his seat. He began to frown bewilderedly, the hard flush of anger leaving him.

'It isn't true, is it, Fanny? Amelia's teasing as usual?'

'Yes, she is,' Fanny said, because at this moment there was nothing else to say.

She looked round, seeing Aunt Louisa behind the shining silver teapot and coffee pot, at one end of the table, Uncle Edgar with his napkin tucked into his waistcoat, his attention apparently solely on his food, Amelia in her fresh blue morning gown keeping her eyelids lowered to hide the wicked sparkle that the result of her sally had aroused, and George momentarily forgetting the food on his place, staring at Fanny in a way that the old George would have thought unmannerly and gauche.

Who would have thought the scene was anything but a pleasant friendly family breakfast? There was a bowl of freshly picked roses, still holding the night's dew on the centre of the table. The furniture gleamed from the daily polish it had had before breakfast had been laid. There was a rich warm odour of well-cooked food and beeswax and roses, an odour as old as the house. Lizzie had come in with more hot water, and Aunt Louisa, lifting the teapot in her beringed hand, was saying, 'More tea, Amelia? Fanny? What about you, my love? Lizzie, bring Mr Davenport's cup.'

And no one would guess that a moment ago she had been hating Fanny intensely. She had never done more than tolerate her, but as a child she had been harmless enough, even useful as a companion for Amelia in the schoolroom, and later in many other little ways. She could still be tolerated if she hadn't developed those disturbing ravishing looks that only a blind or preoccupied person would not realise outshone Amelia's, and if George hadn't got into that irrational infatuated state about her.

Fanny knew all this. But though she knew Aunt Louisa's tolerance had turned to hatred, she didn't know about Uncle Edgar. He was a man. He would have a natural tenderness for a woman, even if she did represent a threat to his own children.

Amelia was young and silly, and affectionate. But she was easily influenced, and her mother could alienate her, too.

George—when his love was not returned? That was a dark question she could not answer.

But all those things lay beneath the calm privileged comfort of the breakfast table. And she was still not sorry she had returned to Darkwater . . .

'Well,' said Uncle Edgar, heavily playful, 'if Fanny didn't lose her heart on this journey, perhaps she will be able to put her thoughts to more practical things. My dear,' he turned to Fanny, 'as soon as my small nephew and niece are presentable, will you be kind enough to bring them to me in the library. I must set about making their acquaintance. They looked quite a promising pair, I thought. Oh, and the amah, too. There will be things she can tell me about my poor brother and the children's mother.'

'She speaks very little English, Uncle Edgar.'

Uncle Edgar looked up, puffing out his moustache.

'Nonsense! She must have spoken it in the household in Shanghai.'

'She says not.'

'Then she's not telling the truth. These Chinese are a devious race, all bows and smiles, and not an atom of their true feelings showing. I've no time for 'em. Frenchmen, either, or Greeks. Even Americans. They had the impudence to turn us out of their country.'

'Or anyone who isn't English, Papa?' Amelia said archly.

'Quite right, my dear, quite right. Oh, I grant you the other races serve some sort of a purpose, although I'm never sure what it is. Italians make good servants. And I remember getting some deuced good gloves in Vienna. But this Chinese woman must talk. I'll make her. Bring her down, Fanny.'

7

THE nursery was the old schoolroom where Fanny and Amelia and George, also, until he had gone away to boarding school, had endured so many years of Miss Ferguson's rule. The blackboard was still in the corner, and the dais where Miss Ferguson used to sit so that she could look down on her rapidly growing 'young ladies'.

Aunt Louisa had not made any extensive alterations for the new children. The old nursery fireguard had been returned to the fireplace, and several low chairs brought in. Fanny had been through the cupboards and brought out such toys and games as had survived George's rough treatment. There was a battered dolls' house for Nolly, and some toy soldiers for Marcus.

But the children had not yet developed an interest in a European child's toys, for when Fanny, obeying Uncle Edgar's instructions, came up to get them she found two small outlandish figures in a state of wild excitement.

Their trunks were standing open and the contents scattered about. Nolly was dressed in a scarlet kimono decorated with black and gold dragons, Marcus in silk trousers and jacket. Nolly not only had a pair of high-heeled shoes much too large for her, but she had earrings hanging precariously from her ears, and rings which she clutched on her fingers. Ching Mei stood scowling fiercely, the situation obviously out of her control.

'Miss Nolly velly bad,' she said to Fanny.

'Marcus is, too,' Nolly declared. 'He wanted his Chinese clothes on. It was his idea.'

Marcus stopped his capering to look at Nolly with open mouth. His slavish following of his sister brought its own bewilderment. But in a moment he was grinning happily and saying that they were being Chinese children.

'That's very amusing,' said Fanny. 'But at this moment your Uncle wants to see you downstairs. So quickly put on your proper clothes.'

Nolly backed into a corner.

'No,' she said. 'We don't want to. We want to be Chinese children.

Her eyes had their hard black stare, there was a high spot of colour in each of her cheeks. But with her drunken jewellery and her shoes askew, she looked too comical to be taken seriously.

'Then I shall have to turn you into an English child again,' Fanny said light-heartedly. 'Take off those ridiculous shoes to begin with.'

'They're not ridiculous,' Nolly said in a low voice. 'They're my Mamma's.'

Fanny looked at the silver brocade shoes, slightly tarnished, too big for Nolly, but small for a grown woman. She felt a sharp pang of pity, thinking of the dead woman with her little feet and her love of flamboyant jewellery. For the stones Nolly was wearing were large dull green ones, not at all like the discreet pearls and garnets which English women wore.

'Miss Nolly velly bad,' Ching Mei said again, helplessly.

Fanny nodded, but a little absently. Her feeling of pity had reminded her of almost forgotten scenes she herself had once created. She remembered shaking Amelia violently in her cradle a few moments after her mother had lovingly kissed her good night. There had been a great to-do and Miss Fanny hadn't been allowed near Baby for some weeks after. There had been tantrums in the schoolroom when Miss Ferguson, newly arrived, had had it explained to her that Miss Amelia was the daughter of the house, Miss Fanny only a sort of cousin. She had hated birthday parties, always, and even Christmas.

The little girl backed balefully into the corner now was not so strange.

Fanny was not concerned with winning a battle, but in making her happy.

She made an abrupt decision.

'Nolly, little sweet, you can't walk downstairs in those shoes. You'll lose them at once. So put on your own, and you may visit Uncle Edgar in your kimono.'

Nolly stared.

'Won't he be angry?'

'He's very kind. Don't you remember last night he promised to show you his watch that plays a tune?'

Uncle Edgar was kind. She counted on that. But if he took exception to the way the children were behaving, Fanny intended to fight on their side. Didn't he know what it was to be so young and alone in a strange place... But of course he didn't. He never had been. She must rely on his kindness only.

She hadn't counted on his amusement. When he saw the two strangely-garbed children he burst into a roar of laughter.

'What's this, eh? A charade? Fancy dress party? Are these all the clothes you could bring with you from China? Is that all that was in those trunks?'

The last question was addressed to Ching Mei who stood in her familiar attitude, with bowed head and clasped hands.

'Uncle Edgar, she doesn't understand,' Fanny said anxiously.

But Uncle Edgar suddenly wasn't listening. He was staring at Nolly. He went towards her, and again put his fingers under her chin, lifting her face.

'What are these gee-gaws you're wearing, child? A bit mature for you, aren't they?' He was chuckling softly. 'By jove, rings, too. Trust a woman to like jewellery. Let me look at the rings. Give them to me.'

Nolly backed away sharply, her hands clutched together.

'No,' she said.

'Come, child, I only want to look. I have no designs on your circus jewellery.'

Nolly's eyes blazed.

'Don't you dare touch them! They're my Mamma's!'

Uncle Edgar's colour had heightened, although he was still smiling.

'Fanny, here's a little girl who must be taught manners. We're not going to indulge in anything so vulgar as a fight. Take her upstairs and send her to her room. The boy——' But Marcus, sensing disaster, had dropped his lower lip, and was beginning to sob.

'Oh dear, dear!' said Uncle Edgar. 'Our acquaintance is scarcely improving. Take the boy, too, Fanny.' He pointed imperiously at the amah. 'You stay.'

'Uncle Edgar, Ching Mei——'

'My dear Fanny, I haven't been deaf. You've already explained several times that the woman doesn't understand English. Leave me to judge that for myself. For heaven's sake,' he finished impatiently, 'what is the boy crying about? He's not going to be a cry baby, I hope?'

'He was expecting to see your watch, Uncle Edgar.'

'And he and his sister thought their behaviour deserved it? Oh, no, that must wait until another day.'

At lunch Uncle Edgar had completely regained his good-temper. He spent some time describing a particularly memorable hunt in detail, and that reminded him of the horse he had promised George. When Amelia, with her modestly downcast eyes, said, 'Papa, if George is to get a horse——' he interrupted good-humouredly, 'So you think you should get something, too.'

'It's only that I *need* so many things, Papa,' Amelia said earnestly.

'We all do, my dear. Or we all think we do. By the way, Fanny'—it was as if he had just noticed her—'have you got your charges into a better frame of mind?'

'My charges, Uncle Edgar?' Fanny's chin was up, her voice cool. She was still upset by the disastrous and disturbing morning.

Uncle Edgar gave his vast chuckle, and went on pursuing his own amusing thoughts.

'Little foreign devils, eh? The girl's got spirit, though. Pity it isn't the boy. He seems a bit of a namby pamby. By the way, Fanny, your aunt will be going through the trunks they brought. It seems there are private papers. I don't want the servants touching anything.'

'Did Ching Mei tell you?' Fanny asked in astonishment. 'But I didn't think she could——'

'Speak English? She certainly doesn't have much of a vocabulary. But I contrived to understand her. Personally, I still think the woman is concealing her talents.'

'She's so strange and homesick,' Fanny said impulsively. 'Adam Marsh thought it would be very generous of you if you could send her back to China.'

'And who is Adam Marsh?' Uncle Edgar asked, with interest.

'Why, the gentleman from the shipping company. He was very kind and understanding.'

'And couldn't mind his own business?'

'Oh, he didn't mean it like that. He was just concerned about her.'

'And does he think an English household offers deadly peril? Are we going to return the woman to her loving family, finger by finger?'

Amelia shrieked in horror. Uncle Edgar explained expansively, 'A charming little custom Chinese bandits have, I believe. Now, don't you worry, Fanny. Ching Mei is perfectly safe in our hands. When she leaves is for me to decide,' there was the smallest hardening in his voice, 'no one else.'

She had been put in her place once more. That was obvious by Aunt Louisa's attitude when she came up to investigate the trunks.

'Take the children out in the garden, Fanny. I don't want a lot of noise and interruption. By the way, I see you have decided to change your room.'

'Yes, Aunt Louisa. If that's convenient.'

'Isn't it a little late to ask now that Dora has moved your things? I might say that room was one of the larger guest rooms.'

'But surely you wouldn't want to put guests next to the nursery, Aunt Louisa.'

'That wasn't the point I was making,' Aunt Louisa said crossly. Her nose had taken on the grape bloom tinge that it did when she was excited or upset. She was already crouched over the battered trunks, like a great over-blown dahlia in her dark red full-skirted dress. Aunt Louisa had a tendency towards flamboyance in her dressing. The next thing, she would be wearing the green earrings in their ornate gold setting, provided, of course, it could be proved that the stones were semi-precious, at least.

'I merely meant,' she went on, 'that you might have had the courtesy to consult me about your new arrangements.'

'But I thought it was taken for granted the children would be my responsibility.'

Aunt Louisa recognised the familiar glint of rebellion in Fanny's eyes. One never knew what the wretched girl was thinking. And the exasperating thing was that she looked prettier than ever when she was indulging in one of her difficult moods.

'Naturally, Mr Davenport and I think it very suitable that you should take an interest in the children. And I agree that sleeping near them is an advantage. But you should have asked. I really think the trust Mr Davenport placed in you by sending you to London has gone to your head. You must try to quell those domineering tendencies in your nature. They're not becoming to a young woman.'

'What are you going to do with those things?' Fanny asked, her voice no less aggressive.

Aunt Louisa was about to make a sharp rejoinder, but her attention was diverted to the heaps of clothing, tossed about untidily after the children's wild scramble through the trunks that morning. She frowned in distaste and perplexity.

'Burn most of it, I should think. It's probably full of germs.'

'What if any of the things should be valuable?'

'If you're thinking of that barbaric jewellery Nolly was wearing, if any of it is of any value, which is most unlikely, considering the impecunious habits of my wretched brother-in-law, it will be put away safely in the bank until the children are of age. Does that satisfy you, miss? Why do you imagine I choose to do this tedious task rather than allow the servants to?'

Fanny resolutely dismissed her vague and unfair suspicions.

'I'm sorry, Aunt Louisa, I shouldn't have spoken like that.'

'Speaking hastily is another of your faults. How many times have I told you that? But we'll say no more, except that even though your uncle and I are trusting you with further responsibilities, we will expect you to still have time for your usual duties. I'm sure I wouldn't care to face either my mother or Amelia if you neglected them. Now what, I wonder, is this meant to be?'

She was holding up a garment of Oriental silk made in no identifiable shape.

'Isn't it a cheongsam, Aunt Louisa? The dress that Chinese ladies wear.'

'So tight,' murmured Aunt Louisa. 'And a split in the skirt. Surely that woman didn't wear anything so indecent. But I suppose one could expect anything—— Well, what are you standing there for, Fanny? I asked you to take the children in the garden. And remember that you're a very fortunate young woman. Boredom, you know can be worse than unhappiness. That's why we must get that idle daughter of mine married as soon as possible.'

Out in the garden Fanny had no envy of Amelia's idleness. It was a cool windy afternoon, with racing cloud shadows and flashes of brilliance from the distant lake when the sun shone out. The peacock was spreading his tail on the lawn against the copper beech, as if he had deliberately planned the rich gleaming backdrop. His mate was picking in the grass near him, ignoring his splendour. But he had an enraptured audience in Nolly and Marcus and the little amah.

Old William, the head gardener, came up and touched his cap, giving a sideways look at the Chinese woman. He said that there were some ripe strawberries in the kitchen garden if the little ones would care for one or two.

After that they went down to the pagoda by the lake. Nolly, her mouth smeared with strawberry juice, was suddenly a natural little girl, excited and happy. She ran happily round the pagoda, wanting to know what the table and chairs were for, and the bamboo screens.

Fanny explained that if they brought tea down to the lakeside and it began to rain, as it often did, they moved into the shelter of the pagoda.

'Can we have a picnic?' Nolly cried. 'Ching Mei, wouldn't it be nice if we hung the windbells up here. See, the wind comes in everywhere. They'd ring all the time.'

'Windbells?' said Fanny. 'But how charming. We'll do that tomorrow.'

Marcus wanted to put his feet in the lake. Where the water-lilies grew thickly he thought it safe to walk.

'No, no!' Fanny cried. 'Only birds can walk on the leaves. You must never try to do that. You'd fall in and drown.'

'Drown?' said Marcus, lifting his dreamy harebell eyes to Fanny.

'The water would go down your throat and choke you,' said Nolly brutally. 'Did you ever drown, Cousin Fanny?'

Ever since that long afternoon the lake had given Fanny a

cool feeling of distaste. It was so smooth, so glassy. When the sun shone on it it looked inviting enough. But she had never gone in the boat since without a shamed feeling of apprehension. She would never forget Uncle Edgar's hands round her throat, dragging her out. And somewhere someone screaming. It had been one of the servants on the bank. The silly woman had had an attack of the vapours, and Uncle Edgar had been angry, because she should have whisked Fanny up to the house for a hot bath and dry clothes. Instead, Aunt Louisa had had to take her. And besides having been frightened to death, Fanny was made to realise that she had spoiled everyone's afternoon. How clumsy to fall out of a boat! Other people could reach for a water-lily without falling overboard.

Even the creamy water-lilies had been distasteful since that day.

The peacock screamed harshly, and Nolly flew to Fanny.

'What was that?'

'Only the peacock. You must get used to strange noises. There are other birds that come to the lake, and they all have different voices.'

'Fanny! Fanny!' That was George standing on the slope of the lawn calling imperiously. 'Come here. I want to see you.'

A child holding each hand, Fanny walked slowly and reluctantly towards him. At the same time a window opened upstairs and Lady Arabella's white-capped head was thrust out.

'Fanny, is that you?' Her husky voice was quite audible across the garden. 'No one has had the courtesy to bring the children to see me. Send them up at once.'

'Who's that?' Nolly said, shrinking against Fanny.

'Your great-aunt Arabella. You must visit her for a few minutes. Dora will take you.'

'She looks like a witch.'

Marcus's eyes had grown enormous. Fanny said sharply, 'Are you frightened, Nolly?'

'Frightened?' said Nolly, with contempt. 'Me?'

'Then don't frighten your brother. Witches, indeed! Ching Mei, ask Dora to take the children to Lady Arabella. Lady Arabella. Do you understand?'

Ching Mei bowed. Marcus's hand dragged at Fanny's.

'Great-aunt Arabella has sugar plums,' Fanny murmured. 'Run along and see.'

She watched them go. Already she had this absurd feeling that she shouldn't let them out of her sight. Why ever should she feel like that? The lake, and the vivid memory of her near-drowning had upset her.

George strolled towards her, scowling.

'Am I never to see you now without those brats?'

'George! Don't speak of your cousins like that.'

'Isn't it true? They've been at your heels ever since you brought them home. And Mamma's quite content to make a servant of you. You know that, don't you?'

'I love the children already,' Fanny murmured, uneasy beneath his intense regard. The little frown was on his forehead. His brown eyes were too bright, almost as if with a fever.

'Come for a walk. Let's go through the woodland on the other side of the lake.'

'Not now, George.'

'But you never will. I scarcely see you. You're so pretty, Fanny. I'd like to——' His fingers were at the neck of her dress.

'George!' she started back. 'Please don't touch me!'

He was immediately contrite. Now his eyes were dull. He suddenly looked years younger, an overgrown schoolboy.

'I'm sorry. I wouldn't do anything to hurt you. But Amelia said you were behaving as if you had fallen in love on your trip to London.'

'Amelia is teasing you,' Fanny said indignantly.

'Yes. Yes, I thought she was.' George passed his hand across his brow. 'You must only love me, Fanny. I won't let—won't let——'

'George, dear, isn't it time for your rest? You know the doctor said you must rest every afternoon.'

'Yes, I suppose it is. I get this headache. Let me walk in beside you, Fanny. I promise not to touch you. But don't let those brats take all your time. If they do——'

'What will happen?' Fanny asked, smiling.

'You know how I got this wound? That Cossack was

swinging his sabre, like a devil. But I could use a sword. I still can. My sword arm isn't hurt. I used to be the best swordsman in the regiment, did you know? You're so pretty, Fanny. None of the girls at the regimental balls could hold a candle to you.'

'Come inside,' said Fanny uneasily. 'The hot sun——'

'Yes, yes, I'm coming. When I stop getting these nightmares I'll be all right. You'll have patience, won't you, Fanny.'

'Of course,' Fanny promised. What else was there to say?

In Lady Arabella's room, with the curtains drawn against the sun because Lady Arabella loved this warm underwater gloom, Nolly stood staring with fascination at the empty birdcage.

Marcus was contentedly stuffing sweetmeats into his mouth, but Nolly held hers untouched in her hand.

'Where is the bird?' she demanded passionately.

'It died, my little darling. I told you. It was ninety-five years old, I believe. And so bad tempered. Although I was dreadfully upset, I was also a little relieved to find it lying in the bottom of the cage one morning. Fanny, these children are charming. The boy's a poppet, but this one, the questions——' Lady Arabella shook her head pleasurably. 'Oh, I shall have some times with her. Look at those bright eyes. They're going to miss nothing.'

'You've been telling me a lie,' Nolly said, turning on her. 'The bird didn't die in its cage. It was in the chimney.'

Lady Arabella blinked and stared.

'Oh, no, little love. You're talking about the white bird that struggles and struggles and can't get out. Not my scruffy old Boney. He was here, sure enough. He wouldn't have been up and down chimneys. Had too much sense. No, that was the white——'

'Great-aunt Arabella!' Fanny interrupted sharply. 'Don't!'

'Don't!' The heavy-lidded eyes looked at Fanny in amazement. 'You suggest I can't tell the child a story?'

'Not that one.'

'Because the bird fell down the chimney this morning,' Nolly said flatly. 'Dora carried it away on a shovel.'

Lady Arabella leaned forward, her cheeks pink.

'*No!* The white one? In your room? But what does that *mean*?'

'It was a starling,' Fanny said. 'It was black. Dora poked it down when she was trying to light the fire. It must have been caught there during the winter. It doesn't mean a thing. And I do wish you wouldn't tell the children these things.'

'So why shouldn't I tell them stories. I told you plenty when you were this size, didn't I? And you enjoyed them. You wanted more. Besides, what is this? Are you making the rules in this house now?'

'Of course I'm not, Great-aunt. But already Nolly——'

Fanny looked at Lady Arabella's flushed hurt face and wondered what was the use. The old Lady was so vain about her story-telling, she would never be stopped. And now the seeds of fear were planted in Nolly. She was brooding over an empty birdcage and imagining she heard things in the night.

But the sounds she had heard in the night had come before she had heard that tiresome eerie legend...

'Couldn't they play with Ludwig?' Fanny suggested.

'Ludwig! At his age! What does he care for romping with children? He creaks with rheumatism, the same as I do. But I have it!' Lady Arabella suddenly clapped her little plump hands. 'We'll have a game of hide the thimble. Now that's something we can all play. Who shall go first? Marcus, of course. He's the smallest. And we girls go into the bedroom while he finds a hiding place. You understand, dear?' The old lady had put a silver thimble into Marcus's sticky hand. 'Dear, dear, covered in sugar already. We shall be very clever and follow your trail. Now I will tell you a secret. Everyone looks under the clock, but nobody in my workbasket. Call when you're ready. Be quick.'

Beginning to smile, Marcus looked round the room slyly. It was clever of Lady Arabella to think of something he could do in which Nolly didn't take the lead. There was no doubt, she could be like an enormous child herself, and throw herself with gusto into any game. This one, at least, seemed to have no pitfalls or sudden shocks.

Nolly was a little put out at not being the one chosen first to hide the thimble, but when Marcus called, she forgot to sulk and rushed eagerly into the room.

It was such a cluttered room, it was almost impossible to find anything that was well hidden. Cushions were tossed about, table-cloths lifted, vases tipped upside down. Nolly had emptied Lady Arabella's hairpin box, disclosing a fascinating collection of buttons, pieces of false hair, pins, and unstrung beads. Lady Arabella was convinced that Ludwig, much discomposed in his demeanour, was sitting on the thimble, and had Marcus in shrieks of laughter at her antics. Nolly was lifting rugs and shaking the curtains.

'He's too clever, your little brother,' Lady Arabella wheezed. 'He's a magician, I believe. Now where is this thimble spirited to? How am I to do my sewing this evening?' She bustled about, looking in the same place twice, getting on her hands and knees to peer under the sofa and chairs.

'It's higher,' Marcus choked. 'It's not on the floor, Great-aunt Arabella.'

'Then it is on a table. Or on the bureau. Or the mantelpiece. Fanny, what are you doing? *Put that down!*'

Fanny stood still in surprise, the pincushion in her hands. She had thought the padded top lifted off to disclose perhaps a small workbox. But the change from glee to sharp command in Lady Arabella's voice immobilised her.

'It's full of pins, you'll only prick yourself.' Lady Arabella watched until Fanny, somewhat bewilderedly, put the pincushion back on the little table in the corner. Then she said in a changed, tired voice, 'Well, Marcus, you've been too clever for us. We give in. Where is the hiding place?'

'Here it is, Great-aunt Arabella!' the little boy cried triumphantly, taking it out of the pocket of his jacket.

'You cheated, you cheated!' Nolly shouted. 'You're not allowed to hide it on yourself. Is he, Great-aunt Arabella?'

'He's very little,' said the old lady. 'And suddenly I am very tired. Come and see me again tomorrow. Now be off with you!'

In the morning, when the mail had been brought up from the village post office, as it was each day, Uncle Edgar sent for Fanny to come and see him in the library.

He had a letter in his hands. He looked puzzled and, Fanny thought, perturbed.

'Fanny, this young man who escorted the children from Tilbury—what did you say his name was?'

Fanny's heart gave a paralysing leap. Had Adam written to say he was coming to the moors? Written to Uncle Edgar himself? Or perhaps to enquire after the children and Ching Mei?

'It was Adam Marsh, Uncle Edgar.'

'And he was a perfectly respectable type of person?'

'Yes, indeed he was. I could swear to that, and so could Hannah. Why, what has happened?'

Uncle Edgar tapped the letter.

'Because the shipping company writes to apologise deeply for their man failing to contact the children. He reported that there was no sign of them, and that he had made a fruitless journey.'

'But that couldn't be so! Why, Mr Marsh seemed to know about them—he even——' Good heavens, Fanny thought in horror, he had even accepted her guinea!

'Then he's an imposter.'

'An imposter? How could that be?'

'*Why* could it be? That's what I'd like answered. What was that young man up to?'

8

THE mystery about Adam Marsh remained unsolved. Of course he had not given her any address, Fanny said indignantly in answer to Uncle Edgar's questions. Ching Mei could give no information in her limited English except that the man had been there and offered his help. 'Him velly kind,' she said simply, her flat yellow face expressionless. It was impossible to tell whether she was puzzled by a complete stranger's action, or whether she just didn't understand what was being explained to her. Yet Fanny found herself remembering Adam Marsh pausing to have that last word with Ching Mei. Had it been as innocent as it had seemed?

'He spoke Chinese,' she said involuntarily, and Uncle Edgar looked at her sharply.

'You didn't tell me that before.'

'I just remembered.'

Nolly and Marcus were also questioned.

Nolly said in her dispassionate voice, 'We liked him. Marcus liked him.'

Marcus, prodded into speaking, merely repeated in his parrot-fashion what his sister had said, 'We liked him,' clearly without having the faintest idea who was being discussed.

'Is he coming to see us?' Nolly asked presently.

'Not that I am aware of,' said Uncle Edgar. 'Although now I begin to wonder. Perhaps this mysterious gentleman will turn up.'

Fanny tried to keep her face as expressionless as Ching Mei's. She knew the attempt was useless. Her mouth, her eyes, always treacherously showed her feelings.

Adam Marsh had said he loved the moors—not that the moors might be his excuse for coming to see the family from China again.

It was the children he had been interested in, not her at all. How could she keep the devastation of that discovery out of her eyes?

The Chinese windbells had been hung in the pavilion by the lake, and their delicate tinkling seemed the voice of the summer days. For one whole week the sun shone.

Then the wind changed, and the mist rolled up again. But not until the evening. In the afternoon they had their first picnic of the summer by the lake. Uncle Edgar had suggested it at breakfast. The Hadlows from Grange Park were coming to tea, and since it was such a fine day surely they would prefer a picnic to stuffing indoors.

His eyes twinkling with heavy roguishness, he added that Amelia would surely like the opportunity to take Robert for a walk through the woods.

Amelia coloured indignantly.

'Papa, he's only a schoolboy!'

'Three months younger than you, to be exact. I grant you a young man hasn't the advantage of springing his grown-up personality on the world, simply by the trick of putting his hair up. But he'll age, my dear, he'll age.'

Amelia pouted, but kept her next thoughts silent. At least Robert was too young to interest Fanny. In the past, young men had shown an infuriating tendency to desert her side for Fanny's, and Fanny had blatantly encouraged them, her eyes shining wickedly. She didn't care two figs for them, yet she thoroughly enjoyed wielding her power over them.

Now that she was grown-up, Amelia thought, tossing her curls, she would prove that she was a match for Fanny. There was this mysterious Adam Marsh, for instance, and the way Fanny had been looking so distrait ever since her trip to London. If that gentleman turned up, as Papa seemed to think he might, she intended to flirt outrageously with him, perhaps even fall in love with him, since he must be quite attractive. She intended to have her own back on Miss Fanny.

Then there was to be Mr Hamish Barlow, the attorney, arriving from Shanghai. He would be here at the time of her ball. One hoped he also would be attractive and interesting, with the glamour of foreign places on him. And he must be a bachelor. It wouldn't do at all if he had a wife. Altogether, Amelia reflected pleasurably, it was to be an exciting summer. She might even be coquettish with Robert Hadlow this afternoon, simply to get some practice.

She lingered in her room, prinking in front of the mirror, until after the Hadlows had arrived, and their carriage been taken to the stables. She intended to saunter down to the lake in a leisurely manner, being the last to arrive so that all eyes would be on her. She would carry her parasol instead of wearing a hat. Everyone would think what a charming picture she made, Miss Amelia Davenport in her lilac muslin, strolling by the lake on a summer afternoon.

As it happened, she wasn't the last to go down to the pavilion, for as she left her room and romped along the passage—her graceful approach could be saved until there was someone to see her—she almost bumped into her father coming out of Lady Arabella's room.

'Oh, Papa! Isn't Grandmamma coming to the picnic?'

It was a warm afternoon. Papa's face glistened faintly with perspiration. He shut the door behind him with a bang.

'She's gone down some time ago,' he said shortly. 'And why aren't you looking after your guests?'

'Why aren't you, Papa?' Amelia retorted.

She had always been able to joke with her father, but she had chosen the wrong moment now.

'Because I'm a busy man and can't be at everybody's beck and call. Where are the servants? No one answered the bell when I wanted someone to go up and see to that atrocious cat. Your grandmother had somehow shut him in the wardrobe.'

'Was he crying, Papa? I didn't hear him.'

'You were too busy listening to your own thoughts, I expect.' Papa was recovering his good humour. He pinched her cheek. 'You're looking very pretty. Who is the toilette for? Robert?'

'I intend only to practice on him,' Amelia confessed, and at last Papa laughed.

'You're a minx. Then let us go down. Don't say anything to your grandmother about the cat. She'll only want to come up and assure herself that he's all right. We don't want the picnic spoilt.'

All the same, he was still strangely absent-minded, and she had to make the same remark twice before he heard her. Also, he had spoiled her plans for an impressive solitary approach. But for all that it was a successful picnic.

Three maids, with flying cap strings, brought a succession of trays with hot scones and muffins, strawberry jam, bowls of the rich yellow Devon cream, and, for the centre of the table, an enormous fruit cake. Mamma poured tea from the Queen Anne silver tea service, into the green and gold Dresden cups. The Hadlows, Mrs Hadlow, Anne and Robert, sat on the light bamboo chairs, but Lady Arabella, distrusting their resilience, had had her own sturdy rocking chair brought down. The Chinese windbells tinkled with a tiny glassy foreign sound. Fanny sat on a cushion on the grass, a little aloof from the rest, not bothering for once to fascinate Robert Hadlow who was looking more grown-up and almost handsome. The children sat quietly beside her. Nolly had her quite hideous Chinese doll in her arms. Ching Mei stood a little distance away. George lounged against a tree, watching. Watching Fanny mostly, but occasionally his quick glance darted over everybody. He made no attempt to talk. He behaved exactly as he pleased now. If polite conversation bored him, he remained silent. Sometimes Amelia wondered how much he was shrewdly exploiting his illness.

The sun shone brilliantly. Dragonflies darted over the gleaming water. The trees rustled gently and the windbells tinkled. It was an idyllic English summer afternoon scene. After Papa's arrival the slightly stilted quality left the party and there was a lot of laughter. Papa adored picnics, and was so good at them. It really was exactly like all the other ones they had had. Even the tiny slender figure of the Chinese woman stopped seeming so foreign and heathenish, and anyway was so unobtrusive among the tree shadows that one could almost forget she was there. Robert Hadlow pretended to think she had been imported to go with the pagoda.

'Is she real? Shall we stick a pin in her and see?'

Really, Robert was growing quite amusing. But all the same ... an older man, more worldly ... someone who would kiss her hand ... Amelia dreamed, and the shadows grew longer, and the first hint of the rising mist obscured the sunlight.

Presently it was chilly, and the ladies were reaching for their shawls, and preparing to go indoors.

'Well, children.' Amelia watched her father take out his fat golden watch. 'You've been as quiet as two harvest mice. So shall we now see if this can make a better sound that those tinkling bells.'

He wound the watch and held it out, smiling at their absorbed faces. The little chiming tune played itself through.

'Oh!' whispered Nolly. 'It's pretty.' Marcus put a shy stubby finger on the watch's plump face. Ching Mei was laughing, a tinkling sound not unlike the windbells, a sound of pure delight.

The mist had rolled up so quickly that it was drifting in opened windows when they returned to the house. The sun had completely vanished, and it was as if it was another day altogether, grey and chilly and filled with the sound of the rising wind. There was a great scurrying to and fro as windows were closed, billowing curtains stilled, and lamps lit. Fogs over the moor were a part of winter, but no one liked the summer ones that rolled up, stealing the light and warmth with sinister rapidity.

Fanny left the children to Ching Mei and Dora, and went to dress for dinner. She had been happier today, because the children had been noisy and completely child-like and even Ching Mei, who had seemed strangely nervous of both Uncle Edgar and Aunt Louisa, but chiefly of Uncle Edgar, had relaxed enough to laugh. All the other days she had been shut in silence. Once she had wanted to write letters to her family and Nolly, who already showed a precocious grasp of her alphabet, had showed her how to laboriously address the envelope, writing the name of her brother in spidery Chinese characters, and the address Shanghai China, in English. Fanny had permitted her to walk into the village to post the letters because it was a pleasant walk for her and the children. It was the only occasion on which she had left the house.

As she went downstairs Fanny heard the hounds barking. It was a far-off sound, fragmentary and melancholy. It made her think of wet heather and scudding clouds, and the smell of fear. Once she and Amelia and George had followed the hunt on their ponies, and seen a fox torn to pieces by the hounds. She had never gone to a hunt again.

Now it was long past the hunting season, and she wondered whose hounds were loose. The baying was so far away that it seemed she might have imagined it. But the prickly sense of apprehension was not imaginary. It stayed with her after the sound of the hounds was lost.

Lady Arabella came wheezing behind her on the stairs.

'Fanny, that was very naughty of you, letting the children in my rooms to play when I wasn't there.'

Fanny turned in surprise.'

'They haven't been in your rooms, surely!'

'Playing hide the thimble,' Lady Arabella grumbled. 'Things upside down. Poor Ludwig taking refuge in my bedroom.'

'When did this happen?'

'When I was down at the lake, I imagine. It was the only time I went out.'

'But the children were there, too,' Fanny said. 'They were with me. Anyway, I'm sure they wouldn't go into your rooms uninvited. They're too——' She stopped. She didn't want to say they were too frightened. Nolly was unduly imaginative about the empty bird cage and Marcus more than half-scared of the old lady herself.

Surprisingly enough, Lady Arabella had begun to chuckle wheezily.

'So that's it, is it?' she said to herself. 'Of course, I should have guessed. We'll say no more about the children.'

'What are you talking about, Great-aunt Arabella?'

The old lady wagged a thick forefinger.

'Fee, fi, fo, fum, I smell the blood of an Englishman,' she quoted enjoyably. 'I've been watching the mist rolling up. Isn't it exciting the way it blots things out, wipes them away? I thought I heard dogs barking a little while ago.'

'So did I,' said Fanny uneasily. 'I don't like the mist as much as you do. It hides things.'

But it wasn't until they were all going in to dinner that George came bursting in, his eyes blazing with excitement.

'There's an escaped prisoner! They've got the bloodhounds out. Did you hear them?'

Amelia screamed.

'Oh, I knew something would happen. I knew it all afternoon!'

'It's because of the mist,' said George. 'They always make a break in the mist. If the search comes this way I'll volunteer to help.'

'You'll do nothing of the kind,' said his mother sharply. 'You're an invalid.'

'I can still fire a rifle and use a sword,' George said indignantly. 'Dash it, I'm not going to miss all the sport.'

'Hunting a fugitive is scarcely sport,' Uncle Edgar said calmly. 'And one doesn't usually shoot the poor wretch down. Anyway, if this fellow has been clever enough to escape, he'll be miles from here by now. I suggest we don't let him spoil our dinner. Come, Amelia, my dear.' Uncle Edgar gave his deep amused chuckle. 'You look as if you imagine he's hiding under your bed already.'

'Oh, Papa!' Amelia said faintly. 'How can you joke about it?'

'I'm not joking. I'm admiring the poor devil's adventurous spirit. Who wouldn't make a bid for freedom in similar circumstances?'

'He may be dangerous,' Aunt Louisa protested. 'Really, Edgar, you can carry your philanthropy too far.'

Uncle Edgar chuckled again. His colour was rather high. He looked as if he had been at the whisky decanter more than once before dinner. He was often mellowed by liquor, while never being overcome by it.

'Don't be alarmed, my love. I should, of course, hand him over to the authorities if, for instance, I tripped over him in the dark. But let's admit we all have a lurking sympathy for him. Fanny? Isn't that true?'

Fanny was remembering the hollowed face and the thin silent figure of the prisoner she had seen on the railway station the other night. She could imagine him now, crouching in the wet bracken, scarcely breathing, praying the hounds would go another way. He was a stranger, yet he had momentarily touched her life, touched all their lives...

'Hunt him like a fox,' said George, the excitement burning in his face.

There was a clatter at the sideboard as one of the maids let a dish slip. The curtains were drawn across the windows, a dozen candles burning on the long table. It was warm and safe in this room. No one was hiding, or hunted, or desperately hungry, or afraid...

After dinner Sir Giles Mowatt arrived on horseback. He stopped for a hasty glass of port, and to warn them that he believed the prisoner was hiding somewhere in that vicinity.

'But if we don't get him, he'll make for the high ground, and try to cross the moors to Okehampton. So you ladies don't need to be nervous.'

'Was it the man who came down from London the other day?' Fanny asked.

'Yes, that's the rogue. He made a break in the fog, and got over the wall. He's as slippery as an eel. But we'll get him never fear.'

'Does luck never go the way of the criminal?' Uncle Edgar asked reflectively.

'Only the ones who never have their crimes brought home to them. And we hope there aren't many of those. But this is hardly a subject for the ladies. And I must be off. I'll send word when we've made a capture. Good night, all.'

Aunt Louisa rang for Barker to go round the house checking that all the windows and doors were locked. She drew her shawl round her ample shoulders, shivering.

'I've always hated the moors. Who else has to live in danger like this?'

'Good gracious, my love, the man's a thief, not a cut-throat.'

'How do you know what he may become if he's desperate? Yes, Dora, what is it?'

Dora had tapped timidly at the open door, and now stood anxiously twisting her fingers.

'Please, ma'am, the children are upset. Master Marcus is crying and Miss Nolly's in a state about her doll. Could Miss Fanny——'

'Can't the Chinese woman control them? Really, Edgar, why are we keeping her here if she can't keep two small children in order?'

'But she's gone to look for Miss Nolly's doll,' Dora broke in. 'It was left down by the lake, and she really won't go to bed without it. It's the only thing she makes a fuss about.' Dora looked round, listening. 'But Ching Mei's been gone an awful long time,' she said uneasily.

Fanny sprang up.

'She's lost her way in the fog, I expect. I'll go and find her.'

Uncle Edgar stepped forward, detaining her.

'No, you won't. Not with a fog, and a prisoner at large.'

'I should certainly think not,' said George vigorously. 'I'll go. I'll take my rifle.'

'Oh, don't shoot anybody!' begged Amelia.

'Barker and I will go,' said Uncle Edgar. 'We'll probably meet this foolish woman on the doorstep. How did she expect to find a doll in pitch darkness?'

'It would have been in the pagoda,' Dora faltered. 'She had a candle to light. Miss Fanny——'

'Yes, I'm coming upstairs,' said Fanny. She wanted to hurry to the distressed children, but more urgently she wanted to go out and find Ching Mei. She didn't know how to explain this feeling of urgency, except that she could have sworn Nolly had had her doll when they had returned from the picnic. Uncle Edgar, in high good humour after his success with his chiming watch, had carried Marcus up to the house on his shoulder, Nolly clinging to his hand. There had been shrieks of excited laughter. One might have known they would later turn to tears. But Uncle Edgar had scored a very big success indeed if he had succeeded in making Nolly forget her beloved doll.

She was thinking of the eerie tinkling of the windbells in the mist, and of the ineffectiveness of one feeble candle in a whole world of darkness. The mist always wreathed closely over the lake, disguising the water as effectively as the water-lilies did. Supposing Ching Mei, unfamiliar with the paths, missed her footing . . .

'How long has she been gone?' Fanny asked, following Dora's little scurrying figure up the stairs.

'Oh, I couldn't say, Miss. Before the children began their bread and milk, and I've bathed them since.'

'But, Dora, that must make it nearly an hour!'

'I wouldn't know, miss. I hadn't thought about it until Miss Nolly wouldn't go to bed without her doll. Then I forgot my-self and said the silly woman must have tumbled in the lake, and Master Marcus began to howl.'

Marcus was still crying, though less uproariously, when they reached the nursery. Sheer exhaustion had left him with only breathless hiccuping sobs. There were no tears on Nolly's cheeks. She was standing at the window, the curtain drawn back, to peer out. When Fanny came in she turned, and Fanny saw her face as white as her nightgown, her eyes angrily accusing.

'What's everyone done with Ching Mei, Cousin Fanny?'

'Everyone, as you say, hasn't done anything with her. She must have lost her way in the fog. Uncle Edgar has gone out to find her. She'll be here presently. Now I want you two children in bed.'

'Then will you kiss us good night, Cousin Fanny?' Marcus asked exhaustedly.

'Of course I will. Don't I always? Come, Nolly. Into bed with you. You shall have your doll when Ching Mei comes.'

'Will you watch for her, Cousin Fanny?'

'No one can see anything in that fog.' Fanny briskly twitched the curtain into place. 'Dora, put some more coal on the fire. I'll sit beside it until the children fall asleep.'

'Will you blow out our candles, Cousin Fanny?' Nolly was coming reluctantly to the bedside.

'When you're asleep. Not before. I promise.'

'Will Ching Mei be afraid in the dark?'

Fanny was tucking Marcus in. She said, 'Ching Mei did a very brave thing coming to England with you. I don't think she'll be afraid of a little dark.' She added offhandedly, 'Nolly, do you remember leaving your doll in the pagoda?'

'No, I didn't leave her there. I had her under my arm all the time. Then we were running up to the house. At least—I think I had her.'

'Then you're not sure, so she is down there. Well, she'll soon be rescued. Dora, you may go now. I'll be here until Ching Mei gets back.'

Marcus was asleep almost instantly. Fifteen minutes later, just as Fanny was about to blow out the candles, Nolly said sleepily. 'I hope those dogs didn't get my doll.'

'Dogs?'

'The ones we heard barking. Marcus said they were wolves. Isn't he silly! Wolves!'

Nolly, too, was sleep, her lashes long and dark on her white cheeks. Neither child stirred when Aunt Louisa came to the door to whisper stridently, 'Fanny! Your uncle says it's no use trying to search any more in the dark. He says either the woman will come back, or she's run away.'

'Run away!' Fanny exclaimed in astonishment. 'She wouldn't dream of doing such a thing!'

Aunt Louisa was a shadow in the doorway, an enormous domineering bossy shadow.

'I don't see how you can claim to know, Fanny, any more than the rest of us how the oriental mind works. I myself have never trusted the woman. I'm perfectly sure she has understood every word we have said. So is your uncle. Now, pray don't spoil the children by sitting there all night.'

Fanny started up.

'But is that all that's to be done about Ching Mei? With a prisoner at large, too.'

'My dear girl, what do you suggest? That we start dragging the lake in pitch darkness? You may sit up and listen for her if you choose. I for one, am going to bed.'

Aunt Louisa probably didn't mean to be callous. She just didn't attach much importance to the safety of one small silent suspicious foreigner, and a servant at that. Uncle Edgar, whose kindness always had a practical element, would be the same. George would think only of discharging his rifle at shadows. So it was left for Fanny to put on her cloak and her outdoor shoes and grope her way across the terrace, past the rose garden, and down the path to the lake.

The wind had dropped. There wasn't a sound until suddenly the tall outlandish shape of the pagoda loomed up out of the fog and the thin intermittent tinkle of the scarcely-swayed windbells sounded.

She had brought matches. She struck them, one after another, as she went into the pagoda and saw the bamboo chairs and the table where, so long ago, they had had the light-hearted tea party.

She called softly, 'Ching Mei! It's me, Fanny. Answer me, if you can.'

The mist formed a halo round the tiny flare of the match. On the lake something made a muted splash. The bells tinkled again, very faintly. There was no other sound, no movement.

Uncle Edgar had been right. There was no use in trying to search in the dark. Ching Mei had obviously strayed out of her way and would shelter beneath a bush until daylight. It was cold, but not dangerously so. She shouldn't come to any harm.

Reassuring herself with those thoughts, Fanny made her way towards the house. Just beyond the rhododendron bank someone sprang on her, holding her fiercely.

'There you are at last, you foreign devil!'

'George! George, let me go at once!'

George's alarmingly strong hands pressed her head back. He was trying to see her face.

'George, it's me! Fanny!' It was as well she had recognised his voice or she would have been scared out of her wits.

'Fanny!' He loosened his hold. The hard substance pressing into her side was his sword, sheathed, thank goodness. Had he had that naked in his hand he could have run her through.

'I thought you were one of the foreign devils.'

'Foreign devils?'

'Russkys, Chinese, what's the difference? Don't you know the dark isn't safe?'

'I came out to look for Ching Mei. I haven't been able to find her. Take me back to the house.'

'Not for a minute, Fanny.' His arm had tightened round her again. He was pushing the hood of her cape back from her face. 'I never have the chance to get you alone like this.'

He had kissed her before she could turn her face away, a hard bruising greedy kiss that filled her first with revulsion, then with furious anger. It was the first time she had been kissed. Her first kiss, and it had to be like this! Her eyes stung with angry tears. She wrenched herself free and resisting an impulse to beat and claw at George, she made herself stand still and face him in the darkness.

'George Davenport, if ever you dare to do that again, if ever you dare——'

'I told you the dark wasn't safe,' George muttered, but the fire had gone out of his voice. Inevitably, the anger in Fanny died, too. She knew how he would look if she could see him, shamefaced, bewildered, sulky, his slowed brain trying to understand the violence that leapt in him.

He wasn't safe, Fanny was thinking uneasily. And yet the

inevitable pity was filling her. It wasn't his fault that he had become like this. Somehow one had to have patience until he got better.

'I'm sorry if I hurt you, Fanny. Truly, Fanny, I wouldn't hurt you.'

'I'm telling you, George, if ever you do that again I believe I could almost kill you.'

'But you wouldn't, would you, Fanny. You only kill enemies, not friends. So stay my friend, Fanny, and you'll be safe.'

Back in her room, Fanny found Nolly's Chinese doll lying face downwards on her bed. She stared at it in stupefaction. Had she absent-mindedly put it there herself? Or had Nolly forgetfully dropped it? Anyway, there it was, the culprit.

It was a very small and innocent toy to have caused the death of one old Chinese woman.

9

For the gardener's boy found her in the morning lying among the water-lilies in scarcely eighteen inches of water. She had been battered about the head. Whether she had been drowned, or had died of those brutal blows, it wasn't possible to say.

But it was clear her death was no accident. There seemed little doubt what had happened. In her search for Nolly's doll she had encountered the escaped prisoner. He, as Sir Giles Mowatt confirmed, was a desperate and dangerous man. He couldn't risk the alarm being given, and had attacked his innocent discoverer violently. A stronger person might have survived his blows, but Ching Mei was a small old woman with fragile bones. She had had no chance.

It was all very tragic, and the search for the prisoner was redoubled. All the comings and goings, men on horseback and on foot, kept Nolly and Marcus at the windows, full of interest, and they even seemed to believe Fanny's story that Ching Mei had suddenly grown too homesick to stay with them. She had crept away quietly last night to catch the train to London, and a clipper ship to China.

'Will she write to us?' Nolly asked. 'She can. I've taught her how to write letters.'

'Then perhaps she will, later.'

'That means in years and years,' Nolly said dispassionately, her nose pressed against the window pane. 'Oh, Marcus, do look at that dog with the white tail. That will be mine. You can have the black one.'

'No, I want the one with the white tail.'

'You're a silly baby, wanting it just because it's mine. You can have the black one.'

'I want the white one!'

'Then very well, you can have the white one, and it's got great big teeth and it will bite you in half!'

'Nolly!' Fanny exclaimed, as Marcus burst into the inevitable loud sobs. 'That wasn't very kind. Tell Marcus you're sorry.'

'Why should I? He always wants my things. He will have to be careful, Papa says, or he will have no mind of his own.'

It was easy enough to see that Nolly's quarrelsome mood came from taut nerves, but that didn't make the task of restoring peace any easier. The child was uncannily intuitive. How much did she guess, or know? Her next question froze Fanny's blood.

'Cousin Fanny, why didn't Ching Mei take her sandals?'

'I expect she did.'

'She didn't. Not her best ones. They're in the wardrobe wrapped in tissue paper. She kept them for feast days and long journeys. That's why I know she hasn't gone on a long journey.'

Fanny thought of Ching Mei's lonely journey, and it was all she could do to answer quietly, 'Then perhaps one day she'll come back. In the meantime neither of you must worry because I will take care of you.'

She thought the hideous day would never end. The mist had turned to rain, and this had obliterated any tracks the fugitive might have left.

If he had been this way . . . Fanny was doing her best to shut out of her mind the episode with George in the dark garden last night. Had she been the first unprotected woman he had sprung on, in his obsession about a foreign enemy?

But surely, surely, what Uncle Edgar, the police, and Sir Giles Mowatt said was true. The prisoner was desperate. In his previous escape from Wandsworth he had bound and gagged a housewife in her kitchen, and stolen bread and half a leg of lamb. There would very likely be more acts of violence in lonely dwellings on the moor before he was recaptured.

One had to believe it was the prisoner who caused Ching Mei's death.

Fanny realised this even more after she had sought out George in the billiard room, and found him in one of his quiet and contented moods.

'Hullo, Fanny. Come to have a game with me?'

'No, I haven't time. I must stay with the children.'

'Can't the servants do that? What about the Chinese—oh, but she met with an accident, didn't she? I forgot for the moment.'

Were servants really of such little importance to him as human beings, or hadn't it penetrated his mind that Ching Mei was dead? Watching him place the balls with skill, his handsome face completely absorbed, Fanny was genuinely bewildered.

'George, you do remember being in the garden last night?'

'When I bumped into you? Sorry if I scared you. I was only fooling.'

'Fooling!'

'Lord, Fanny, you don't think I'd kill a woman, do you? I thought you were the escaped prisoner, until I got my hands on you. Knew then you were a woman—skirts and things.'

'George!' Fanny breathed. 'Ching Mei wore trousers.'

'What's that got to do with it? Dash it, Fanny, you don't think I go about fumbling an oriental!'

The horror in his voice was convincing. He looked so affronted that Fanny almost found the situation comical. She compressed her lips. She found herself longing to laugh, light-heartedly, carelessly, at anything. Laughter seemed a very long way away.

'No, you save those favours for an English woman,' she said with asperity. 'And I won't have it, George. I told you last night.'

George looked abashed. 'Sorry,' he mumbled. 'Lost my head. Guess the opportunity won't come again. If it does—can't promise——'

At this moment it was impossible to imagine George a murderer, he was merely lovestick and embarrassing. But his moods changed, and he was, perhaps conveniently, unable to remember. Sometimes he was still pursuing Russians. Asking him questions got one nowhere at all.

To Amelia, the day had been intolerable. She had had to spend most of it alone, for Mamma was with Papa, talking first to Doctor Bates, and then to the hastily summoned police. Grandmamma, on an occasion like this, was someone to be avoided. She would have been talking about omens and portents, and probably that ghastly bird in the chimney. And Fanny wouldn't let Amelia come into the nursery, because she had foolishly wept (not for the strange little Chinese woman, but from shock and depression, and curious strung-up state of expectation), and her eyes were still reddened.

'I won't have the children upset,' Fanny had said. 'They think their amah has gone back to China, but they're quick enough to guess anything. Anyway, why are you crying?'

Amelia sniffed and mopped at her eyes.

'Fanny, you're getting altogether too bossy. Mamma says so, too. And why must you spend all day with the children? I need some companionship as well.'

'But, Amelia, they're so little!'

Amelia pouted.

'Then they don't understand this terrible thing. I do. I can't bear to be alone. I keep thinking——'

'Thinking what?' Fanny asked curiously, seeing Amelia's furtive and frightened eyes.

'That that dreadful man might break into the house. You know—that a curtain might draw back and there he would be.'

'Oh, Amelia, darling! Hunted people like him don't come into houses. They hide on the moors, in caves, under hedges. He'll be miles away by now. Sir Giles says so.'

'I wonder where,' said Amelia fearfully.

The day, of course, did end. Even dinner was over. Only Amelia and Lady Arabella had stayed downstairs afterwards. Lady Arabella had fallen asleep by the fire, and Amelia unable to face the thought of her bedroom all alone, stayed at the piano, picking out tunes, singing a little, but only half-heartedly. To cheer herself up, she had put on her best blue silk, and tied blue ribbons in her hair. She had expected Mamma to scold, but no one, not even Papa, had made any comments, or seemed to notice her. It had been a horrible day, and thank heaven it was almost over.

A log fell with a muffled crash in the big fireplace. Lady Arabella didn't stir. Amelia gave an exclamation of exasperation and bad temper. She brought her fingers down on the keys with a resounding chord, but still Grandmamma, sunk deep in her slumber, didn't wake. Something made a pecking sound at the window behind her. A bird? A branch of the wistaria climbing the wall? Amelia turned and stared fascinatedly at the drawn curtains.

Actually, they were not quite drawn. There was a space of two inches that showed dark window pane—and was that something moving?

Amelia's hands flew to her throat. The tapping came again, peremptorily.

She didn't know where the courage which impelled her to the window came from. She really wanted to scream until Papa or George or Barker, or anyone, came. Instead, she was drawing aside the curtain, and looking into the wild shining eyes of the man outside.

He made urgent motions for her to open the window.

Again she didn't know what kind of hypnotism compelled her to obey. But in a moment the window was open, the cold wind in her face, and the man, pressed against the wall, under cover of the wistaria was whispering harshly, 'Get me some food! I'm starving. You look like an angel.'

'You're the p-prisoner!' Amelia gasped.

'Never mind what I am. Shut the window and get me the food. Quick! Don't wake her.'

He nodded towards Lady Arabella, still fast asleep, her cap tilted sideways, her chin sunk into her plump breast.

Amelia suppressed an hysterical giggle.

'Nothing wakes Grandmamma.'

'Then hurry! You wouldn't let a man starve.'

Just for one horrifying thrilling moment his fingers, cold and hard, touched hers. Amelia snatched her hand away and held it pressed in her other palm as if it had been wounded.

'Will you promise not to get into the house?'

'Yes, yes, I promise. Shut the window. Draw the curtains again. I'll be here. But hurry.'

Suddenly Amelia realised that her fright was really intense excitement. She did as he told her to, closing the windows softly, and pulling the curtain across. Then she flew out of the room and down the stairs to the kitchen where the lamps were lit and a fire burning cosily in the big stove. Lizzie was washing dishes, and Cook sitting at the long scrubbed table finishing her supper.

The kitchen was familiar and comforting territory to Amelia. Her plumpness was largely due to her fondness for coming here to be petted by the maids, and consume freshly made biscuits and hot scones.

'Cook, make me a sandwich, please. A big one.'

Cook, who also found food the chief pleasure in life, threw back her head and shouted with laughter.

'Miss Amelia, you'll never get an eighteen inch waist this way, bless your heart.'

'Please, Cook. Cold meat, if you have it, and a piece of plum cake. Honestly, I couldn't eat a thing at dinner. Everyone was so quiet and glum, as if it was one of us who had died.'

(And was that the murderer crouched beneath the wistaria, trustfully waiting for her?)

Cook was shaking her massive head. 'We couldn't make anything of that heathen idol. She gave us the creeps, to tell the truth. All right, Miss Amelia, don't fidget so. I'll make your sandwich. Lizzie, get me that cold joint out of the safe. And the bread. Lizzie will bring it up to you, Miss Amelia.'

'No, I'll wait and take it. But hurry. I'm so tired, I could die.'

She yawned convincingly. She hoped the high colour in her cheeks was put down to over-tiredness by Cook and the inquisitive Lizzie. They seemed to dawdle so over cutting the bread and buttering it that she could have screamed with impatience. But at last it was ready, with the large slice of plum cake, and Cook was chuckling with admiration at the thought of Amelia's unashamed greediness.

Clutching the plate to her, praying she wouldn't encounter anybody, and that Grandmamma hadn't woken, she hastened back to the drawing room.

Everything was as she had left it, the songbook open on the piano, the fire crackling, Lady Arabella snoring gently. It was such an innocent scene. She scarcely believed that when she drew back the curtain and opened the window the hungry hand would enter and snatch at the food.

Indeed, for a moment, when she had undone the catch, there was no movement without. She had a crazy feeling it had all been a dream. She was wildly disappointed.

Then the leaves rustled, and the shock of dark hair, the thin face, appeared.

He didn't snatch at the food. Instead, he looked steadily into

Amelia's face.

'I think I have never seen anyone so beautiful,' he said.

Amelia felt the hot flush of startled pleasure flood her whole body.

'Here's your food. Take it and go.'

He emptied the plate quickly, putting the sandwiches and the cake carefully in his pocket. Then, much as she wanted him to go, taking the fearful excitement with him, Amelia detained him.

'Have you been hiding about here all day? How was it the dogs didn't find you?'

'Because I haven't been here. I went the other way last night, then at midday I doubled back to fool them. I'm making for Plymouth. I'll get aboard a ship.'

'You—weren't in this vicinity last night?'

He grinned, showing remarkably good white teeth.

'Sure, I was not. I slept under a boulder stinking of sheep.'

'Why do you trust me?' Amelia whispered.

'Because when I saw you sitting at the piano there, with the light in your hair, I knew you could be nothing but an angel. I'll never forget you. Now I'm off. God bless you.'

There was an infinitesimal rustling in the leaves, and he was gone. He was as quick and silent as a fox. Amelia had no doubt he would get to Plymouth, and get safely aboard a ship sailing for France or Holland, or perhaps one of the Americas. She was glad she had helped him, glad! She would never breathe a word about him having been there. If necessary, she would lie until the day she died. For he had done something for her that so far no other man had done. He had made her feel beautiful, and a woman. She didn't think she could ever talk to a schoolboy like Robert Hadlow again.

As she softly closed the window, Lady Arabella woke.

'Ugh!' she exclaimed, shaking herself. 'It's cold. The room's full of draughts. What are you doing at the window?'

'Just looking to see if it's a clear night,' Amelia said.

'And is it?'

'Yes, the moon's shining.'

'Then they'll most likely catch that criminal. He won't have the fog to hide in. Ugh!' She shuddered again. 'It's cold. I feel as if I have that dead woman's blood in my veins. Now what is it, child? Why are you looking so frightened?'

Amelia pressed her hands to her pounding heart. She had just realised a terrible thing. Only she knew that the prisoner had not killed Ching Mei, but by keeping her secret, no more effort would be made to find the real culprit. And who was it? *Who?*

10

THE hunt moved the other way, towards Okehampton and Ashburton, and the Somerset border. Trains going to London were searched, and shopkeepers in small villages warned to be watchful. It seemed as if the prisoner's break for freedom might have been a success.

The episode had passed like a disastrous storm over Darkwater. The villagers, from having been hostile and unfriendly towards the little foreign woman, were now belatedly sympathetic and shocked. It was arranged that she should be buried in the village churchyard, her grave lying between honest Joseph Briggs, a blacksmith, and Old Martha Turl, centenarian, dead a few weeks previously. She was in respectable company now, people said with satisfaction, but Fanny kept thinking of how Ching Mei, Chinese to her core, must be fretting for the paper house, the food and the cooking utensils, which she would require for her long journey. Even her feast day sandals, which Hannah had briskly bundled up, together with her other modest belongings, and taken away to be destroyed.

There couldn't be letters written to her family in Shanghai because no one knew who they were. Hamish Barlow's arrival would have to be awaited, to see if he could produce any information. Fanny had the strange suspicion that Adam Marsh, too, might have been able to throw some light on the subject.

But Adam Marsh remained as great a mystery as Ching Mei's Chinese relatives, and the gloom hanging over life at present was hard to dispel.

Strangely enough, Amelia seemed to be touched by it, too. She was restless and distrait. Amelia without her boisterous talkativeness was another person. Lady Arabella noticed the change in both girls and although she approved their extreme sensibility—delicately-reared young woman must naturally be deeply shocked by violent death—she finally grew impatient of it.

'Louisa, those girls either need a good dose of rhubarb or a change. Why don't you take them to London for a week or two? I'll speak to Edgar if you like.'

'Thank you, Mamma, but I'm quite able to speak to my husband myself. Why should he listen to you more than to me?'

Lady Arabella rocked back and forth in her rocking chair, smiling gently.

'Because he has a respect for old age, probably.'

Louisa looked at her mother suspiciously. The reply was too innocent. She hadn't noticed her husband's respect for age lead to any great generosity. Though there was the matter of George's new hunter which Mamma had wheedled out of him.

'Anyway, there's no need to speak to him. He has agreed that we may go to Plymouth and shop, particularly for Amelia. This is her year, after all. Edgar has been very generous.'

Indeed, he had. He had thrown a pile of sovereigns on to the bed last night and said offhandedly, 'See how far you can make that go. I don't expect wild extravagance, but make Amelia—and Fanny, of course—look as they should. Eh, my love?'

Then he had kissed her on the cheek.

'You see, I'm not such a bad husband after all.'

Louisa, for once, was at a loss for words. At that moment she found his portly figure impressive and admirable, his eyes not merely tolerant and a little facetious, but loving.

'Have you overcome your financial difficulties?' she asked.

'Things are looking more optimistic, yes. There are still problems, but I hope and expect to overcome these.'

'You will, I am sure. You always have.'

'And then you will begin to think about your ermines?' His eyes twinkled with the kindness he could show so many people, orphans, impoverished villagers, people struck by misfortune, but not always, Louisa had to admit, herself. Nevertheless, at this moment, he was showing it to her. She was sceptical but pleased.

'Edgar, sometimes I believe you really are a good man.'

For some reason he found this remark diverting. His heavy jowls and his stomach shook as he chuckled rumblingly.

'Then let us settle for that. Sometimes I am good, and sometimes you are tolerable. But I must admit'—he laid his hand on her shoulder—'you pay for dressing. I expect you and my daughter to do me credit at this ball.'

'Is Fanny to go to Plymouth also?' Lady Arabella asked.

'If she wishes to,' Louisa replied shortly.

But Fanny didn't wish to go on the shopping expedition. She couldn't bring herself to leave the children. She didn't know why she had this obscure dread that the tragedy of Ching Mei might spread to them . . .

So Aunt Louisa and Amelia, with Trumble on the coachman's seat, went, and arrived home after dark, laden with silks and brocades, lawn and striped taffeta, also trimmings for bonnets, ribbons and braids, and feathers, and an enchanting white fur muff and bonnet to match for Amelia. The children had not been forgotten. Uncle Edgar had particularly asked that they be fitted out as became their new position in life, so there was a plaid coat and bonnet for Nolly, frilled pantaloons and petticoats, and shiny black-buttoned boots, and for Marcus a sailor hat and suit, and a cord with a whistle on it.

There was even a length of the new foulard silk for Fanny. It was for her ball gown, Amelia explained. Amelia had quite recovered her spirits and chattered endlessly.

'We do hope you like the silk, Fanny. Mamma and I took ages to choose it. And the next time we go to Plymouth you're to come, too, so that you can go to Miss Egham for your measurements to be taken. She's to make all our gowns. Lady Mowatt says she's terribly clever, and even makes things for the Duchess of Devonshire. Isn't it jolly, because it means several visits to Plymouth, and although it isn't London, at least it's better than being cooped up here. Miss Egham has let us bring home some of her fashion books. Do you want to see them?'

'Later,' said Fanny, absently.

She had to admit that Aunt Louisa and Amelia had chosen well for her ball gown. The silk was a deep rose instead of the pastel colours worn so much, and it would set off very well her black hair and vivid colouring.

But they had had to choose carefully, because Amelia's ball

was going to be a large important one, and everyone belonging to the family must do her credit.

Fanny hated herself for her thoughts. She hated dressing the children in their new clothes and telling them that they were for Sundays only, when they would be going to church. Afterwards, they must be taken off and hung away carefully until next Sunday.

'I don't think Marcus likes his,' said Nolly.

Marcus stood uncomplainingly in the sailor suit. Indeed, there was an innocent look of pleasure on his face.

'I think he likes them very well,' Fanny said.

'Then Ching Mei won't when she comes back. She doesn't like us in any clothes but the ones she gets ready for us.'

This was all too true. Ching Mei had been extremely vain and particular about her washing and ironing of the children's clothes. But how did one explain to a highly suspicious little girl that time didn't stand still, that clothes wore out and unfamiliar hands had to prepare new ones. That Ching Mei was never coming back . . .

It seemed impossible that Nolly, aged six and a half years, could have divined what had happened and kept the knowledge to herself. Yet there was that look of austere acceptance in her face and she had never cried.

She made scenes instead. There was the scene when she couldn't find the marbles.

'What marbles?' Fanny asked patiently. 'Dora, do you know anything about Miss Nolly's marbles.'

'I've never seen them, miss.'

'But you must know about them. Everyone knows about them!' Nolly stamped her foot, her black eyes sparking. 'They were in a little bag that Ching Mei sewed for us, and Marcus and I are always playing with them. Aren't we, Marcus?'

'What?' said Marcus.

'Playing with our marbles, stupid!'

'We haven't for a long time,' said Marcus. 'Where are our marbles?'

'Don't you understand, that's what I'm asking Cousin Fanny!' The loss of the marbles, whatever they were, was not serious enough to provoke such anguish in Nolly's face.

Fanny averted the real tantrum by suggesting a walk.

'We'll go to the village, and I'll show you the church where you'll be wearing your new clothes on Sunday.'

It was late afternoon and the sun had left the long windows over the altar. The church was dim. Fanny walked slowly up the aisle, the children tiptoeing after her.

'What's that?' whispered Marcus. 'What's that, Cousin Fanny.'

Fanny looked round. He was pointing to the tomb of a long-ago Davenport, the one who was reputed to have built the house at Darkwater. Hugo Davenport, born 1521, died 1599. He lay, tall and thin, carved in cream-coloured stone, his shoes narrow and pointed, his beard trim, his long nose rubbed flat with the centuries. His wife, Elizabeth, lay beside him, her Elizabethan ruff holding erect her small firm chin. Their feet rested against a greyhound, which lay humbly loyally curled, not deserting them in death.

It was the dog which fascinated Marcus.

'I'd like it,' he said.

'You can't have it, it's stuck there,' said Nolly.

'It's a memorial,' Fanny explained. 'It's so people will always know that once there lived a man called Hugo Davenport and a woman called Elizabeth, and they had a faithful greyhound. What would you like to be at your feet?'

'When we're dead!' said Nolly in astonishment.

It couldn't happen to a little girl of six years. It could scarcely happen to someone who was almost twenty-one. But it had happened to the homesick, alien Chinese woman, as loyal as the Davenport greyhound. It could happen to anyone.

'I'd have a dove, I think,' said Fanny.

'I'd have a peacock!' said Marcus.

'And what about you, Nolly?'

Nolly lifted her small chin. It looked remarkably like that of her ancestor Elizabeth. It didn't need supporting by a stiff ruff.

'But I'm not going to die!'

Someone had opened the church door. It creaked, and sunlight fell across the flagstones. Then the door closed softly, and the man stood within.

His face was in shadow. There was something about his

bearing that was familiar. Why did he just stand there as if he hoped to remain unseen? Marcus gave a small whimper as Fanny's fingers tightened on his. Nolly said in her clear low voice, 'Cousin Fanny, there's a man watching us.'

Fanny stepped briskly into the aisle, a child at each side. She hoped to reach the door without her palpitating heart rendering her speechless. She was almost sure... She *was* sure...

She held out her hand with easy grace.

'Why, Mr Marsh! So you have come on your visit to the moors.'

She had thought she had remembered every detail of his face, but she found she had forgotten the squareness and strength of his chin, the faint disturbing grimness of his eyes before they left her face and turned to the children with a look of assumed surprise and delight.

And the unwanted thought flashed through her head—how long had he been in this part of the country without making his presence known?

'Miss Davenport!' her hand was all but crushed in his grip. 'And Miss Olivia and Master Marcus! I had hoped to see you hereabouts. I fancied it was you I saw going into the church.'

'We were looking at the dead lady,' Marcus said.

'Dead lady?' repeated Mr Marsh, and Fanny tried to signal to him that if he had heard about Ching Mei, not to say her name.

'The one on the box over there,' Marcus said. 'She's squashing a dog with her feet.'

'She's not squashing it, Marcus,' Nolly said severely. 'She's just resting her feet on it. It likes it, anyway. It's a faithful and true dog. Would you like to see it, Mr Marsh?'

'Very much.'

So the little procession filed back to the tomb, and while the children, brought to life by his sudden appearance, rushed forward to caress the dog's cold ears, and trace its stony outline, Fanny said softly, and hurriedly, 'Ching Mei—the Chinese woman—I don't know if you remember her, has d-died——' To her horror she heard her voice trembling. Belatedly, and at this highly inconvenient time, she felt herself about to weep for the patient silent loyal woman who also would have curled up at the feet of her master and mistress in eternal devotion.

'I know. They told me in the village. I'm staying at the Darkwater Arms.'

His fingers had barely touched hers before the children were looking round, demanding attention. But the gesture had warmed her to her heart, and more than ever her tears were difficult to control.

'Mr Marsh, will you be coming to call on us?' That was Nolly, remembering her manners and her dignity. 'Ching Mei, we're sorry to say, has left us, but we have new clothes, and a great many toys to play with.'

Mr Marsh bowed.

'I hope to, Miss Olivia. I have been meaning to renew my acquaintance with you ever since the day I said good-bye to you in London. Wasn't it good fortune, Miss Davenport, that I was able to give assistance to these small travellers when they arrived in a strange country in such bewilderment.'

He realised that she must know by this time that he had not been the shipping company official, and that an explanation was due. But it was a little belated. Why couldn't he have told her at the time and saved her the embarrassment of the guinea tip? At the thought of that, Fanny's colour rose angrily.

'It was very kind of you, Mr Marsh,' she said in a clipped voice. 'But it has since caused my uncle, and myself, also, some mystification. Perhaps you might have explained your identity a little earlier.'

'My identity?' He was smiling. Had she imagined that earlier grimness in his eyes? Now they seemed to hold nothing but gentle amusement. 'What am I? Let us say, a traveller in search of a home. The same as Olivia and Marcus. Perhaps that's why I had sympathy for their plight. I apologise deeply for any misapprehension I caused. Later I will apologise to Mr Davenport personally.'

'Later?' She was furious for letting the anticipation be heard in her voice.

'I told you I love the moors. I intend to spend some few weeks here. Perhaps longer if I find a suitable house.'

'You would—live here?'

'I explained, Miss Fanny, that I am a traveller in search of a home. I have moved about too much in my youth, but now I intend to settle down. Indeed, you're uncle may be able to give me advice. Do you think it would be convenient if I present myself tomorrow afternoon?'

'I think—yes, I am sure it would be.' Fanny felt herself behaving more like a schoolgirl than Amelia did. 'He'll look forward to having the mystery of the traveller on the train cleared up. It has puzzled us all.'

(And you particularly? his intent gaze was asking.)

'And now, perhaps I may see you part of your way home?'

'Oh, no. Please don't. I think it would be better—I mean, if you were to call formally——'

'As you wish, Miss Fanny. We shall meet, of course. And talk of what has happened.'

He was referring then to Ching Mei's death. Naturally he would want to talk of it, since he had been interested in her welfare, and spoken to her in her own language.

But was it coincidence that his arrival had taken place so soon after her death?

'I wonder what brought him just now.'

She realised she had spoken aloud, as she and the children made their way down the narrow lane, deep-set between hawthorn hedges.

'I wrote him a letter,' said Nolly, tossing her curls.

Fanny stopped short. 'Nolly, what are you saying?'

Nolly's bright black gaze faltered.

'I know how to spell and write.'

'But you didn't write and post a letter. Where would you have sent it? You're not telling the truth, Nolly.'

'Marcus posted it. He pushed it into the box.'

'Marcus, did you?'

Marcus's wide innocent eyes were full of indignation.

'That was Ching Mei's letter to China. Nolly, you're not telling the truf.'

Nolly burst into loud sobs.

'I hate you! I hate you both! You say I tell lies.'

'Nolly, darling!' It was the first time the child had cried like this. Fanny recognised it as a release of her pent-up grief for Ching Mei's disappearance. She welcomed the tears, noisy and untidy as they were. 'Nolly, my pet, come here. Let me dry your eyes. No one's cross with you. We love you. Don't we, Marcus? And you see, even without a letter, Mr Marsh has come. So all is well, isn't it?'

It was only when they got home, and Fanny had left the children with Dora, and was in her room thinking she had only ten minutes to dress for dinner, that she realised her appearance. Her poplin gown was darned in two places, the cloak she had thrown over her shoulders, was threadbare, and quite the oldest one she possessed. She had had a scarf tied over her head. There was certainly no grand lady about her this time. She must have looked like a servant.

Looking into the mirror at her flushed cheeks, Fanny began to dimple with mirth. She had been saved the trouble of an explanation to Mr Marsh of her own position. He must by now be as puzzled about her as she had been about him!

11

BUT this situation didn't seem so amusing the next day.

Marcus had developed a slight fever during the night, and had to be kept in bed. He was fretful and restless, and wept every time Fanny left his bedside.

'Cousin Fanny, are you going on a journey, too?'

Ching Mei's disappearance had shaken him as much as it had Nolly. He remembered his mother and his father disappearing. He distrusted everybody.

Fanny scarcely had the opportunity to dress, or tidy her hair. When, half way through the morning, Lizzie came up with a message that the master wanted her in the library, she had an impulse to send back a message that she was unable to come. Then the thought sprang into her mind that Uncle Edgar might have come to hear of Adam Marsh's presence in the village, and wanted to speak of it.

She hurried downstairs straight from Marcus's bedside. Her long black hair was escaping from its hasty pinning up, and, because of her nursing chores, she had put on her oldest gown.

Voices in the library should have warned her. She was so intent on getting the interview over, and hurrying back to Marcus that she failed to realise that the voices were not only Uncle Edgar's and Amelia's.

She saw him standing near the window immediately she entered the room. He had been talking to Amelia, bending a little towards her attentively. Amelia, her fair hair brushed and shining, and tied with black velvet bows, and a spotless muslin fichu draped over the shoulders of her pretty blue morning gown, looked charming and animated and deliciously young. The contrast between her and Fanny, at that moment, could not have been more marked.

It showed on Adam Marsh's face as he turned and saw her. She was aware of his moment of keen assessing regard before he bowed and smiled.

'Miss Fanny! We meet again.'

Uncle Edgar, wearing his most benevolent expression, came forward.

'Fanny, my dear, why didn't you tell us you spoke to Mr Marsh yesterday, and that we could expect a visit from him?'

'Why, I——' Why had she wanted to keep their meeting secret? Because she had anticipated that scene of him bending so attentively over Amelia?

No, no, Amelia was only a gauche schoolgirl. Or had been until very recently. One couldn't quite decide when, in the last week or two, she had suddenly acquired moments of dignity and a certain mystery. Had it been since the tea party in the pagoda, when she had conversed so animatedly with Robert Hadlow? She didn't giggle so much, and she dreamed, and now, with the stimulation of a personable man's attention, she was really pretty.

They were all waiting for Fanny to finish what she had begun to say. Aunt Louisa was there, too, and George. They had been having glasses of Madeira and biscuits, showing hospitality towards the stranger even though they must want to know a great deal about him.

'Marcus has developed a fever,' she said. 'I've thought of nothing but him. Anyway, I was under the impression that Mr Marsh said he would probably call in the afternoon.'

'Marcus ill!' Mr Marsh exclaimed. 'I'm sorry to hear that.'

'It's only a little fever——'

'We must call Doctor Bates,' Uncle Edgar interrupted. 'Why hasn't it been done already?'

Aunt Louisa's nose, whether from the Madeira, or the pleasure of entertaining a good-looking and presumably unattached young man, or her husband's implied rebuke, had taken on its familiar grape colour.

'Fanny said the fever was slight. As you can see, Mr Marsh, Fanny is a practical young woman, and already so devoted to the children. My own daughter, I am afraid, has still to learn the practical things of life.'

At her mother's indulgent tone, Amelia's lashes drooped on her pink cheeks. She looked unbearably smug. And suddenly Fanny hated them all for what they had just done to her, letting her come unaware into the room looking as she did so that the comparison between her and Amelia was inevitable.

They had meant to do it. She wished passionately that she had run away that day in London. Then she remembered the children upstairs, utterly dependent on her, and was ashamed of her selfishness. But the anger stayed in her eyes, and in her jutting lip. Let Amelia smile coquettishly. She would be herself, refusing to be meek and humiliated.

'Fanny, Mr Marsh has been telling us how he came to be of such inestimable help to the children on the train that day. The shipping clerk was dilatory. Mr Marsh found Ching Mei in a state of distress. Being able to speak Chinese, he soon ascertained the facts. Isn't that so, Mr Marsh?'

'Miss Fanny expressed surprise that I spoke Ching Mei's language.' Mr Marsh's eyes as they rested again on Fanny were ironic. 'I didn't explain to her, as I have to you, that my father was a well-known collector of Chinese porcelain and jade. He made several trips to the East, and on two occasions I accompanied him. I should add that I was at Tilbury that day because the *China Star* was bringing some new pieces for the collection which I now own.'

'And he is looking for a house in which to keep it,' Amelia exclaimed, unable to keep silent any longer. 'And in which to live himself, of course. Mr Marsh, if it were to be somewhere in this vicinity I should be delighted—I mean, we shall all be delighted.'

She blushed at her transparency and Adam Marsh smiled. 'That is charming of you, Miss Amelia.'

It was funny, thought Fanny, that when he looked at Amelia that almost grim expression left him, and he looked light-hearted and gay. He wasn't summing her up as he was Fanny. But then Amelia needed no summing up. She didn't look like the daughter of the family one day and a servant the next.

'Yes, I'm tired of wandering,' he went on. 'I intend to settle down. As I told Miss Fanny, I have a great fondness for this part of England. Our meeting has been quite a coincidence, hasn't it?'

'A fortunate coincidence, Mr Marsh,' said Aunt Louisa warmly. 'I hope we can persuade you to come to some of our gaieties this year. We are giving Amelia a ball later.'

'And by jove, my brother's attorney from Shanghai will be here, too,' said Uncle Edgar. 'A Mr Hamish Barlow. I don't suppose you have heard of him?'

Did something flicker in those dark brown eyes? They were unreadable eyes, Fanny had decided from the first. Amelia could get out of her depth in them. So, for that matter, could she.

'I'm afraid my acquaintance of China is confined mostly to Peking. But I shall be interested in meeting Mr Barlow.'

'I have suddenly remembered!' Amelia cried. 'The other day Robert Hadlow said that Heronshall was going to be put up for sale. Old Mr Farquarson is going to live entirely in London. That's scarcely ten miles from here. It's a Georgian house, Mr Marsh, with lovely light rooms. Not nearly so dark and dreary as these.'

'But this is a beautiful house,' said Mr Marsh.

Fanny found she couldn't bear to stay there while Amelia excitedly arranged this stranger's future. Surely he wouldn't allow her to do it! Though if he were speaking the truth and wanted to buy a house, Heronshall was eminently suitable. The long windows would display to perfection his collection of Chinese porcelain—if it existed...

She interrupted the conversation, speaking quite calmly.

'If I may be excused, I would like to return to Marcus.'

'Certainly, my dear,' said Uncle Edgar. 'But don't make yourself a prisoner in the sickroom. You know there's no need for that.'

'Fanny used to think she had a vocation for nursing,' said Aunt Louisa indulgently. 'Then later she began to talk of convents. I think she used to imagine she had something of the martyr in her. It's her Celtic ancestry, I expect.'

'She's much too pretty for convents or hospitals,' Uncle Edgar boomed. 'And to add to our festive year, Mr Marsh, Fanny has a twenty-first birthday which of course will be suitably celebrated.'

How clever they were, Aunt Louisa suggesting that her tendency to martyrdom made her stay in Marcus's sickroom and wear her oldest clothes, Uncle Edgar hinting that twenty-one was so much more than the delicious freshness of seventeen.

Or did she imagine these things because she had fallen in love and all her senses were unbearably heightened? She knew she would have to walk a tightrope to achieve happiness. She was more likely to fall and hurt herself irremediably.

She had got out of the room and longed only to escape to the children, now her allies and her uncritical unquestioning friends. With dismay she heard Adam's voice at the door.

'I was greatly taken with the children. I promised them to come. Would I be out of place for two minutes in the sick-room?'

'But how thoughtful of you, Mr Marsh.' Aunt Louisa's voice was acquiescent as courtesy demanded, but a little bewildered, a little put out.

'It may be the measles, Mr Marsh. Pray don't catch them.' Amelia laughed, but she was a little put out, too.

Fanny hurried up the stairs, not thinking at all. She didn't want him in the nursery. He had already been too officious, too overpowering. He made glib explanations and got his own way. He probably broke hearts right and left. She wouldn't have Nolly and Marcus fretting for him.

'Miss Fanny!'

They were at the turn of the second flight of stairs. There was no one about. From the nursery Fanny could hear Marcus whimpering.

'I've heard how Ching Mei's death happened. Is it true?'

She had to turn and look at him.

'How could it not be?' she asked slowly.

'There was no other reason?'

'Not that I know of. My cousin George—you must have noticed how he is. He hasn't yet recovered from his war wound. But he has been trained to kill with a sword, not—not with his hands.'

'Then it was the escaped prisoner?'

'It must have been. The coroner decided so at the inquest.' She looked into his intent eyes. 'Why do you care?'

'Because I find a mystery provoking. Very provoking.'

'You are staring at me,' said Fanny. She put her hands to her hair, an inevitable feminine movement, trying to smooth it. 'Is there anything wrong?'

'Everything.'

'Then you had better go back and talk to my cousin Amelia. She has had time to make her toilette this morning.'

He began to laugh as if her tartness amused him, then stopped, and said thoughtfully, 'Yes, your cousin Amelia is a delightful creature. I fancy we shall be seeing quite a lot of one another. If I had known I would have come much sooner.'

'Known what?'

'Why, that the moors can be so fascinating. Exciting, dark, unpredictable, stormy, tragic, and then warm and glowing like a summer's day, full of light, innocent, irresistible.'

He was talking of the moors. But he made them sound like a woman.

12

LADY ARABELLA had awoken with a start to the knowledge that something was going on about which she knew nothing. This had happened also the other evening when she had opened her eyes to find Amelia at the window and the room full of cold air. She never had discovered what Amelia had been doing, which was aggravating. She didn't intend to be left out of what was happening upstairs now, with Nolly laughing hysterically and the sound of a man's deep voice.

Had Doctor Bates been sent for to examine Marcus? But Doctor Bates was elderly, prime, and serious, and most unlikely to make a child laugh.

Sighing and struggling, Lady Amelia heaved herself out of her low chair, put her cap straight, and waddled off to her vantage point at the head of the stairs. The windowseat was shadowed by the heavy velvet curtains. It was surprising how often she had sat there quietly in her black dress and never been seen, though occasionally a startled maid had dropped what she was carrying and exclaimed in confusion. She had heard many intriguing fragments of conversation from there, and if they hadn't always been interpreted correctly, that made it all the more interesting. Lady Arabella was all for a little embellishment of the truth.

Her harmless ploy was well-rewarded today, for she had scarcely sat down before the door of the nursery on the second floor opened, and footsteps began to come down the stairs.

Fanny led the way, followed by a stranger, who seemed to be on terms of some intimacy, for he was saying in a low almost conspiratorial voice, 'I will come again, I hope frequently. I've taken a fancy to those children. I shall be interested in their future.'

Fanny, bless the girl, never minced matters.

'If you have such paternal feelings, Mr Marsh, I wonder that you don't do better than borrow other people's children.'

'Perhaps I intend to.'

Amelia must have been lurking at the bottom of the stairs,

for she called in her high assured young voice—now there was someone who was rapidly learning the artifices, the gushings, and the vapourings, that Fanny despised—'What is it you intend to do, Mr Marsh?'

'He intends to find a wife,' Fanny answered.

'How interesting.' Amelia's voice bubbled with interest. 'We wish you luck, Mr Marsh. Don't we, Fanny?'

As Lady Arabella had expected, no one noticed her sitting quietly in the shadow, but she was able to take a swift look at Fanny with her geranium-flushed cheeks and ruffled hair—that girl would look beautiful in sackcloth, in childbirth, in extreme old age—and then a much longer one at her companion. She noted the hard chin and the broad clever brow. She also noticed or divined a look of intense speculation in the almost black eyes. This, however, disappeared as the man caught sight of Amelia in the hall below. He paused a moment, looking down with a smile and an unruffled face. He could change his expression like an actor. He was someone to be watched, this young man. Lady Arabella made a sharp guess at his thoughts. Of the two girls, Fanny was the prettier, but Amelia was the richer. The children upstairs? They merely provided an original and convenient excuse for establishing himself in the house. Lady Arabella itched with curiosity. Who was he?

She had to wait until her pre-lunch glass of Madeira before her son-in-law satisfied her curiosity. Edgar, also sipping Madeira, was as anxious to discuss his uninvited guest as Lady Arabella was to hear about him.

'Well, that's cleared up the mystery of the man on the train. Fellow's story seems plausible. With his connections with China, the Chinese amah attracted his attention, naturally enough. Any gentleman would have done what he did.'

'Even to coming all the way to Devon?' Lady Arabella murmured.

Edgar paced up and down, reflectively.

'He seems to want to live in these parts. Call that coincidence, if you like. If he buys a property, we can't doubt his integrity.'

'And do you now?'

'Eh? Doubt a gentleman's word? I should hope not.'

'What are you worrying about, Edgar? That he will run off with Fanny?'

'With Fanny!'

'Didn't it occur to you that it might be Fanny who has brought him to these parts?'

It was obvious that such a thought had not occurred to Edgar. His brow cleared. He gave his rumbling chuckle.

'Well, now, I must have been blind not to see that. Of course, Fanny is an attractive young woman. But I'm afraid this won't suit my wife and daughter. They plan to lay claim to Mr Marsh. I've said they must wait until we know more about the gentleman, but you know what women are. Louisa sees him as an asset to our entertainments this summer, and Amelia'—Edgar shrugged his shoulders with tolerant amusement—'you may have noticed that what that young lady wants she intends to get.'

'I've noticed,' said Lady Arabella. 'I've also noticed that Fanny isn't completely without a will of her own. She hasn't Amelia's material assets, of course. That should provide a test to Mr Marsh's character. The contest should be remarkably interesting, don't you think?'

'Remarkably,' said Edgar shortly.

Lady Arabella watched him beneath her eyelids.

'I notice you worry less about the young man now you realise his interest is of the heart only.'

Edgar shot her a quick glance.

'What other object did you imagine he had in coming here?' Lady Arabella murmured. She waved her small white hands. 'No, don't bother to invent an answer, because I know that is all you will do. But I wouldn't underestimate even this romantically-inclined gentleman.'

'Wouldn't you?' said Edgar sharply.

'He is strong. Very strong. I feel it. I feel—no, never mind. I can see you despising my old woman fancies. And anyway, as you say, Louisa intends to fête the young man, Amelia intends to pursue him, so even if we think him a menace we're helpless.'

'Really, Mamma, you would make a country bumpkin, a clod, into a menace.' Edgar stared at her angrily, accusingly, 'You do it to amuse yourself.'

'Oh, yes, my dear, I make up stories. I turn the frog into the prince and vice versa. It's a harmless occupation. Like my little forays into local history. By the way, isn't it strange how that letter that I was telling you about has disappeared, so that neither of us can find it?'

She lifted her eyelids, letting him have her full round innocent gaze. He returned it, puffing his cheeks out in angry frustration.

'Whatever that letter is, if it exists, it's nothing to do with me. It's only against my better judgment I'm making arrangements to buy George a new hunter. Does that satisfy you?'

'In the meantime,' said Lady Arabella meekly.

Edgar made his voice genial.

'What else is it you want, you old witch?'

'What else? Only George's happiness. Even to his marrying Fanny, if he insists.'

'Marrying Fanny!' Edgar exploded. 'What poppycock! I'll never hear of it. Neither will his mother.'

'Edgar, you're getting red in the face. Is your health what it should be? I only made this comment now because I don't think it will do for Fanny and Mr Marsh to form an attachment. George wouldn't care for it.'

'George, George, George! Is he to run this house?'

'One day, we hope.' The old lady gave Edgar her heavy-lidded glance, a sly secret look she invited him to share. 'If things go as I suspect they must.'

'I am the master here!'

Lady Arabella seemed to be falling into one of her sudden naps. She didn't appear to notice his changed and furious face.

Outside the window, on the sloping lawn, the peacock suddenly set up its harsh penetrating squawking.

Lady Arabella opened her eyes.

'I have never disputed that, Edgar. But even you won't live for ever. Though longer than some, perhaps. And if you are the master, could you demonstrate it by finding out why the luncheon gong is two minutes late. I, for one, am famished.'

It was true that Amelia had already set her heart on having as much of Adam Marsh's company as she could get. Her mother was cautious, pointing out that although Adam seemed a perfect gentleman they didn't yet know anything about him.

'Your Papa will make enquiries,' she reiterated.

'Oh, Mamma, it's perfectly plain what he is by his face and his manners. I think it rather impertinent to even suggest investigating him. Anyway, no matter what you might find out, I intend to have him here a great deal.'

'None of that talk, miss.'

'He likes me,' said Amelia. 'He will help me to forget.'

Her mother turned in astonishment.

'To forget what, for goodness sake?'

'All faces are not as easy to read as Mr Marsh's.'

'Amelia, *what* are you talking about?'

Amelia flung her arms round her mother passionately.

'Oh, Mamma, I want a kind safe husband. I don't want to be—tortured.'

'Good gracious, child! Whatever books have you been reading to get such ideas? Tortured, indeed! As if your Papa or I would allow you to meet that kind of man.'

Amelia gave a small hollow laugh. 'No, I know you wouldn't if you could help it.'

'I still don't know what you're talking about,' said her mother, losing patience. 'You're a very fortunate girl. You live a sheltered life.'

'Yes, Mamma,' Amelia whispered, her eyes dark. 'I know.'

Amelia's prediction about Marcus's illness came true—he did have the measles, and by the end of the week Nolly had come down with them, too. So the children were not able to wear their new clothes to church on Sunday. The Davenport pew was occupied by Uncle Edgar, Aunt Louisa, Amelia, and George. It was taken for granted that Fanny should stay in the sickroom since, by her own behaviour, she had made the children so dependent on her that they were unmanageable when she was absent. No one else seemed to understand that two such little ones, deprived cruelly first of their parents, and then of their faithful nurse, must have some security in their lives.

Though perhaps Lady Arabella understood a little. She had taken it on herself to come and sit for long intervals in the sickroom, sometimes bringing Ludwig to sit in her capacious lap, sometimes her many-coloured wools and embroidery. She urged Fanny to take walks in the garden so as not to lose her pretty colour. At first Fanny was reluctant to do this, knowing Lady Arabella's propensity for making children nervous. But she had become so quiet and gentle that Nolly and Marcus seemed to like her sitting in the big armchair, as dozy as the cat in her lap. It was only when after a day or two, they grew better, and restless, that she began to tell them stories.

The outcome of this was that when Amelia came rushing up to the nursery after church Nolly burst into loud hysterical screams.

No one could tell what was the matter. The day was bleak and rainy, and Amelia had taken the opportunity to wear her new white fur hat and muff.

It emerged, at last, that on her first glimpse of it Nolly thought it was a white bird.

Fanny turned on Lady Arabella.

'You've been talking about that bird again!'

'No, I haven't, dear.' Lady Arabella's eyes were milky and innocent. 'Except to point out to the child that it was white, and not that wretched black skeleton she found the other day. A white bird. A beautiful pure creature. And on that day the mistress of the house shall die.'

Amelia said scornfully, 'Grandmamma, you can't scare us now with that old myth. It isn't true, anyway. Do you think a silly old bird is going to warn Mamma when she is going to die!'

'Need it be your mother?' said Lady Arabella softly.

'Well, who else, if it is to be the mistress of the house? Pay no attention, Nolly. See, I'll take my hat off and you can touch it. It's only white fur, so soft.'

But Nolly wouldn't be lured into touching the fur. She shrank away, hiding herself beneath the blankets, and although later she protested loudly that she hadn't been frightened, Fanny knew that that particular fear had been tucked deeply into her mind and that it would be a long time before it ceased to haunt her.

That was when it came to her that Lady Arabella might be more than a foolish, imaginative and mischievous old woman. In her desire to shock and in her desire to wield power she might be dangerous.

But why she should feel that, Fanny couldn't have said. She was becoming as overwrought as Nolly. Perhaps poor old women were happier than rich ones. They might be tired to the bone with washing and ironing great baskets of laundry, or scrubbing and cleaning, or hoeing the potato patch or caring for a clutch of grandchildren, but they were not so hopelessly bored with their idleness and uselessness that they weaved strange schemes in their heads.

It appeared that Amelia had rushed up to the nursery on her return from church for the express purpose of telling Fanny that she had talked with Adam Marsh. She had to wait until Fanny came down for her brief walk outdoors to seize her, and say, 'Don't you want to hear about Mr Marsh? He looked so elegant and everybody talked to him. And what do you think, Sir Giles Mowatt had heard of his father and of his famous collection of Chinese ceramics So Papa has to admit now that all his actions have been perfectly innocent.'

'Innocent?' said Fanny.

'Mamma and I believed him on sight, but I suppose fathers of marriageable daughters have to be careful, and even suspicious.'

'How can you *be* so smug?' Fanny breathed passionately.

Amelia opened her eyes wide.

'Smug? But why? Mr Marsh is unattached and we expect to be seeing a great deal of him this summer—by the way, he intended looking at Heronshall—and after all I am considered something of a catch. That isn't being smug, Fanny. It's simply looking at things the way they are.'

Fanny pulled her shawl more tightly round her shoulders. The wind was chilly. It was because of her that Adam had come here! Not because of this bright-eyed baby of a cousin, this plump naïve creature scarcely out of the schoolroom.

But then he hadn't known about Amelia in London. He had imagined her, Fanny, the pampered daughter of the house... As Amelia had said, one had to look at things the way they were.

'Do be a little more sympathetic, Fanny. Otherwise I won't be able to tell you my affairs of the heart.'

Fanny laughed out loud.

'Affairs of the heart, indeed! You're only a child.'

Amelia flushed indignantly. 'Mr Marsh doesn't think so. He complimented me on the way I looked. You had only to see the expression in his eyes.' Already she had forgotten her anger with Fanny, and was carried away with the happiness of her recollections. 'He is so masculine. He makes me feel truly like a grown woman. Only one other—person has ever made me feel like that.' Amelia's eyes were suddenly inward-looking, strange. 'Do you know,' she said in a rush, 'all the time I was in church I kept thinking of that wretched Chinese woman buried outside. Sometimes I am frightened . . .'

Fanny stared at her.

'Why? Because the prisoner may come back?'

Amelia shook her head.

'Sir Giles says he is afraid he has got away completely. To France or Belgium, or the Hook of Holland.' Her next words were almost inaudible. 'I think that is why I am frightened . . .'

George, tapping his riding crop against his leg, said to Fanny, 'You're not having your head turned by this fellow Marsh, too, are you?'

'I think my head is fairly securely attached.'

'Mamma and Amelia are behaving as if they had never seen a man from the city before. He must be laughing at them.' George's eyes, with their look of feverish excitement, were on Fanny with the intensity she was beginning to dread. 'You won't let him laugh at you, will you?'

'I don't suppose he's laughing at anybody.'

'I saw you looking at him yesterday. Don't do it again, Fanny.' His voice was very soft. 'I don't care for you to look at another man.'

'Oh, George, leave me alone! I can't bear this possessive attitude of yours. It's suffocating me. You used to tease me and despise me. Be like that again. Please!'

'Never!' said George. 'Never!'

'You will be when you are well.'

'I love you, Fanny. Being well won't change that.'

Fanny was near to tears with exasperation and tiredness and strain.

'Then if you must love me, you must. But please don't persecute me, or I'll have to tell your father.'

An indescribably sly look came into George's eyes.

'That wouldn't be much use, you know. Not poor old Papa.'

Then he turned and left her, the once handsome young lieutenant of the 27th lancers, who had flirted shamelessly with every pretty girl, a shambling young man whose once immaculate clothing was now always a little untidy, and whose breath frequently carried the fumes of brandy.

George was a tragedy. But how long could one have patience and forbearance with that kind of tragedy! How long was it safe to do so? Fanny couldn't help thinking constantly of Ching Mei's death and the convenient way in which it had been blamed on the escaped prisoner. Had anyone else seen George in the garden that night? Uncle Edgar? For why had George begun to speak of his father with pitying contempt? Poor old Papa . . .

It didn't seem, after all, as if Adam Marsh were laughing at Amelia with her transparent admiration for him. For he invited her to accompany him to look over the property, Heronshall. They went on horseback across the moors. Amelia rode almost as well as George did. On her mare, Jinny, she lost her dumpiness and her coquettish flutterings, and was a figure worth watching. They made a fine pair as they rode away. Fanny could scarcely bear to watch them go.

There was a shuffling sound behind her.

'A well-matched pair,' said Lady Arabella's throaty voice. 'Don't you agree?'

'Amelia scarcely comes to his shoulder.'

'She is on a level with his heart. That used to be the thing in my young days. Don't girls have these romantic notions nowadays?'

'You know that Amelia has her head stuffed with romantic dreams,' Fanny said irritably.

'And you? You're too practical for such things?'

Fanny turned away.

'You know I am not,' she said in a low voice, as if the words were forced from her.

Lady Arabella patted her hand.

'Your turn will come, my dear. Don't despair.'

Fanny snatched her hand away. She found the old lady's

kindness more intolerable than her sarcasm. How could she not despair when Amelia and Adam rode through the honeyed sweetness of the moorland air, talking perhaps intimately, perhaps touching hands. It was no use to wonder what Adam Marsh saw in an empty-headed rattle like Amelia. He would discover that she had beautiful small white hands, that her yellow curls blew across her throat when disordered by the wind. A man didn't then seek for a high intelligence.

They arrived back late in the afternoon. Amelia came flying upstairs calling, 'Fanny! Mr Marsh has things for the children. Are they well enough to see him? Oh, and you should have seen that divine house. Mr Farquarson's things are gone and the rooms are empty, but one can imagine exactly what is needed. Mr Marsh has a fine Arabian carpet which he says will perfectly fit the drawing room. The staircase must have portraits on either side. It is so light and airy compared with all the dark stairways in this house. And the master bedroom has the most beautiful views across the moors.'

'Did you furnish that, too?'

'Fanny! What a thing to say. We merely discussed what could be done. And it was all perfectly respectable as Mr Farquarson's housekeeper was still there. Mamma naturally wouldn't have let me go otherwise. Then is Mr Marsh to come up?'

Fanny wanted to refuse to have Adam in the nursery, but it would give the children pleasure. She said he might come for five minutes, no more.

The wind had raised a glow in his sallow skin. Although he was smiling he looked strangely serious. He had brought gingerbread cookies, bought from old Mrs Potter in the village that morning.

'For the invalids,' he said. 'I hope they are recovering fast. You see, Mrs Potter gave the gingerbread men spots too.'

The children studied the figures liberally sprinkled with coloured sugar, and laughed with delight.

'Marcus got the measles first, Mr Marsh, but I had the most spots,' Nolly declared.

'I had the most spots,' Marcus said.

'You did not, Cousin Fanny said I had more. And anyway my gingerbread man has more spots than yours.'

'No, it hasn't. Mine has.'

'Then count them. Come over here and I'll teach you to count.'

While they were wrangling, Adam turned to Fanny.

'Miss Amelia has been telling me a great deal about you.'

'About me!' Fanny exclaimed in astonishment. She could scarcely believe that they could find nothing to talk of but her on that long ride across the moors. She couldn't prevent a dimple appearing momentarily in her cheek.

'Amelia usually finds herself the most absorbing subject.'

'Perhaps it was because I asked her questions.'

'What kind of questions?' Fanny's face had gone still.

'Why, how you came to be in this position.'

'Yes, I suppose you must find it rather different than what you imagined it to be when we met in London.'

'Amelia tells me your parents died when you were very young. Your mother—your father—tell me what you know about them.'

'I know so little. My father died of a consumption. He had artistic leanings, I believe. I can't remember him at all.' Fanny frowned, feeling the old familiar bafflement. 'My mother was Irish, of landed but poor gentry, Uncle Edgar has told me. Her name was Francesca, like mine. I try to imagine what she was like, but I know so little. I feel as if I had dropped from the sky. What I do know,' she finished briskly, 'is that poor Papa's illness took all his money. That's why he left me in my uncle's care. To be quite accurate, Uncle Edgar isn't my uncle, but a second cousin.'

She realised, all at once, his interest and was startled and a little disturbed.

'Why do you ask me these things?'

'I have an inquisitive bent,' he said pleasantly.

Fanny frowned again. 'I think I find your inquisitive bent, as you call it, a little presumptuous. So now you know without any doubts that I am a poor relation. Have you some better position to offer me?'

'Cousin Fanny, Cousin Fanny! Marcus has eaten all his gingerbread.'

Nolly's imperative voice broke in on their small duel. For duel it was, and Adam seemed to welcome the interruption.

He went over to sit on Nolly's bed.

'When you are quite recovered how would you like a picnic on the moors? We could take a hamper. Have you seen the moorland ponies? They will come for crusts of bread.'

'Sandwiches like we eat?' Nolly asked.

'Yes, indeed. They have cultivated tastes. But they all need a brush and comb taken to their manes and coats.'

Nolly laughed delightedly. Marcus clamoured, 'Me, too. Can I come, too.'

'Naturally. And Cousin Fanny, of course. One day when the sun shines.'

He had a way of making people adore him, Fanny was thinking coldly. Not only children, but adults, like Amelia. Even Aunt Louisa. But the strange conversation they had just had had confirmed her suspicions about him. She knew now what he was about.

He was looking at her to see if she shared the children's enthusiasm about the proposed picnic.

'If you are disappointed I am not an heiress, I am sorry,' she said. 'I am afraid no amount of conjecture can achieve that.' She wanted to go on and say that he would have to be satisfied with Amelia, a compromise that didn't seem too displeasing to him.

She wasn't prepared for his frowning anger.

'I must have been very clumsy to deserve a remark like that. I assure you——'

But at that moment Amelia came bursting in.

'Mr Marsh, Mamma insists that you stay to dinner. We're not going to dress. Say that you will.'

He inclined his head. 'Your mother is very kind.'

'Then come downstairs.' She had taken his arm proprietorially. Miss Ferguson's patient lessons about etiquette and modesty seemed to have escaped from her flighty little head. 'I think it's sweet that you should be so interested in my little cousins,' Fanny heard her saying as they went. 'But you mustn't let them monopolise you.'

That was the moment when Fanny decided he was never to have the satisfaction of knowing what he had done to her.

In spite of Amelia's lofty decree that because Adam was in riding clothes, no one should dress, Fanny took great pains with her appearance that night. She wore her grey taffeta, old to be sure, but she let the neckline fall as low as possible over her shoulders, and she decided, with deliberation, to wear the sapphire pendant Uncle Edgar had given her. Above all, pity was not the emotion she wanted Adam Marsh to feel for her. She brushed her hair into a state of velvet softness and instead of wearing it in ringlets, as was all the rage, she twisted it low on her neck so that her ears and all of her round white forehead were visible.

She went downstairs late, so late that the gong had gone and everyone was just about to go to the dining room. Everyone looked at her. Aunt Louisa was about to scold when Uncle Edgar saw the sapphire and beamed with pleasure.

'And very well it looks on that pretty neck,' he whispered conspiratorially, making sure, nevertheless, that his words were quite audible.

'I had a fancy to wear it,' Fanny murmured. 'Somehow I was feeling happy. The children are recovered, and it's summer, and everything is so beautiful.'

She looked vaguely out of the window, suggesting that her remark about beauty meant the garden, and the trees heavy with mid-summer leaf. But her lingering gaze went round the room.

'May I sing to you later, Uncle Edgar. It seems a night for singing, I hardly know why.'

'You may indeed, my dear.'

'Fanny has a very pleasant voice, Mr Marsh,' Aunt Louisa said repressively.

'It's more likely we may hear a nightingale if we go outdoors,' said Amelia. 'Are you an admirer of the nightingale, Mr Marsh?'

So now he was caught between the two of them. Fanny found herself waiting for his answer with more amusement than pain. The pain would come later, when he strolled in the warm dark scented garden with Amelia, as inevitably he would, while she sang to Uncle Edgar, or Lady Arabella, dozing in her chair, or George with his worshipping eyes—or the uncaring moon.

'Perhaps if the windows were to be opened, we would hear both nightingales.'

'Bravo, Mr Marsh! Worthy of a diplomat,' applauded Lady Arabella.

'Coward, Mr Marsh!' Fanny murmured.

Adam's eyes met hers over Amelia's ringletted golden head. They had a strange intense glitter that shook all her resolutions and left her silent for the rest of the meal.

But later, half way through a song, when the wind from the open window was causing the candle flames to gutter in their own grease, she realised that he and Amelia had disappeared.

'Don't stop, my dear,' said Uncle Edgar. He was a bulky shadowy figure in the winged chair. 'But perhaps something a little more gay.'

Fanny's hands came down on the keys in a jagged discord. She saw that the room was empty except for Lady Arabella sunk, as usual, in her gentle after-dinner slumber, and Uncle Edgar. Even George had not stayed. But George didn't care for music. He could be forgiven. No one else could.

'Most songs are sad,' she said.

'But not all of them are about death. Although, indeed,' Uncle Edgar was sipping his second glass of port, 'we must be practical and realise our ultimate destiny. And that reminds me that now you're almost twenty-one, Fanny, my dear, you must make a will.'

'A will! But I have nothing to leave to anybody.'

'It's more tidy to do so. After all, where would you have been, as indeed where would Olivia and Marcus have been, if your separate father's hadn't left instructions about you. True, you haven't children. Nor have you a fortune. But you do have a little jewellery, my dear, some of it of a certain value. And your aunt and I intend you shall have more. So one day we'll draw something up. I'm sorry if I sound morbid. Some people think that by signing a will they hear the nails going into their coffin. George made his before he went to the Crimea, and naturally Amelia will also do so later. My own has been made this thirty years, and look at me! No nails in my coffin.'

Fanny was taken aback, more surprised than repelled.

'What made you think of such a thing just now?'

'Your song about death. And seeing you wear that sapphire tonight. You will naturally want to choose your own recipient for that.'

It was ironic, macabre, hilarious, even vaguely flattering, since it indicated she wasn't completely without possessions. She had come down meaning to be so gay and to steal the evenings into her hands, and this was what happened. She and Uncle Edgar had an absorbing conversation about death!

Amelia and Adam came in just as she was laughing with uninhibited mirth.

'Whatever is the matter now?' Amelia demanded. She had been flushed and a little sulky all evening, knowing Fanny's ability to steal a scene. 'I only took Adam out to insist that he smell the new red rose William is so proud of, and immediately we go you and Papa start having private jokes.'

'About mortality,' said Fanny. 'A very amusing subject. Although I don't imagine Ching Mei found it so. I hardly——' She stopped what she was going to say—what had it been going to be? The wind from the open window was making her shiver violently, to the exclusion of all thought. One of the candles on the piano had blown out. The room seemed too dark, the faces all looked at her too intently.

George and Aunt Louisa had also come back, and, about to ask what was going on, the words had died on their lips. It was a strange petrified moment, without rhyme or reason. Did anyone else but herself perceive that all at once Darkwater had turned treacherously into its haunted state?

Someone walked about here who thought too much about death. Was it the name, Ching Mei, that had brought the silence?

13

AMELIA'S ball was only six weeks away, and Hamish Barlow, the attorney from Shanghai, was due to arrive within a month or so. Everyone seemed to be on edge. Uncle Edgar was probably wondering how he was going to explain Ching Mei's death to Mr Barlow, and Aunt Louisa was constantly fussing about the arrangements for the ball.

Finally, instead of making frequent journeys to Plymouth, Miss Egham, the dressmaker, had been installed in the house, and Amelia divided her time between fittings, riding on the moors with George, or alone (did she have a rendezvous when she went alone?) and wandering about with a moony look on her face.

Adam Marsh kept his word about the children's picnic, and Amelia, who hitherto had found Marcus and Nolly little but a nuisance, suddenly discovered that she couldn't resist so delightful an outing, and was sure that there would be room for her in the pony trap, too.

Fanny thought that Adam looked put out when he met them at the crossroads. But if he had, his ill-humour was gone in a flash, and he was welcoming them all with the news that if they followed the uphill road a little farther he had found a perfect spot, out of the wind. Sheltered by an outcrop of rocks they spread their rugs on the turf and prepared to bask in the sunshine. Amelia had brought her parasol, a frivolous affair of purple lace. She said how fortunate Fanny was to have a complexion that was not harmed by the sun, and could even toss aside her wide-brimmed hat. Her own skin was so delicate it would be burned to a cinder without protection, and with her ball so near Mamma was constantly chiding her about her appearance.

'It's a terrible thing to be a woman,' she said, sighing deeply.

'It certainly seems a pity to have to sit upright under a parasol on a picnic,' Adam agreed gravely, and then said that he was taking the children to find some moorland ponies.

Perhaps Fanny would care to come, since Amelia had her complexion to protect?

Fanny resisted both the invitation and her desire to laugh. She said that she would busy herself unpacking the luncheon basket. She meant to keep Mr Adam Marsh at arm's length, and anyway Amelia would look so forlorn if she were left, sitting primly under her parasol, playing at being a lady when all the time she wanted to throw dignity to the winds and romp after the children.

'I think he was laughing at me,' Amelia declared indignantly.

'I sometimes thing he is laughing at us all,' Fanny said.

'Why? What is ridiculous about us?'

'Perhaps I used the wrong word. Perhaps, "examining" would be a better one.'

'He does ask a great many questions,' Amelia admitted. 'He says he is interested in human nature. I wonder, Fanny, if he is a dilettante.' Amelia's eyes shone. 'I confess I would find that irresistible.'

'Getting your heart broken?' Fanny asked dryly.

'Oh, I shouldn't allow that to happen. But he does make all the other men we know seem dreadfully dull. Do you know,' she finished in a burst of confidence, 'it is my ambition this summer to make him fall in love with me. If he isn't already,' she added dreamily.

'I think you are a silly little girl,' Fanny said.

And so she was, sitting there in her too elaborate clothes, the ridiculous parasol outlined against the wild beautiful landscape.

But her silliness could not be entirely dismissed. She was the one with the dowry which was undoubtedly a feature of great attraction. It could compensate for her affectations and her constant chatter and her childish enthusiasms. And she would develop poise. Indeed, she had disturbing moments of it already, when one saw the woman too prematurely. She was irritating and endearing, and Fanny would love her if only she would fall in love with Robert Hadlow, or some other harmless young man.

But now she had to be an enemy, because, innocently, she was exposing Adam's weakness. Or what one imagined was his weakness . . .

The children came back, with flushed cheeks and happy laughter.

'Cousin Fanny, Marcus thought the pony was going to bite him. It took his sleeve, like this!' Nolly nuzzled at Marcus's jacket, and he shrieked with laughter.

'It had big teeth, Cousin Fanny. Mr Marsh said it used them to gnash at its enemies.'

'There were hundreds of ponies, Cousin Fanny. And Marcus is hungry. Can he have something to eat?'

Whatever this man was, he knew how to make children happy.

'Let us all sit down and eat,' said Fanny calmly. 'Adam—have you a large appetite, too?'

He didn't fail to notice her use of his first name. He gave her his quiet unsmiling look.

'I don't know which looks the more edible, the food or the young ladies.'

Nolly giggled wildly. 'Pray don't eat them, Mr Marsh! At least, not Cousin Fanny. She puts us to bed and listens to our prayers.'

'I would leave her eyes to the last,' Adam said. 'Because they are the colour of heaven.'

'That's where Mamma and Papa are,' said Marcus in surprise.

Nolly plucked nervously at Adam's sleeve.

'You wouldn't actually? Would you, Mr Marsh.'

'I am a maker of bad jokes. I deserve to go without anything to eat at all.'

'That child would be afraid of a mouse,' Amelia put in, with some peevishness. She hadn't cared for the conversation.

'And so would you, I don't doubt,' Adam retorted. 'Come, Nolly. You be a mouse, and scare Cousin Amelia from under her pretty parasol.'

Amelia shrieked wildly, forgetting to be a lady, as her ruffled and starched petticoats were threatened. And Fanny found herself storing in her memory what Adam had said in his flippant voice.

At the end of the day, as if he were tossing them a trivial piece of information, Adam said that he had arranged with Mr

Farquarson to take a year's lease of Heronshall, and that his Aunt Martha would be arriving to organise the household.

'If at the end of the year I want to buy, I will do so,' he said. 'But in the meantime it's a place to call home. I have travelled so much I can scarcely remember what it is to have a home.'

Amelia was excited and too unsophisticated not to show her jubilation.

'But how wonderful! I believe you have done it this year, for me, because it is my coming-out year. Anyway, it pleases me to think so.'

Adam bowed. 'If it pleases you, Miss Amelia, then it is true, of course.'

'Your Aunt Martha?' said Fanny involuntarily. This latest information surely made him a completely honest person.

'Yes, you must meet her. She's delighted that I seem to be settling down at last. She has a particular fondness for children, so one day I will send for those two to come to tea.'

'Surely you will give more than children's tea parties,' Amelia said, pouting.

'To be sure, if Miss Amelia Davenport has time to spare from her numerous social activities.'

Amelia giggled. 'The most I do at present is stand and be poked and prodded and pinned by Miss Egham. Really, you have no idea what it is like to be a woman.'

Amelia's light chattering voice went on, but Fanny no longer heard what she was saying. For her own first overwhelming feeling of pleasure at Adam's news had died. Why was he merely taking a lease of Heronshall? His reason, to be sure, sounded plausible enough. But was the true reason the fact that he hadn't the capital to put down, that first he must marry to advantage? And was his Aunt Martha, so respectably sounding, a willing conspirator to this end?

Amelia, with her feather brain, would be the last person to recognise this. But would it matter, if she married someone she ardently loved? Miserably, Fanny knew that it wouldn't. She would do the same herself. Only she would never never have the chance.

As Trumble took the pony trap away and they went into the

house, George appeared and took Fanny's arm. He didn't say anything, but just welcomed her in this possessive manner, as if she were already his wife.

Fanny shook herself free, trying not to be irritated.

'I must take the children up.'

'I wouldn't go up there just yet. The doctor's there.'

'Doctor?'

'Doctor!' echoed Amelia. 'Who's ill?'

'Grandmamma had a fall. It's nothing serious, I believe.'

'But how did she fall?' Fanny asked.

'She tripped over Ludwig. Poor Ludwig.' George gave a high-pitched giggle. 'It's a wonder he survived.'

Amelia and Fanny hurried upstairs. They met Aunt Louisa coming out of Lady Arabella's room. She looked harassed and worried.

'Oh, there you are at last. Grandmamma's had a fall. Doctor Bates is going to bleed her.'

'Then it is serious!' Fanny exclaimed.

'He doesn't think so, but at present she's dazed and he can't be sure'—Aunt Louisa lowered her voice—'that it isn't a slight apoplexy. She says she fell over a cushion on the floor, but it must have been the cat, of course. Poor Mamma sees so badly.

'She broke her spectacles,' Aunt Louisa went on, 'so now she can't see at all. Oh dear, this is very vexing, just at this time. We can only hope she won't be an invalid for long. And Amelia, Miss Egham has been wanting you. She can't get on with the tarlatan until she has had another fitting. I did think you might be back a little earlier. Let me see your face, child!' Aunt Louisa's voice reached a new pitch of anxiety. 'Oh, I do declare you've got your nose sunburnt! Really, how could you be so careless?'

Fanny felt a rubbing against her skirts, and looked down to see Ludwig, the fat tabby, ingratiating himself. He had missed his tea, no doubt, with Lady Arabella in bed. He usually had a small dish of cream, and a sardine. He showed no sign of having been stumbled over by a very heavy person.

'Why is Great-aunt Arabella so unkind?' Nolly asked.

'Unkind?'

'To step on poor Ludwig like that. Like on a beetle.' She stamped noisily on the floor to establish her point.

'It was an accident. She didn't do it on purpose.'

'Ludwig doesn't let me step on him. He runs away too quickly.'

It was uncanny that the child had had the same thoughts as herself. Fanny said sharply, 'Stop making so much noise. You can be heard all through the house.'

Nolly ignored her defiantly.

'Come on, Marcus. Stamp on beetles. Like this.'

Marcus needed little encouragement to join in such an original game. Fanny had to seize them both and hold them firmly.

'Such behaviour!'

'Ching Mei would let us play that game.'

'Ching Mei would,' Marcus echoed.

It was the first time Ching Mei's name had been mentioned for days.

Nolly's eyes were flat and hard and bright.

'Is Great-aunt Arabella going to die?'

'No, she isn't, foolish little one. Kiss me, and be good.'

Hannah was sitting with Lady Arabella when Fanny tapped and asked if she might come in.

'Go and get some rest, Hannah,' she whispered. 'I'll stay here.'

'But what about your dinner, Miss Fanny?'

'Lizzie can bring me something on a tray later.'

'Bless your kind heart,' said Hannah. 'Miss Amelia, I suppose, is too concerned about her fripperies to have time to come and see her old grandmother.'

Hannah, for all her long service, was getting too outspoken. Ever since the journey to London and the arrival of the children who had touched a chord in her soft heart, she had been an ally of Fanny's.

'Never mind Miss Amelia, Hannah. How is Lady Arabella?'

'Very hazy, Miss Fanny, but it's from the doctor's medicine to quieten her more than the fall.'

'Who found her?'

'Lizzie, when she brought up her tea tray. She let out such a squawk, you'd have thought the peacocks had got indoors. And then the master and Barker had to get her on to the bed. It was quite a task.'

Fanny looked down at the inert form in the big fourposter. Sunk into the feather bed Lady Arabella looked unexpectedly small. Her frizzed grey hair stuck out from under her night-cap, her cheeks were pink and white like a child's. Her eyes, too, when she opened them, had a surprising childlike innocence. It was because they were without the customary spectacles, of course, and so short-sighted as to be almost blind.

She stared up at what must be a very hazy form at her bedside, and said testily, 'Who is it? Come nearer, can't you?'

'It's me, Great-aunt Arabella. Fanny.'

'Bend closer. Let me see.'

As Fanny obeyed, the old lady grasped her shoulders with unexpected strength and pulled her so close that the pale round myopic eyes were a few inches from Fanny's. Her breath was on Fanny's cheek.

'Have to be sure,' she muttered. 'Can't trust anyone. They said I tripped over Ludwig. Stuff and nonsense. Who tells such lies? It was a cushion, put there purposely to trip me. They picked it up, of course.'

'Who is they?'

'Now how would I know?' the old lady said in her husky irritable voice. 'Someone with a tidy mind, I expect. There are tidy minds in this house. But my poor Ludwig. He never got in the way of my clumsy feet. Bring him in to me, Fanny. My prince.'

Fanny did as she was bid, because Lady Arabella didn't seem in a mood to be crossed. She was definitely wandering a little in her mind, and very petulant.

The elderly cat settled down comfortably on the bed, and the fat ringed hand caressed his head.

'My prince. He wore a sky-blue uniform. He had such elegant moustaches. And his manners. He would click his heels and bow and kiss my hand and say I was adorable. I was too,' Lady Arabella added sharply. 'You may look disbelieving, as I know you are. My skin, my eyes—ah well—and I had such a figure. Louisa has all my husband's worst features. That was why she had to marry a plain man like Edgar Davenport. Still'—a sly smile lay on the curved pussy-cat mouth—'he has proved quite a man. Fanny, bring me my needlework.'

'Now, Great-aunt Arabella? But you're ill.'

'Stuff and nonsense. I'm only in this condition because that ridiculous doctor had leeches clamped to my neck while I was still unconscious. Said there was probably neither cushion nor cat, but that I had had a seizure. Oh, yes, I heard him. I heard a great deal while they thought I was still beyond listening. But bring my work basket, as I told you. My scissors, my tapestry, everything.'

Fanny obeyed, knowing that without her spectacles Lady Arabella wouldn't be able to see a stitch.

'And my pincushion,' the autocratic voice followed her. 'Bring all those things and put them at my bedside.'

When Fanny had done so, the old lady groped to feel the shape of the objects, satisfying herself that the wicker work basket, overflowing with coloured wools, the fat round pincushion, and the half-finished tapestry were there.

Then she subsided with an odd sigh of relief.

'There's nothing wrong with me that a new pair of spectacles won't cure,' she said in her hoarse husky voice. 'But I may find being an invalid quite amusing.' Her eyelids were closing. Doctor Bates' soothing dose was beginning to take effect. 'Send George to me,' she murmured. But she was already asleep.

When Hannah came back some hours later Fanny had been almost asleep herself. She felt in a dream that was half nightmare. She knew that both Aunt Louisa and Uncle Edgar had tiptoed to the bedside, satisfying themselves that the invalid would do until the morning, but that now seemed so long ago. The wind was blowing softly, and the slightly moving curtains, the shadow of the fourposter wavering across the ceiling in the moving candlelight, and the gentle snoring of Lady Arabella were all somnolent. She had had to struggle to keep awake, welcoming the familiar and sometimes unfamiliar creakings and murmurings of the old house. Even a sudden flurry in the chimney, and then a fall of soot, stirred by a wayward breeze, had been not so much startling as another means of keeping her heavy eyes open.

'What time is it, Hannah?'

'Midnight, Miss Fanny, and you must get some sleep.'

Hannah was bundled up in a crimson flannel dressing gown. She, too, looked another person, a friendly succourer in the alien world of the night and the sick.

'She hasn't moved since eight o'clock. I don't think there's anything to be alarmed about.'

Fanny took the candle Hannah held out to her. She stumbled a little from weariness as she went into Lady Arabella's sitting room. She noticed that Ludwig was back in his favourite place on the rocking chair. The couch was littered with cushions and it seemed very possible that Lady Arabella, stirring from her afternoon nap, had dislodged one without noticing, and then had stumbled over it. In the flurry of finding her prostrate, someone must have picked it up without remembering doing so.

Did it matter what she had fallen over, if anything at all, since her fall had been an accident? So why was Ludwig being blamed so strenuously?

14

Lady Arabella recovered to a certain extent. She maintained, however, that her legs gave way, and that she couldn't walk without assistance. She refused to be a prisoner indoors, and said that she must have a wheelchair. When this contraption arrived, Dora was ordered to push it. Lady Arabella chose Dora for the reason that the girl was timid and wouldn't be tempted to go too fast down slopes, or push her chair, occupant and all, into the lake.

Within the family, it was decided that poor Grandmamma had grown a little weak in her mind. Uncle Edgar said the persecution complex was a common one. All this talk about dangerous cushions, for instance (Lady Arabella refused to have any in her room now), and not allowing anyone she didn't trust near her. Also, there was her insistence that she must have her embroidery, her wools, her work box, and paraphernalia with her all the time, although her plump idle fingers never touched it. The whim to work might come on her, she said. So she sat cosily in the chair, cashmere shawls round her shoulders, a jet-trimmed bonnet nodding on her head, a fringed parasol erected above her, for all the world, Amelia giggled, like some eastern potentate taking the air.

Presently she became expert with the mechanism of the chair, and indoors was able to operate it herself, taking pleasure in coming up silently behind people and waiting for them to discover her. Fanny had the suspicion that the wheelchair was nothing but a pretence, that Lady Arabella could walk very well if she tried, but she kept this thought to herself because the old lady was kind to the children, and occasionally let them ride with her, the three of them whooping with delight as they negotiated slopes or startled the gardeners at their work.

Sometimes George took time from his riding or his billiards to wheel his grandmother. He was the only other person permitted to push the chair.

Summer moved on, the roses were over and the dahlias and

michaelmas daisies out. A haze of heat lay over the moors. The dabchicks' family on the lake had grown to full size, the strawberries were finished and the blackbirds had had their fill of sun-reddened cherries. The carriage, coming round the curve of the long drive, raised a trail of reddish dust. It was a hot summer, and Amelia prayed that the weather would last until the night of her ball. It would be so much more romantic if couples could take the air on the terrace, or even wander daringly across the lawns beyond the illumination from the ballroom.

'Have you ever been kissed?' she asked Fanny. She didn't expect an answer. She was quite sure it would be in the negative. For only a serious suitor would kiss a girl, and only a flighty girl would allow herself to be kissed under any other conditions. Amelia pursed her red lips and determined that she would be kissed on the night of her ball. She also knew who would kiss her. She spent a great deal of time in front of her mirror nowadays, studying her reflection from different angles. She was growing vain. She could never forget the words of that wild and hunted man, 'I have never seen anyone so beautiful,' and sometimes, by candlelight, when her face looked older, more fragile and shadowy, she saw exactly what he meant.

She intended Adam to see her that way, in the half-light near the fountain, on the night of the ball.

But when he bent over her, would she see that other face beyond him, ruthless, half-starved, desperate... Amelia pressed her hands to her own face, afraid to look any more, afraid of the unknown within herself...

A stranger, a Mr Solomon, short, heavily-built, with small sparkling black eyes, came to spend a night. He had business to do with Uncle Edgar. It was obvious Aunt Louisa didn't think much of him. She was cool and distant with him at dinner, and afterwards, when Uncle Edgar took him to the library she sighed with relief and said to Amelia and Fanny, 'There will be no need for you girls to wait up to entertain Mr Solomon. Papa has affairs to discuss with him.'

Mr Solomon departed immediately after breakfast in the morning. The business must have been concluded satisfactorily, for he and Uncle Edgar exchanged a cordial handshake.

'Remember, Mr Davenport, I will be happy to be at your service at any time.'

He had scarcely noticed the women of the household. Fanny, who had often preferred to be overlooked, and Amelia, who had discovered the pleasures of male admiration, found it strange to meet a man who was much more deeply interested in something other than them.

'Who is he, Papa?' Amelia demanded. 'What does he do?'

'Busybody!' said Uncle Edgar, ruffling her hair affectionately. 'If you must know, he is a diamond merchant from Hatton Gardens in London.'

Amelia's eyes became round.

'And now you may ask questions until your voice wears out, but you will get no answers at present.' He went off, smiling to himself, in high good humour.

And it was no good Amelia persecuting her mother with questions, either, for Aunt Louisa declared she knew nothing whatever about the matter. Although Fanny thought there was something distrait about her manner, and a look almost of uneasiness in her eyes.

The next visitor was Hamish Barlow.

Trumble met him at the station and he arrived before lunch. Amelia, always eager to meet someone new, went down early. Fanny was late. She hadn't meant to be, because she didn't want to make any kind of entrance. But Marcus had been difficult over his lunch and she had stayed to help Dora get him into a better mood. So that eventually she came flying undecorously down the stairs just as everyone was going into the dining room.

She was aware of the stranger's face looking up at her with sudden intent interest. It was a narrow pale face, with reddish eyes, neat ginger-coloured eyebrows, and a small ginger moustache. Hamish Barlow was meticulously dressed in a black frock-coat and dark grey trousers with braided sideseams. He looked a gentleman. But there was a quick alertness about him that immediately made Fanny think of a fox.

'And this late arrival,' Uncle Edgar was saying, 'is my niece

Fanny. She has taken the children completely under her wing. You must talk to her about them. Fanny, this is Mr Barlow.'

He bowed exaggeratedly like a pigeon to its mate, Fanny thought, his head well down, coat-tails in the air. Involuntarily she smiled at her foolish imaginings. Foxes, pigeons ... was Mr Barlow an animal, a bird, or simply a human being, very anxious, for some reason, to make a good impression.

It was pleasant enough to have a visitor from the other side of the world, who talked well about China and his travels in the East. Fanny planned to have him gratify her curiosity about the children's parents, especially their mother, at a later time when they might have a few moments alone. Though she wasn't sure that she particularly desired a tête-à-tête, for he was proving to be one of those men who couldn't keep his eyes off her. He ignored Amelia, and only good manners made him turn occasionally to Aunt Louisa.

'The wonders of the ancient Chinese civilisation,' he said directly to Fanny, 'are uncountable, but against them you must put their primitive and barbarous habits. Binding women's feet, cold-bloodedly murdering female infants, or selling their unwanted daughters into slavery. When it comes to a woman's country, Miss Fanny—Miss Amelia,' he added belatedly, 'you must be very content with your own.'

Fanny was reflecting that there were different subtle forms of slavery when George suddenly leaned forward.

'Why do you look at Fanny all the time, Mr Barlow?'

No one could have warned Mr Barlow about George's strangeness. It must have come as a shock to him that this handsome adult young man was asking the question of an ill-mannered and jealous child.

Aunt Louisa said quickly, 'George, don't be foolish. Mr Barlow is talking to all of us, and most interestingly.'

'Perhaps,' said Mr Barlow easily, turning to George, 'because I find an English woman such a pleasant sight after years of lemon-coloured faces.'

He was quick-tongued and clever. But George was clever, too, in his fumbling intuitive way. He saw what was already happening. Fanny noticed that Uncle Edgar's eyes were narrowed in thought. His expression was bland. Only her own heart was beating more quickly in nervousness and frustration.

Hamish Barlow. She had instinctively disliked him on sight.

But she had to be polite to him because he was a guest in the house and because she wanted to talk to him a great deal about the children's parents.

Nolly and Marcus did not remember him.

'But Miss Olivia is such a young lady now,' Mr Barlow said admiringly. 'She was only so high when I last saw her.' His hands, spread out, were pale-skinned with a dusting of large coffee-coloured freckles. 'And Marcus in his cradle. That was when I visited your Mamma and Papa in Shanghai, but you won't remember.'

Nolly would have nothing to do with him. She forgot her manners and hung back against Fanny, giving her malignant stare. But she was not good with strangers. That was all that was wrong. Adam was the only stranger who had known the way past her prickly defences. Marcus was pleased enough to be noticed, and answered Mr Barlow's questions as best he could.

'Ching Mei went away,' he said quite happily. 'She left her sandals. Cousin Fanny looks after us now.'

'And very lucky children you are.'

'Yes we are. I have a new suit. It's red velvet. It's to wear to the ball. Nolly has pink ribbons on her dress. Would you like to see my toy soldiers, Mr Barlow?'

Nolly tugged at him sharply.

'You're showing off, Marcus.'

'And I wonder what Cousin Fanny is to wear to the ball,' Mr Barlow said softly.

Nolly's hand tightened in Fanny's. She seemed to recognise the unwarranted intimacy as much as Fanny did.

But there were questions to be asked. She had to be pleasant. She didn't intend Nolly to spend her whole life wondering what kind of a woman her mother had been, grasping at half-memories.

'I haven't heard your plans, Mr Barlow. Are you to stay for my cousin's ball?'

'Your aunt has been kind enough to invite me. I am looking forward to it with the greatest anticipation. You can't know what this means to me after so many years in exile, a gracious house, this truly English garden, with its ancient oaks and cedars, the wonderful hospitality your aunt and uncle are giving me, and now beautiful women at a ball. I was only nineteen when I left England and I have been away for seventeen years. I feel almost like that nineteen-year-old young man again, full of hopes and dreams. Does that sound foolish to you, Miss Fanny?'

He spoke sentimentally and quite movingly. One wouldn't have thought those emotions dwelt behind his narrow and calculating face. Was he inventing them to gain her sympathy?

'Then you have been an unwilling exile, Mr Barlow. I wonder why.'

'No, you mustn't misunderstand me. The East has me in its spell, just as it had these children's Papa. I intend going back as soon as my business here is completed. But apart from winding up the late Mr Davenport's affairs and assuring myself that his children are happy, as I promised him I would—it was my last assurance to him, poor fellow—this interlude makes me absurdly sentimental.'

Fanny made no reply to that. She wished he wouldn't look at her so boldly.

'But I must talk alone with you sometime, Miss Fanny.'

'Why?' she asked bluntly.

'For this reason and that. I hope you will give me the opportunity.'

Amelia teased her mercilessly.

'I believe you have made a conquest, Fanny. The way he looks at you. It's almost ill-bred, but I suppose the poor man can't help it if he's so overcome by passion.'

'Amelia, be quiet!'

Amelia giggled. 'But he really is. I've even remarked on it to Mr Marsh.'

Fanny's face became still. 'And what did Mr Marsh say?'

'Why, that you deserve a good husband.'

Such rage swept over Fanny that she could scarcely speak coherently.

'He dares to say that! He dares to patronise me! I won't have it. And I won't have you, Amelia, running to him with every bit of foolish tittle-tattle. What must he think of you? That you're empty-headed and a gossip and a silly little rattle.'

Amelia refused to be drawn.

'I know exactly what Mr Marsh thinks of me,' she declared complacently. 'And really, Fanny, if you get so upset over a simple remark like that you must be entertaining some feelings towards Mr Barlow.'

Everyone else seemed to like the man, and there was no doubt that he set himself out to be entertaining. Aunt Louisa took even more care than usual over her toilette, coming down in the evening looking like the rich and well-bred matron she was, and Uncle Edgar was frequently in Mr Barlow's company, showing him over the estate, or sitting closeted in the library with him when no doubt every aspect of poor Oliver's affairs was discussed.

Once the door was left slightly ajar, and in passing Fanny heard Uncle Edgar speak the word 'Gee-gaws' in an amused and slightly rueful voice.

'Are you absolutely certain, Mr Davenport?'

'But of course. I had them examined. If there had been anything else, the Chinese woman must have disposed of it. Tell me, can you trust these Chinese? You've lived among them long enough to know. It seems to me that they say one thing and think another. They're like icebergs, their words are a fragment on the surface, their thoughts—oh, very deep.' He laughed delightedly at his metaphor.

Mr Barlow laughed, too, and agreed, and added, 'I'm sorry that after the debts were paid there was no cash left at all. But you expected that.'

A faint whispering sound behind her made Fanny turn to see Lady Arabella wheeling her chair expertly away across the polished floor.

'No change there, my girl,' she said over her shoulder, and then laughed hoarsely at her unwitting pun. 'Come and help me upstairs.'

As Fanny heaved the large soft body, like nothing so much as a bag overstuffed with wool, out of the chair, she was sure again that Lady Arabella was much more active on her legs than she let anyone know.

'I've listened at doors all my life and never learnt anything pleasant yet. It's not a habit to be commended.'

Fanny flushed but made no excuses.

'I was thinking of Ching Mei. I hoped Mr Barlow might have been her friend.'

Lady Arabella gave Fanny her opaque unreadable stare.

At last she said, 'Ching Mei doesn't need friends now,' and leaning heavily on Fanny's arm struggled slowly up the stairs.

It appeared, however, that Ching Mei was in Hamish Barlow's thoughts also, for a day or two later he joined Fanny and the children in the pavilion by the lake.

He had cleverly learned that the best way to cope with Nolly's hostility was to ignore her. Seeing that the children were absorbed in their own game of building a house with toy bricks and twigs, he asked quietly if he might sit by Fanny and talk to her. He admired the tinkling windbells, saying they almost made him homesick, then, with a suddenness that made Fanny draw in her breath sharply, asked what her version of Ching Mei's death was.

Adam Marsh, she remembered, had asked a similar question. Adam's interest had been in Ching Mei as a person, this man's was for some other reason.

'Why, it was an accident, of course.'

'You're a very intelligent young woman, Miss Fanny. You really believe that?'

'What else would I believe? Didn't my uncle tell you the story? It was a thick mist that night and there was this escaped prisoner, desperately anxious not to be seen. If he had been caught——'

'I understand all that. The laws for prisoners are harsh enough. Then if this is what you believe, I accept it.'

Fanny frowned. 'You mean, you accept what I say when you doubt—other people's views?' She had no intention of discussing her Cousin George with a stranger.

'I repeat, I admire your intelligence.'

Fanny's eyes fell beneath his regard.

'You think it your duty to make these enquiries, of course.'

'Naturally. I take the trust imposed in me quite seriously. Does that surprise you?'

She could have talked to him if only he would leave the personal note out of the conversation.

'Mr Barlow, I have heard so little about Oliver Davenport's wife. One day Nolly is going to ask what her mother was like and no one will know. I understand this, because I too was orphaned very young. Won't you tell me about her?'

'I knew very little of her background. Her family had returned to England after she had married. I believe they had only been travelling in the East when she met and fell in love with Oliver. She was young and beautiful——'

'Who was young and beautiful?' came Nolly's voice, her ears alert at precisely the wrong moment.

Mr Barlow sprang up.

'I see a boat tied up at the jetty. Won't you come on the lake, Miss Fanny? The children are fully occupied with their own affairs.'

Extraordinary as it seemed to her afterwards, Fanny forgot her dislike of water and assented eagerly. On the lake they would be safely out of earshot of the children and she could hear more about the woman who had worn the flamboyant green earrings and the high-heeled dancing slippers.

She allowed Mr Barlow to assist her into the boat, and push it smoothly out from the jetty. Away from the shadow of the willows the sun was deliciously warm, the summer wind on her face. The reflections of the yellow flag irises hung like lamps in the water. Dragonflies skimmed in darts of light. There was no sound but the far-off chirping and chattering of the children, mingled with bird cries.

Mr Barlow sent the boat forward with a long pull on the oars.

'At last,' he said, 'I have you to myself. The only way to escape me is to jump overboard, and personally I don't care for the look of those water weeds. They could drag a person down.'

The sun was not so warm after all. But it was silly to feel this chill. He was only joking.

'Once, when I was a child,' Fanny said, 'I did fall in. Uncle Edgar rescued me. And why do you think I want to escape you, Mr Barlow?'

'Am I wrong? I had the impression that Miss Fanny was fully occupied with the children, or reading to her great-aunt, or perhaps doing some highly important needlework. She always seemed to be just a flick of a skirt round a corner when I came near. Except at mealtimes, of course, and then she had to be polite.'

'I lead a busy life,' said Fanny coolly, 'as you have noticed. And now I think we came out here to talk about Nolly and Marcus's mother. You said she was beautiful?'

'But not one half as beautiful as you.'

Fanny made an impatient exclamation.

'Mr Barlow, please be serious, or I shall have to ask you to take me ashore.'

'But I am serious. Never more. You are the most beautiful woman I have ever seen. I recognised it the first moment I saw you.'

'Mr Barlow——'

'No, please listen.' His face was quite pale. Perspiration glistened on his brow. There was no doubting his intensity. 'I know your circumstances. All that makes not the least difference to me. I want to marry you. I want to take you back to China with me. I've spoken to your uncle. Now it only requires your consent. Fanny! Fanny, are you listening! I want you to be my wife.'

She had been gazing into the distance, trying not to hear his words. Trying not to hear Adam Marsh's words, if ever they had been spoken, *'She deserves a good husband . . .'*

She had known this was going to happen at some time during Hamish Barlow's stay. A woman couldn't fail to sense that kind of thing. But she would have given anything for it not to have happened. Now she had to be graceful, grateful, and flattered. Her first kiss had been George's violent searing one, and now her first proposal—perhaps her only one—came from a man with a foxy face whose hands were covered with blemishing freckles.

She wasn't grateful or flattered. She was furious with the fate that had done this to her.

'Mr Barlow, you've tricked me, and I don't enjoy that. Will you please take me back to the shore immediately.'

'But, Fanny! How extraordinary you are! How different! You came out here to hear about a dead woman and you're angry because I offer you life. Yes, life, my dearest. Don't think I haven't seen how you live here only through your uncle and aunt's courtesy and sense of duty. You're a woman who needs her own household, her own family. And I would give it to you. I'm not a poor man. I'd show you the wonders of the East, and later you could choose your own house, in Peking, Shanghai, Hong Kong, wherever you pleased. I'd show you the world, Fanny. Doesn't that interest you? Answer me!'

'Mr Barlow—later I will thank you for the compliment you have paid me—just now I am not interested. I never will be interested. So please row back to the shore.'

He stared at her in growing resentment and incredulity.

'You can't mean this! To choose to be a poor relation, little more than a governess——'

'Cousin Fanny! Cousin Fanny!'

The children were on the bank staring across the lake. Nolly had sensed something. She was agitated.

'Cousin Fanny, come back. Our house fell down.'

'Come back!' Marcus echoed.

'What is wrong with me? Why do you dislike me!' He was leaning nearer. His eyes had a reddish glow. 'Don't you want a husband who would adore you?'

His hand was on her skirt. It came nearer, intent on clasping hers. Fanny drew back sharply, forgetting the precariousness of her position, and her movement made the boat rock violently. For one heart-stopping moment she felt the water coming up close to her face, and that other long-ago memory swept over her, the cold, the choking, the darkness...

Then the boat steadied, and she was aware of Mr Barlow, temporarily forgetting his ardent courtship, looking at her anxiously.

'I am afraid of water,' she murmured. And then, unaccountably, 'Ching Mei drowned.'

He picked up the oars.

'I'll take you back,' he said curtly.

She would have given a great deal not to go down to dinner that night. She was still shivering intermittently. Nolly had been wiser than she. Nolly had known Hamish Barlow for an enemy immediately. An enemy? When he wanted nothing but to love and cherish her? The thing was, what he might do if he didn't get his desire. She recognised the driving force in him, the refusal to be thwarted.

What *could* he do?

She was overwrought and hysterical, or she would not be imagining that disasters could follow a simple refusal to marry a man she did not love. She would go down to dinner simply to disprove any accusation of cowardice.

And as it happened, the conversation at the candlelit table couldn't have been more innocuous.

Hamish Barlow, impeccably dressed, was calm and seemingly contented. He had turned the conversation to his youth, comparing it with that of the children today.

'Our toy soldiers wore a different uniform,' he said. 'The Duke of Wellington was the great hero. Poor old Boney was in prison, and harmless, but we still played at battles defeating him. Then we had hoops, and skipping ropes, and of course marbles. By the way, Marcus seems to be grieving about the loss of his marbles. Do you know anything about them, Miss Fanny?'

It could not have been a more innocent question. She could only wonder why the table seemed so silent.

'I never saw them here. I think they must have been left behind on the ship. Yes, he has complained about their loss.'

'If that's all he wants,' Uncle Edgar said, 'we must get the little fellow some more. Nothing could be easier.'

15

UNCLE EDGAR sent a message to Fanny that he must talk with her. She found him in the library, strolling up and down, his thumbs tucked in his waistcoat pocket—he was wearing a silk waistcoat of maroon stripes on silver grey that gave him a peacockish air. He had a habit of showing small vanities in his dress that was pleasing because he carried it off with such an air of boyish pleasure. He was, Fanny saw at once, in an affable and relaxed mood.

She hoped the traces of her own disturbed night didn't show too clearly on her face. Last night she had never felt so alone. There was no one to whom she could talk or turn to for sympathy. Hamish Barlow's taunt had kept returning to her, 'To choose to be a poor relation, a governess!' and at last she had wept into her pillow. Courage belonged to daylight. In the morning, she would face her chosen future more calmly.

'Well, Fanny,' said Uncle Edgar pleasantly, 'Mr Barlow has been surprising me.'

'Surprising you, Uncle Edgar?'

'Indeed, yes. I didn't think you would be foolish enough to refuse an offer such as, speaking candidly, you are never like to receive again. You have decided hastily, of course.'

So Uncle Edgar wanted this to happen. Probably Aunt Louisa did, too. Only by marriage would they be rid of her. Otherwise she was likely to remain an encumbrance to them, and later to George or Amelia, until the end of her life.

Fanny bit her lip, and answered, 'Hastily, perhaps, Uncle Edgar. But quite finally.'

Uncle Edgar smiled and patted her shoulder. 'Finally is a long word, my dear. Mr Barlow will be here another three or four weeks. He understands young women can be over-emotional and too precipitate. He will give you an opportunity to change your mind.'

'Would you have me marry a man I not only don't love, but actually dislike?'

'There you are, you see. You are over-emotional. Now sit

down and let us talk about this. What is it about Mr Barlow that you don't like?'

'How can I explain that? It isn't a list of criticisms, it's a matter of one's senses.'

'Illogical, too!' Uncle Edgar chuckled gently. 'I told Barlow you wouldn't be able to put a finger on your reasons for refusing him.'

'But I can!' Fanny cried hotly. 'It would be terrible to travel to a foreign country with a man one didn't love. To spend the rest of one's life...' She paused a moment, contemplating the appalling prospect. Then she added more quietly, 'Besides I can't leave the children. I have promised them.'

'The children don't come into this question.' For the first time Uncle Edgar's voice had a hint of harshness. 'You can't sacrifice your life for them. They will be cared for very well whether you are here or not. After all, you didn't have a kind Cousin Fanny when you came here as a child. And you survived, didn't you? So put them out of your mind, and think of the brilliant future you can have. Mr Barlow has told me his financial position, and his prospects, and all I can say is that for a young woman without a dowry you are extraordinarily fortunate. Now, Fanny, your aunt and I won't let you throw away this chance.'

'But Uncle Edgar, marrying Mr Barlow is the last thing I wish to do.'

'The young man has been a little impetuous, I grant you. I told him so. But you must be tolerant, Fanny. He is quite infatuated with you. By George!' Uncle Edgar chuckled again, 'I've never seen a man so smitten. I want you to reflect again. For instance, would you regard my brother's children as an obstacle if you were really in love?'

If it were Adam Marsh who had sat in the gently rocking boat telling her of his undying love? Fanny's eyes fell. What could she answer?

'You want to be rid of me,' she murmured.

Uncle Edgar leaped up, his face flushed with distress.

'Fanny! Don't you ever dare suggest such a thing again! Haven't you always been one of the family! Haven't George and Amelia been a brother and sister to you? This makes me ashamed. How have I failed you?'

Remembering a thousand things she remained mutinously silent. If she showed gratitude at this moment she would be lured into making a promise she could never keep.

She watched Uncle Edgar stare at her with such earnest appeal that at last she had to say defensively, 'It's just that I won't marry a man I don't love.'

'And you think your unfeeling and heartless uncle is forcing you to? I won't force you, child. But I will do my best to make you change your mind. Have you contemplated the life of an unmarried woman in this country?'

'Do you imagine for a moment I haven't!'

'And yet you still say no to such an eligible suitor? Illogical, emotional, romantic ... I think you have more than a little of your Irish mother in you, my dear. Amelia, three years your junior, has far more good sense.'

(*But Amelia has a dowry and is free to choose. The wonderful forbidden wealth of that word, choose!*)

'All the same,' Uncle Edgar had regained his comfortable placidity, 'I think you will come to look at this matter in a different light. Mr Barlow is remaining with us until after Amelia's ball. Between now and then I expect you to have a complete change of heart.'

It was an order. Uncle Edgar's most serious orders were always given in that over-soft kindly voice.

Fanny lifted her chin.

'Am I the kind of person to have a change of heart, Uncle Edgar?'

His eyes narrowed.

'It is a possibility for everyone. Everyone, my dearest Fanny. What is more, your aunt and I will give you as fine a wedding as we intend for Amelia. And you will make a very beautiful bride.' He patted her hand again. 'Now run along and make Amelia jealous. She always expected to be the first to marry, the little rogue.'

Amelia, it was true, was full of curiosity, but it was Aunt Louisa who behaved in the most disturbing way. While Fanny was being fitted for her ball gown Aunt Louisa said to the dressmaker, 'You had better make arrangements to stay on for a little while, Miss Egham. Miss Fanny will be requiring a bridal gown.'

'But I won't, Aunt Louisa! Didn't Uncle Edgar tell you——'

Aunt Louisa behaved as if she were nothing but a dressmaker's dummy.

'She has a pretty waist, hasn't she, Miss Egham? I am always telling my own daughter to control her appetite for sugar plums.'

'Fancy, ma'am! And where will you be going to live, miss?'

Miss Egham's eyes were popping with curiosity. The roundabout question was intended to give her a clue as to whom the bridegroom was to be. If there were to be one, since this seemed to be a remarkably reluctant bride...

But the question presented a much bigger problem to Fanny. Where would she be going to live when this dismal affair was over? Supposing they wouldn't let her stay with the children...

'You have made the waist pinch a little, Miss Egham. Aunt Louisa, can't we discuss this—other matter another time?'

'Certainly, my dear. But I wasn't aware there was anything to discuss.'

So Aunt Louisa had adopted her husband's bland attitude that Fanny would allow herself to have a change of heart. A reluctant bride was no uncommon thing. She was none the worse for that in the end.

Amelia, knowing Fanny's stubbornness, was not so certain. She was only cross that Fanny refused to talk to her about either Hamish Barlow or her own feelings.

'A proposal and you won't tell me how it happened,' she sighed. 'Fanny, you are mean. Did he kneel at your feet? Did he kiss your hand? Or your lips, Fanny? Is that why you won't tell me?'

George said nothing at all. He only seemed to be around more than usual, seldom now going out to ride although he was inordinately proud of his new hunter. He watched Fanny, but he watched Hamish Barlow even more. For once Fanny was not afraid of what he might do. She even had a dark dream of Hamish Barlow at the bottom of the lake, tangled in the waterweeds...

It was inevitable that Nolly should sense what was happening. She said very little, but it was difficult to persuade her to eat, and Dora reported that she pined all the time Fanny was not in the room. Fanny worried, and wondered what to say to the child, and then was saved an explanation by Nolly herself suddenly clinging to her and saying fiercely, 'You promised! You promised!'

'I promised what?'

'That you would never leave us. Marcus thinks you're going to leave us.'

'Then you must tell Marcus that he's wrong.'

Nolly's face was taut and unchildish. She wouldn't let it relax.

'I don't think he will believe you.'

'Then he's a silly little boy. I'm sure you have much more sense, and know that people don't leave other people they love. Nor go away with people they don't love . . .'

The child's black eyes bored into her. What she saw must at least have satisfied her for she gave the smallest nod.

'That's what I told Marcus,' she said.

What Adam Marsh thought—and he must surely have heard such a brilliant piece of news through Amelia—she hadn't the faintest idea. She only suspected that he, too, didn't care for Hamish Barlow. Or had she imagined that faint antagonism when the two men had met?

There was no reason for antagonism, she thought bitterly. Mr Barlow must have noticed how Mr Marsh was Amelia's lapdog, a role that couldn't have suited him less. But perhaps it would get him what he wanted, where Mr Barlow's own tempestuous tactics in love had failed.

It was as well that the night of the ball was almost on them, and there was little time during the daylight hours to think of anything else.

16

HANNAH had been sent away to see that Amelia was safely dressed and not prostrate with too much excitement. Louisa and Edgar were alone in their bedroom. Louisa's face already echoed the wine colour of her low-cut wide-skirted velvet gown. She wore the diamond earrings which Edgar had given her just a few minutes previously.

He had kissed her brow, and murmured, 'A mere trifle, my love. Just a memento of the coming-out of our daughter.'

It seemed a very short time ago that Edgar had been preaching economy. Louisa didn't understand business, but she imagined the stock market must have greatly improved, or some other windfall which naturally was her husband's affair, had come Edgar's way. Nevertheless, her delight over the unexpected gift was vaguely tinged with uneasiness, she didn't know why.

'So that explains Mr Solomon's visit.'

'As usual you are right, my dear. Well now,' Edgar adjusted his waistcoat, and took a glance at his sideview in the mirror, 'isn't it time we went down? Let me say you are looking extremely well. If Amelia looks as well, she'll be safely launched.'

Louisa preened herself, knowing very well that for all her weight, she was still a fine figure. But she was too hot already. Whatever had made her choose velvet? She had thought it a regal material, forgetting its suffocating warmth. She waved her feather fan jerkily. Although the windows were wide open no coolness, only a dark tide of warm air, came in.

'Edgar! I'm worried about Fanny.'

A little of the satisfaction left Edgar's face.

'So am I. Does she show signs at all of changing her mind? Tonight is her last chance.'

'She doesn't confide in me,' said Louisa shortly. 'I know there's that problem, too, but what I'm worried about is tonight. She's in a strange mood. She can spoil Amelia's ball.'

'Spoil Amelia's ball! Come, my dear!'

'You know how she can be if she sets out to gain attention. Nobody looks at anyone else. Certainly not men. She has only to lift her eyes and give them that bold look.'

'Bold? Fanny bold?'

'Oh, you know what I mean,' Louisa said snappishly. 'She has never learnt it in this house, but she knows how to use her eyes, in a way our innocent daughter never will. I believe men feel they are drowning, or something equally stupid. Mr Barlow tried to explain it to me, but of course he's in a state of ridiculous infatuation.'

'I am quite aware that Fanny has magnificent eyes,' Edgar said slowly. 'And also great vivacity when she pleases. Sometimes, I am reminded—— No never mind. What makes you think she won't behave well tonight?'

'Because she is desperate. She will finally have to marry Mr Barlow, of course, but first she may throw discretion to the winds. And you have insisted in dressing her in a gown that will make every other woman in the room look insipid,' she added bitterly.

'I haven't even seen her gown,' Edgar said mildly.

'Oh, well, perhaps that was Amelia's fault. She insisted the rose-coloured silk was Fanny's colour, that pastels didn't suit her.'

'Then haven't you taken care that Amelia looks just as well?'

'Amelia is suitably dressed in white. She looks like a rose. But Fanny will look like—I don't know—a poppy perhaps. Something too vivid.'

Edgar smiled reassuringly.

'You're understandably suffering from nerves, my dear. At least Adam Marsh seems to prefer a rose to a poppy, and that, I can make a guess, is all Amelia wants of this night.'

'That's another thing, Edgar. Who is Adam Marsh? We have never satisfactorily discovered. Oh, I know Sir Giles has heard of Matthew Marsh the famous collector. But it has never been proved he really is Adam's father. We've never met any of his family. I grant you he's a pleasant young man, but how do we know he tells the truth?'

'That's a thing we can go into another time,' said Edgar,

with faint exasperation. 'I believe Adam's aunt is arriving to live at Heronshall in a week or so. So that will be someone of his family whom you can meet. Our immediate worry, and I've emphasised this to you before, is to see that Fanny accepts Hamish Barlow.'

'Yes,' said Louisa, following her own thoughts. 'I think it will be a relief to have her out of the house.'

'We will miss her, naturally. But we must think of her future. It is vitally important that she should do this. Vitally important.'

'Edgar!' Louisa's vague unexplainable uneasiness had come back. 'You speak as if she has no alternative.'

'Neither she has. Now I believe I hear the first carriage. It's time we went down.'

Amelia was by no means prostrate. She was revolving round her room in a waltz, making the candles dip madly, and catching glimpses of herself, a fairytale figure, she thought, in the mirror. Hannah and Lizzie were watching admiringly.

'Do you think my dress will be admired, Lizzie?'

'Only them as is blind wouldn't, Miss Amelia,' Lizzie said, unable to take her eyes off what she thought was the most beautiful dress in the world. Its low round neck and puffed sleeves showed Amelia's pretty, plump neck and arms, the crinoline skirt, looped up in front and trimmed with white roses, revealed a crisply flounced underskirt. Amelia's bead-trimmed reticule hung on her wrist, her fan was made of silk and ivory, her white satin slippers peeped beneath her wide skirts. She looked like a dressed-up ringletted very shining and clean doll.

Then there was a tap on the door and Fanny came in. Lizzie went on thinking loyally that Miss Amelia was the prettiest thing ever, but Hannah was aware at once of the superior elegance of Miss Fanny.

The rose colour was not fashionable, her shoulders were too thin, there were faint hollows at the base of her throat (she seemed to have grown thinner in the last week), but when the heavy dark lashes of those blue eyes, the exact blue of the jewel she wore round her neck, lifted, then who could not be shattered by their brilliance? Certainly not that little man from the East, or any other man, unless his thoughts were entirely on a fortune in the bank, and not on what he might hold tenderly in the curve of his arms. Hannah was an old woman and had not missed any of the aspect of life which came within her province of bedroom and upstairs sitting room. She saw her ladies before and after gaieties, she saw them unrobed or in their finest feathers. She saw their smiles fall off like their gowns, their undisguised weariness, their boredom, their secret hopes, and their unsuccessfully hidden fears. She heard the chatter of women alone, or the whispers of the husbands, the scufflings, the sometimes raised voices, or the muffled sobs. She had learned human nature in the most revealing room of all, the bedroom.

And she knew in that moment that no one could meekly make Miss Fanny take second place, or marry a man whom she detested. She would rather proudly remain alone all her life.

'Fanny,' said Amelia, 'you look very nice, but I do think that dress needed a little decoration. Miss Egham thought so, too. Some beading, or at least some ribbon bows. It's quite severe, isn't it? Now me, don't you admire my roses? And the necklace Papa gave me?' She fingered the pearls round her neck. 'He got it from that Mr Solomon. He says I am too young for diamonds, but they'll come all in good time. He is such an indulgent Papa.'

She was wholly wrapped up in herself, and certainly wasn't sharing her mother's fears that Fanny might spoil her evening.

'You ought to go down,' said Fanny. 'It's time.'

'Yes, I know. Oh, dear, I'm so excited I could die. What about you, aren't you coming down?'

'In a little while, I'm bringing the children. We'll wait until the dancing begins.'

'Fanny! Aren't you going to tell me I'm beautiful.'

'Really, Amelia! You're growing impossibly vain. You look very well, certainly.'

Amelia pouted and tossed her head.

'I don't look just "very well". Already one man has told me I'm beautiful, so I don't imagine it.'

Fanny watched her go down the stairs, her ringlets bobbing, her feet hardly able to resist breaking into a run. Certainly she did look pretty enough tonight, to turn any man's head—whose head, like Adam Marsh's, was not already turned. Fanny should have been more generous in her praise. She should have tried, for a moment, to forget her breaking heart.

The first dance was almost over when Fanny, with Nolly in her starched petticoats and Marcus looking pale and fragile in the rich scarlet velvet, came downstairs. The servants were in a huddle at the foot of the stairs, trying to see into the ballroom. They made way for Fanny, and cook said boldly, 'The foreign gentleman was looking for you, Miss Fanny. Dora will keep the children if you want to dance.'

'Cousin Fanny!' whispered Nolly penetratingly. 'You promised you would stay with us.'

'And so I will. But do come and look at the lights and the fine dresses.'

Nolly stared into the brilliant room. All the windows were thrown wide open, but the hundreds of candles, swaying like yellow broom flowers, made the room already unbearably warm. The musicians on a raised dais played with verve and energy, and the dancers, the ladies with their great skirts ballooning, passed in small gales of wind. Uncle Edgar was dancing with Aunt Louisa, both of them looking flushed and triumphant, Amelia with, of course, Adam Marsh. Fanny made her eyes slip over those two, and sought for George and Hamish Barlow. Neither appeared to be on the floor. She sighed with resignation and led the children to chairs along the wall. She would have liked to stay in the anonymous darkness of the hall with the servants, but that wouldn't have been fair to Nolly and Marcus. So let everyone see her sitting here, looking like a governess.

'Cousin Fanny! Cousin Amelia's dress is only white. It isn't nearly as beautiful as yours.' Nolly leaned smugly against her.

'There's Mr Marsh,' cried Marcus, pointing.

'He's looking at us,' said Nolly. 'Mr Marsh! Stop dancing and come and talk to us.'

'Nolly! What behaviour! People don't stop in the middle of a dance to talk to children.'

'Mr Marsh would to us.'

'Yes, Mr Marsh likes us.'

'Be quiet, both of you, and listen to the music.'

But their unobtrusive entrance had not gone unnoticed. They were not to be left in peace. Fanny had just noticed Lady Arabella sitting in her chair at the other end of the ball-room, and was pondering joining her, when Hamish Barlow stood over her, giving his exaggerated bow.

'Miss Fanny! I have been looking for you. May I have the pleasure of the next dance?'

'Cousin Fanny——'

Fanny shushed Nolly silent.

'Thank you, Mr Barlow, but I have promised the children to sit with them for a little. This is a great event for them.'

'I appreciate your kind heart, Miss Fanny, but surely their nursemaid——'

At that moment the music stopped, and the dancers began returning to their seats. Fanny was aware of Uncle Edgar, pompous and benign.

'By George, it's a warm night. This tells on an old fogey like me. Well, Barlow, are you persuading Fanny to dance. I promise myself one with her a little later if she will bear with me.'

'Uncle Edgar, the children have never seen an English ball. I've promised to stay with them.'

'And not dance! God bless my soul, what nonsense! Where's that girl, Dora.' He snapped his fingers. A servant came hurrying. 'Tell Dora to come and take charge of these children. Your zeal, my dear Fanny, does you credit, but it's quite unnecessary.'

Nolly aimed her little pointed boot at Uncle Edgar's shin and administered a sharp kick.

'I hate you!' she said under her breath.

Uncle Edgar burst into a roar of laughter. It was loud enough to make many heads turn. The little group was the centre of attention.

'So! You would bite the hand that feeds you, little girl? And you looking like an angel in that pretty white dress. Just like a woman, eh, Mr Barlow? You pamper and cosset them, and what happens? Something displeases them and they let you know it. By George, I love the dear creatures. Whims, pouts, tempers, and all.'

Marcus's lip was trembling. Nolly prepared to outstare her uncle, her eyes glittering, but Dora had come and Uncle Edgar gave a sign of satisfaction, and moved away to his guests. The little incident was brushed-off as completely trivial, yet for all she had meant it otherwise, Nolly had played into Uncle Edgar's hands. Once more he was able, in his jovial benevolent way, to show the assembled company his generous heart.

'Do you dislike dancing with me so much?'

She was so thankful that he wore gloves. At least those freckles which gave her such a feeling of revulsion would not touch her. But his curved pale mouth beneath the sandy moustache, his narrowed eyes, his sharp alert face, were too close to her. She couldn't escape his gaze while she danced with him.

'I love to dance,' she murmured non-committally.

'And you do it beautifully. Those little feet are like birds flying. What's wrong now? Don't you like my choice of words?'

'I would prefer you not to compliment me.'

He gave a short unamused laugh.

'Really, Miss Fanny! For a woman not to care for compliments! I've scarcely seen you lately. I think you've been avoiding me.'

Fanny seemed to be intent on the dance. She looked beyond him to see who Amelia was dancing with. The Talbot boy. Then who was Adam with? She failed to see him.

'Miss Fanny! I asked if you had been avoiding me?'

'I have been busy.'

'Oh, yes, I know about that. But I hoped also you were taking time to reflect on my proposition. Your uncle promised me that you were.'

'Really!' Fanny's eyes flashed angrily. 'It is wrong for one person to guarantee another's thoughts. At least that is something one has in private.'

'And these so private thoughts—have they been a little kind towards me?'

It was too late for mere politeness, too late to cover a rebuff in carefully chosen words. This man would understand only finality.

'Mr Barlow, I gave you my answer on the lake. I am not the kind of person to change her mind.'

He returned her gaze. His eyes hardened, seemed to gleam with some curious kind of triumph, as if he were turning disappointment to something he almost enjoyed. But Mr Hamish Barlow had looked a self-centred man who would pamper rather than inflict hurt on himself.

'Then I seem to have been wasting my time,' he said stiffly. He added, almost under his breath. 'I wonder if you realise what you have been doing. You are a fool. Your uncle will never forgive you.'

Fanny had a moment of remorse. Hamish Barlow had paid her the biggest compliment it was possible for a man to pay a woman. She should have been more appreciative. But at this moment she wanted only to escape from his gaze, and his touch on her arms. She wanted never to see him again. She scarcely paid any attention to his impertinent remark about Uncle Edgar's feelings. She merely said, 'That is scarcely your business. Besides, you exaggerate.'

'Miss Fanny, what do you think I came to England for?'

'To wind up Oliver Davenport's affairs.'

'Precisely.'

'Perhaps it was to find a wife as well?'

'Perhaps.' He seemed to be reflecting with himself. 'You will see. You will see.' He added, almost with humility, 'I wish you could have liked me a little. It would have been so much simpler for everybody.'

Fanny forced herself to say, 'I am sorry. And now I can see that Marcus is crying. Will you excuse me?'

'Certainly.'

They found they had stopped dancing immediately in front of Lady Arabella, ensconsed in her chair, her only concession to the grandeur of the occasion a jewelled comb in her hair.

She insisted that Fanny stay and talk to her, and Hamish Barlow bowed politely and left.

Lady Arabella smiled conspiratorially.

'So I see you have got rid of the fox from China.'

'How do you know?'

'My dear child, too much gets written on your face. Learn to conceal your feelings. That is the beginning of power. Well,

I thoroughly agree with you. The man is a poor little runt.' She waved her fan impatiently at Uncle Edgar who was approaching. 'Go away, go away! I am talking to Fanny.'

'I'm sorry, Mamma, you can't monopolise Fanny at a ball. Come, Fanny. Dance with me.'

'I was about to go to Marcus, Uncle Edgar. He is in tears.'

'Then let the servants dry them. You're spoiling those children. I'll have to put my foot down. Come!'

He had taken her hands and drawn her towards him. She knew precisely why he was doing this. He had seen Mr Barlow leave her and had to know the outcome of their conversation. But she was saved the awkwardness of telling him, for Lady Arabella was waving her fan, and saying in her hoarse carrying voice, 'You've been foiled, Edgar. Ha, ha, ha! But if Fanny hadn't had the courage, I should have come to her rescue, you know.'

'What does she mean, Uncle Edgar?' Fanny asked.

Uncle Edgar didn't answer for a moment. He seemed to be finding dancing too agile an occupation for a man of his years and weight. His face was almost the colour of Aunt Louisa's dress.

'Your Great-aunt Arabella,' he said at last, 'I am sorry to say, is a mischief-maker. I suppose it is a danger that threatens all old ladies with too little to do. So am I to understand that you've dismissed Mr Barlow, Fanny?'

'Yes.'

'That was very foolish. Very foolish indeed.' Uncle Edgar's voice had gone soft with what seemed like sincere regret and even sympathy.

'Uncle Edgar, my future at present is with the children.'

She hated having to plead. But supposing he took Nolly and Marcus away from her.

'Yes, yes.' He dismissed that subject as if it were of little importance. His eyes were rather persistently on her throat. 'Do you know, you look extremely well tonight. You remind me of——'

'Of whom, Uncle Edgar?'

'Eh? Oh, of someone I knew a long time ago. The long white throat...' The inward look in his eyes was strange, it seemed to hold more loathing than admiration. Who was the woman he was thinking of? Someone who had hurt him as she had just hurt Hamish Barlow?

'Well,' he said, and he seemed to be speaking to someone else, 'let us be friends in spite of all. Now I will release you to go to those pampered children.'

But Dora had taken the children out, and Fanny, still affected by Uncle Edgar's oddness which she would not admit had frightened her, suddenly had to escape from the hot ballroom. She slipped into the conservatory hoping no one would be there. It was such a mild still night that most people seeking air would go on to the terrace.

She was unlucky, of course. There was someone there already. She knew him instantly from the set of his shoulders. And in the same moment he must have sensed her approach for he turned.

'Well, Miss Fanny!' said Adam Marsh. 'You look distressed. I realise some of us are not expert dancers.'

'I have more than sore feet,' Fanny burst out, and then was angry that the temptation to confide in him was so great. What did he care for her and her problems?

He came towards her, his eyes twinkling maddeningly.

'You are looking very charming. Has someone been telling you so too pointedly? Mr Barlow perhaps?'

'They can't make me marry him?'

'They?'

Uncle Edgar's strange look, a mixture of love and hate it had seemed, was still with her. She couldn't understand why the shiver of fear had gone over her.

'I would marry you,' said Adam Marsh, in an undertone, as if speaking to himself.

She flung round on him furiously. 'Don't joke with me. Go back to Amelia. She will be missing you.'

He didn't move. His eyes, too, were on her throat. But not in the way Uncle Edgar's had been.

'That's a very valuable jewel you are wearing for someone who says she is penniless.'

'If you imagine I have a jewel box overflowing with these things, Mr Marsh, you are mistaken.'

Their eyes met in a hard unflinching stare.

It was Adam who spoke first.

'I wasn't imagining anything of the kind. I expect your uncle gave it to you.'

Fanny's hand was over the sapphire pendant. Why did he have to make his harmless words suggest that the gift had been some kind of bribe? The unreasonable fear caught at her again.

'What is the matter?' she heard him asking in concern.

'I have tried,' she said intensely, 'I have tried to get away from here. But the children came to stop me, and now——'

'I beg you not to go.'

'You? Why?'

He came closer, not answering. His eyes had that deep strange glitter she had noticed once before.

'Because I would hate you to go.'

Her voice had lost all its assurance.

'Go back to Amelia.'

'You said that before. I have no intention of doing so'—his arms were actually about her waist and she was weakly letting herself be drawn towards him—'until I have kissed you.'

She felt the hardness of his body against hers. She knew she should struggle, but her lips were parting, her eyes closing. Very well, he would kiss her. What was a kiss? Surely not this strange bewildering ecstasy that made her so dizzy. She had to lean against him, waiting for the touch of his lips which never came.

For a moment later she was snatched back so roughly that she almost fell.

'Don't do that, Marsh,' came George's voice.

His grip on Fanny's shoulder was so firm that she would have had to struggle ignominiously to get away. She said furiously, 'George, you are a devil!'

George laughed with pleasure and triumph. His eyes were too bright with what seemed to be an uncontainable excitement.

'Fanny is mine, Mr Marsh, as you must have observed. I've had to make that clear to Mr Barlow, too.'

Adam was very pale, his mouth angry.

'Don't you think you are taking too much on yourself, Davenport? I fancy your cousin isn't a person who can be dictated to. I suggest you take your hands off her?'

'So you can kiss her in a dark corner! Not a chance!'

No one had heard Aunt Louisa come. Suddenly she was standing there, like a great crimson peony, visibly palpitating with annoyance.

'Fanny! What's going on here? Are you letting these foolish men quarrel over you? George! Mr Marsh! I'm surprised. Is Mr Barlow here, too?'

'Mr Barlow isn't here, Mamma,' George said smugly. 'Fanny and I have sent him packing. And I've just had to explain to Mr Marsh here the lie of the land. Now Fanny is coming to dance with me. You don't need to worry, Mamma. I have the situation under control.'

Fanny wrenched her arm away from George. She was blazing with anger.

'I'm not going to dance with you, George. Now or ever! I'm not going to dance with anybody. I have a headache. I ask to be excused.'

'But, Fanny——'

'No, George! The situation isn't under control after all.'

'But, Fanny——'

'Fanny!' Aunt Louisa exclaimed. 'You can't leave the ball!'

'Would you have me faint at your feet, Aunt Louisa?'

'What nonsense! You have never fainted in your life.'

Fanny was already at the door. George, flushed and perplexed, made an impulsive movement towards her. Adam stood perfectly still, his face composed and expressionless. He might have opposed George, but he was too gentlemanly (or too cowardly?) to oppose Aunt Louisa. Once again she faced her disillusionment. As George had said, he had wanted only a snatched kiss in the dark.

So her beautiful dress, her pleasure in the dancing, her eternal optimism that perhaps tonight something wonderful would happen to her, were all wasted. She had not had the opportunity to dance with Adam once. She had only quarrelled with him, and then weakly surrendered to him. Now she despised him only slightly less than herself.

It was true that she felt dizzy and faint, and for the first time without hope.

She turned and ran up the stairs before anything more could be said.

Hannah came to her room to see if she would have a soothing drink, or needed help to undress. Fanny sent her away. She only wanted to be alone.

She had let her ball dress slip to the floor, and lay on the bed in her petticoats. She could hear the violins and the sound of voices and laughter. They were distant, because her room was at the opposite end of the house, facing the yew garden and beyond it the copse. She supposed it would be almost daylight before the carriages rolled away and the guests who were staying overnight came upstairs.

Her head ached badly, and it was a long time before she could fall asleep. When she did she was woken with shattering suddenness by a hoarse scream.

She started up in terror, the nightmare darkness pressing on her.

Oh, but it was the peacock, she realised, almost but not quite able to laugh at her foolish imagination. Although it still seemed so dark it must be nearly dawn.

17

AMELIA already dressed in her morning gown of lavender muslin stood at the door.

'How are you feeling now, Fanny? Wasn't it sad that you had to leave the ball? Mamma said you were feeling faint.'

Fanny had overslept. She struggled up on the pillows, feeling heavy and dull.

'I'm better, thank you. What's the time?'

'It's after ten. Mamma said we were both to sleep all morning, but I couldn't. I scarcely slept at all. I can still hear the violins.' Amelia began to waltz round the room. 'Wasn't it all heavenly. Except——' She began to frown a little, and Fanny asked, as she was expected to, 'Except what?'

'Oh, well!' Amelia decided to be philosophic. 'It isn't something that can't be remedied. It's only that I had expected to be kissed, I was determined to be. But somehow I was never able to get the opportunity. There were so many people round me, wanting to dance, or talk to me. Mamma says I was a great success.'

'And it wouldn't have mattered who kissed you, so long as you achieved this great event?'

'Fanny! How can you be so stupid? Oh, I see, you're teasing me as usual. But, Fanny!' Amelia was able to stop thinking of herself for long enough to tell the news which had brought her up to Fanny's room. 'Whatever happened between you and Mr Barlow last night?'

Fanny's heart missed a beat. She was suddenly sharply apprehensive. 'Why do you ask?'

'Because he's left! Either he walked, or got a lift with some of the guests leaving last night, and caught the early train to London this morning.'

Relief swept over Fanny. She could have heard nothing that pleased her more.

Then suddenly she was remembering George's peculiarly smug look last night, his words, 'Fanny and I have sent him packing.'

Fanny and I . . . What had George had to do with it?

'But didn't he say good-bye?' she asked breathlessly. 'Didn't anyone know he was going?'

'Oh, yes, Papa did. He said Mr Barlow asked for his bags to be sent on. Now that he has suffered such a great disappointment—that was the way Papa said he expressed it—he only wanted to be away as quickly as possible. I suppose no one can blame the poor man. Fanny, you were cruel to him.'

If he had told Uncle Edgar he was leaving, it must be all right. She had no reasons for these superstitious fears. She tried to concentrate on what Amelia was saying.

'Would you marry a man you didn't love?'

'No, of course I wouldn't,' Amelia admitted honestly. 'I don't blame you. Neither does Papa.'

'Doesn't he?'

'Well, he thinks you have thrown away a wonderful opportunity, but he has decided to forgive you.'

Hamish Barlow, in that strange almost deadly voice, had said, 'Your uncle will never forgive you . . .'

'Papa is the kindest man,' Amelia said. 'You needn't be afraid he will be angry with you.'

But would he have been very angry indeed if Lady Arabella hadn't taken her side? Why the old lady had done that was now perfectly plain. George must not be made unhappy. And for some reason Uncle Edgar always listened to Lady Arabella, even though he thought her a mischief-maker.

So on the one side there had been Hamish Barlow, and on the other George. There was always George who, even without his grandmother's help, would get his own way by any means. She didn't think she wanted to live.

Dora brought her hot chocolate and fresh brown bread and butter.

'There you are, miss,' she said, her rosy face full of affection. 'The mistress said I was to bring it because you were poorly.'

Instead of chiding her they were cosseting her. Fanny couldn't understand it.

'I hope you're feeling better, miss, though what we all need after last night is a good sleep. Just fancy, even the peacock was upset. Screeching at three o'clock!'

Fanny had forgotten that moment of frozen horror. Now it came back to her vividly.

'Did you hear it, too, Dora?'

'I swear I did, miss. Hannah and cook say I'm crazy, what would the peacock be doing awake at that hour. But I heard it as plain as daylight. Or else it was——'

Had it been only three o'clock? What a strange time for the peacock to cry out. Some of the dancers must have sought it out on its perch and disturbed it.

She was only half listening to Dora.

'Or else it was what, Dora?'

'Why, that—that other bird, miss!'

'In the chimney! Making all that noise! Dora, don't be daft!'

'No, miss,' said Dora, relieved. 'It was only the peacock. He's cranky in his old age, William says.'

The strange thing was that Hamish Barlow's name was scarcely mentioned again. Uncle Edgar made only one reference to the matter. His voice was uncharacteristically humble.

'Your aunt and I were thinking of your own good, Fanny. But if you're content to stay with us, we're content to have you.'

Something impelled her to say, 'Did you see Mr Barlow leave, Uncle Edgar? Was he very upset?'

Uncle Edgar pinched her cheek.

'Little rogue! It's too late now to worry whether he was upset or not. But he was, I assure you. He looked like a man in a daze, poor fellow.'

Aunt Louisa's silence was perhaps more eloquent. She had obviously been instructed by her husband that Fanny was not to be scolded. So she contented herself with looking cold and reproachful every time Fanny appeared. But even this attitude was hard to maintain, for she was so busy with the aftermath of the ball which everyone had pronounced a great success. Invitations were rolling in, and it seemed that Amelia was to lead at last the social life for which she craved.

When Fanny's name appeared on invitations, Fanny begged that apologies be made for her. She wished to devote herself to the children, she said. They were about to begin lessons in the schoolroom.

Aunt Louisa interpreted this as a desire on Fanny's part to retire into the kind of life that would now be her future, since she had refused what was probably her only chance of marriage. She willingly agreed, since who knew when the wretched girl would behave unpredictably and disastrously. But Fanny sincerely wanted to be with the children and avoid all those empty social festivities where she was always 'Amelia's cousin', some nameless person who was there by courtesy only. Even her slightly malicious pleasure in stealing the limelight had ceased to be an amusing game. She preferred the company of Nolly and Marcus.

She was nearly twenty-one and she must grow sober, quiet and restrained. In another ten years she would have lost her love of attractive clothes and be content with her governess's grey gown. She didn't suppose she would ever wear the rose-coloured ball dress again.

Those were her resolutions and she thought she made them with calm resignation.

They all vanished to the four winds when the invitation came from Heronshall for Miss Fanny, Miss Amelia, and the children, to come to tea to meet Miss Martha Marsh, Adam's aunt.

There was no hint as to whether Adam would be there. Fanny hadn't seen him since that brief scene in the conservatory when she had as near as possible accused him of being a fortune hunter. Also, Amelia was to go, and Amelia was now as possessive of Adam as George was of Fanny.

Yet Fanny's lethargy had vanished, and she was filled with life and vigour. She hadn't known she could despise a man and still love him. Nor had she realised that just to set eyes on the person one loved, even if no words were spoken, was the most acute and bittersweet pleasure. Perhaps even if he married Amelia she would still feel this. But he was not yet married and she was not a half-dead elderly young woman after all. She could no more keep the light out of her eyes than she could stop the sun shining.

Heronshall, in contrast to Darkwater, was full of light. It was already most tastefully furnished with turquoise velvet curtains and rose-coloured carpets, a startling combination of colours that set off perfectly the plain white walls, and the few well-chosen paintings and ornaments. There were several pieces of Chinese jade and porcelain.

The effect was so simple as to be extremely luxurious. Could Adam need to marry a fortune when he could live in a house like this? But she had heard of men expending their last shilling on the gamble of making the correct showing.

She despised herself for her thoughts as they were welcomed by Adam's aunt. Miss Marsh was a tall bony commanding-looking old lady with unexpectedly gentle eyes. From the beginning, although she greeted Fanny and Amelia with the greatest courtesy, it was evident she was almost entirely taken up with the children.

'I love children,' she explained, and then made no effort not to devote her attention to them.

Amelia began to fidget. This was not her idea of a visit at all. She was accustomed to being the centre of attention.

'Is your nephew home, Miss Marsh?' she at last asked boldly.

'Adam? Oh, yes, he'll be in shortly. Then we'll have tea.'

Amelia settled more happily then, patting her curls, and retying her bonnet strings. The children fortunately had taken to this rather unexpected elderly woman, and were shyly but politely answering her questions. She must have a good deal of Adam's gift for dealing with children, for even Nolly's hostility had not been aroused.

But when Adam came in he, too, devoted himself to the children and what remarks he addressed to the young ladies were made chiefly to Fanny regarding Nolly and Marcus. Had they enjoyed watching the ball? How were they progressing with their lessons? What were their favourite games?

Nolly answered that question herself. She clamoured for a game of Hide the Thimble when they had finished tea.

This was not Lady Arabella's cosy dishevelled room with a thousand hiding places. Nevertheless, Miss Marsh agreed good-naturedly to the game and suggested the morning room should be used, also. This necessitated a great deal of running to and fro, and so it was that Fanny, at one stage, found herself alone in the drawing room. She was fascinated by the Chinese ceramics, and was standing studying a small camel in some kind of earth-coloured pottery that looked older than the tors on Dartmoor when she was aware of Adam at her side.

'Do you like that? It's a Bactrian camel. It was one of my father's favourite pieces.'

'It has such a look of age.'

'Yes. The craftsman who made that has been dust for many centuries.'

Adam had picked up the piece and was studying it. Fanny no longer saw it, but only his strong square hands holding the fascinatingly ugly creature so surely. She was conscious of the most overwhelming desire that it should be one of her hands he held like this, turning it over, examining it lovingly. She felt hot and on the verge of trembling. If he were to take her in his arms now she would make very sure that his lips reached hers. The very thought made her draw in her breath sharply, and to cover her odd behaviour she said in a rapid voice, 'Mr Marsh, I am sorry for the things I said to you on the night of the ball.'

'What did you say?'

Had he forgotten? Had her words had so little effect on him?

'Why, that you might be interested in whether I had other valuable jewellery besides the sapphire pendant.'

'And so I was interested. But entirely for your sake. Fanny, if ever you are in doubt——' His hand was on her, gripping her wrist. He had a look of wanting to say something of the greatest importance. But it was never to be said, for the children, followed by Amelia, came running in.

'Cousin Fanny, Marcus found the thimble! Wasn't he clever. It was in—Cousin Fanny, why are you looking at that funny camel. A thimble couldn't be hidden in it.'

'Have you ever heard about camels, Olivia?' Adam asked. 'They are beasts of the greatest courage. They can keep going in the desert when it seems certain they will die of hunger and thirst. But they never stop expecting to find the oasis with green palms and cool water and date trees.'

'And do they find it?'

Adam balanced the Bactrian camel on his hand.

'This one did. And you see it became too happy to die. It has lived for hundreds of years. But it is important always to remain optimistic, to be sure the oasis is there.'

Nolly laughed delightedly.

'Tell us more stories, Mr Marsh. Marcus likes stories.'

'Fanny!' Amelia's voice cut sharply across the conversation. 'Isn't it time we left? We have a long drive.'

'Yes. Yes, indeed.' Fanny's voice was distrait. She was only vaguely aware of Amelia's petulance, and had scarcely heard Adam's fanciful tale of the happy camel. Her fingers were clasped lightly round her wrist, as if they would preserve the unbearably exciting feel of Adam's grip. She had the most foolish desire to burst into tears.

At the last minute, as they were saying their farewells, Nolly remembered the most important thing.

'Cousin Fanny, can we ask Miss Marsh and Mr Marsh to Marcus's birthday party? Marcus will be five next week, Mr Marsh. Cousin Fanny says we can have tea in the pavilion if it's a nice day.'

'But it isn't really a party, Nolly dear.'

Amelia leaned forward in the carriage, her face suddenly much more cheerful.

'Why don't we make it a party? I'm sure Mamma will agree. We could play Hunt the Thimble outdoors, or have a real treasure hunt. Let's, Fanny. You're clever at thinking up things. Do you remember when we used to play paper chases? Miss Marsh, do say you will come. Mamma will write to you. And we can ask the Hadlows, and the Grey children for Nolly and Marcus.'

'A party seems to be being born,' said Adam, 'What about it, Aunt Martha?'

His aunt gave the remarkably sweet smile that transformed her stern face.

'I should like nothing better than to go to Marcus's party.'

'I'm five,' said Marcus, realising his importance.

'Not until next week, you silly!' said Nolly. Her face relapsed into resignation. 'I shan't have a birthday until next April. It's an awfully long time to wait. Cousin Fanny has one before then. Shall we have tea in the pavilion for you, too, Cousin Fanny?'

'Hardly, in October. There are fogs then, and the leaves are falling.'

'Oh, do come, Fanny! We must go.' Amelia was petulant

again. For some reason Fanny had had far too much attention today. Who was interested in a woman's twenty-first birthday? So old!

'I do think, Fanny,' she said aggrievedly, as Trumble whipped up the horses, and they began their long drive across the moor, 'that you didn't behave very well while we played that game. Just making it an excuse to talk to Mr Marsh alone. No wonder Mamma says you're a born flirt. What with poor George, and poor Mr Barlow, and now Mr Marsh.'

Fanny was in too dreamy a state to be annoyed by Amelia's maliciousness.

'Why don't you say poor Mr Marsh, too?'

'Because he is much too intelligent to be taken in.'

'Have you discovered that yourself?' Fanny asked innocently.

Amelia coloured angrily.

'Don't be ridiculous! I don't flirt. I'm entirely sincere.'

When they had alighted from the carriage, at Darkwater, Amelia hurried inside, still sulking. Dora came out to get the children, but Fanny, following them, was called back by Trumble.

'Miss Fanny! I have a package for you.'

'A package?'

Trumble took a neat brown paper parcel from beneath his driver's seat.

'Mr Marsh asked me to give it to you when we reached home. Quiet-like.' The old man almost winked. His faded blue eyes were twinkling kindly.

'Oh!' Fanny had that absurd feeling of being about to tremble again. She took the package, and automatically slipped it inside her cloak. She would wish passionately to keep it private even if Adam hadn't already hinted that she should do so. She could scarcely get up to her room quickly enough to open it.

It was the Bactrian camel.

'Oh, no!' she whispered. 'It's too valuable. Oh, Adam!'

If he had been there she would have flung herself into his arms.

So it was as well he was not, she told herself soberly. But why did he give her a present like this? Was it to disprove her sordid doubts that he might be a fortune hunter? Did he care so much for her good opinion?

She could only stand there, lost in delight.

It was some minutes later that she noticed the thin sheet of white paper that had fallen to the floor with the wrappings. It was a hastily scrawled note.

My dear Fanny—what I was interrupted in saying to you—if ever you have doubts as to what is happening, if ever, I repeat, you are uneasy, will you tell me, or send a message to me or my aunt? If this injunction seems like nonsense to you now, it may not always be nonsense. I will be very happy if you will accept this small gift as a—let us say—happy omen.

And then, at the bottom, was written, 'I would not have let you marry Barlow.'

18

'WELL, how do I look, Master Marcus?' Uncle Edgar demanded in his rollicking voice. He stuck out his stomach, and patted his elegant striped satin waistcoat. 'Made especially for your birthday party, my boy.'

The children adored Uncle Edgar in this expansive mood. Marcus judged it a good moment to ask to hear the fascinating chiming watch, and Nolly, delicately touching the fine new waistcoat, remarked judiciously that she thought it beautiful.

'So you've forgiven me, have you, young lady?'

Nolly lifted her unafraid eyes.

'Marcus thinks you're being kind on his birthday. But I shall kick you, if I please.'

Uncle Edgar roared with laughter.

'By George, we'll never find a husband for you, you little spitfire. Don't say you're going to be as stupid as your Cousin Fanny.'

'Cousin Fanny isn't stupid!'

'All right, all right, we won't malign your paragon.' Uncle Edgar sounded suddenly irritable, his good humour a veneer that could easily crack. 'But remember, your Cousin Fanny isn't indispensable, and you children can't monopolise her life.'

'What does indispensable mean, Uncle Edgar?' Nolly demanded, following him out of the room.

'God bless my soul, child, keep off my heels. It means that I could find you and your brother quite dispensable, except that it's my duty to keep you, and except that it's Marcus's birthday and I believe we're having a picnic in the garden. Or aren't we?'

'Yes, yes, yes!' shouted Marcus.

'Does dispensable mean not being here?'

'In a way it does.' Uncle Edgar's voice was growing more testy. 'Where's your nursemaid? Where are the servants?'

Nolly stood quite still.

'Then isn't it your duty to keep Cousin Fanny?'

'It is my duty to keep your Cousin Fanny until she is twenty-one years old, which means she is of age, and free to do as she pleases. If she chooses to go away I will have no legal right to stop her. Now, miss, will you leave me in peace?'

'Who is going away?' came George's voice from the stairs.

Nolly and Marcus had treated George warily, not understanding his alternating hearty friendliness, and moodiness. But now Nolly darted to him.

'Cousin Fanny!'

'Never!' said George.

He suddenly seemed very tall, and Nolly shrank back, although he wasn't looking at her but at his father with that look of frowning frightening anger. His blue eyes burned.

'Well, God bless my soul,' Uncle Edgar muttered in assumed helplessness. 'I am good-humoured enough to indulge this child in her interminable questions and like all women she immediately jumps to the wrong conclusion. No one is going away, as far as I know, anyway. I was merely explaining the legal situation, which I am sure, my boy, you understand already. If you don't, I've no doubt your grandmother will explain it to you. So would you mind having the good manners to look at me with some respect. I am your father, I would remind you, not your enemy.'

The tense little situation was broken up by the ladies, Aunt Louisa, Amelia, and Fanny, coming down the stairs in their light summer dresses and wide straw garden hats with fluttering ribbons.

The scene had been like the day, gloomy with thunder threatening. But now the sun had come out again, and it was very hot and bright.

'George,' said Aunt Louisa, 'your grandmother is waiting for you to help her downstairs. See that she brings an extra shawl. I don't trust the weather. It's too warm. Well, children, what are you waiting for? Why don't we go down to the lake? Our guests will find us there. Fanny, see that Olivia and Marcus look after little Charles and Amanda Grey. They're old enough to begin understanding their social responsibilities. We don't want any tears or tantrums.'

'I can't keep it, of course,' Fanny said in a low voice, later.

'Why not?' demanded Adam Marsh. His voice was hard. 'Why not?'

'It's much too valuable. And besides, why——'

She had known the opportunity to speak privately to Adam would only last a moment. Already Amelia was at their side at the lake's edge saying vivaciously, 'Has Fanny explained the list of things to be found on the treasure hunt? Some of them are awfully difficult. Twelve varieties of wild flowers, a lady's handkerchief—you should have no difficulty with that one, I am sure, Mr Marsh—a windfall apple, a toadstool, a bird's feather. And what else, Fanny?'

Fanny laughed. 'It is mainly for the children, Mr Marsh.'

'But everyone must join in,' Amelia insisted. 'And I shall need help because I confess I scarcely know two varieties of wild flowers. I shall prick my fingers or get caught up in a hedge.' She contrived to make the picture of herself caught in a hedge a beguiling one. Adam laughed.

'I shall be glad to assist you, Miss Amelia. And to whom do we bring our offerings?'

'To Fanny, of course.' Amelia looked from one to the other of them. She sensed something and said impatiently, 'It's only a game, of course. You're not actually making her a gift.'

No, it couldn't have been a gift, any more than Uncle Edgar's giving her the sapphire pendant had been a gift. Yet she persisted in believing that the little camel was a wholly impulsive offering, with no underlying intention. Even in the dark water of the lake her face looked up at her rosily. She was happy. She knew that happiness was the most fragile of all emotions yet while it was there she never imagined it departing.

When the game began she watched without a pang Adam accompany Amelia. She was beginning to know her strength, yes and her power. Lady Arabella had been right. Power lay behind a calm and secret face.

In spite of having been told they must look after the Grey children, Nolly and Marcus stubbornly ran off hand in hand, Nolly's white dress and wide-brimmed straw hat blown on to the back of her neck, and Marcus's fair head flickering behind the rushes on the far side of the lake. Robert Hadlow, now that Amelia had gone, was left to rather sulkily escort his sister, and Uncle Edgar, declaring sportingly that he could at least pluck a feather from the peacock's tail, sauntered off in a leisurely manner. George refused to play the childish game, unless Fanny joined him. Lady Arabella could surely be trusted with gathering the trophies and announcing the winner.

But George's method of playing would be to attempt to put his arm round her waist the moment they were out of sight. Fanny refused pleasantly.

'No, George dear. If you want to please me, help Charles and Amanda. They don't understand where to look for things.'

George looked at the shy and gaping children with the greatest distaste.

'There's a prize,' said Fanny softly.

'By jove, is there!' George's voice had the anticipation of a small boy. But his eyes were on Fanny's lips. He looked as if he meant to demand another sort of prize.

Fanny sighed, and then forgot the perpetual worry of George as she observed the way Aunt Louisa and Miss Martha Marsh were getting on so amicably. For some reason this seemed to amuse Lady Arabella, or something amused her, for she sat a little distance away in her wheelchair, smiling to herself, her idle fingers resting on her work basket and her hopelessly tangled wools.

The close airless heat had increased. There wasn't a breath of wind. Black clouds loomed, then parted and exposed the sun's blazing heat, only to gather again after a few minutes, threatening imminent thunder. Bird cries were sudden and sharp, the lake was a black mirror, the dipping dragonflies making stitches across its gleaming surface.

'You were taking a risk, Fanny,' Lady Arabella observed. 'Sending everybody out with a heavy shower about to descend. Amelia, I've no doubt, will enjoy it. She can huddle under a tree with Mr Marsh.' Her eyes were sly. 'Had you that in mind, Fanny? But what about the children? If it thunders they'll be frightened.'

'Charles and Amanda have George,' said Fanny calmly. 'And Nolly and Marcus aren't in the least afraid of thunder. Indeed, Nolly enjoys it.'

This was true, for the last storm there had been had filled Nolly with a delighted excitement that kept her at the windows on tiptoe, wanting to dance every time the thunder rolled.

'But I hope they'll take cover if it begins to rain,' she added, and as she spoke the first drop fell.

It was isolated, but the clouds had converged overhead, and the first broken roll of thunder sounded.

Aunt Louisa sprang up, exclaiming in vexation.

'Now isn't this just like our English weather! Having lived in London, Miss Marsh, I expect you haven't had the experience we have of ruined picnics. That's no doubt why my husband's ancestor had this pavilion built.'

'And which Davenport was that?' Miss Marsh asked politely.

'Well, now—I'm not exactly sure. My husband acquired the property from a cousin. He knows its history better than I do.'

'Perhaps Fanny knows,' Miss Marsh suggested, her long gentle face turned towards Fanny.

Fanny, who had never been encouraged to feel that Darkwater was any part of her lineage, was startled that she should be addressed.

'I believe it was the father of the previous owner, John Davenport,' she answered. 'He would have been my great-great-uncle and I expect Uncle Edgar's great-uncle. That would be right, Aunt Louisa?'

'My family,' said Aunt Louisa in her most lofty tones, 'were more inclined to follow the Greek and Italian style of architecture. We had a lot of statuary, and a folly, of course. Ah dear, there's the thunder again. And which children are those?'

She was peering across the strangely darkening landscape. Fanny followed her look, and saw the children running on the edge of the copse, Nolly's white dress glimmering, and Marcus following some yards behind.

'They must have all their trophies,' declared Miss Marsh. 'They're hurrying.'

This was true, for Nolly, her long starched skirts billowing out behind her, was literally flying out of the copse, with Marcus stumbling valiantly behind her.

It was Marcus's sobs that reached their ears. Nolly wouldn't wait for him. She wasn't usually unkind like that. Taller and light on her feet, she had outstripped him and he was bawling.

Fanny went towards them, calling, 'Wait for Marcus, Nolly. There no need to hurry like that. No one else has come back yet.'

She realised at once that her words hadn't reached Nolly, that even if the child had paused to hear, she was in no condition to take anything in. As she came within reach, Fanny saw that she was half-crazed with fear.

At last she flung herself into Fanny's arms, panting and trembling. In spite of the violence of her exertions her face was colourless, her eyes absolutely black.

'Nolly! Nolly, what is it?'

She had lost her hat somewhere. Her hair was tumbled and damp with sweat. Some wild flowers, hopelessly crushed, were held forgotten in her clenched hands.

'Nolly darling, what frightened you?'

The other ladies were gathering round. It was Miss Marsh who went to Marcus's rescue, picking up the hot noisily sobbing little boy.

'N-Nolly wouldn't wait!' he accused. 'She ran away from m-me.'

'The thunder's frightened them both,' said Aunt Louisa practically. 'They shouldn't have gone into the wood. It probably got very dark in there. Get them calm, for goodness sake, Fanny, before the others come back.'

Nolly's grip round Fanny was unbreakable. The child obviously couldn't stop trembling.

Perhaps it had been the thunder. Safely indoors watching a majestic sky was one thing, but in a gloomy wood it was another. Perhaps a startled bird had flown in their faces.

'You're safe now, darling. Tell me what it was.'

Nolly's face, pressed into Fanny's breast, didn't move.

'Marcus, what happened in the wood? Can you tell us?'

Marcus's sobs had died to hiccups. His drowned blue eyes held nothing but reproach.

'Nolly ran away. And I fell over a stick, and she said "Quick!" and she wouldn't wait for me.'

'Perhaps there was a wild pig,' said Lady Arabella. Her eyes gleamed pleasurably. 'Was there a great old boar snorting and snarling, Marcus? Or did your sister think the thunder was one? I expect that's the explanation, you know. She thought the thunder was an animal. And perhaps it is, or perhaps a herd of huge animals, bigger than elephants, growling and stamping about in the clouds.'

'Please, Great-aunt Arabella!' Fanny begged.

'Oh, Nolly isn't afraid of that. She likes my stories. Come on my lap, child, and I'll find you a sugar plum.'

The others were drifting back with their spoils. Uncle Edgar stood over Fanny demanding to know what had happened, and listening intently. He was perspiring, Fanny noticed. He was too heavily built for exertion in the heat. Adam listened intently, too. Amelia said that the thunder had scared the wits out of her.

'Didn't it, Mr Marsh? You saw how terrified I was.'

George came back, his two small companions, the Grey children, trailing a long way behind him as if he had deliberately lost them. Everyone declared that he or she had not been in the copse and seen Nolly and Marcus.

'They shouldn't have been allowed to go in there alone,' said Uncle Edgar. 'They could have got lost, apart from being torn on brambles. It's too wild. I intend to get it cleared up one day. They probably did meet a wild pig.'

The rain was about to descend in volumes. Aunt Louisa sensibly decreed that they should all hurry indoors, and the servants would gather up the chairs and the picnic things.

There was a great scurry to get to the house before the rain began. The thunder reverberated again, and a flash of lightning sent Marcus scurrying for Fanny's other hand.

The lake was as black as ebony when they left it. The willows were just beginning to sigh in the rising wind. With a sound of eerie gaiety, the windbells began to chime. For no reason at all, Fanny was vividly remembering Ching Mei's death.

Nolly had to be put to bed. She would neither talk nor eat. Her white face was a little alarming. Fanny stayed with her, so didn't know how the party ended, although Dora reported that Master Marcus had behaved nicely, and blown out the candles on his cake quite cleverly.

The thunderstorm was over in a very short time. Afterwards

everything dripped in a brilliant yellow light. The lifting of the gloom seemed to lesson Nolly's fear, or else she was naturally recovering from some shock she had had. She sat up and was persuaded to drink a little warm milk. At last it looked as if she would be persuaded to speak. Only by talking about what had happened, Fanny realised, would the nightmare leave the child.

'What was it, little pet? Did it grow too dark? Did you see a wild pig?'

'No,' said Nolly. 'I saw a black bird.'

Birds—the child's phobia. The dead starling tumbling down the chimney. The empty cage in Lady Arabella's room. Amelia's white fur hat that had made Nolly scream.

One might have realised it had been a bird, perhaps a blackbird or starling fluttering out of a bush. But that wouldn't have sent Nolly into such an ecstasy of terror. Fanny sensed more to the mystery. She probed gently.

'Nolly darling—was it the white bird you saw? You know, it would have been a pigeon, or even a white owl who thought it was night time with the dark clouds.'

'No, it was black,' Nolly's voice was shrill. 'It was black, black, black!'

'But you wouldn't be frightened by a harmless little blackbird. You often see them in the garden.'

Nolly's fists beat at her.

'You are stupid, Cousin Fanny! Uncle Edgar says you are stupid! It wasn't a little blackbird. It was big, big like this!——' She stretched out her arms dramatically.

'And where was this bird? In a tree?'

'No, it was on the ground. Marcus didn't see it. I told him to run. We both ran. I tore my dress.'

Suddenly she had flung herself into Fanny's arms, trembling and saying in her high shrill voice, 'You are so stupid! You have to keep saying it was white when it was black.'

Once, in the dark, she had gone out to look for Ching Mei. Now it was only twilight, the half-light. Dawn and dusk, Lady Arabella used to say, were the times when frightening things happened, when nothing was quite real.

Fanny wasn't afraid now, only tense and just vaguely apprehensive. She was sure she would discover the thing that had frightened Nolly, a dead hawk perhaps, or even something that wasn't a bird at all. What was echoing in her mind was Nolly's insistence that she was stupid because Uncle Edgar had said so. Nolly's hysteria had given the remark a significance out of all proportion, and now, in the gloom of the copse with its tangle of bracken and brambles, it came back to haunt Fanny. Why was she so stupid? What was it she hadn't seen? That black was white, or white was black?

Now she was allowing her fancies to take possession of her just as Nolly's had. She must concentrate on what she had come to do, pick her way, her skirts held up, down the vague track which Nolly and Marcus had followed.

The bracken shook with raindrops. The heat had been swept away with the storm, and the air was full of a damp chill, as if autumn were truly here. The young birches shivered audibly in the dying wind. A blackbird, a real vociferous blackbird, plummetted out of a bush and flew scolding into the dusk. Fanny stopped at a glimmer of white on the ground. It was an uprooted toadstool, obviously dropped by Nolly in her flight. So she was on the right track.

The strange thing was that as she stopped there was the faintest crackling of bracken which ceased almost at once, as if someone else had stopped, too.

She must have imagined it. She stood very still, listening. There was no sound but the shiver of the beeches. The half-light gave very little perspective. Surely nothing moved behind that broad tree trunk!

She gave herself a little shake, telling herself that if she were going to be afraid she should have sent someone else to find out what had startled Nolly; George, or Uncle Edgar, or Adam, or one of the gardeners. It was foolish to think that they might not have eyes to recognise what would frighten a sensitive child, or perhaps they would not tell the truth about what they found.

Was there anything to find? The children could not have gone very far through the tangle of bracken and moss-grown logs. There was a strong smell of damp rotting leaves and earth. Had she noticed that before? But of course she had. The bracken seemed to have been trampled down a great deal as if indeed a wild pig, or some animal had crashed through here.

A twig snapped behind her. She was instantly motionless, petrified. Her own footstep hadn't snapped that twig. She turned her head, listening. Her thumping heart deafened her. It seemed to have grown very dark.

Who was following her?

'Who's there?' she called softly. 'Is it you, George?'

There wasn't the faintest sound.

'George, I'm not an enemy to be stalked.'

But supposing she were to stumble on to something she shouldn't see, just as Nolly had... Just as, perhaps, Ching Mei had ... *Fanny is so stupid... The white bird is a black one... There is no escaped prisoner tonight...*

Was that someone breathing? Or just the whisper of the beech leaves? It was so dark, she couldn't *see*. The tree trunks were men. She had to go back, but somebody, something, barred her way.

To George, with his blurred brain, everything that moved in the dark was an enemy. She found she didn't dare to go back. She had to go to the left, in the direction of the lake, leaving the half-formed track behind and plunging through the nettles and fallen logs and drifts of dead leaves. It couldn't be very far. She would come out on the far side of the lake directly opposite the pavilion. She had been crazy to come here so late in the day. She shouldn't have waited for Nolly to talk, she should have come immediately the rain had stopped.

Had that other person come then, and waited ever since?

She didn't stop to listen now for pursuing footsteps. She was intent only in bursting out of the copse, as out of prison. Her skirts would be ruined. She would have to ask Uncle Edgar for another dress. She would have to explain she had ruined this one in running away from his son, and Lady Arabella would tell him not to be so foolish as to encourage her to run away from George, let George have his way ...

The light hadn't gone from the sky after all. When Fanny at last emerged only a few yards from the lake she saw that the water held the last glow of sunset, and was the colour of candlelight. It looked beautiful and reassuring, and even warm. And a few yards away a figure stood motionless, watching her.

Fanny froze. She could feel her feet sinking into the damp

rushy ground. She couldn't have turned and run. Her breath had left her.

'Fanny! Whatever are you doing bursting out of the woods like a witch.' Adam Marsh was standing over her. 'Your hair is tumbling down.'

'What are you doing here?'

'Reflecting, in the quiet of the evening. But my aunt will be getting impatient. It's time we were leaving.'

'Weren't you in the copse?'

'A short time ago, yes?'

She searched his face, his figure. She saw that he was perfectly calm, that his clothing was unruffled, no dead leaves clung to his trousers as they did to her skirts.

'I thought someone was there,' she said uneasily.

He looked over her head to the dark line of the trees.

'Perhaps there was. I believe we've all been down at one time or another searching for Nolly's scarecrow. Or perhaps it was that wild pig your uncle said was there.'

'Uncle Edgar said there was a wild pig?'

'Both he and George and one of the gardeners found indisputable evidence, I believe. So there is Nolly's ghost.' His eyes searched her. 'And what did you find?'

'Nothing at all. It was too dark.'

'What did the child finally tell you?'

'Oh, only some exaggerated story about a black bird. Nolly has this unnatural fear of birds. I'm afraid it's Great-aunt Arabella's fault. I expect it was a crow or a starling. Nolly has a weakness for exaggerating. But I wanted to reassure myself, all the same.'

'And you didn't reassure yourself?'

'I thought someone followed me.'

Adam took her arm.

'It wasn't me. It should have been. Pin up your hair, my dear. Or we will look guilty when we are innocent.'

She was still too disturbed and distressed to notice the regret in his voice.

19

'WELL, aunt, what did you think of her?'

'She's a nice enough child. Empty-headed, of course.'

'Empty-headed! Fanny!'

'How was I to know which one you meant. You give so much attention to the other.'

They stared at each other across the jolting carriage. Adam saw the humorous gleam in his aunt's eyes and knew that she hadn't been missing anything. He laughed softly, in appreciation.

'And sometimes at that I fancy Miss Amelia isn't so empty-headed.'

'She must be if she is taken in by you.'

Adam stopped laughing, and frowned.

'Yes. That's what I hope and count on. Then she won't be hurt too deeply. But don't you agree that I must go on. There is something. That child wasn't in a state of absolute terror today over nothing at all.'

Miss Marsh leaned forward.

'What do you imagine it was?'

'Not the wild boar everyone is talking about. Although I grant you there were traces of a boar. I saw them myself. No, I haven't the slightest idea, aunt. Or if I have, it's too fantastic to put into words. No, no, aunt, I don't know. I thought I was in the copse before anybody else, but there was nothing to find, nothing that hadn't flown away.'

'If you ask me, Adam, it's time you stopped being so secretive.'

'No, I disagree entirely. As I explained to you, it isn't only the children, it's Fanny.'

'Tut, boy! You have no grounds whatever for your suspicions. Besides, Fanny is a grown woman, and by the look of her, very capable of taking care of herself. The children——' Miss Marsh sighed, it seemed with longing. 'You shouldn't have let Mr Barlow get away like that without having it out with him.'

'How was I to know he would behave like that? Like a sulky child, not like a man at all. Good lord!'

Miss Marsh tapped his knee with her fan.

'And how would you behave in similar circumstances?'

Adam looked out of the window at the darkening moor.

'You must have noticed her beauty, aunt,' he said in a low voice.

'I have noticed that, and all her other qualities. You have my sympathy, but not my patience. I'm nervous, Adam. I confess it. Find out whatever it is you have to, and be done with it.'

'Another two months,' Adam murmured. 'I don't think it can be any longer than that.'

'Winter,' said Miss Marsh. 'The leaves fallen, that old house full of draughts. Rain, wind, snow. Why must we wait until the winter?'

'Because that is when Fanny becomes of age.'

20

IT was later that Fanny thought how strange it was that Adam Marsh seemed always to be there at the unexpected moment. On the railway station on that first day of all, in the church in the village, at the lake in the dusk when she had been so frightened, and when the other men had been indoors—or were when they themselves returned. All those meetings could not have been accidental. Perhaps none of them had been . . .

Once she had had the thought that he was watching over the children, because, having come to their rescue on their arrival in England, he fancied he had some responsibility for them. But lately he had seemed always to look first at her. If he were trying to warn her about something, why didn't he tell her what it was? Or didn't he know? Was he, too, haunted by this feeling of premonition?

Nothing was different, and yet somehow everything was. Nolly had never quite recovered her spirits since her mysterious fright, for some time she refused to be left alone and cried at a shadow moving. It was never established exactly what she had seen, but it seemed certain it had been a wild pig, for Uncle Edgar organised a shoot a few days later and two boars and a sow were slaughtered.

Lady Arabella told her rumbustious stories, as usual, and was in high good spirits when the children visited her, letting them handle all her treasures, and even coax Ludwig to play with a ball of wool. But she ended every session with the words, 'I'm so glad, Fanny, you had the good sense to send that little red fox of a man back where he came from. We'll keep her safely here, children, won't we?' Later, she had secret sessions with the children from which Fanny was excluded. It was something to do with making her a birthday present, an occupation that made Nolly's eyes shine with happy importance.

Amelia was quite openly talking of an Easter wedding, although no one had yet proposed to her. Her thoughts were easy enough to read. And George, with just a shade more confidence and possessiveness, kept trying to persuade Fanny to bring the children down to the stables where they could grow accustomed to the horses before beginning riding lessons. He was shrewd enough to know that that was the only way he might persuade her to go with him, since she refused to be in his company alone.

Aunt Louisa had dismissed Miss Egham, and told Fanny that if she needed a good workaday gown to wear in the schoolroom she was at liberty to choose the material and make it herself. That was the way the wind blew in that quarter. Poor Aunt Louisa, Fanny thought, stuck with her unwelcome niece after all, but perhaps making the best of it, since when Amelia married the house would be very quiet.

Uncle Edgar was exactly as he had been before the Hamish Barlow episode, affable, good-tempered, laughing just as heartily at his own jokes, becoming a little more conceited, perhaps, in his dress, and showing a great propensity for social occasions. There were always visitors at Darkwater, or the carriage was ordered for some dinner party or another. Uncle Edgar vowed every morning that he was exhausted, worn out, too old for all these gaieties, but that it was his duty to arrange them for the sake of the girls.

That was the subtle difference. Whereas previously Fanny had been allowed to make excuses for her absence, now Uncle Edgar insisted that she accompany them everywhere.

'You know why Papa is behaving like this,' Amelia said. 'He's giving you another chance to find a husband. He's quite forgiven you, you see. He's so kind-hearted, dear Papa.'

But Fanny didn't think that was the reason at all. She thought that Uncle Edgar was merely making it publicly known once more how generous and worthy a man he was, and how sincerely he loved the waifs thrust on him. It would have broken his heart if his dearest Fanny had gone to live in far-off China . . .

It was the only way she could reconcile his present fond demeanour with his previous emphatic insistence that if she did not marry Hamish Barlow she would never be forgiven.

The letter with the London postmark arrived for her one late October morning when she had just returned from a walk with the children. Usually all mail was taken to Uncle Edgar who enjoyed distributing it, though the bulk of it was for himself. But today Amelia happened to be there when the postman arrived, and caught sight of Fanny's name on the top envelope.

'Fanny!' she shrieked. 'Have you an admirer you've never told me about? Do you think this is from Mr Barlow? Do open it quickly and tell me.'

Her interest was forgiveable. Fanny never received letters. There had been no one from whom to receive them. And the London postmark was highly intriguing.

Fanny's own fingers trembled as she tore open the envelope. The thin delicate writing didn't look like a man's. Mr Barlow didn't come to her mind. She had no clue to the writer, only again this unreasonable disquiet.

The thick sheet of notepaper was open in her hand. She read, *My dear Miss Davenport, You will not perhaps recognise my name since I have been retired for some years, and am now a very old man. But as your late father's attorney and friend, I would like to extend to you my very best wishes on your coming of age. Indeed, since I have not seen you since you were virtually a baby, I have an old man's whim that you might, when you next make the journey to London, call on me at my house in Hanover Square. I have no doubt that under your uncle's excellent guardianship you have bloomed. It would please me to see this with my own eyes. Would you be so kind as to bear the thought in mind? Your obedient servant, Timothy J. Craike.*

It was like a hand reaching out from the past. Someone who had known her father, and perhaps her mother. Fanny had to read the letter twice to assimilate its contents, and then, forgetting all propriety, she went flying into the library.

'Uncle Edgar! Oh, I am so glad to find you here!'

'I scarcely had time to disappear, since you gave me no warning,' said her uncle dryly.

'I'm sorry. I should have knocked. I was so excited. Look, Uncle Edgar! I have a letter. Read it!'

She thrust the sheet of notepaper at Uncle Edgar, wondering for the first time as she waited impatiently for him to read the thin careful writing, why he had never mentioned Mr Craike to her.

But in a moment he had unwittingly explained her doubt.

'God bless my soul, I thought the old man dead long ago.'

'Then you know him, Uncle Edgar?'

'Certainly. He attended to your father's affairs after his death. But it's years now since I had occasion to see him, and as he was an old man then I'd no idea he was still alive. Let me see, he must be as near ninety as anything.'

'Then how wonderful of him to remember me. Oh, I should like to meet him.'

'For a young woman who seems to show a remarkable scorn for males of her own age, I find this deep interest in a gentleman approaching his century very strange.'

'Uncle, please be serious!' Fanny begged. 'It isn't Mr Craike I'm interested in. He remembers my father, and perhaps my mother. I should dearly like to talk about them to him.'

Uncle Edgar clasped his hands on his stomach, leaning back in his chair. His eyes were inscrutable.

'So you want to make another journey to London?'

'Oh, I do, please! I know it's a tremendous favour to ask, but if you would try to understand how I have felt with no memory of my parents, and now here is an opportunity of getting one.'

'And supposing you hear something you wouldn't care to know?'

'What do you mean? There is nothing like that about my parents. What could there be that I shouldn't know?'

Uncle Edgar was chuckling gently.

'Be a little calmer, my dear. If I know anything at all, Mr Craike will tell you you are your mother over again, wilful, turbulent, a proper handful, eh? That's how he'll describe you.' He was patting her hand in his familiar reassuring way. 'Don't look so anxious. You shall go to London and see this gentleman. We shall both go.'

'You mean you will come with me!'

'I will certainly come with you. Looking as you do at this moment you could certainly not be trusted to travel alone.'

He submitted to Fanny's impulsive hug with amused tolerance.

'Perhaps you'll even have a good word to say for your uncle when we get to London.'

'But of course, Uncle Edgar. When can we go? Tomorrow?'

'One day next week, perhaps.'

'Oh, but, Uncle——'

Uncle Edgar made a sudden impatient movement, as if his goodwill were only superficial. Fanny had a cold feeling that he already regretted his promise.

'Am I to cancel all my appointments, no matter how important, for a sentimental old man who has already waited almost twenty-one years to see you? Come, my dear, be reasonable.'

'Yes, of course. It must be at your convenience. I didn't think.'

'Never mind thinking.' He reached in his pocket for his snuff-box. 'Pretty women shouldn't think.' As he opened the box some of the snuff was spilt. How strange. Uncle Edgar's plump fingers were never clumsy. But he was laughing softly again. 'And a man should never allow himself to be upset by a pretty woman.'

'Have I upset you, Uncle Edgar?' Fanny asked bewilderedly.

'Yes, you have. The hunting season begins in ten days. I shall have to miss the first meet. The devil take old Craike who should have been in his grave ten years ago.'

Amelia had found the little Chinese camel. She was holding it in her hands when Fanny came into the room. She started guiltily at Fanny's entrance, and Fanny exclaimed, 'Amelia, how dare you! Going through my things!'

'I was only looking for some cotton in your work box. Why did Adam give you this? Did you ask him for it?'

'*Ask* him for it!' Fanny snatched the camel from Amelia in high indignation. 'No, I did not. He merely saw that I admired it.'

'And so, as if you were the Queen, he had to give it to you!' Amelia's face was flushed, her voice sneering. 'Why is it that you have to get everything these days, even another trip to London to see a silly old man in his dotage. I don't know what has come over Papa. But now, all the time, it's Fanny must do this, Fanny must have that, as if—I don't know. Why didn't you marry Mr Barlow and go away?'

'Amelia!'

'You needn't think Adam cares for you just because he's given you that ugly old camel. To tell the truth, he's just sorry for you. He told me so.'

'And why is he sorry for me?' Fanny asked in a low voice.

'Good gracious, how could he not be? Everyone's sorry for poor relations.'

'I think you're just being spiteful.'

'No. I'm speaking the truth. Mamma says it should be me getting the trip to London. It's time I went to operas and theatres. But I don't really grudge it to you. You'll have little enough.'

'Will I?' Fanny asked dreamily. The little camel cradled in her hands felt like the whole world.

'Don't look like that!' Amelia cried, stamping her foot. 'You look lovesick and silly. Adam isn't going to marry you. He's going to marry me.'

'Has he—told you so?'

'I'm not blind!' said Amelia and suddenly burst into tears and ran out of the room.

In his own way George made a worse scene than that. He had got it into his head that Fanny was going to meet Hamish Barlow in London. It was useless to tell him that she wasn't, that Hamish Barlow had long ago sailed for the East, 'Then who is it you're going to meet? It must be a man. You wouldn't look excited like that for a woman.'

'Yes, it is a man, but a very old man. Nearly ninety. Does that satisfy you?'

'It would if I believed you,' said George. His eyes were sulky and smouldering. 'Are you going to come back?'

'Of course I'm going to come back!' Fanny said exasperatedly. 'Though sometimes, the way you behave, I'd like to stay away.'

'If you do, I'll follow you. I'll follow you and kill you both.'

One day George would do something like that—if he hadn't done so already. Fanny's thoughts inevitably went back to Ching Mei and the riddle of that tragic evening. Then he would have to be put away, either in a mental hospital, or behind the grim grey walls of Dartmoor prison. How terrible to ride past the prison and know that Cousin George was there. And yet what a relief it would be. Neither his parents nor his besotted grandmother recognised his potential danger. She had loyally tried not to recognise it herself, but the time was coming when she couldn't endure his persecution any longer, when something would have to happen.

Aunt Louisa was the other person who thought the trip to London a piece of extravagant folly.

'Why can't Fanny write to Mr Craike?' she asked her husband.

'Because she wants to see him and talk to him. It's very understandable.'

'Then why don't you have the old man come here?'

'Because he is quite beyond travelling. I gather he has only a short time to live. One can't refuse a dying man's whim, my dear.'

Aunt Louisa tossed her head impatiently.

'Oh, you and your sense of duty! Do you ever stop to consider the inconvenience caused to others by it? Fanny has already spoiled those children until the servants can scarcely manage them. There'll be trouble the moment she's gone, and the brunt of it will fall on me. Really, Edgar, I seem to have spent the whole of my married life coping with your obligations. What other woman would have done it—no less than three strange children—the house practically an orphanage——'

Uncle Edgar bent to press his lips against his wife's plump neck.

'You have been an angel, my love. Angels are sometimes rewarded.' He gave his throaty gurgle at her face suddenly full of anticipation. 'Not another word at the moment. But you haven't the worst husband in the world'—his fingers found her breast—'I assure you . . .'

Once again Fanny packed her neat carpet bag with the essentials for a journey. But this time she could leave out her most precious possessions, for she very definitely was coming back. She would have liked to have had the opportunity to tell Adam about her journey. She fancied he would have been pleased for her. But he had not called lately, and it hardly seemed sufficient reason to write to him since she would be back within three days. Two days for travelling, and one to visit Mr Craike. Yet it would have been a wonderfully satisfying thing to write a note to Mr Marsh. Even forming his name on paper would have made her lips curve with pleasure. So he was to marry Amelia was he! She would see about that!

'Cousin Fanny, why are you always smiling? Is it because you are leaving us?'

Nolly's eyes were black with hatred.

Fanny began to laugh, and shook the child gently by the shoulders.

'If you continue to look like that I will be very glad to leave you.'

'Marcus says you won't come back.'

'Marcus says nothing of the kind. And you are to be good children while I'm away. If Dora tells me you haven't been, there will be no gifts in my bag.'

Marcus immediately began to clamour for a toy trumpet.

'I need one to blow for my soldiers. Cousin George says there must be a trumpeter to sound the alarm. What does alarm mean, Cousin Fanny?'

'It means when the enemy is in sight.'

'Then you mustn't blow it, Marcus! You mustn't!' Nolly cried, in agitation.

Marcus, five years old, was at last beginning to realise his superiority over a mere girl. He strutted about saying derisively, 'You're scared. Cousin Fanny, Nolly's always getting scared of something.'

Nolly made a wild dash at him, to tug at his hair.

'I am not scared! I am not scared!'

'Lawks!' cried Dora, running to separate the screaming children. 'Miss Nolly, you'll be going to bed without your supper.'

Nolly stood glowering.

'I am not scared at all. I am only over-sensitive. Great-aunt Arabella says so. She says I must be treated gently and not frightened. She says this house is enough to frighten any child.'

'And now that speech is over,' said Fanny, 'what is there about the house to frighten a child?'

There was a red spot in each of Nolly's cheeks. Otherwise her face was paper white and looked alarmingly delicate. She was a bunchy little figure in her starched petticoats and her wide-skirted gingham dress, but Fanny knew that when the clothes were stripped off her she was far too thin and light. And her flat little chest was the storing place for too many conflicting emotions.

'Nolly,' Fanny said, 'I will be back for my birthday. You know that, don't you?'

This was suddenly, to Nolly, an irrefutable argument. Her face lit up, showing its infrequent dazzling prettiness.

'You will have to be, Cousin Fanny. Because I am making you a present. You wouldn't be too stupid not to come back for your presents.'

In spite of that victory, Fanny was still not entirely easy about leaving the children. It was only that she wanted so badly to go and see Mr Craike, and besides Hannah had assured her that she was wrong to let the children possess her too much.

'You're only making a rod for your back, Miss Fanny,' she said. She looked round quickly to see that no one else was within hearing, and added, 'You know what it's been, running errands for Miss Amelia all your life, and now being tied to the nursery when you should be living your own life. All this nonsense about not getting a husband. You had only to see how that gentleman from China was turned silly about you, so why shouldn't others be. You ought to be thinking of children of your own, Miss Fanny.'

'Bless you, Hannah. I don't know why I worry about Nolly when you're here. It's only if she gets one of her frights——'

'And them all imagination!' Hannah said briskly. 'It's a pity she ever heard that old story about the bird in the chimney. I know it can be scary for a child. You found it scary yourself when you were a little one. But if you ask me, half Miss Nolly's frights are invented.' Hannah shook her grey head wisely. 'She sees she gets plenty of attention from them.'

'Perhaps you're right, Hannah. Anyway, she's convinced, for some reason, that I'm stupid. Perhaps that's the reason.'

Fanny wanted so much to be convinced that she allowed herself to be. The children could come to no harm in three days. Dora would sleep in the nursery with them. Hannah would be within call.

But in the late afternoon of the day before her departure everything changed. Nolly and Marcus went to Lady Arabella's room as usual, Nolly to work on the mysterious birthday present, and Marcus to amuse himself with whatever new fascinating object Lady Arabella might produce.

A few minutes later there were piercing screams.

When Fanny rushed into the room it was difficult to get a coherent story from anybody. Lady Arabella was just shuffling on her sticks from her bedroom, the lamps had not been lit, and the living room with its claustrophobic collection of furniture and knick-knacks was in gloom. Nolly was standing in the middle of the room screaming with terrifying regularity. Her figure was rigid. As that other day by the lake, she obviously was in no condition to say what had happened, and it was left for Marcus, beginning to sob with infectious fear, to stutter that Nolly had touched the bird.

'What bird?' Fanny demanded.

Marcus pointed towards the empty birdcage. 'In there.'

Lady Arabella shuffled forward. 'There's no bird in there. The cage has been empty for months. Didn't I tell you about my parrot. He died—but my goodness, Fanny! Look! There is a bird.'

The white shape, wings outspread, was clearly visible. It was hanging motionless against the bars of the cage. All unawares, Nolly must have brushed against it and it had pecked at her.

Marcus had caught Nolly's fear, and now, in an unreasoning overwhelming wave it swept over Fanny.

There was only a not very large white bird hanging motionless in a cage in a gloomy room yet the atmosphere was heavy with dread.

'Where are those lazy servants?' cried Lady Arabella. 'Why aren't the lamps lit?' She fumbled for the bell rope, and suddenly, from the deep chair in the corner, George began to laugh.

'Ho, ho, ho! You've all been nicely taken in. It's only a

dead bird.'

Fanny spun round on him.

'George! Why are you hiding there? Is this a horrible joke you've played?'

'I didn't play the joke. I didn't put the bird there. But it was funny to see Nolly jump. You'd really think it had bitten her.'

Lizzie had come hurrying to answer the bell. Lady Arabella turned on her angrily.

'Why haven't you lit the lamps half an hour ago? You know Miss Olivia comes here to sew. Do you expect her to do it in the dark?'

'But I did light them, ma'am!' Lizzie protested. 'Really I did. They must have gone out. Look, this one's still warm.'

Nolly's face was buried hard against Fanny's breast. Fanny only hoped her own rapidly beating heart was not further upsetting the child. But she couldn't help her feeling of unexplained dread. Someone had played a horrible trick on the children, put a dead bird in the birdcage, blown out the lamps . . . Why?

'Then didn't you fill them?' Lady Arabella snapped. 'Can't you be a little more thorough in your work? Here I fall asleep on my bed, and am woken by banshee shrieks all because you've been too lazy to see that the lamps were burning properly. The child wouldn't have got a fright if she could have seen this bird properly. Let's have a look at it.'

Lizzie, muttering something under her breath about the lamps being properly attended to, re-lit them, and in the soft glow the poor mute motionless creature was clearly visible. It wasn't even a real bird, but just a realistic concoction of feathers, with a small sharp beak. Fanny remembered seeing it somewhere before, and suddenly recognised it as belonging to one of Aunt Louisa's bonnets. She had used to wear it to church last winter, nestling among veiling and ribbons.

It was only someone who knew Nolly's phobia about birds who realised how much of a fright this would have given her. But who, apart from George with his retarded sense of humour, would have wanted to frighten a child?

The disturbance had brought Aunt Louisa and Amelia hurrying upstairs.

Aunt Louisa was furious.

'Who has been destroying my bonnets? Mamma, surely——'

Lady Arabella's eyes went completely cold.

'I'm not senile yet, Louisa, much as you might like to think I am. No, I don't go about blowing out lamps and frightening children.'

But she had always enjoyed frightening them with her stories, Fanny remembered, and then comforting them with sugar plums. She had enjoyed her power over them.

'George! Amelia——'

'Mamma, don't be idiotic,' said Amelia. 'A silly old artificial bird. I wouldn't even think of such a thing.'

George was laughing again, the snigger of a schoolboy who has enjoyed a practical joke.

'I don't know who did it, but it was deuced funny. I say, make the child get over it, Fanny. She can't have been that scared.'

But Nolly, Fanny realised, was not going to get over this last shock. Too many shocks had been accumulating inside her. She had gone suddenly limp in Fanny's arms, and seemed as if she were really ill.

'I'm taking her to bed,' she said. 'I'm sorry, Aunt Louisa, but I think this time the doctor ought to be sent for.'

There was a great fuss about that. Aunt Louisa pooh-poohing pandering to what were probably only tantrums, but at that moment Uncle Edgar came upstairs to see what was going on and was instantly alarmed.

'The child's sickening for something. By all means, the doctor must come. I'll have him sent for immediately.'

'She isn't sickening for something, Uncle Edgar,' said Fanny. 'She's merely had a very bad fright. But can we talk about that later?'

She was carrying Nolly's limp, too light body back to the nursery, Marcus clinging to her skirts whimpering. She heard Uncle Edgar's loud voice as she went, 'God bless my soul, Mamma, what next! If you want a new parrot I'll buy you one, but to play games with dead birds!'

'If I play a game, Edgar,' came Lady Arabella's voice, slow, distinct, and far from senile, 'it will be a much cleverer one than that. And one that I will win.'

By night-time Nolly had a high fever. The doctor had been, and given her a sedative which had sent her into a heavy sleep. He had heard the story of what had happened and said that contrary to sickening for some disease, the fright, to such a highly-strung child, might well bring on a brain fever. The utmost quiet and good nursing were essential. And there must be no more shocks. Her short life had held too many already.

Leaving Hannah (Dora was infected with the uneasiness in the house and jumped every time a door opened or a curtain billowed in a draught) beside the sleeping child, Fanny went downstairs. She didn't want dinner, she was too distressed for that, but there were things that must be said. She had reached a conclusion in the last hour that made her more angry than afraid.

The meal was over, and the family was in the drawing room.

George sprang up eagerly at her entrance, and Amelia asked, 'How is poor little Nolly?'

'Sleeping,' said Fanny briefly. 'Uncle Edgar, I shall not, of course, be able to accompany you to London tomorrow.'

Uncle Edgar pushed aside his glass of port, and said in distress, 'My dear child, is that sacrifice really necessary? You had set your heart on this expedition.'

'Yes, Uncle, I had. But someone is equally determined that I shouldn't go.'

Now she had everybody's startled attention.

'Whatever is this, Fanny?' Aunt Louisa demanded. 'I admit I never thought that extravagant journey to see an old man who has probably lost his memory was at all necessary. But this stupid childish joke with the bird in the cage was meant only to amuse the children, surely. It had nothing to do with you. I never heard anything so extraordinary.'

'I think it had everything to do with me,' Fanny said clearly. 'Someone must have been jealous of my going, or perhaps had an even more serious reason for stopping me. Anyway, you all knew Nolly's fear of birds. Whoever put the bird in Great-aunt Arabella's room was quite aware that the child would be scared out of her wits, and probably ill. And that consequently I wouldn't leave her. It's really very simple indeed.'

As they all stared, she added, 'If it was only meant to frighten the children, then that's even worse. I think whoever would do that is a devil.'

She rubbed her hand across her forehead, wearily, and heard Aunt Louisa saying in a put-out voice, 'Edgar, surely it isn't necessary to question the servants. Fanny is making a mountain out of this silly business. After all, I should be the one who is upset. It was my bonnet that was ruined.'

'It isn't a trifling business, Aunt Louisa,' said Fanny. 'Nolly is seriously ill.'

Uncle Edgar was on his feet, looking as perturbed as his comfortable after-dinner flush would allow.

'Now come, Fanny, if you're finding hidden meanings in a prank, I can surely find one in your implication that neither your aunt nor Amelia nor any of the servants, even Hannah who has seen you all through enough illness, is capable of looking after that extremely spoilt little girl. Stop talking nonsense, and prepare to leave for London in the morning, as we arranged.'

'You know I can't. You know I won't. You must have heard the doctor say Nolly could develop brain fever. She has already been crying for Ching Mei. She hasn't mentioned her amah's name for weeks. Next she will cry for her mother. And if I disappear, too, then what do you imagine the consequences will be? No'—her eyes went round the room—'if someone played this horrible trick to keep me here they have succeeded very well. I will write to Mr Craike explaining the position.'

Nobody had wanted her to go to London, she knew that. They had all had their separate reasons. Even Uncle Edgar hadn't wanted to miss the hunt. But now, because she had made the accusation, they all had smooth astonished faces, as if incredulous that she could think herself so important.

The fact that no one could deny was that the bird had been put in the birdcage, and had succeeded far too well in providing the necessary upset.

George was the most likely culprit, and yet it seemed at once too clever and too simple a plot for him. Perhaps he had had his grandmother whisper in his ear. Aunt Louisa had grudged the money spent on Fanny, and Amelia the attention. Uncle Edgar's seeming acts of generosity were not usually such unselfish ones . . .

'Oh, poor Fanny!' Amelia cried, suddenly springing up and throwing her arms round Fanny. 'It is true, she gets all the worry. Let's make up to her for her disappointment, and give her a really wonderful birthday next week.'

'A splendid idea,' said Uncle Edgar in a relieved voice. 'And you write a letter to Craike, Fanny. Ask him all the things you want to know. He'll answer them as well in writing, as in an interview. Get it done tonight, and give it to me. I'll see it gets away by the post in the morning.'

'And Fanny, don't sit up with that child all night,' Aunt Louisa ordered. 'I'll look in before I go to bed, and the servants will take turns. You've really brought this indispensability on yourself, by your own behaviour.'

'If Ching Mei hadn't died, it wouldn't have happened,' said Fanny, and again the blank faces looked at her.

'Well, you'd better have that out with Sir Giles Mowatt,' said Uncle Edgar. 'He let the prisoner escape. He's tightened up regulations now, he tells me. Vows there'll be no more escapes. Fellow's away to Australia by now, I believe.'

'Aus-Australia!' echoed Amelia unbelievingly.

'That's what they think. A ship bound for the Antipodes sailed from Plymouth a day or so later. And there goes a murderer scot-free. He'll probably make his fortune in the goldfields. Ah well, life's a funny thing. Most unfair at times. Most unfair.'

Amelia made a movement as if to say something, then stopped. Her face was white, her eyes darkened.

'Papa——'

Her father waited indulgently for her comment. When none came, he said, 'What is it, my dear?'

'Are you all right, Amelia? You look pale.'

'I'm quite all right, Mamma. It's just that talk of escaped prisoners makes me nervous. Sometimes at night—the ivy taps on my window—and I almost scream.'

'My poor darling, you mustn't be nervous. I tell you, Sir Giles declares not even a weasel could slip out of that jail now.'

Amelia looked at her father with her dilated eyes. Then Lady Arabella, who had been dozing the entire time, woke with a great start, and murmured in her hoarse voice, 'Fanny is a good girl. She deserves more than a party.'

And it seemed as if after all she might have been listening all the time.

21

SHE was caught—she was the bird struggling and suffocating in the chimney. The bird had died...

Fanny, dozing in her chair at Nolly's bedside, started up, wide awake again, the questions without answers going round and round remorselessly in her brain.

The fire was dying, and the room almost dark. She got up to carefully shovel on more coal. In spite of her care, Nolly stirred, and muttered, as she had several times in her half-delirium, 'Cousin Fanny! When will Ching Mei come back for her shoes?'

Soon the coal caught alight, and the room grew more cheerful. Nolly slept again. The Chinese doll that lately she had wanted much less was tucked in beside her. It had seemed to comfort her. That it had been the innocent cause of Ching Mei's death, fortunately the child didn't know. And, just as it was likely she would never discover who had put the bird in the birdcage, Fanny had never known who had tossed the doll on her bed that night.

But none of the queer episodes, not even Nolly's fright in the copse, had seemed quite as sinister as the imitation bird tonight.

Or perhaps Fanny felt that simply because she was so tired and overwrought and disappointed about her cancelled journey to London. So alone...

She had no one to whom to turn except Adam Marsh. Should she turn to him? Could she trust him? She kept remembering his injunction in his letter to her, '*if ever you have any doubts...*'

Now she had too many doubts. Whether they were the kind to which he referred, she didn't know, but on an overwhelming impulse she tiptoed to her room and got writing paper from her bureau.

'... *It isn't for myself, but for the children that I am worried. Someone is deliberately trying to frighten them. Nolly is ill tonight. I can't leave her to go to London. I am wondering if that pleases our tormentor, if it is what was intended. I confess now that I have never been entirely convinced that Ching Mei's death was due to the accident of her encountering the escaped prisoner. I think someone outside the family should know that my cousin George is more seriously ill than it was at first thought. Families can be too loyal . . .'*

Putting her anxieties on paper gave her intense relief. She finished the letter, melted wax over the candle flame to seal the envelope, then slipped it into her pocket to ponder later how she would see that it reached Adam. She couldn't leave it in the hall to be taken with the rest of the post. Everyone would want to know why she was writing to Adam Marsh.

That letter finished, she began the one of apology to Mr Craike. She begged him to write to her telling her all he could of her parents. Perhaps at a later date she would be able to visit him.

There was no worry about the posting of this letter. Uncle Edgar had promised to see that it was dispatched first thing in the morning.

The wind had risen and it had begun to rain. The summer was over, and the leaves were falling. With this wind, the ground would be carpeted in the morning and the lake scattered with drowning leaves. The misty days and the long dark nights were coming. That was when the house really came to life, not with fires and parties and gaiety, but with its multitudinous creakings and sighings in the gales that swept over the moors, with the moonlight caught in uncurtained windows, and the snuffings of candles by immense disembodied breaths. Fanny shivered. She loved the drama of the winter, but this coming one she dreaded. She couldn't see its end.

Nolly was better in the morning. She drank a little warm milk, stared at Fanny with a shadow of her old truculence, said, 'Stay here beside me! All the time!' and fell asleep again this time deeply and quietly.

It was still raining in a fine drizzle by mid-morning when Amelia came flouncing in, wet and bad-tempered. She had been out riding and Adam hadn't met her.

Fanny looked at her in astonishment.

'Do you mean to say you have a rendezvous with Mr Marsh

when you go riding?'

Amelia nodded. 'Of course. I never did enjoy riding alone. Oh Fanny, don't look so shocked. This is the nineteenth century. Or is it that you're jealous?'

'Then your meetings were never by accident?'

'The moor's a bit big for accidental meetings, isn't it? No, he waits for me by High Tor. But he didn't come today, the coward. Surely he's not afraid of a little rain.'

Fanny's fingers were closing over the letter in her pocket, crumpling it viciously. *If ever you are in doubt*, he had said. What was she in at this moment but the most miserable doubt?

'And does he encourage you—to confide in him?' she asked.

'Of course. I tell him everything. He's so wonderfully sympathetic. Fanny. I really think I'm in love.'

'Think!' said Fanny contemptuously.

Amelia frowned, 'How can one ever be absolutely sure? Could you be sure?'

'No, I couldn't,' Fanny admitted, her colour high. 'Sometimes I don't know which is which, love or hate. Or whether they're both the same thing.'

'You looked as if you hated us all last night,' Amelia agreed. 'So I understand what you mean. Because I'm sure you really do love us all. Even maddening George.'

'I hate whoever frightened Nolly so badly,' Fanny said in a low voice. 'Who was it? I must know.'

'Then don't ask me.' Amelia was uncomfortable. 'I expect it was Grandmamma, really. But she'd meant to amuse Nolly, not frighten her. You've made an awful scene out of such a trivial happening, Fanny. Mamma was very angry with you.'

'Does she think Nolly being ill trivial?'

'No, of course not. How is she this morning, anyway?'

'Better,' said Fanny briefly. 'Dora is with her. She must be kept quiet.'

'Will she be allowed downstairs for your birthday?'

'I don't know. How can I say.'

'Oh, well!' Amelia sighed and yawned. 'You're lucky to be so interested in children. What am I to do for the rest of this dreary day? I hate sewing, I hate reading, there's absolutely nothing to do. That silly Adam, why couldn't he have come out in the rain!'

When she had gone Fanny took the letter out of her pocket and tore it into small pieces. Then she burst into tears which she had to hastily dry when Dora came knocking at the door to say Miss Nolly was awake and fancied a little jelly. There was no peace for her, not even the peace of having a sympathetic ear into which to pour her troubles. Amelia had stolen that from her. It seemed that Mr Adam Marsh had a pair of very inquisitive ears, and enjoyed the secrets and heart-searchings of young women.

'Now, Fanny,' said Uncle Edgar that evening, 'we must be business-like. You come of age on Monday, so, as I mentioned once before, you must make your will.'

'But I have nothing——'

'I don't want to remind you of the value of a gift I have made to you,' Uncle Edgar interrupted, 'but I would point out that that sapphire pendant has a cash value as well as a sentimental one. Surely you would like to choose who is to be its recipient?'

And there was the little Chinese camel, Fanny thought, with a pang. Adam's gift. Of course, Uncle Edgar was quite right, she must choose her own beneficiary.

'I would like to leave the pendant and—other personal things to Nolly,' she said unhesitatingly.

'I thought you would say that, my dear. And a very nice gesture on your part. The day will come, a very far-off day, I trust, when the child will appreciate this. The other essential thing in a will, as you probably know, is that you must name a trustee. I make the suggestion from a purely practical point of view that that task should be left in my hands. If you agree, we'll draw up a very simple document that can be signed on your birthday.'

'Do what you think best, Uncle Edgar.'

She was too tired, after her long vigil at Nolly's bedside, to think clearly. Anyway, the subject was a minor one. It was only men who had this passionate desire for tidiness in their business affairs. She would give the pendant to Nolly long before she died, anyway. But the camel—that would remain her own until the end, no matter what memories it gave her.

'Craike will get your letter, and write again,' said Uncle Edgar as an afterthought. 'I hope you've forgotten all that nonsense you talked last night. Your aunt and I understand that you were overwrought. You spoke as if we were all your enemies. Oh, I know that someone played a prank, but not a malicious one. A fine brainstorm you turned on, eh, my dear? But it's all forgiven and forgotten.'

So she was the one to be forgiven! Fanny was too tired even to be indignant about that. Tired and hopeless. Unless Adam had had private reasons for meeting Amelia and listening to her garrulous tongue.

Perhaps that was it, Fanny thought, her mood turning to sudden high excitement. He was aware that somehow all was not well—as indeed he had hinted to her—and was pursuing his own methods of obtaining information. If that were so, she must see him. Yes, she positively must see him, and have the whole matter out with him. Why torture herself with doubts when ten minutes' conversation would solve the whole thing?

She would ride over to Heronshall. When? Tomorrow, when the family was at church. If Nolly continued to improve she could be safely left for three or four hours with Dora and Hannah. When the family returned from church and found her missing she could explain, on her return, that she had been impelled to get some fresh air.

The next day it was still raining and blowing a half gale. On Amelia's horse, Jinny, Fanny took the short cut across the moor. Even so the ride took her more than an hour, but the wind and rain in her face were wildly exhilarating. After being shut in a sickroom she felt one of her swift changes of mood to an almost intoxicated state of hope and freedom. It even occurred to her that she might find Adam waiting at his rendezvous beneath High Tor for Amelia. She would surprise him by her appearance, tease him, ask him if he were not bitterly disappointed.

But there was no horse and rider beneath High Tor, only a grey huddle of sheep sheltering from the rain.

Fanny rode on, and came at last to Heronshall. She was soaked through, but glowing with warmth. She didn't give a thought to her dishevelled appearance, knowing that Miss Martha Marsh would at once invite her in to dry herself by the fire, and drink hot tea. And Adam—she could already visualise the expression on his face, puzzled, pleased, welcoming.

Strangely, she had to lift the heavy knocker and pound on the door twice before it was opened.

Then a manservant, dressed rather casually in a leather apron, whom she hadn't seen before stood within, looking at her in some surprise.

'Is Miss Marsh or Mr Marsh at home?' she asked. 'Would you be so good as to tell them that Miss Fanny Davenport has called?'

'I'm sorry, miss. They be away.'

Fanny stared at the man, scarcely taking in his words. Both Miss Marsh and Adam couldn't be away—not after her picture of a glowing fire, a warm welcome.

A gust of wind blew her wet hair across her face. She pushed it back impatiently.

'Oh, they've gone to church, of course.'

'No, miss, they be gone to Lunnon. There be only Bella and me here. The house is shut.'

'To London!' Fanny repeated. 'But he never told us. He didn't even tell Amelia. He let her ride out——' She realised she was thinking her astonished thoughts aloud, and said quickly, 'When did they go?'

'Day before yesterday, miss.'

'For long?'

'That I can't say, miss. But the servants was to have yesterday and today off.'

Fanny tried to collect herself after her profound disappointment, her unreasonable sense of having been abandoned.

'Is there someone who could rub my horse down? Could I rest her for half an hour?'

'I'll see to it myself, miss,' said the man good-naturedly. 'Will you step inside, into the dry, while you wait?'

The hall which she had thought so light and airy and attractive was as cold as doom. She sat on the edge of a carved oak chair and shivered. No one came near her. She tried to rationalise what had happened. Adam and his aunt had probably found the grey windy weather depressing and had decided on an impulse to go to London to see friends, an opera perhaps, or a new play. They had no obligation to inform any one at Darkwater of their plans. They would be back before anyone knew they had gone.

But Fanny failed to comfort herself. Apart from Adam's thoughtless behaviour towards Amelia, he had given her the unmistakable impression that he would always be there if she needed him. And now he just wasn't there, the house was cold and empty, and she had the greatest difficulty in controlling her tears. Could nobody at all be trusted?

On the way back across the moor in the early dusk she saw a rider approaching, and her heart suddenly leaped. Adam, after all! He had returned. He had ridden out looking for her.

The rider on the superb black horse who galloped up, reigning in his mount with easy authority, was George. His highly-flushed face was full of pleasure at having found her.

'They said you'd gone out riding. Amelia's furious that you took Jinny. How far have you been?'

'Only to High Tor.'

'That's where Amelia waits for Mr Marsh. I've seen them.' George's face was suddenly suspicious. 'You haven't been looking for him, too?'

'Of course I haven't. I only had to get some fresh air. I'm going back now. Don't wait for me. Jinny can't keep up with your horse.'

George laughed. 'Don't be silly. I've been looking for you. Simon can suit his pace to Jinny's. Let's take as long as we like getting home.'

'Not in this weather. I'm frozen.'

'You don't look frozen. Your cheeks are scarlet.' George suddenly leaned across and took Jinny's bridle. 'Wait a minute, Fanny. I was jolly glad to hear you'd gone riding. I knew I'd get a chance to see you alone at last. I want to know when you're going to marry me.'

'*Marry* you!'

'Well, don't sound so surprised! What do you think I've been trying to tell you for the last six months?' George's voice had turned sulky. Already Fanny's reaction had hurt him. 'Look here, Fanny, I've waited long enough. You'll be twenty-one tomorrow. Even if Mamma and Papa oppose us, you'll be free to decide for yourself. So I want your answer then.'

Jinny moved restlessly as the hold on her bridle tightened.

George's face, flushed, too bright-eyed, oddly triumphant, was uncomfortably near to Fanny's. She felt caught and pinioned, unable to escape. And Adam had deserted her.

'George, let me go!'

'All right. I'll let you go now. But tomorrow I want your answer. And after that I'll never let you go. Never!'

He gave a sudden wild laugh, and abruptly releasing Jinny's bridle, spurred his horse and galloped off. But before he had gone far, he turned and came back, circling round Fanny on her slower mount, laughing and showing off his superb riding skill. He did that all the way back to Darkwater. It was, Fanny thought, like being hovered over by a bird of prey.

22

SHE was twenty-one. Everyone had gifts for her. Amelia gave her a cameo brooch and Aunt Louisa a cashmere shawl. Uncle Edgar kissed her soundly on the cheek, and handed her a small packet containing ten sovereigns. 'Buy yourself some gee-gaw,' he said affectionately. Great-aunt Arabella's gift was a topaz ring set in heavy silver, but George was mysterious about his, saying that whether he gave it to her or not depended on her answer to his question yesterday.

Fanny knew that it must be an engagement ring, and her heart sank. She dreaded the scene she would have to face sometime today. She was physically afraid of George's reaction.

She tried to forget this in her pleasure at the children's gifts. Nolly, downstairs for the first time since her illness, importantly handed her a flat parcel, then went back to sit on Lady Arabella's lap while Fanny opened the parcel.

It was a sampler, 'Remember Life's Sunny Hours' and 'This sampler was worked by Olivia Davenport, aged six years, in the year of our Lord, eighteen hundred and . . .'

'It isn't quite finished,' Nolly explained. 'I had only that last bit to do when I got sick. But Great-aunt Arabella said I should give it to you on your birthday and finish it later.'

Tears sprang to Fanny's eyes. She went to take Nolly in her arms.

'It's the very nicest gift of all.'

'You haven't got mine!' shouted Marcus. 'Here's mine.'

This proved to be a box of sugar plums, and everyone laughed and agreed to sample one, and Fanny said tactfully that certainly Marcus's gift had been the sweetest.

'Well, Fanny, don't you feel awfully old?' said Amelia. 'I intend to be married and have children by the time I'm twenty-one. Just think, if you had married Mr Barlow you would have been celebrating your birthday in China.'

'She isn't in China, she's here, where she belongs,' said Lady Arabella, with finality.

It was still misty and dark outdoors, the trees almost leafless after the gale. In contrast, the warm room with the fire blazing, and the comfortable circle of people, had an illusion of happiness and security. Was it really an illusion? Had she been unfairly suspicious and mean-spirited to imagine under-currents? It almost seemed possible this morning to wipe away all her doubts and enjoy the pleasure of being the day's most important person in the bosom of her family.

Uncle Edgar said, 'Since we are all here, and since it's a solemn occasion, I think we might read a chapter out of the Bible. Then, Fanny my dear, we'll get a couple of the servants to witness that brief document I drew up last night, and you'll really be your own mistress. Does that alarm you?'

She was thinking that the ten sovereigns, more money than she had ever had at once before, would pay for her journey to London if it became necessary to go. Or to Exeter or Bristol or Liverpool or any part of England. She need no longer feel completely a prisoner. The knowledge gave her a great sense of freedom and lightness of heart. She could even take the children...

'No, Uncle Edgar. I am not alarmed.'

'She's a rich woman,' said George unexpectedly. When everyone looked at him, he said, 'How does a woman spend ten sovereigns? I'd know what to do with it, mind you.'

'Then never mind your dissertations,' said his father, with some sharpness. 'Now be quiet. I am going to read the twenty-third psalm.'

He had a good voice for reading aloud, rich and sonorous. Fanny had heard it every day of her life, when the servants gathered with the family for morning prayers. She had also heard it thrown out impressively from the pulpit in church when Uncle Edgar frequently read the lesson. But it had never sounded more moving than now on this, her twenty-first birthday, when she was in the grip of so many emotions. Excitement, pleasure, uneasiness about George, anxiety for the children, a most bittersweet feeling about Adam Marsh, and above all an unexplainable tense anticipation of some event about to happen.

Though I walk through the valley of the shadow of death I will fear no evil...

'There,' said Uncle Edgar, closing the big Bible with a clap, and reaching for the bell rope.

When Lizzie answered the bell he said, 'Can you write?'

Lizzie looked bewildered, bobbed a curtsey, and said proudly that she could.

'Good. Then I want you here, and someone else who can write a good hand.'

'Cook can't, sir, but Rosie in the dairy can.'

'Then ask Rosie to come.'

'Yes, sir.'

As Lizzie bobbed and hurried away, Uncle Edgar produced the narrow sheet of parchment which he had inscribed in his own thick deliberate writing.

'If you want to peruse this, Fanny, you may. But I assure you it isn't necessary. I've done exactly as you asked. I am your Executor, Olivia your ben—well, never mind. That child will want to know the meaning of the word, and I've already had experience of trying to answer her questions. She will at once imagine you—har-har-harumph.' He chuckled good-temperedly, and handed Fanny the parchment.

Fanny glanced quickly at the script. She saw her own name in large letters, 'Francesca Davenport' and further down 'to my cousin Olivia Davenport all my personal effects including one sapphire and diamond pendant' (now there would be the cameo brooch and the topaz ring as well for Nolly to receive). Further down she read 'to my said Executor Edgar Davenport all the rest and residue of my estate' and thought, with slightly grim humour, that if she died quickly enough, Uncle Edgar was ensuring that he got back his ten golden sovereigns!

The two maids had arrived, Rosie nervously hanging back in the doorway.

Uncle Edgar dipped his quill pen in the silver ink-well, and handed it to Fanny. She took it and signed her name where he indicated. She was in a curious state of unreality, the words *Though I walk through the valley of the shadow of death* ... mingling in her head with the formal phrasing of the will.

'Where did you learn these legal phrases, Uncle Edgar?'

'Ah, that's easy. I've signed enough documents in my time. Now, if you'll just stand there, Fanny, while Lizzie and Rosie append their names as witnesses.'

With much heavy breathing, the two women complied.

Rosie gasped in dismay as a small blot formed beneath the nib, but Uncle Edgar swiftly blotted it away and said kindly, 'Take your time, my girl. Don't be nervous. You're not signing your death sentence.'

Fanny found Nolly at her skirts, whispering agonisedly, 'What are you writing, Cousin Fanny. Does it mean that you'll go away, now you're twenty-one?'

Fanny said, 'S-sh, Nolly! It's only something grown-ups do. Something you'll do one day. Ask Uncle Edgar.'

'Yes, child,' said Uncle Edgar absently. 'Yes, if you have some jewellery and a little money. It's everyone's duty.'

'You're wasting your time, Fanny,' said George suddenly and harshly. 'A married woman's property becomes her husband's.'

Uncle Edgar lifted his heavy white eyebrows blandly.

'A married woman, George? But our dearest Fanny isn't married. So what can you be talking about?'

'George——' began his mother, uneasily.

'Be quiet, Mamma, Papa. I've waited long enough to speak. I knew you wouldn't allow Fanny to marry me before, but now she's her own mistress, as you just said. So she's free to do as she likes. And I'm asking her to marry me. I won't be put off any longer. Fanny, I want your answer now.'

In that moment George sounded strong and dignified. But the speech had cost an effort of concentration that had made the moisture stand out on his forehead and heightened his colour alarmingly. His blue eyes had a fixed expression of determination and desire that made Fanny wince. She was only glad that this unwelcome proposal had been made in company where she was safe. Had they been alone George would have inevitably tried physical persuasion.

Aunt Louisa made a movement to speak again, but this time Uncle Edgar stopped her.

He said himself, in a perfectly quiet reasonable voice, 'Well, Fanny? What is your answer?'

Fanny felt Nolly's small hand holding her own in a hot and panic-stricken grip. She felt almost as panic-stricken as the child, but she made herself speak calmly, 'The answer is no, as George has always known it would be. I have never given him the slightest encouragement. I am sorry, George, but you can scarcely be surprised——'

George took a step forward. His brow was creased in concentration, his big hands held out. He seemed to be having trouble in understanding her words.

'Fanny, I told you yesterday on the moor that today I would be doing this. I want you to be my wife. We'd be happy together. You'd be mistress here——'

'Fanny! Mistress of Darkwater!' cried Amelia suddenly, deeply shocked. 'But she's only——'

'Be quiet, Amelia!' That was Lady Arabella, her husky voice full of authority. 'What is there about Fanny that makes her unsuitable to be the mistress here? She is beautiful, kind—oh, hot-tempered, I agree—but a lady. I commend George's taste.'

'Mamma, you're talking as if I were dead!' exclaimed Aunt Louisa in high dudgeon. 'I anticipate being mistress here for the next thirty years, at least, and this whole conversation is nonsensical. George is still ill and quite unfit to marry. I won't hear of such a thing. I thoroughly disapprove of cousins marrying, anyway. Fanny, be good enough to take the children upstairs. They shouldn't be listening to this conversation. And George, you are very flushed, I'm afraid your head is bad again. You had better rest.'

Aunt Louisa's tactics had always been to reduce them to the status of children. To speak in a loud bossy voice, and wield her authority.

This time, however, George, at least, was not to be intimidated.

'My head is fine, Mamma, and I don't intend to ask the doctor's permission to marry. I shall do so when I please. So, Fanny! Listen to me! I warn you whether you do or not, I shall get my own way.'

Fanny's refusal burst from her. 'No!' she cried. 'No, no, no! I won't be persecuted in this way. I can't stand it any more. What do you think I am? A servant to be bribed and bullied into giving in to your wishes? You're nothing but a bully, George. You always were. I'm glad to say it at last.'

George's hands slowly opened and closed. His face had gone a curiously dark colour.

'I've told you I would kill anyone who came between us.'

His hands closed again, convulsive. 'I can kill. I've been trained to.' He gave a sudden high laugh. 'That's one thing the Crimea taught me. It's no trouble at all. A sword and a dark night...'

'George!' His father's voice was icy. 'There are young ears listening. Have a little self-control. Or if you can't, leave the room.'

George's face suddenly and distressingly collapsed into that of a harshly scolded child.

He turned momentarily to Lady Arabella.

'I must have her, Grandmamma!' he exclaimed, and then rushed headlong from the room.

In the shocked silence that followed, Aunt Louisa put her handkerchief to her face and began to cry. Amelia ran to her side.

'Mamma, it was only George in one of his moods. He'll forget it. It's ridiculous that he should want to marry Fanny. Imagine—Fanny!' But her eyes sought Fanny's in astonishment and resentment. 'That's two proposals you've had in three months. At least, you won't be able to say you've never been asked.'

'How could I marry George who is practically my brother?' Fanny demanded. 'And I've said before I will only marry for love.'

'A nice sentiment,' said Uncle Edgar, 'though sometimes difficult to fulfil.' His eyes rested very briefly on his wife. 'Amelia, get some smelling salts for your mother.'

'Yes, Papa,' Amelia hurried from the room.

'A nice sentiment, indeed,' came Lady Arabella's deliberate voice. 'But quite impractical, Fanny. Quite impractical.'

Her grey eyes, round as a cat's, met Fanny's with a look of stony hostility. Fanny's heart missed a beat. She had never thought Lady Arabella her enemy.

The tense atmosphere was broken by Marcus demanding whether Cousin George would sound his trumpet before he used his sword.

'I wanted a trumpet,' he said wistfully.

'Did you, my boy? Then you shall have one.' Uncle Edgar was trying to restore the previous mood of happiness and normality. 'And Miss Olivia? What are her present desires?'

But Nolly wouldn't answer. She was very white and still clung to Fanny. Fanny wished uselessly that that scene hadn't taken place in front of the children. She murmured something about taking Nolly upstairs, it was time she rested. She didn't want to look at anyone any more, Aunt Louisa weeping angrily because always, always, this interloper, this girl with more looks and spirit than her own daughter, ruined things, Uncle Edgar earnestly trying to retrieve the happy birthday spirit while his eyes glinted with other thoughts, and Lady Arabella with her look of implacable hatred.

But a flicker of her never quite extinguished optimism came back as she saw the postboy coming up the gravelled drive.

'Uncle Edgar, here's the post. Do you think there might be a reply from Mr Craike?'

'Couldn't be yet, my dear. Don't be so impatient. He's an old man and sick. Give him at least ten days, if he replies at all. Cheer up, child, cheer up. Forget that affair with George. He's not himself, and you did quite right. Don't be afraid of his wild threats. We all know him, eh? But I'll have the doctors back, if necessary.'

'Uncle Edgar, I've always wondered about that night Ching Mei——' She had to stop, because again the children were listening.

Uncle Edgar, surprisingly, didn't deride her unspoken suspicion. Instead he said, soberly, 'I can't deny I've had my own thoughts, too. But that's over, past, can't be undone. So run along and begin to enjoy your birthday. Marcus, Olivia, if within an hour you have made your Cousin Fanny laugh you shall each be allowed to make my watch play a tune yourselves.'

So, on the way upstairs, Marcus enquired earnestly the best way to make Fanny laugh, but Nolly, with a shadow of her former spirit, remarked dispassionately that when next she saw Cousin George she would cut his throat.

'Nolly!' Fanny exclaimed. 'Such a thing to say.'

'How?' Marcus asked with deep interest.

'With a knife, of course. Like William uses for wild pigs. He told me.'

'I thought you'd use a sword,' said Marcus.

'Children!' said Fanny, almost on the verge of laughter after all.

Life was so crazy. It swung from the fearful and the grotesque to the absurd and the touching without giving one time to change one's mood. Now she found that the alarming scene with George had jolted Nolly out of her apathy. There was colour in her cheeks, and her ingeniously macabre imagination was hard at work to find a way to protect her beloved Fanny. A little warmth and happiness had come back to the day, after all.

When Amelia came into the nursery to report that George had gone out riding, galloping his horse wildly across the parkland to the moors, she relaxed a little more. That meant he wouldn't be back for hours and when he came he would be tired and wanting only a hot bath and a brandy. So the house was safe until dark.

Safe? That was the word that had instantly sprang to her mind.

'Goodness, Fanny, you've upset everybody.'

'I!' said Fanny indignantly.

'Mamma says it's your fault. She's talking of sending George to London for the winter. She says he needs a change of people and scene, and he'll come back cured. Grandmamma just says, "Try, Louisa. See if he'll go."' Amelia was amusing, the way she could imitate Lady Arabella's hoarse voice. 'And Papa says nothing at all except that this will blow over. George is merely suffering from a foolish infatuation, like most young men. But you must admit, Fanny, that it wasn't a very *romantic* proposal of marriage. It was more like a threat, somehow. I'd hate my first one to be like that.'

There was something wistful in Amelia's voice that made Fanny say, generously, 'You don't need to worry. Your first one will probably be from the right man.'

'Will it?' said Amelia, and strangely looked about to weep.

She didn't, however. She sprang up, crying, 'Poor Fanny! What a birthday. First it was so nice, then so horrid. Let's make it nice again. Let's play games this afternoon. Everyone is to dress up as some well-known character, and the rest must guess who it is. Nolly and Marcus, too. Grandmamma will lend us things. It won't frighten Nolly, will it?'

'I don't think so. But it might be better if she sat and watched. She isn't strong yet.'

'Yes, I suppose so. Then I wish we had some guests. I wish Adam were here. But who knows, he might ride over.'

'He might be away,' suggested Fanny.

'Oh, no. He'd have told me if he were going away. Anyway, let's do this, Fanny. We must do *something* this long dark afternoon. Why don't you dress up Dora and Lizzie too? And I'll take Marcus.'

It was a very long time since Fanny had been up to the long narrow room in the very eaves of the house where a miscellany of articles over the years had been stored. She and Amelia and George had used to go there as children, opening the old chests to explore the musty and quaintly old-fashioned clothing stored in them, and playing carriages with the discarded furniture. But one day a rat had run across the floor and scared them out of their wits, and they hadn't been up there since.

Now, when Fanny took Dora up the final almost vertical flight of stairs, she found that the door to the attic room was stuck, or locked.

This was odd, since no one ever went there nowadays. Both girls pushed valiantly, but the door remained fast shut.

'Perhaps Hannah has a key, miss,' Dora suggested.

'Yes, run and find her, Dora.'

But Hannah, when she came said she had never had a key to that particular door. She didn't know there was one.

'Anyway, I wouldn't have locked the room,' she said. 'There's nothing but old junk in there.'

'Shall we get Barker or one of the gardeners?' Fanny asked.

'Wait a minute, Miss Fanny. Sometimes these keys I have fit two or three locks. All the linen cupboards can be opened with the same one, and I wouldn't be surprised if this one for the ironing room fits here.'

After a little manipulation, to everyone's delight, the rusty lock gave and the door creaked open.

'Goodness, it's dark,' said Fanny. 'And musty. Dora, run down and get candles. How cold it is in here. Ugh!'

The long dim room with its peaked ceiling was full of strange shapes. Fanny knew that they were made only by upturned furniture and chests, but she waited with Hannah on the threshold until Dora returned with the branched candlestick.

Quickly the candles were lit, and the wavering light made the conglomeration of rocking chairs, tables, a child's high chair and wooden cradle, a paint-faded rocking horse, dark pictures in heavy frames, and old-fashioned travelling trunks quite unsinister.

'Put the candles there,' Fanny instructued, indicating a dusty table. 'Goodness, here's the old newspaper reporting the Battle of Waterloo. I remember reading that years ago, and George made me be Buonaparte and Amelia the King of Prussia, while he, of course, was the Duke of Wellington. We knocked over the furniture while we fought and made a terrific noise. Do you remember, Hannah?'

'That I do, Miss Fanny. Master George was never happy without a sword in his hand. He should have ended up a general, if—well, then, he's shed his blood for his country, and we must just remember that.'

'Yes, Hannah. I do. Always.' There was no need to explain that that was the only reason she had tolerated George's persecution. Hannah was not blind. She must know, too, by the servants' infallible grapevine, what had happened this morning.

In the candlelight, in the dark musty room, Fanny found Hannah's unspoken loyalty more comforting than anything that had happened today.

Dora had opened a chest and was exclaiming over the smell of the clothes.

'Faugh! They do need an airing, Miss. If you knew what things you wanted I could take them out and give them a good shaking.'

'Yes, there's a ball gown that I think was Lady Arabella's—it's the Empire style, in white lace. There should be a shawl and shoes and a fan that goes with it. I know, because I wore it once at Amelia's birthday party when we dressed up. I don't suppose it's been touched since. And I remember a velvet cloak—I think that was in one of these chests——'

She was engrossed now in the clothes and the old memories. She impatiently pushed the wrong trunk aside, and there was a little cascade as several boxes slid down. This disclosed two unexpectedly new-looking travelling bags, quite modern in design.

Fanny looked at them in surprise.

'These must have been put here by mistake. They're not in the least antique. I wonder what's in them.'

She lay one on its side and undid the straps and fastenings. The lid opened and displayed the neatly folded Norfolk jacket, which lay on top of a miscellany of masculine clothing.

'Goodness!' said Hannah. 'That's certainly got here by mistake. It's a good new garment. I wonder who it belongs to, miss.'

Fanny was staring at the neat brown checks of the good expensive tweed in a fascination of horror. She could almost feel the boat rocking beneath her, see those hot eager red-brown eyes fixed on her, the freckled hands reaching towards her. She knew every detail of the jacket Hamish Barlow had worn that day because she had had to keep her eyes fixed on it rather than on his face.

'But he's gone. His things were sent on!' she whispered in desperation.

'Whose things, miss?'

'Mr Barlow's. The gentleman—from China.' She couldn't bring herself to touch the jacket. She stared at it in horrified distaste.

Hannah had caught her feeling of unreasoning horror.

'But he did go. His things were packed. The master gave orders.'

'He couldn't have travelled to London in his evening clothes!'

'Then who brought the bags up here? To a room locked for goodness knows how long.'

'Why hasn't he sent for them? What's he been wearing in the meantime?'

Dora, who had said nothing, only stared with enormous eyes, suddenly exclaimed, 'I heard rats, one night. Don't you remember, Hannah?'

'Yes,' said Hannah derisively. 'And you thought you heard the peacock, too! In the dark, long before morning.'

'The peacock!' whispered Dora. 'Screaming!' And clapped her hand to her mouth.

23

'WHAT will you do, Miss Fanny?' asked Hannah at last.

'I don't know.' (Ching Mei had left her shoes, Nolly kept saying. But compared to that, Mr Barlow was practically naked. He had gone out into the world in a set of evening clothes which, no matter how distraught or even drunk he may have been, would have to have been changed by morning when he took up his ordinary life.)

'I'll have to tell my uncle,' she added. 'I wish we hadn't come here. I wish that door had stayed locked.' Again, her eyes met the fearful eyes of the two servants. Who had locked the door?

'I'll go down now,' she said at last, standing up and brushing her skirts. 'Lock the door again, Hannah, and Dora, go to the children. Suggest another game for them to play. Not dressing up. Tell Miss Amelia I said so.'

Was she only twenty-one today? She felt older than Hannah, older than Lady Arabella. She walked down the three flights of stairs and along the twisting passages as slowly as if already her body were fragile, and dried-up. She moved in a dream and for the first time in her life forgot to knock as she entered the library.

The two men looked up in surprise. Sir Giles Mowatt's expression immediately changed to a welcoming smile, Uncle Edgar's to an annoyed frown.

'Fanny, my dear—here is Sir Giles—we were having a private conversation.'

'I'm sorry, Uncle Edgar! But I must speak to you at once. There's been a—a strange discovery. Uncle,' she burst out, 'where is Mr Barlow?'

There was the smallest silence—of surprise, of consternation?

'Gone back to where he came from, I believe. And entirely due to you, young lady.' Uncle Edgar was fiddling with a paper knife. His voice was slightly jesting and affectionate because Sir Giles was there. Fanny knew that he would not have been so tolerant, otherwise. 'I hope you haven't suffered a change of heart at this late day.'

'No, uncle. We only wondered how he could have travelled without luggage.'

'We?' said Uncle Edgar sharply.

'Hannah and Dora, and me. We found his bags and all his clothes in the attic room. They looked as if they had been hidden there. The door was locked. Hannah had a key that opened it. Uncle Edgar, he *couldn't* have travelled in his evening clothes!'

'Is this the gentleman from the East who was your brother's trustee?' asked Sir Giles with interest. 'Why, Davenport, you didn't tell me this young lady had sent him packing with quite so much speed that he abandoned his luggage.'

'But I didn't mean to,' Fanny cried. 'He had seemed to accept my decision with fortitude. I thought——'

'Never mind about your female intuition just now, Fanny,' Uncle Edgar interrupted. 'And Mr Barlow's bags will keep. They seem to have done so for some time already. Sir Giles and I——'

'Let us know what she thought,' put in Sir Giles. 'I'm interested in this. It sounds quite a mystery.'

'Yes,' said Fanny. 'I think perhaps you should know. Everyone should know. Uncle Edgar, you heard George say this morning that he would kill anyone who came between him and me. Well, it isn't the first time he has said that. And he warned me about Mr Barlow, I'm so afraid——'

'Of what?' asked Uncle Edgar, smiling, amused by the nervous imagination of the feminine sex.

'The peacock screamed that night. Both Dora and I heard it. But it was still dark, and the sound came from the yew Garden. I have never seen the peacock in the yew garden. And it never calls after dark. Then, in the morning, Mr Barlow—had gone.'

Sir Giles sprang up with a decisive movement.

'Davenport, I don't know what this means but you'll have to have it investigated.' Uncle Edgar made to interrupt him, but he motioned him to be silent. 'Miss Fanny, you're an observant young woman. I wonder if you can throw any light on another affair. It has just come to my knowledge that that escaped prisoner was seen in another area altogether on the night he got away. A farmer in the Okehampton district, an illiterate fellow, has chanced to mention it at this late day. That was the night, you will remember, that the unfortunate Chinese woman died.'

'What does this mean?' Fanny breathed.

'It's up to the police, whether they decide to re-open the enquiry or not. But your suggestion that your cousin George is, let us say, not entirely responsible for his actions, throws another light on the affair.'

'He was in the garden that night,' Fanny said. 'I know, because I ran into him.' She caught her uncle's eye, and declared agitatedly, 'I must say this, Uncle Edgar! I must. George isn't safe. He will kill sometime—if he hasn't done so already . . .' Her voice died away. She was shuddering at the thought that she had been kissed by a murderer, almost with the blood still on his hands . . .

'Now if I may at last be allowed to speak,' Uncle Edgar said mildly. 'First, George had nothing to do with Hamish Barlow's bags. He hadn't furtively disposed of a body—forgive me, Fanny, but that is what you intended to suggest—and then tried to dispose of the evidence. No, it was I who put the bags in the attic room.'

'You, Uncle Edgar!'

Uncle Edgar smiled, as if he were enjoying the effect of his revelation.

'Yes, I. At the dead of night and like a criminal. But my intentions were innocent, I assure you. It was merely to stop gossip among the servants. The wretched fellow, in his hasty departure, promised to let me know where to have his bags sent, but he never did so. So I merely had them put out of sight, pending hearing from him.'

'You mean he's never let you have a word!' Sir Giles said in disbelief.

'Well, he had a broken heart, so I suppose we must forgive him. And he did have an overcoat, Fanny. He would have arrived in London, or wherever he went, quite respectably. Also, he was a man of means, you know. A little lost luggage would scarcely worry him. These fellows seem to make their fortunes in the East, Sir Giles.'

'But your brother failed to, I understand?'

'Ah, Oliver. My brother, I am sorry to say, was always the exception to the rule. But there's your little mystery explained, Fanny. You see, there was no need to exercise your very fertile imagination over it. You and that child Olivia are a pair. Now Amelia may be a little flighty, but she has a sensible head on her shoulders. None of these melodramas for Amelia, thank heaven.'

'But where is Mr Barlow, Uncle Edgar?'

'Oh, forget the man. It was you who sent him packing. If you must know, I wrote to the shipping company enquiring for his whereabouts, and they replied that they thought he had decided to travel back to China overland. Adventurous fellow. I suppose it's as good a way as any of getting over a broken heart.'

Uncle Edgar stood up. 'Can I offer you a little brandy, Sir Giles?'

'No, thank you. I must be getting on my way. I thought it only fair to warn you about this other matter in case the police should call.'

'Thanks, my dear fellow. Very good of you. But you can put that poppycock about my son out of your head. What on earth was the Chinese woman to him? I don't believe he'd ever spoken to her. She was only a servant, you know.'

Fanny couldn't help lingering after Sir Giles had gone. At the risk of completely offending her uncle she had to say, 'I don't believe a word of what you said, Uncle Edgar!'

His eyes narrowed, and became a foggy unfathomable grey. 'So?'

'No, I believe you made it all up to protect George. And that you're just as afraid as I am.'

She clenched her hands. She could hardly put into words her final fear.

'Mr Barlow is still here, Uncle Edgar. I know.'

24

NOLLY and Marcus were in Lady Arabella's sitting room where Nolly was painstakingly finishing her sampler. They were pleased to see Fanny come in, but too occupied to pay much attention to her. Fanny sat quietly beside Lady Arabella on the other side of the room. The high back of the sofa separated them from the children. She didn't want to talk, or even to think, but neither of these things could be escaped.

She should have asked Uncle Edgar to show her the letter from the shipping company saying that Mr Barlow was on his way by overland route to China. But Uncle Edgar would merely have said he couldn't lay his hands on it. Fanny was quite certain that no such letter existed.

'The child has the wrong text on her sampler,' Lady Arabella said suddenly. 'It should have been one about charity.'

Fanny kept her voice low so that the children sitting in the window getting the last light of the day wouldn't hear.

'Great-aunt Arabella, I couldn't agree to marry George.'

'No. You are too selfish for sacrifices. Or charity. Not that marrying George would have constituted either. Humour him and you'd have found a kind considerate husband.'

'I don't want a husband who has to be humoured all the time,' Fanny said, with asperity.

Lady Arabella gave a derisive laugh.

'H'mm. You've a lot to learn, my girl. What do you think every wife has to do?'

'But not to be humoured like a child,' Fanny persisted. 'George is quite childish most of the time. And when he isn't he——'

'He what?' Lady Arabella's eyes were stony.

'He's frightening, Great-aunt Arabella. I think he's dangerous.'

'Fiddlesticks! You only have to know how to manage him. I hadn't noticed you being particularly quailed by anyone before. I had thought you a young woman of remarkable spirit.' Lady Arabella was stroking Ludwig on her lap. His fur crackled. He stretched sensuously and showed his claws. 'I am very disappointed,' said Lady Arabella. 'But you will see reason eventually. You will marry George and have a child and become a contented woman.'

'I won't marry a mur——' Fanny stopped abruptly, remembering the children.

Lady Arabella's eyes flickered. She gave no other sign of having understood what Fanny had been about to say.

'Why do you all want me to marry against my wishes?' Fanny went on. 'But you will forgive me, Great-aunt Arabella, just as Uncle Edgar forgave me about Mr Barlow.'

'I am a great deal stronger than your uncle,' said the old lady. 'Also, I am not a forgiver. I love George dearly, more than any other person in the world. I shall see that he gets what he wants. I have ways.'

'You may have ways of intimidating other people, but not me!'

'You, a young dependent creature with no future,' said Lady Arabella cruelly. 'You must learn to know yourself, Fanny. And life. My daughter had to marry against her wishes. Almost all women do. You will see.'

Fanny was at last goaded into saying, 'But hasn't Uncle Edgar told you about Sir Giles Mowatt's visit? Don't you know the police may re-open the case about Ching Mei?' She was whispering now, her eyes warily on the children in the window. 'And if they do—if they do. Great-aunt Arabella—I shall tell them how I met George in the garden that night, how——' She pressed her hands to her face, shuddering uncontrollably. 'Mr Barlow has disappeared, too,' she said. 'I don't need to remind you of George's—insane jealousy.'

Lady Arabella's face was old, older than Fanny had ever imagined it could look.

'There must be an investigation,' Fanny insisted.

Lady Arabella straightened herself.

'Nonsense! Nonsense! George is as innocent as the day he was born.'

'Only because he is mentally irresponsible——'

Marcus suddenly came running across the room.

'Cousin Fanny! Look what Great-aunt Arabella found for me. You turn it upside down and all the leaves fall.'

It was a glass kaleidoscope filled with a shower of autumn leaves. When they had fallen, in their pretty amber pattern, to the bottom, they lay in a heap round a miniature dead tree. They stirred some obscure memory in Fanny's mind.

'It's pretty,' she said to Marcus. 'It's like the story of the Babes in the Wood. Do you remember how they covered themselves with leaves?'

The smell of wet dead leaves recently stirred...

'Oh, it's too dark!' Nolly cried exasperatedly. 'Why doesn't somebody bring the lamps? Cousin Fanny, I'm tired. I want to sit in your lap. What are you and Great-aunt Arabella talking about?'

There was a tap at the door and Amelia came bursting in.

'Is this where you all are? Fanny, why didn't you dress up after all? Dora came in looking as if she'd seen a ghost. But I hadn't time to find out what was wrong. I had to be with Mamma. She's terribly upset. Do you know that just now Papa has been saying George may have to be put——'

'Amelia!' said Lady Arabella in a voice of thunder.

Amelia, for once, was not intimidated by her grandmother's anger. Her words were tumbling over themselves as usual, but now Fanny noticed there was a look of intolerable excitement in her eyes.

'Hasn't Papa told you about Sir Giles' visit? Don't you know that poor escaped prisoner was miles from here that night?'

'Hearsay!' declared Lady Arabella contemptuously. 'We won't discuss this in front of the children, if you please, Amelia. You ought to have more sense. And must we sit in the dark? Fanny, ring for lights. And take the children to the nursery. Wait! Before they go I have a gift for Nolly.'

'Me, too,' cried Marcus.

'No, greedy. You have the kaleidoscope which you may keep. Nolly is to have my pincushion. The one I cherish particularly.'

Nolly's eyes opened wide.

'But, Great-aunt Arabella, you don't let anyone touch it.'

'I will let you touch it.'

Nolly's nose wrinkled in distaste.

'It's only an old thing. I don't care for it.'

'Of course it's an old thing. It's an antique. It belonged to my grandmother, and perhaps to her grandmother before her. It has held the pins used to make gowns for the Court of Charles the Second. Now do you call it merely an old thing in that rude voice?'

'I still don't care for it,' Nolly muttered, but she took the fat faded pincushion in her hand and went off with it to the nursery.

When Marcus boasted that he had the best present she hissed, 'I will stick a hundred pins in you! Needles, too!'

Before Fanny could follow the children Lady Arabella called to her peremptorily, 'Fanny! Help me downstairs. I must see your uncle.'

Amelia, deprived of her audience, cried with strange desperation, 'Don't leave me alone! I'm afraid.' She gave a ghost of her old happy giggle, 'Of I don't know what.'

Her grandmother's eyes went slowly over her, from head to foot.

'That's a pity,' she said at last. 'That you should be afraid of your own brother. Fanny!'

The old Lady was heavy on Fanny's arm. She had an odour of lavender water and wool, a familiar odour that in the past had represented some security. Lady Arabella's broad lap which welcomed children had been all the mothering Fanny had known. It was impossible to think of her as too implacable an enemy. She was merely indulging in her favourite game of intimidation.

'He'll be in the library,' said Lady Arabella, panting slightly. 'Don't come in. Leave us alone.'

Her chair was at the bottom of the stairs in its usual place. Lady Arabella got into it and rapidly wheeled herself across the hall. She disappeared into the library and the door closed, but not completely, behind her.

'Fanny!' came Amelia's voice from the top of the stairs. 'Why should I be afraid of George? What's Grandmamma got in her head?'

Fanny ignored her. There were no servants about. The hall was empty. She crossed it softly, and stood with her ear against the chink of light from the library, listening.

But only for a moment. She had to move away quickly into

the shadows beneath the stairs for hurried steps were approaching. Uncle Edgar's voice was raised in agitation.

'Thank God, Mamma! I was just coming for you. One of the servants has seen George down at the lake. He's behaving oddly. Walking up and down, in a distraught way.'

'He's not going to drown himself!' Lady Arabella cried.

'I don't know. What with the disappointment about Fanny this morning and the state of his damaged mind—if anyone can stop him, you can.'

'Fanny can. He loves her.'

The door of the library had opened and Lady Arabella, wheeling her chair furiously, had appeared, followed by Uncle Edgar.

He was saying in a low hurried voice, 'No. The sight of her may send him over the edge. Poor fellow! Let me push you, Mamma. Quietly. We don't want all the servants rushing down, and a scandal. You and I can handle this. I expect the truth is he's taken a little too much to drink.'

They had almost reached the big oak door with its heavy fastenings. Fanny never knew what made her run forward.

'Great-aunt Arabella! Don't go!'

The two stopped, turning startled heads.

'Don't go!' Fanny cried again. She was, quite irrationally, remembering the kaleidoscope in Marcus's hands, with its little flurry of leaves settling, settling. And Hamish Barlow saying coldly and finally, 'Your uncle will never forgive you...' It was Great-aunt Arabella who was the person who didn't forgive, not Uncle Edgar... And perhaps poor distraught George really was hesitating on the edge of the lake, trying to make up his mind to plunge into the blackness and the iciness.

Amelia was flying down the stairs.

'What's happening? Where is Papa taking Grandmamma at this hour?'

'Great-aunt Arabella, don't you remember? The cushion. The fall you had. It's dark outside. Your chair runs away down the slope...'

Fanny was aghast at what she had said. The words had come compulsively, without coherent thought. But Lady Arabella was turning her chair round, and slowly getting out of it.

When Uncle Edgar put out his hand to assist her she pushed it away.

'No, Edgar, I can manage alone. Fanny! Come here at once. What is in your head?'

Nolly's little Chinese doll tossed negligently on her bed, Fanny was thinking, the dead bird in the cage, the cancelled trip to London, Uncle Edgar's insistence that she signed her will.

'You're not signing your death sentence,' he had said to the two maids . . .

'Nothing that makes sense,' she said. 'But let us all go down to the lake and find George. *All* of us. Amelia! Barker, Hannah, and Lizzie and Cook! Barker will push your chair, Great-aunt Arabella.'

Her hand was on the bell rope.

'Fanny! Leave that alone!' Uncle Edgar ordered. His voice went soft. 'You interfering creature! You have defied me long enough. There's a limit——' But before he could finish what he was saying, and before Fanny could realise the fury in his face someone rapped on the door, lifting the heavy knocker and letting the sound thud through the house.

'George!' Lady Arabella gasped thankfully.

Barker appeared, looked surprised at the gathering in the hall, and retired discreetly, as Uncle Edgar himself opened the heavy door and saw the light shine on the tall figure without.

'Marsh!' he exclaimed. He recovered himself quickly, stepping back for Adam Marsh to come in. 'I wasn't aware you were expected. Did my wife—Amelia, perhaps——'

Amelia had made a sound of pleasure, but it was Fanny who ran forward, whose feet, acting as compulsively as previously her tongue had, carried her straight to Adam Marsh's arms.

'Fanny!' ejaculated Lady Arabella.

'Fanny!' shrieked Amelia. 'How could you?'

Fanny's face was pressed hard into Adam's bosom, her waist was likely to be crushed by the strength of his grip. The pain was ecstasy, she wanted to suffer it forever.

'You went away without telling me!' she said furiously. 'I rode over. There was no one there.'

'It was urgent,' said Adam. 'I couldn't help it. But I got back in time for your birthday.'

'Back from where?'

He pushed her away.

'From London, of course. And I brought you a present.'

'Ah!' said Lady Arabella icily. 'So now Fanny, your behaviour becomes clear. How long has this intrigue been going on? And don't stand there, the two of you, as if you were on the moon. Mr Marsh, we are suffering the most intense anxiety as to the whereabouts of George, and you burst in, uninvited, full of your private affairs!'

Adam bowed with the greatest courtesy.

'Lady Arabella, forgive me! I was carried away. And if you're worrying about George, he is at present drinking in the village inn. Or was, not half an hour since. I imagine he'll be there for some time yet.'

'So!' The old lady had collapsed back into her chair. Her chin was on her breast. Fanny knelt quickly beside her, but in a moment she was waved vigorously away. Lady Arabella's chin was up, her eyes as cold as the lake water on a grey day. Nevertheless, her voice was almost grotesquely gay.

'Edgar, we will have things to talk of later. But not in front of these young people. I suggest you sit down, Amelia, and try not to indulge in anything as futile as an attack of the vapours. Mr Marsh, it seems, simply has a birthday gift for Fanny. A charming sentiment. Perhaps we may be permitted to look at it.'

'Certainly,' said Adam. He handed Fanny a small jeweller's box of red morocco. 'You might be interested to hear, Mr Davenport, that I patronised your friend, Mr Solomon. He has an interesting collection in that extraordinarily dark shop of his, hasn't he?'

Before Uncle Edgar could reply Aunt Louisa came hurrying downstairs, exclaiming in her petulant voice, 'Is this where everyone is? Fanny, Dora finds it impossible to control those children. You'd better go up—oh, Mr Marsh, we weren't expecting you. Did I hear the name Solomon? Surely you haven't been buying diamonds from him!'

'Louisa, be quiet!' Hastily Uncle Edgar tried to smooth over his anger. 'We are all bursting with curiosity to see Mr Marsh's gift. Open it, Fanny.'

Fanny knew it wasn't a real gift. She knew it was being

made like this, publicly, for a purpose. As Adam's eyes reassured her, she pressed the catch and the little box sprang open.

She almost dropped it.

'But no! They're Nolly's. The green earrings!'

'Emeralds,' said Adam casually, as if he might have been mentioning green bottle glass. 'And they're yours now, Fanny. I bought them. You may, of course, like to give them to Nolly at some future date.'

'What right have you, Mr Marsh, to stick your nose into my affairs like this?' Uncle Edgar demanded stiffly. 'It seems to me like damned inquisitive impertinence. And I don't apologise for my language. I am within my rights, as my brother's trustee, in disposing of his property as I think fit.'

'And I within mine for buying property legally for sale,' Adam replied. 'Your brother must have done better than you expected him to do in China, Mr Davenport. Weren't you a little hasty in labelling him a failure? Could it be that you had always disliked him? Perhaps envied his popularity? I know how a prejudice will arise. But you shouldn't have assumed he died penniless.'

Uncle Edgar's brows rose in angry astonishment at Adam's attack.

'I assumed nothing of the kind.'

'I think you did at first. And you made no statement to correct that impression when you made that rather momentous discovery.'

Aunt Louisa started forward.

'Edgar, do you mean that bag of green stones, the things the childrens called their marbles, were emeralds! Why, you told me they were some sort of inferior jade.'

'A fortune,' said Adam softly. 'Your wastrel brother, Mr Davenport, was making sure of his children's future after all.'

Aunt Louisa pointed a trembling finger.

'But you lied to me, Edgar! You must have stolen those jewels!'

Strangely, her words gave back to Uncle Edgar his poise. He thrust his fingers into the pockets of his elegant flowered waistcoat with an air of negligent ease.

'Not stole, my dear wife. Merely invested. Mr Marsh, who seems to have a passion for secret investigation, may care to inspect my investments. I would remind him again that I am legally the children's guardian, and perfectly within my rights to dispose of property. Mr Barlow would bear me out. We talked of this at length.'

'But could it be,' said Adam, in his deceptively soft voice, 'that there was a conspiracy between you and Mr Barlow? Unlucky fellow that he was.'

'Unlucky?'

'I understand the bargaining point was your niece Fanny. He was to take her off to China, and nothing more would be said about the children's assets. Am I right?'

'Adam! Adam!' Fanny cried, unable to be silent any longer. 'Mr Barlow's bags are still here. We found them today. I'm so afraid——'

Adam's grip on her fingers was remarkably soothing. Almost in a moment her terror quietened. She could even think of that pile of autumn leaves without such great distress.

'You think the poor fellow is still here? Perhaps he may be. Wild pigs can be destructive, can't they, Mr Davenport?'

Uncle Edgar stared at him, his pale eyes expressionless. Adam went on, 'A man buried not very skilfully, and in evening dress, could easily seem like a large black bird to a child, if a wild pig had previously investigated the grave and some part of the body, perhaps an arm, protruded. You followed the children that day, didn't you, Mr Davenport? And made some quick repairs. I expect you made a much more thorough job later in the night. But I have taken the liberty of asking the police to investigate. They're in the copse now, with lanterns.'

He looked at the horrified women, and said, 'I apologise for the grisly nature of this conversation. But it isn't really as distressing as a hunt for a live prisoner. A man, a human being, hunted like an animal. And conveniently at hand when the little Chinese woman, who knew too much about the wealth of her charges, was lured down to the lake looking for a doll that had already been safely secreted.'

'And encountered a desperate man on the run,' Uncle Edgar said, speaking at last his well-rehearsed statement. It had been said to the police and the coroner many times.

'Did she?'

'Of course. Oh, there's recently some hearsay evidence against it, but——'

'Papa!' That was, surprisingly, Amelia. White-faced, with brilliantly shining eyes, she faced her father. 'It isn't true about the prisoner. You know it isn't. And so do I!'

There was all the usual indulgence in Uncle Edgar's voice as he answered his daughter.

'Your kind heart does you credit, my dear, but you know nothing whatever of this. Kindly stay silent.'

Amelia's head was up, her face strangely mature.

'I do know something about it, Papa. I must speak. The prisoner was here the night after Ching Mei's death. The next night! He told me he had come from Okehampton, miles away. I gave him food. Cook will tell you. She wonders'—Amelia's voice trembled in a travesty of her light-hearted giggle—'where my appetite has vanished to lately. I don't want sandwiches and slices of fruit cake after dinner any more. But the prisoner wasn't here the night Ching Mei died, Papa. I know.'

Uncle Edgar's eyes went from one to another. He seemed to come, regretfully, to a long-expected decision.

'Then I am afraid the police will have to interview my son.'

Aunt Louisa made a violent movement.

'Edgar! How dare you! putting the blame on your innocent son!'

The eyes of husband and wife were locked. Twenty-five years of marriage culminated in that moment of Aunt Louisa's bitter disillusionment, no longer hidden, and Uncle Edgar's aggressive dislike.

Yet Uncle Edgar spoke quite quietly and gently.

'It's something we can no longer make a secret of, my dear. George isn't safe. The police should also be told about his hatred for Hamish Barlow.' He threw out his hands. 'I hate to disappoint you, Marsh, but I myself am entirely innocent. Your assumptions are fantastic. I merely sold some jewels and invested the proceeds on behalf of my nephew and niece. And may I add I find your whole manner and actions extremely offensive.'

'But there is another thing,' said Adam insistently. 'I didn't travel alone from London. I persuaded a very old gentleman to travel with me. He's staying at the inn in the village at present. He needed to rest. But he will be calling on Fanny tomorrow. He has some extremely interesting and vital information for her. His name, I scarcely need to tell you, is Timothy Craike.'

25

THAT was when the disintegration of the man who, with his jokes, his whimsicalities, his naïve pleasure in himself, his vanity, his desire for public esteem, and his autocratic will, as befitted the master of the house, began.

He sat down very slowly in one of the carved hall chairs. His chubby hands were fiddling restlessly with his watch chain. His jowls had dropped, his face had grown thinner and lost its ruddy colour. His eyes were very tired.

'What an extraordinarily interfering young man you are,' he said to Adam, almost mildly. 'So now you know everything, and I observe you are quick to have an eye for an heiress into the bargain. All the summer, it was my poor little Amelia, with her promise of a substantial dowry. But your affections seem to be easily transferable.'

'My affections,' Adam said quietly, 'have always been with Fanny, as I think she knows. To my great regret I have had to hurt her and puzzle her occasionally. I also can't apologise sufficiently to Amelia for misleading her so wilfully. But she was too useful to my purpose. She made me welcome here. She talked a great deal, and unwittingly gave me important information. It was she who told me about Fanny's disappointment over not getting to London to see this Mr Craike who had written to her. It was my first real clue about Fanny's affairs. I had waited all summer for it. But I am deeply sorry it had to be discovered at the risk of hurting Amelia.' He turned to Amelia, holding out his hand. 'Can you forgive me?'

Amelia promptly burst into tears, and ran to her mother. Aunt Louisa said in a strangled voice, 'I don't understand one word that has been said. Fanny can't be an heiress! Why have I never been told? Is this another of my husband's machinations?'

'But it isn't true!' whispered Fanny incredulously.

Her eyes were caught by Lady Arabella's expression. It was

unreadable. Her eyelids drooped until her eyes were mere slits. But it seemed as if she might be hiding triumph. Almost, as if she might have been waiting for this hour.

'Adam?' said Fanny urgently. 'What has Mr Craike to tell me? Have I got a fortune, also in jewels? Was the sapphire pendant really my own all the time?'

It was at that moment there was a flurry at the top of the stairs. Dora was crying helplessly, 'Miss Nolly! Come back at once. Oh, I declare!' But her words were useless, for Nolly was flying down the stairs in her nightgown.

'Cousin Fanny! Cousin Fanny!'

Fanny started towards her. 'What is it? Nothing's happened to frighten you——'

But it was not fright, she saw at once, that possessed Nolly. The little face was illuminated with excitement, and had its moment of blazing prettiness.

'Cousin Fanny, this dear little pincushion Great-aunt Arabella gave me opens! Look, the top comes off and makes the sweetest little box. I shall keep my jewels in it.'

'Is that all?' said Fanny. 'Does it please you so much?'

'Yes, it does. And I found this letter in it. I think it's about you. See, here is your name. F-a-n-n-y.'

Suddenly and rather frighteningly Lady Arabella began to laugh.

Ah, Edgar! You searched so hard. And such a simple hiding place. I used to keep my love letters there and when I was very young. I baffled you, didn't I? And I wasn't bluffing about that letter. But it would never have been discovered if I hadn't realised you would kill for it.' Her mirth had left her. Her eyes were fully open now and full of implacable revenge. 'Fanny, send that child upstairs!'

'Yes, Nolly. Run up to Dora.'

'But don't you think the little pincushion is delightful?'

'I do. And tomorrow we'll find some treasures to keep in it. Run along.'

Nolly went reluctantly and Lady Arabella continued her conversation as if she hadn't interrupted it.

'I decided to dismiss that clumsy accident you arranged for me, Edgar. Just the threat of a schoolboy, I thought. Give her a fright and who knows, the old lady might have a stroke. But today, this evening, everything has changed. I would have had another accident down at the lake, wouldn't I? Just a feeble old woman tripping in the dark. Fanny knew. I underestimated you, Edgar. I even despised you. Now I must admire your—how shall I put it—diabolical simplicity. But I don't forgive it. You would have blamed your son. I share my daughter's feelings for you at this moment. I hope, Edgar,' she finished, slowly and distinctly, 'that you hang.'

Uncle Edgar made no attempt to defend himself. He sat with his head slumped, his eyes far-off, almost as if he were in a dream.

Then he said, 'I am very tired. It has all been a great strain for too long.'

Looking at him, Fanny had the impression of reading him as if his life were written in his face—the over-sensitive pompous young man laughed at by the girl he loved, looked down on by his wife and mother-in-law, scorned by his gay reckless brother as dull, given only the qualities of steadiness and reliability by relatives who found him useful—no wonder he had had to puff himself up into a turkeycock of importance, seeking and finding the wherewithal for his family, his household, his village and the whole community to revolve round him.

'Uncle Edgar——' she began.

Uncle Edgar lifted his extinguished eyes.

'No, child. Don't come near me. I would have killed you, too. Don't you realise that? I could never have let you find out that I had spent your capital and taken possession of your property. Yes, you would have died. A fall off the train, I thought, on a journey to London. Or perhaps a skating accident on the lake. There were so many possibilities.'

'Edgar!' Aunt Louisa had difficulty in speaking. Her face was so alarmingly flushed that it seemed she would have a seizure. 'Do you mean to say that Darkwater, everything, belongs to Fanny!'

'Completely, my dear. It is a pity you were such an avaricious woman. Always wanting, wanting, wanting.'

'I had to have something!' Aunt Louisa cried thickly.

'You had me. And I had never told you about Marianne—always there behind your eyelids. You didn't know my private ghost. Fanny sometimes reminds me of Marianne. That long white throat.' He curved his strong thick fingers thoughtfully. 'It's a matter of love and hate. You can kiss and kill—yes, almost simultaneously. But there it was. I comforted myself by marrying an earl's granddaughter and acquiring property. I bought diamonds for my wife. My son had a commission in a famous regiment and my daughter a dowry. But finally Fanny's fortune was not sufficient for the needs of my extravagant family. I hardly knew where to turn when the second plum fell in my lap. My brother's orphaned children, and a bag of uncut emeralds. How was that for luck? And the intricate plotting, the timing, the manipulating of people. The stimulation of it! But of course one's luck couldn't last forever. Time runs out.'

'Edgar, you are mad!' cried Aunt Louisa, horrified.

The shrunken man, with his enormous calm, said, 'Don't let those men you brought knock all the copse down, Marsh. I can take them to the exact spot. I agree that I did a careless job on that. I never realised the fellow would be so heavy. I had to risk leaving the body concealed by leaves and do the burying the next night when I could wear suitable clothes. Even so, it was quite a task getting garden debris cleaned off myself so as to present myself back in the ballroom. Luckily there was no blood. I have strong hands. And a man taken by surprise—I had asked him to step outside to discuss some business—has little defence. I must have a discussion with Sir Giles about these spontaneous crimes. They seem to be the most successful. Haphazard, but unsuspected.' Uncle Edgar seemed almost to relish re-living the success of his macabre tactics. 'Barlow was an unlikeable fellow, anyway. I can't think how my brother trusted him. Well, that's how it was. And now,' he moved wearily, 'I suppose I had better be getting along.'

'Where are you going, Edgar?' Aunt Louisa cried.

'To the police, naturally. Marsh will perhaps accompany me, since he has already assumed so much responsibility. One knows when the game is over. One must behave with dignity. Time—oh, speaking of time, Fanny,' he had taken the large gold watch, as yellow as a pumpkin, from his pocket, 'give this to Marcus in the morning. The little fellow was always fascinated by it.'

He wound it absently, and the tiny delicate tune hung in the air, as frail as a dream.

'Don't fret, Louisa.' Uncle Edgar spoke with a shadow of his old pompousness. 'I haven't wasted my time with a petty crime. The case will be a *cause célèbre,* of course. And it isn't as if we have a son able to inherit the estate. Poor George is finished. We both know it.' He stood a moment surveying his wife's highly-coloured and tear-stained face dispassionately. 'It's a great relief to tell you my true feelings at last. I trust you to see that Amelia's life isn't ruined by an unfortunate marriage.'

'Papa!' cried Amelia in a heartbroken voice.

'My little girl——'

But Lady Arabella dismissed the one emotional moment with an authoritative movement of her hand.

'Let him go, Amelia. He is your father, but he is a monster.'

Something made Fanny re-wind the watch she was holding and listen again to the tinkling tune. The shortish stout figure going out through the door into the hall was nothing without his watch, she realised. How strange. He had simply diminished away.

26

So there it was at last, the voice of her father speaking. Fanny re-read the much-creased letter that had been concealed in Lady Arabella's pincushion.

Dear Uncle Leonard,

How can I express my gratitude for your intention to leave me your property and capital. I fear my ownership will be of short duration for I am a dying man with perhaps one, perhaps two years to live, but if only you could know how you have eased my mind. Now I can die confident that my daughter Francesca is well provided for. She is only a baby who looks like her mother, but is a true Davenport in spirit. I am making my cousin Edgar, a man of the highest integrity, her guardian . . .'

It was quite impossible to sleep. At some time in the night, she wasn't sure how late, Fanny got up and tiptoed down the dark passages to Lady Arabella's rooms.

As she had guessed, a night light was burning in the bedroom. She tapped, and went in swiftly.

'Great-aunt Arabella? I thought you wouldn't be asleep!'

The old lady was propped up with pillows. She had been reading her large shabby Bible. She closed it, her finger holding the place she had been reading.

'Naturally I wouldn't. Sleep is for the innocent. What do you want?'

'You were never really my enemy, were you?'

'And what makes you think I am turning soft in my old age? Of course I was your enemy, until I realised I was wasting my time. Your will was stronger than mine. Which makes it formidable. I pity the man who marries you.'

'I would like to think kindly of you,' Fanny said earnestly. 'I know you would have sacrificed me for George, but I can understand that because you loved him. And you did, in the end, give Nolly the pincushion so I would find Papa's letter.

I want to thank you eternally for that.' She looked very young, with her black hair tumbling over her shoulders, and tears on her lashes.

Lady Arabella said impatiently, 'Pshaw! You and your extravagant emotion. You thank me eternally for something I should have done months ago. It could have saved lives. Do you realise that? I am a wicked old woman. But I'd do the same again.' Her husky voice broke between a sob and a chuckle. 'My son-in-law should have made more of a study of the human mind. He didn't even bother to discover that his great-uncle Leonard loved poetry and that his favourite was Chaucer. A well-worn volume of the Canterbury Tales was marked at the place where the old man had stopped reading with your father's letter. I thought such carelessness on your Uncle Edgar's part deserved a little punishment. I always did hate the pompous little man, anyway. Daring to marry my daughter! But he was George's father, and—I apologise to you, Fanny—at that time that was far more important than demanding justice for you. Anyway,' she said irritably, 'you were to marry George and be mistress here, and it would all have come to the same thing.'

'Uncle Edgar must always have wanted me to die,' said Fanny sadly. 'Do you remember the day I fell out of the boat? Perhaps he hoped I had inherited my father's delicate constitution, and would catch a chill and go into a decline. But I suppose he really thought it was tidier to let me come of age and make my will, almost as if he enjoyed the years of anticipation.' She buried her face in her hands, shuddering. 'It's all so horrible. How can a man's ambitions and ego turn his mind so? He would have killed, and killed again.'

'They say it's easy after the first time,' the old lady said. 'I believe it even grows on one, like gambling, or drinking. And one doesn't look for a criminal where none is suspected, as your uncle pointed out. Besides, no one cared about the Chinese woman, no one was unduly concerned about that detestable fox Barlow. My death would have been an unfortunate accident caused by age and senility. Senility, ho!'

'And mine?' Fanny whispered.

For a moment the old lady's hand rested on her head.

'That was a habit of thought in your uncle's mind, a task

that must one day be done. He would blame that wretched girl who once jilted him, and my daughter for her demands and her extravagances, caused, as he very well knew, by discontent in her emotional life. He would have retained a singularly innocent mind. But it didn't happen. Let us not talk of it. Here, sit beside me, and we'll read together.'

Her stubby finger found the place. She began to read, 'They are like chaff which the wind scattereth away... No sugar plums, tonight,' she said. 'George was always the one who liked them best.' Her voice was full of desolation.

George, very flushed and unsteady, had come in late the previous evening, and gone straight to his room. In the morning he came downstairs dressed in the uniform of an officer of the 27th Lancers. He was shouting for his horse to be brought to the door. It seemed dangerous to oppose him, so the groom brought the magnificent animal, his father's last gift to him, to the door, and George mounted, and sat still in the saddle for a moment, very young and heroic and incredibly handsome. Then he shouted wildly, 'I can smell the cannon smoke. Goodbye all!' and with his superb horsemanship, he galloped madly away, the sun gleaming on his helmet, his white plumes streaming. When he came back hours later his horse was exhausted, and he was dazed and muttering something about the Cossacks and the deadly fire of the cannon.

'You realise, Louisa,' Lady Arabella said with great gentleness, 'that he will have to go away for a time, at least. We must find a suitable hospital. Come, George. Come Georgie, my lamb. Retreat has sounded.'

Aunt Louisa was a ghost of herself, listening to everything her mother said, and agreeing mechanically. Yes, she would go and live in the Dower House on the Dalston estate. Although it was small and dark and inconvenient. It was no place for a young girl just beginning life, but with the change in Amelia's fortunes she must be thankful for a place to which to retreat until some of the terrible scandal had blown over.

It was then that Amelia surprised everyone.

'No, Mamma. I'm not coming with you.'

'And what, pray, are you planning to do? Live on Fanny's charity?'

'Aunt Louisa, please!' Fanny protested. 'I have tried to tell you all morning how welcome——'

Amelia didn't let her finish. She lifted her round young chin, unexpectedly stubborn, and said that she had quite made up her mind, she was going to find a position as lady's maid with some nice family going to Australia.

'I know I can't sew very well,' she said, 'and I know almost nothing about starching and ironing. But Hannah is going to teach me, and I can learn quickly if I set my mind to it. I shall be quite a success.'

Aunt Louisa was completely shocked.

'Australia! Are you mad? There's no need to go to the other side of the world. I know your father's case will be a terrible scandal, but people soon forget. There are plenty of young men who will admire you for yourself.'

Her expression, overfond and distraught, did not deter Amelia.

'Yes, Mamma. I know one of those men already. But he is now in Australia, I believe, hoping to make his fortune in the goldfields. I am going out to find him.'

'Amelia!' Fanny exclaimed. 'You can't mean the escaped prisoner! But you only talked to him for a moment.'

Amelia's eyes were shining brilliantly. There was nothing of the plump immature girl left about her. She was a woman, with a proud confidence that at that moment made her beautiful.

'It wasn't just a passing thing. It was more. It was like—you might almost say like a moment in eternity. I told myself I was foolish and romantic. I tried to forget about him and fall in love with Adam. I thought I had. But I hadn't. I can't forget this man.'

Fanny took her hand.

'I believe I see now what he saw. I believe you will find him. I pray that you do.'

'I will,' said Amelia.

'And anyway,' Amelia had added after that conversation, 'who is Adam Marsh?'

'I don't know,' said Fanny. (But I know how his heart feels beating against my cheek . . .)

'Papa was right when he said he was interfering and inquisitive. Is he a fortune-hunter? Or is he a policeman in plain clothes? Would you marry a policeman, Fanny?' Amelia asked, in her old inquisitive way.

'I would marry Adam whoever he was. If ever he asks me,' she added under her breath.

For the first time the house oppressed Fanny. She dressed the children in their outdoor things and said they were all going for a walk. Marcus could bring his hoop if he wished, but Nolly was to pay attention to everything Fanny told her. She was to learn more about English birds.

She didn't miss the flicker of fear in Nolly's eyes, and went on calmly, 'You are deplorably ignorant about them, my love. You scarcely know a robin from a crow. We'll take some crumbs to feed them.'

'Put our hands on their beaks!' Nolly gasped. 'Touch their feathers!'

'After weeks of patience you may perhaps entice one of them to eat out of your hand. You must remember that they're much more frightened of you than you are of them.'

Nolly looked extremely sceptical.

'How can they be? They have beaks and claws.'

But she allowed herself to be buttoned into her warm cape and gaiters and Fanny, half way through the task, thought how absurd this was. She was the mistress and doing the nursemaid's work.

'And I always will,' she said aloud.

'Always will what? Cousin Fanny, why are you smiling?'

'I don't know. Perhaps I was thinking how happy I am to have you and Marcus.'

Nolly made her usual attempt to scoff.

'Marcus doesn't care for being here. He would rather be in China. But I shall tolerate it'—Nolly's mouth pursed judiciously—'if I learn not to be afraid of birds.'

It was a cold windless day, the sun shining from a clear colourless sky. The children raced across the garden, kicking up flurries of leaves fallen in yesterday's gale. Inevitably, their destination was the lake where there might be wild ducks and perhaps a swan.

The water was not dark and sinister today, but the colour of the sky, pale and translucent. The floor of the pavilion was littered with dead leaves. It looked as if it had not been visited for years. The summer tea parties had vanished as completely as the yellow flag irises and the water-lilies from the lake.

Fanny suggested a reward for the first person to see a robin, then forgot to look herself as she became lost in thought. She was so tired, so crushed by the weight of events, and yet so full of a sense of joy which surely she had no right to feel in the midst of tragedy.

'Cousin Fanny! I saw one. In that tree. He flew away. Cousin Fanny, Lizzie's coming down. Don't let her make us go back to the house yet.' Nolly's face, healthily pink and happy, looked out from her blue bonnet. 'You promised we could feed the birds.'

'Miss Fanny!' That was Lizzie, breathless, scarcely knowing yet how to speak to the new mistress. 'Mr Marsh has arrived with the old gentleman from London. Barker has put them in the library.'

Fanny sprang up. 'I will come at once.' But in the next instant she saw Adam strolling across the autumn-yellowed grass. She waited, her heart beating too fast, until he came up.

He bowed and said good morning, and added that he hadn't the patience, like Mr Craike, to wait in the library.

Fanny was almost as breathless as Lizzie, but had the presence of mind to say, 'Lizzie, ask Barker to be kind enough to pour Mr Craike a glass of Madeira. Mr Marsh and I will be up immediately.'

'In fifteen minutes, Lizzie,' Adam amended. 'Miss Fanny and I have things to discuss.'

'Yes, indeed,' said Fanny. 'Poor Uncle Edgar—poor George. And Amelia planning to go to Australia. Did you know?'

'And you?' said Adam softly. 'Are you going to slap my face if I kiss you?'

Fanny strove for composure.

'Mr Marsh, naturally I can't keep those very valuable earrings. I realise the gift was a gesture——'

'You said you couldn't keep the Bactrian camel, either. That was mine. The earrings were my sister's.'

'Your—*sister's*!'

Adam's smile was quizzical, a little amused.

'You shouldn't always have been accusing me of ulterior motives. The explanation is so simple. I merely wanted to observe, incognito, whether my brother-in-law had made a suitable choice of guardian for his children. When I saw you in London my doubts were completely allayed. I knew that if you had the care of the children they would be happy. But I still wanted to make the acquaintance of Edgar Davenport. And when I received the letter from Ching Mei——'

'A letter from Ching Mei!' Fanny had to interrupt. 'Nolly said she had written to you and I didn't believe her.'

'The letter was written with Nolly's help. I had arranged it with Ching Mei in London. If anything troubled her she was to let me know. Naturally, your uncle taking possession of the children's fortune alarmed her very much.'

'Of course,' Fanny breathed, remembering the conversation in the Chinese language between Adam and Ching Mei.

'Anyway,' he went on, 'I came at once, intending to state my business immediately. But you will remember I chanced to meet you in the church. You were so different from the fashionable young lady I had seen in London. You were plainly, even poorly dressed. My curiosity, and, I must admit, my suspicions, were aroused. When I made the discovery that you, too, were a ward of Edgar Davenport I began to wonder. I knew about my niece and nephew's fortune for a great part of it was my sister's. Had you, too, perhaps had one? Meeting your uncle increased my suspicions. He was too hearty, too affable, too apparently generous, a façade, I suspected, that hid the real man. I decided the only way to remain on the scene and make investigations was to go on concealing my identity and cultivate the family, particularly the charming garrulous Amelia. Fortunately your uncle displayed no curiosity at all about the family of the girl his brother had married, or my game would have been up. He shouldn't have so under-rated Oliver who was a nice fellow, and who made Anne Marie, whom he met when she travelled with my father on one of his trips to the East, very happy.'

'Oh, how glad I am about this!' Fanny cried. 'You will be able to talk to Nolly and Marcus about their mother. They will have someone to keep her alive for them.'

'More than one person. My Aunt Martha is longing to have them with her at Heronshall. We will apply for their guardianship, Fanny, and bring them up with our own children.'

Fanny caught her breath, the colour rising in her cheeks.

'We will live at Darkwater if you wish. It is very lovely. And plenty of lively children about will banish its ghosts, or make them happier ones. But I have a property just as beautiful in the Western Highlands of Scotland. My father used to come back to it after his trips to the East.'

'You have—decided all this?'

'Long ago. When I first saw you on the railway station in London. You knew.'

'Yes, I knew,' said Fanny, and forgot that she had ever doubted it.

'Cousin Fanny! Cousin Fanny!' called the children in their imperious voices.

All at once the windbells were chiming. Or was it the windbells, for no wind stirred. The sound had been remarkably like Ching Mei's high delightful tinkle of laughter.